The Best
AMERICAN
SHORT
STORIES
1992

The Best
AMERICAN
SHORT
STORIES
1992

Selected from
U.S. and Canadian Magazines
by ROBERT STONE
with KATRINA KENISON

With an Introduction by Robert Stone

HOUGHTON MIFFLIN COMPANY
Boston • New York • London 1992

ISSN 0067-6233
ISBN 0-395-59304-2
ISBN 0-395-59353-0 (PBK.)

Printed in the United States of America

AGM 10 9 8 7 6 5 4 3 2 1

Contents

Foreword

THE YEAR 1991 was a good one for the American short story. While many of us are tightening our belts, cutting our budgets, and struggling to economize, short story writers are producing new work of extraordinary depth and magnanimity. In fact, the year's best fiction — full-blown and brimming with energy — is a welcome antidote to these lean economic times. Even as we add another blanket against the chill and huddle our chairs closer to the hearth, our storytellers seem to be loosening the stays on their imaginations and allowing themselves to stretch, as if in preparation for a long night's work ahead. This is a happy development indeed.

The eighties were years of excess, and American writers seemed to react to all that reckless consumption by wresting their art in the very opposite direction. Pared down, peeled back, and psychologically acute, the decade's best fiction achieved tremendous emotional impact through dispassionate observation and rigorous economy. But after a decade of minimalist fiction, some readers began to feel deprived, suffering a hunger that would not be sated by one more technically impressive black-and-white snapshot of emotionally constricted characters failing to recognize the emptiness of their own lives.

If the stories in this collection are any indication, there is change afoot. There is a great generosity of spirit, an exuberance of language and imagination, a sense of expansiveness, even gusto, in this year's best stories. The authors represented here approach the age-old art of storytelling with an urgency and passion that cannot help but engage the reader. As I read this year's short fiction (about 2400 stories in all, published in 267 different periodicals), I sensed that our finest writers are approaching their work with tremendous confidence — confidence in their own abilities, confidence that they will be well served by traditional forms and solid craftsmanship, and confidence that we, the readers, are ready once again to lose ourselves in stories. Eudora Welty once wrote that her mother "sank as a hedonist into novels." The stories in this anthology invite just such luxurious immersion.

This year's guest editor, Robert Stone, has chosen stories that are big in the best sense of the word. These are mature works, fully conceived, beautifully executed, and deeply felt. There are no quick sketches here, no dazzling little doodles, no minimalist miniatures. Instead there are twenty stories that draw us into other worlds. While novels demand that we live within their pages for a time, short stories rarely ask us to inhabit them for long. But these are stories of unexpected breadth and scope. They are not easily dispensed with; rather, they haunt the imagination and tug insistently at the heart long after the last lines have been read. Within these pages you will meet a two-hundred-pound schizophrenic with a voice like an angel; a thirteen-year-old boy momentarily paralyzed as he prepares to plunge into the rest of his life; a white man who finds the first true happiness he's ever known in the arms of his black mistress; a young monk struggling to uphold his vows in the face of proffered love; a college student searching for insights into his dead father; a woman driven by boredom to an act of murder; even the ghost of Ho Chi Minh.

The authors have been profligate with their creations, constructing not just rooms but mansions, big enough to accommodate life-size characters, full-scale plots, and the whole gamut of human emotion. Alice Munro presents nothing less than the entire history of a woman's life, all within the confines of a short story. Annick Smith, in her first published fiction, traces the long trajectory of love, from youthful hope, through tragedy, to middle-aged acceptance. Robert Olen Butler lifts an old man's reflections into the realm of literature. And each of these authors has something valuable to reveal, compelling us to pause for a moment and view the world from another vantage point. In the Contributors' Notes at the back of the book, the authors comment on the genesis of each story, providing us a rare glimpse into the mysterious process by which a particular image or flash of insight takes root and blossoms into fiction.

During the past year, Robert Stone spent many hours away from his own work in service to the short story. When first asked if he would be willing to edit this year's volume, he said, "I would be honored. I think this is a duty of fiction writers, and my time has come." He embarked on this year's pile of reading with a keen sense of responsibility, and he concluded his task with the happy realization that he had thoroughly enjoyed himself. I think his pleasure, not to mention his keen appreciation for fine prose, is reflected throughout this volume.

The stories chosen for this year's anthology were originally published in magazines issued between January 1991 and January 1992. The qualifications for selection are: (1) original publication in nationally distributed American or Canadian periodicals; (2) publication in English by writers who are American or Canadian, or who have made the United States or Canada their home; (3) publication as short stories (novel excerpts are not knowingly considered). A list of magazines consulted for this volume appears at the back of the book. Publications that want to make sure that their fiction will be considered each year should include the series editor on their subscription list (Katrina Kenison, *The Best American Short Stories*, Houghton Mifflin Company, 2 Park Street, Boston, Massachusetts 02108).

K.K.

Introduction

IN 1842, reviewing Nathaniel Hawthorne's *Twice-Told Tales* for *Graham's Magazine,* Edgar Allan Poe delivered his famous appreciation of the short story as a form. "The tale proper," Poe wrote, ". . . affords unquestionably the fairest field for the exercise of the loftiest talent which can be afforded by the wide domains of mere prose." At the time Poe wrote, he, Hawthorne, and Washington Irving were arguably the leading practitioners of the story in English. British writers had yet to recognize its possibilities.

As a critic, Poe tended to overintellectualize the process of composition. He loved the image of himself as a monster of rationality like his fictional detective C. Auguste Dupin, all icy premeditation and fearless logic. Nevertheless, his insights were of the first order. His observation that a short story presents "a mystery which it obscurely typifies" well described the form's somewhat ineffable satisfactions.

After Poe, at least until the flourishing of Henry James, the art of the short story declined in America, becoming the medium of regional humorists and other purveyors of local color. Meanwhile, in Europe and particularly in Russia at the hands of Ivan Turgenev, the short story was being forged as a subtle psychological tool. "It's strange how things happen in life," Turgenev once remarked. "You live with someone for a long time, you are on the best of terms, yet you never once speak to him frankly and from the heart; with someone else, you've hardly even got acquainted — and there you are: as if at confession one or other of you is blurting out all his intimate secrets."

Turgenev and the writers who followed him conditioned the short story's future. For their purposes, character was fate. The cardinal virtue was perception, which assumed a moral dimension. Maintaining the interior intensity of Poe, while largely abandoning grotesque incident and exotic setting, the short story became in their hands a vehicle for inquiry into and exposition of the human condition. These artists became pioneers of sensibility. Their work, as much as that of scientists and philosophers, served to put the conscious mind in touch with its own frontiers. Claiming less, they often saw more clearly.

Many of the terms associated with the short story in its formative years are pictorial. Stories were scenes, sketches, vignettes. But the concentration of effect, the economy and precision necessary to a good story, suggest an analogy to music. A tale requires a voice, a quality of sound in the mind's ear. Every word has its resonance, and a story is told word upon word. At its best, a story emerges as something quite close to poetry, demanding an equally intimate blend of effective form and content. As the most impacted and precisely timed form of "mere prose," it is particularly subject to Joseph Conrad's celebrated principle, that fiction must justify itself in every line. Its essentials are vividness, clarity, economy, and precision.

A few well-known examples of virtuosity come readily to mind. Hemingway's story "Hills Like White Elephants" is a fine example of that master's work at its most effective. Short and tight as can be, it has an almost mystical spareness and perfectly illustrates Hemingway's capacity for making the very white space between lines tremble and shimmer with meaning.

The well-named Eudora Welty story "Powerhouse," about black jazz musicians, is another example of the uncanny force a good story can bring to bear. Its sound replicates the music in the narrative, being both elusive and haunting, at once elemental and sophisticated, indirect, mocking and wise, humorous and full of mystery. It may be the most ambitious and most effective invocation of African American sensibility ever attempted by a white artist.

Some of the stories in James Joyce's *Dubliners*, created during Europe's great outburst of artistic energy before the First World War, remain unsurpassed in their intensity and eloquence. One of them, "Araby," perhaps not the best known, has always seemed to me a thing close to perfection, a work of genius, answering forever the requirements we ask of art. It was through understanding, over time, how much Joyce was offering his readers in "Araby" that I came closest to some perception of what the short story was for and what it ought to be. I can think of no better way of representing the editorial sensibility informing this volume than by reproducing here and commenting on the opening pages of that work.

"North Richmond Street, being blind, was a quiet street except when the Christian Brothers' School set the boys free. An uninhabited house of two storeys stood at the blind end, detached from its neighbours in a square ground. The other houses in the street, conscious of decent lives within them, gazed at one another with brown imperturbable faces."

That the street is blind means simply that it is a dead-end street; still the word has its weight, suggesting here blighted vision as well as no exit. The brown imperturbability of the houses speaks of sterile *embourgeoisement.*

The previous tenant of our narrator's house had been a priest, a solitary man in black, who died in a back drawing room. The house itself is musty and moribund. The priest's only leavings are an oxidizing pump in the rank garden outside and the decaying pages of lifeless tomes; an ancient historical novel, an incitement to piety, the recollections of a police spy whose trade was concealment. Everywhere the suggestion of cloister, labyrinth, and mortality.

Then:

When the short days of winter came dusk fell before we had well eaten our dinners. When we met in the street the houses had grown sombre. The space of sky above us was the colour of ever-changing violet and towards it the lamps of the street lifted their feeble lanterns. The cold air stung us and we played till our bodies glowed. Our shouts echoed in the silent street. The career of our play brought us through the dark muddy lanes behind the houses where we ran the gantlet of the rough tribes from the cottages, to the back doors of the dark dripping gardens where odours arose from the ashpits, to the dark odorous stables where a coachman smoothed and combed the horse or shook music from the buckled harness. When we returned to the street light from the kitchen windows had filled the areas. If my uncle was seen turning the corner we hid in the shadow until we had seen him safely housed. Or if Mangan's sister came out on the doorstep to call her brother in to his tea we watched her from our shadow peer up and down the street. We waited to see whether she would remain or go in and, if she remained, we left our shadow and walked up to Mangan's steps resignedly. She was waiting for us, her figure defined by the light from the half-opened door. Her brother always teased her before he obeyed and I stood by the railings looking at her. Her dress swung as she moved her body and the soft rope of her hair tossed from side to side.

Among the "sombre" houses, on this landscape of death-in-life, the youthful vitality of the boys flares like street lamps under the violet sky, a temporal, extinguishable glow but signifying life nonetheless. Their games are beginning to bring them into contact with the larger world and also with sexuality and its mysteries. For it is this, I submit, that is suggested by the pungent "dark dripping gardens" in the lines that precede the author's introduction of the girl known only as "Mangan's sister." Our narrator, an intelligent and sensitive orphan, is alive to the outline of her figure, the movements of her body and, all at once, to "the soft rope of her hair." Not only sensuality is prefigured in the earlier lines of the paragraph. The coachman, smoothing and combing, shakes music from a buckled harness, music that the reader can plainly hear, music that indicates the lyrical aspect of love's longings. For Joyce, as is well known, was a musician.

One of the great wonders of "Araby" is the way it renders so precisely and insightfully the humors and emotional storms of early adolescence. It does so by creating as its narrator a literate, eloquent adult who projects an exquisite imaginative sensitivity enabling him to summon past confusions with perfect clarity. It is hard not to speculate on the character of this narrator. He seems to have undergone a passage from solitary motherless childhood to what we might guess to be the literary life. He resembles Stephen Dedalus, but, an orphan, he cannot be Stephen. One might imagine him as kinder and wiser than the Stephen Dedalus of *Portrait of the Artist* but no less angry. At the end of "Araby," when the boy has had his first embittering taste of disillusionment, a shattering and sublime moment occurs.

"Gazing up into the darkness I saw myself as a creature driven and derided by vanity; and my eyes burned with anguish and anger."

In this final moment the cultivated narrator is suddenly transformed into the unhappy child of the past, the child who has always been alive inside him.

As of the last decade of the twentieth century, the pleasures and principles of the short story seem to remain generally what they were in Joyce's day. The selections included represent many varieties of experience and modes of life. Amy Bloom's "Silver Water" combines a life-affirming tough-minded humor with the essence of tragedy. Joyce Carol Oates's "Is Laughter Contagious?" conveys hysterical denial with disturbing immediacy. David Foster Wallace's "Forever Overhead" isolates some significant moments in time and freezes the frame to examine them in several dimensions.

A number of stories reflect the cosmopolitan nature of late-century America. The events in Marshall N. Klimasewiski's "JunHee" take place within a consciousness that spans two temporal cultures and at least one metaphysical realm. Robert Olen Butler's "A Good Scent from a Strange Mountain," Thomas Beller's "A Different Kind of Imperfection," and Lorrie Moore's "Community Life" all show the intersection of far-flung historical lines. Some stories portray those who populate the margins of society, whose America is formless and frenetic; the orderlies in Denis Johnson's "Emergency," the rural drifters of Tim Gatreaux's "Same Place, Same Things," Christopher Tilghman's "The Way People Run," and the genteelly displaced mother and son in Tobias Wolff's "Firelight." Others, like Elizabeth Winthrop's "The Golden Darters," invoke the traditional middle-class American life that continues to be lived out amid the alarms and confusions of change.

Nine of the stories included in this volume were originally published in *The New Yorker*. The large number of *New Yorker* inclusions I think results from the fact that while *The New Yorker* is still able to attract first-rate submissions, the days are past when there was such a thing as a *"New Yorker* story." A magazine publishing works as different from each other as "Emergency," "A Different Kind of Imperfection," and Alice Munro's "Carried

Away" cannot really be accused of perpetrating one brand of fiction.

In their variety, these stories reflect what is probably the most significant development in late-twentieth-century American fiction, the renewal and revitalization of the realist mode, which has been taken up by a new generation of writers. This represents less a "triumph" of realism than the obviation of old arguments about the relationship between life and language. As of 1992, American writers seem ready to accept traditional forms without self-consciousness in dealing with the complexity of the world around them.

ROBERT STONE

The Best
AMERICAN
SHORT
STORIES
1992

ALICE ADAMS

The Last Lovely City

FROM THE NEW YORKER

OLD AND FAMOUS, an acknowledged success both in this country and in his native Mexico, though now a sadhearted widower, Dr. Benito Zamora slowly and unskillfully navigates the high, sharp curves on the road to Stinson Beach, California — his destination. From time to time, barely moving his heavy, white-maned head, he glances at the unfamiliar young woman near him on the seat — the streaky-haired, underweight woman in a very short skirt and green sandals (her name is Carla) who has somewhat inexplicably invited him to come along to this party. What old hands, Benito thinks, of his own, on the wheel, an old beggar's hands. What can this girl want of me? he wonders. Some new heaviness around the doctor's neck and chin makes him look both strong and fierce, and his deep-set black eyes are powerful, still, and unrelenting in their judgmental gaze, beneath thick, uneven, white brows.

"We're almost there," he tells the girl, this Carla.

"I don't care; I love the drive," she says, and moves her head closer to the window, so her long hair fans out across her shoulders. "Do you go back to Mexico very often?" she turns now to ask him.

"Fairly. My very old mother still lives there. Near Oaxaca."

"Oh, I've been to Oaxaca. So beautiful." She beams. "The hotel —"

"My mother's not in the Presidente."

She grins, showing small, white, even teeth. "Well, you're right. I did stay there. But it is a very nice hotel."

"Very nice," he agrees, not looking at her.

His mother is not the doctor's only reason for going to Oaxaca. His interests are actually in almost adjacent Chiapas, where he oversees and has largely funded two large, free clinics — hence his fame, and his nickname, Dr. Do-Good (to Benito, an epithet replete with irony, and one that he much dislikes).

They have now emerged from the dark, tall, covering woods, the groves of redwood, eucalyptus, occasional laurel, and they are circling down the western slope, as the two-lane road forms wide arcs. Ahead of them is the sea, the white curve of beach, and strung-out Stinson, the strange, small coastal town of rich retirees; weekenders, also rich; and a core population of former hippies, now just plain poor, middle-aged people with too many children. In his palmier days, his early, successful years, Dr. Zamora often came to Stinson from San Francisco on Sundays for lunch parties, first as a semi-sought-after bachelor ("But would you want your daughter actually to marry . . . ?" Benito thought he felt this question), and later, less often, with his bride, the fairest of them all, his wife, his lovely blonde. His white soul. Elizabeth.

After Elizabeth died, now some five months ago, in April, friends and colleagues were predictably kind — many invitations, too many solicitous phone calls. And then, just as predictably (he had seen this happen with relatives of patients), all the attention fell off, and he was often alone. And at a time impossible for trips to Mexico: rains made most of the roads in Chiapas impassable, and he feared that he was now too old for the summer heat. Besides, these days the clinics actually ran quite well without him; he imagined that all they really needed was the money that came regularly from his banks. (Had that always been the case? he wondered. Were all those trips to Chiapas unnecessary, ultimately self-serving?) And his mother, in her tiny stucco villa, near Oaxaca, hardly recognized her oldest living son.

Too much time alone, then, and although he had always known that would happen, was even in a sense prepared, the doctor is sometimes angry: Why must they leave him now, when he is so vulnerable? Is no one able to imagine the daily lack, the loss with which he lives?

And then this girl, this Carla, whom the doctor had met at a dinner a month or so before, called and asked him to the lunch, at Stinson Beach. "I hope you don't mind a sort of last-minute invitation," she said, "but I really loved our talk, and I'd wanted to see you again, and this seemed a good excuse." He gratefully accepted, although he remembered very little of her, really, except for her hair, which was very long and silky-looking, streaked all shades of brown, with yellow. He remembered her hair, and that she seemed nice, a little shy; she was quiet, and so he had talked too much. ("Not too unusual, my darling," Elizabeth might have said.) He thinks she said she worked for a newspaper; it now seems too late to ask. He believes she is intelligent, and serious. Curious about his clinics.

But in the short interval between her call and this drive a host of fantasies has crowded old Benito's imagination. She looked about thirty, this girl did, but these days most women look young; she could be forty-two. Still a long way from his own age, but such things did happen. One read of them.

Or was it possible that Carla meant to write about him for her paper? The doctor had refused most interviews for years; had refused until he noticed that no one had asked, not for years.

"What did you say the name of our hostess was?" he thinks to ask her as they round the last curve and approach the first buildings of the town.

"Posey Pendergast. You've never met her?"

"I don't think so, but the name — something goes off in my head."

"Everyone knows Posey; I really thought you would. She's quite marvelous."

"Quite marvelous" is a phrase that Benito (Elizabeth used to agree) finds cautionary; those marvelous people are almost as bad as "characters." All those groups he is sure not to like, how they do proliferate, thinks old Benito sourly, aware of the cruel absence of Elizabeth, with her light laugh, agreeing.

"I'm sure you'll know some of her friends," adds Carla.

Posey Pendergast is a skinny old wreck of a woman, in a tattered straw sun hat and a red, Persian-looking outfit. She breathes heavily. Emphysema and some problems with her heart, the doctor thinks, automatically noting the pink-white skin, faintly bluish mouth, and arthritic hands — hugely blue-veined, rings buried in finger flesh. "I've been hearing of you for years," she tells Benito, in her raspy, classy voice. Is she English? No, more like Boston, or somewhere back there, the doctor decides. She goes on. "I can't believe we've never met. I'm *so* glad Carla brought you."

"This is some house," he says solemnly (using what Elizabeth called his innocent-Indian pose, which is one of his tricks).

It is some house, and the doctor now remembers walking past it, with Elizabeth, marveling at its size and opulence. It was right out there on the beach, not farther along, in Seadrift, with the other big, expensive houses, but out in public — a huge house built up on pilings, all enormous beams, and steel and glass, and diagonal boards.

"My son designed it for me," Posey Pendergast is saying. "Carla's friend," she adds, just as some remote flash is going off in the doctor's mind: he used to hear a lot about this Posey, he recalls, something odd and somewhat scandalous, but from whom? Not Elizabeth, he is sure of that, although she was fond of gossip and used to lament his refusal to talk about patients. Did he hear of Posey from some patient? Some old friend?

This large room facing the sea is now fairly full of people. Women in short, silk, flowered dresses or pastel pants, men in linen or cashmere coats. Rich old gringos is Benito's instant assessment. He notes what seems an unusual number of hearing aids.

He and Carla are introduced around by Posey, although Carla seems already to know a number of the guests. People extend their hands; they all say how nice it is to meet the doctor; several people say that they have heard so much about him. And then, from that roster of Anglo-Saxon names, all sounding somewhat alike, from those voices, nasal Eastern to neutral Californian, Benito hears a familiar sound: "Oh." (It is the drawn-out "Oh" that he recognizes.) "Oh, but I've known Dr. Zamora *very* well, for a *very* long time."

He is confronted by an immense (she must weigh two hundred pounds), short woman, with a huge puff of orange hair, green eyeshadow, and the pinkish spots that skin cancer leaves marking her pale, lined forehead. It is Dolores. Originally Dolores

Gutierrez — then Osborne, then Graham, and then he lost track. But here she is before him, her doughy face tightened into a mask, behind which he can indistinctly see the beauty that she was.

"Benito Zamora. Benny Zamora. What an absolutely awful name, my darling. So *spic*," said Dolores, almost fifty years ago.

"How about Dolores Gutierrez?"

"I can marry out of it, and I certainly plan to. Why else would I even think of Boy Osborne, or for that matter Whitey Satterfield? But you, you simply have to change *yours*. How about Benjamin Orland? That keeps some of the sound, you see? I really don't like names to begin with 'Z.' "

"This is an extremely ugly room," he told her.

She laughed. "I know, but poor dear Norman thinks it's the cat's pajamas, and it's costing him a fortune."

"When you laugh I feel ice on my back." He shivered.

"Pull the sheet up. There. My, you are a gorgeous young man. You really are. Too bad about your name. You don't look so terribly spic."

They were in the pink and gold suite of a lesser Nob Hill hotel, definitely not the Mark or the Fairmont, but still no doubt costing poor Norman a lot. Heavy, gold-threaded, rose-colored draperies, barely parted, yielded a narrow, blue view of the San Francisco Bay, the Bay Bridge, a white slice of Oakland. The bedspread, a darker rose, also gold-threaded, lay in a heavy, crumpled mass on the floor. The sheets were pink, and the shallow buttocks of Dolores Gutierrez were ivory — cool and smooth. Her hair, even then, was false gold.

"You know what I'd really like you to do? Do you want to know?" Her voice was like scented oil, the young doctor thought, light and insidious and finally dirty, making stains.

"I do want to know," he told her.

"Well, this is really perverse. *Really*. It may be a little too much for you." She was suddenly almost breathless with wanting to tell him what she really wanted, what was so terrifically exciting.

"Tell me." His breath caught, too, although in a rational way he believed that they had surely done everything. He stroked her smooth, cool bottom.

"I want you to pay me," she said. "I know you don't have much

money, so that will make it all the more exciting. I want you to
pay me a lot. And I might give it back to you, but then again I
might not."

After several minutes, during which he took back his hand,
Benito told her, "I don't want to do that. I don't think it would be
fun."

And now this new Dolores, whose laugh is deeper, tells him,
"This is a classic situation, isn't it, my angel? Famous man runs
into an old lady friend, who's run to fat?" She laughs, and, as
before, Benito shivers. "But wherever did you meet my darling
old Posey?"

"Just now, actually. I never saw her before."

"The love of my life," Dolores declaims, as the doctor reflects
that this could well be true, for he has just remembered a few
more lines from their past. "I really don't like men at all," Dolores confided back then. "I only need them, although I'm terrified of them. And now I've fallen in love with this beautiful girl,
who is very rich, of course. Even thinner than I am. With the
most delicious name. Posey Pendergast. You must meet her one
day. She would like you, too."

Wishing no more of this, and wishing no more of Dolores,
ever, Benito turns in search of Carla, who seems to have vanished or hidden herself in the crowd that now populates this
oversized room, milling around the long bar table and spilling
out onto the broad deck that faces the sea. As he catches sight of
the deck, the doctor instinctively moves toward it, even as Dolores is saying, "You must come back and tell me how you made
all that money, Dr. Do-Good."

"Excuse me," he mutters, stiffly, making for the door. He is
not at all graceful in the usual way of Latins; Elizabeth said that
from time to time.

From the deck San Francisco is still invisible; it lurks there behind the great cliffs of land, across the surging, dark-streaked
sea. The tall, pale city, lovely and unreal. Benito thinks of his
amazement at that city, years back, when he roamed its streets as
an almost indigent medical student — at Stanford, in those days
a city medical school, at Clay and Webster streets, in Pacific
Heights. How lonely he used to feel as he walked across those
hills and stared at massive apartment houses, at enormous family

houses — how isolated and full of greed. He *wanted* the city, both
to possess and to immerse himself in. It is hardly surprising, he
now thinks — with a small, wry, private smile — that he ended in
bed with Dolores Gutierrez, and that a few years later he found
himself the owner of many sleazy blocks of hotels in the Tender-
loin.

But that is not how he ended up, the doctor tells himself, in a
fierce interior whisper. He ended up with Elizabeth, who was
both beautiful and good, a serious woman, with whom he lived
harmoniously, if sometimes sadly (they had no children, and
Elizabeth was given to depression), near St. Francis Woods, in a
house with a view of everything — the city and the sea, the Far-
allon Islands.

Nor is that life with Elizabeth how he ended up, actually. The
actual is now, of course, and he has ended up alone. Childless
and without Elizabeth.

The doctor takes deep breaths, inhaling the cool, fresh wind,
and exhaling, he hopes and believes, the germs of self-pity that
sometimes enter and threaten to invade his system. He looks
back to the great Marin headlands, those steep, sweeping hills of
green. Far out at sea he sees two small, hopeful white boats, sails
bobbing against the dark horizon.

Looking back inside the house, he sees Carla in intimate-seem-
ing conversation with withered old Posey. Fresh from the inti-
mations of Dolores, he shudders: Posey must be even older than
he is, and quite unwell. But before he has time for speculation
along those lines, he is jolted by a face, suddenly glimpsed behind the glass doors: bright-eyed and buck-toothed, thinner and
grayer but otherwise not much aged, in a starched white embroi-
dered shirt (Why on earth? Does he want to look Mexican?), that
lawyer, Herman Tolliver.

"Well, of course they should be condemned; half this town
should be condemned, are you crazy?" Tolliver grinned sideways, hiding his teeth. "The point is, they're not going to be condemned. Somebody's going to make a bundle off them. And
from where I'm sitting it looks like you could be the guy. Along
with me." Another grin, which was then extinguished as Tolliver
tended to the lighting of a new cigar.

In that long-ago time (about forty years back) the doctor had just opened his own office and begun his cardiology practice. And had just met a young woman with straw-blond hair, clear, dark-blue eyes, and a sexy overbite — Carole Lombard with a Gene Tierney mouth. A young woman of class and style, none of which he could ever afford. Elizabeth Montague: her very name was defeating. Whoever would exchange Montague for Zamora?

None of which excused Benito's acquiescence in Tolliver's scheme. (Certain details as to the precise use of Tolliver's "hotels" Benito arranged not quite to know, but he had, of course, his suspicions.) It ended in making the doctor and his wife, Elizabeth Montague Zamora, very rich. And in funding the clinics for the indigent of Chiapas.

After that first encounter with Herman Tolliver, the doctor almost managed never to see him again. They talked on the phone, or, in the later days of success and busyness, through secretaries. Benito was aware of Tolliver, aware that they were both making a great deal of money, but otherwise he was fairly successful in dismissing the man from his mind.

One morning, not long before Elizabeth died, she looked up from the paper at breakfast (Benito only scanned the *New York Times,* did not read local news at all) and said, "Didn't you used to know this scandalous lawyer, this Tolliver?"

"We've met." But how did Elizabeth know that? Benito, shaken, wondered, and then remembered: some time back there had been phone calls, a secretary saying that Mr. Tolliver wanted to get in touch (fortunately, nothing urgent). Just enough to fix the name in Elizabeth's mind. "Is he scandalous?" Benito then asked his wife, very lightly.

"Well, some business with tax evasion. Goodness, do all lawyers do things like that these days?"

Aware of his own relief (he certainly did not want public scandals connected with Tolliver), Benito told her, "I very much doubt it, my darling."

And that was the end of that, it seemed.

Carla is now talking to both old Posey and Herman Tolliver, but the doctor can see from her posture that she doesn't really like him much, does not really want to talk to Tolliver. She is barely giving him the time of day, holding her glass out in front of her like a shield, or a weapon. She keeps glancing about, not smiling, as Tolliver goes on talking.

Is she looking for him? the doctor wonders. Does she ask herself what has happened to old Benito? He smiles to himself at this notion — and then, almost at the same moment, is chilled with longing for Elizabeth.

A problem with death, the doctor has more than once thought, is its removal of all the merciful dross of memory: he no longer remembers any petty annoyance, ever, or even moments of boredom, irritation, or sad, failed acts of love. All that is erased, and he only recalls, with the most cruel, searing accuracy, the golden peaks of their time together. Beautiful days, long nights of love. He sees Elizabeth at their dining table, on a rare warm summer night. Her shoulders bare and white, a thin gold necklace that he brought her from Oaxaca shines in the candlelight; she is bending toward their guest, old Dr. McPherson, from med-school days. Benito sees, too, McPherson's wife, and other colleague guests with their wives — all attractive, pale, and well dressed. But none so attractive as his own wife, his pale Elizabeth.

"Oh, there you are," Carla says, coming up to him suddenly.

"You couldn't see me out here? I could see you quite clearly," he tells her, in his sober, mechanical voice.

"I was busy fending off that creep, Tolliver. Mr. Slime." She tosses her hair, now gleaming in the sunlight. "I can't imagine what Posey sees in him. Do you know him?"

"We've met," the doctor admits. "But how do you know him?"

"I'm a reporter, remember? I meet everyone."

"And Posey Pendergast? You know her because —"

But that question and its possible answer are interrupted, cut off by the enormous, puffing arrival of Dolores. "Oh, here's where you've got to," she tells Benito and Carla, as though she had not seen them from afar and headed directly to where they stand, leaning together against the balcony's railing. "Carla, I'm absolutely in love with your hair," says Dolores.

Carla giggles — out of character for her, the doctor thinks — and then, another surprise, she takes his arm for a moment and laughs as she asks him, "Why don't you ever say such flattering things to me?"

Is she flirting with him, seriously flirting? Well, she could be.

Such things do happen, the doctor reminds himself. And she seems a very honest young woman, and kind. She could brighten my life, he thinks, and lighten my home, all those rooms with their splendid views that seem to have darkened.

"Don't you want some lunch?" she is asking. "Can't I get you something?"

Before he can answer (and he had very much liked the idea of her bringing him food), Dolores, again interrupting, has stated, "He never eats. Can't you tell? Dr. Abstemious, I used to call him."

"Well, I'm really hungry, I'll see you two later." And with an uncertain smile (from shyness? annoyance? and if annoyance, at which of them?), Carla has left. She is pushing back into the room, through the crowds; she has vanished behind the glass.

Looking at Dolores then, the old doctor is seized with rage; he stares at that puffy, self-adoring face, those dark and infinitely self-pitying eyes. How he longs to push her against the railing, down into the sand! How he despises her!

"My darling, I believe you're really hungry after all" is what Dolores says, but she may have felt some of his anger, for she deftly steps sideways, on her high, thin, dangerous heels, just out of his reach.

"Not in the least," says Benito rigidly. "In fact, I think I'll go for a walk on the beach."

Down on the sand, though, as he walks along the dark, packed strip that is nearest to the sea, Benito's confusion increases. He feels the presence of those people in that rather vulgar, glassed-in house behind him — of Dolores Gutierrez and Herman Tolliver, and God knows who else, what other ghosts from his past whom he simply failed to see. As though they were giants, he feels their looming presences, and feels their connection to some past year or years of his own life. He no longer knows where he is. What place is this, what country? What rolling gray-green ocean does he walk beside? What year is this, and what is his own true age?

Clearly, some derangement has taken hold of him, or nearly, and Benito is forced to fight back with certain heavy and irrefutable facts: this is September, 1990, the last year of a decade, and the year in which Elizabeth died. He is in Stinson Beach, and if he continues walking far enough along the coast — he is heading south, toward the Golden Gate — he will be in sight of beautiful, mythical San Francisco, the city and the center of all his early dreams, the city where everything, finally, happened: Dolores Gutierrez and his medical degree; Herman Tolliver and those hotels. His (at last) successful medical practice. Elizabeth, and all that money, and his house with its fabulous views. His fame as Dr. Do-Good.

His whole San Francisco history seems to rise up then and to break his heart. The city itself is still pale and distant and invisible, and he stands absolutely still, a tall figure on the sand, next to an intricate, crumbling sandcastle that some children have recently abandoned.

Hearing running feet behind him, at that moment the doctor turns in fright (expecting what? some dangerous stranger?) — but it is Carla, out of breath, her hair streaming backward in the wind. His savior.

"Ah, you," he says to her. "You ran."

"And these aren't the greatest running shoes." She laughs, pointing down to her sandals, now sand-streaked and damp.

"You came after me —"

She looks down, and away. "Well. It was partly an excuse to get out of there. It was getting a little claustrophobic, and almost everyone I talked to was hard of hearing."

"Oh, right."

"Well, shall we walk for a while?"

"*Yes.*"

Walking along with Carla, the doctor finds that those giants from his dark and tangled past have quite suddenly receded: Dolores and Tolliver have shrunk down to human size, the size of people accidentally encountered at a party. Such meetings can happen to anyone, easily, especially at a certain age.

Benito even finds that he can talk about them. "To tell you the truth" — an ominous beginning, he knows, but it is what he intends to do — "I did some business with Herman Tolliver a long time ago, maybe forty years. It came out very well, financially, but I'm still a little ashamed of it. It seems to me now that I was pretending to myself not to know certain things that I really did know."

"You mean about his hotels?"

"Well, yes. Hotels. But how do you — Does everyone know all that?"

"I'm a reporter, remember? Investigative." She laughs, then sniffles a little in the hard, cold ocean wind. "He had an idea a few years back about running for supervisor, but I'm sure he was really thinking mayor, ultimately. But we dug up some stuff."

"Here, take my handkerchief —"

"Thanks. Anyway, he was persuaded to forget it. There were really ugly things about preteen-age Asian girls. We made a bargain: the papers would print only the stuff about his 'tax problems' if he'd bow out." She sighs, a little ruefully. "I don't know. It might have been better to let him get into politics; he might have done less harm that way."

This walk, and the conversation, are serving both to calm and to excite the doctor. Simultaneously. Most peculiar. He feels a calm, and at the same time a strange, warm, quiet excitement. "How do you mean?" he asks Carla.

"Oh, he got in deeper and deeper. Getting richer and richer."

"I got richer and richer, too, back then. Sometimes I felt like I owned the whole goddam city." Benito is paying very little attention to what he is saying; it is now all he can do to prevent himself from speaking his heart, from saying, "When will you marry me? How soon can that be?"

"But that's great that you made so much money," Carla says. "That way you could start those clinics, and do so much good."

Barely listening, Benito murmurs, "I suppose . . ."

She could redecorate the house any way she would like to, he thinks. Throw things out, repaint, reupholster, add mirrors. His imagination sees, all completed, a brilliant house, with Carla its brilliant, shining center.

"How did you happen to know Dolores?" Carla is asking.

By now they have reached the end of the beach: a high mass of rocks left there by mammoth storms the year before. Impassable. Beyond lie more beach, more cliffs, more headlands, all along the way to the sight of the distant city.

"Actually, Dolores was an old girlfriend, you might say." Since he cares so much for this girl, Benito will never lie to her, he thinks. "You might not believe this, but she was quite a beauty in her day."

"Oh, I believe you. She's still so vain. That hair."

Benito laughs, feeling pleased, and wondering, Can this adorable girl be, even slightly, jealous? "You're right there," he tells Carla. "Very vain, always was. Of course, she's a few years older than I am."

"I guess we have to turn around now," says Carla.

"And now Dolores tells me that she and that Posey Pendergast were at one time, uh, lovers," Benito continues, in his honest mode.

"I guess they could have been," Carla muses. "On the other hand, it's my impression that Dolores lies a lot. And Posey I'm just not sure about. Nor any of that group, for that matter. Tolliver, all those people. It's worrying." She laughs. "I guess I sort of hoped you might know something about them. Sort of explain them to me."

Not having listened carefully to much of this, Benito rephrases the question he does not remember having begun to ask before, which Dolores interrupted: "How do you know Posey?" he asks Carla.

"It's mostly her son I know. Patrick. He's my fiancé, I guess you could say. We keep planning to make it legal, and I guess we will. Any day now." And she goes on. "Actually, Patrick was supposed to come today, and then he couldn't, and then I thought — I thought of you."

The sun has sunk into the ocean, and Benito's heart has sunk with it, drowned. He shudders, despising himself. How could he possibly have imagined, how not have guessed?

"How nice," Benito remarks, without meaning, and then he babbles on, "You know, the whole city seems so corrupt these days. It's all real estate, and deals."

"Get real," she chides him, in her harsh young voice. "That's what it's like all over."

"Well, I'll be awfully glad to get back to Mexico. At least I more or less understand the corruption there."

"Are you going back for long?"

The wind is really cold now. Benito sniffs, wishing he had his handkerchief back, and unable to ask for it. "Oh, permanently," he tells Carla. "A permanent move. I want to be near my clinics. See how they're doing. Maybe help."

The doctor had no plan to say (much less to do) any of this

before he spoke, but he knows that he is now committed to this action. This permanent move. He will buy a house in San Cristóbal de las Casas, and will bring his mother there, from Oaxaca, to live in that house for as long as she lasts. And he, for as long as he lasts, will work in his clinics, with his own poor.

"Well, that's great. Maybe we could work out a little interview before you go."

"Well, maybe."

"I wonder if we couldn't just bypass the party for now," says Carla. "I'm just not up to going in again, going through all that, with those people."

"Nor I," the doctor tells her. "Good idea."

"I'll call Posey as soon as we get back. Did she tell you the house was up for sale? She may have sold it today — all those people . . ."

Half hearing her, the doctor is wrestling with the idea of a return to the city, which is suddenly unaccountably terrible to him; he dreads the first pale, romantic view of it from the bridge, and then the drive across town to his empty house, after dropping Carla off on Telegraph Hill. His house with its night views of city hills and lights. But he braces himself with the thought that he won't be in San Francisco long this time. That as soon as he can arrange things he will be back in Chiapas, in Mexico. For the rest of his life.

And thus he manages to walk on, following Carla past the big, fancy house, for sale — and all those people, the house's rich and crazily corrupt population. He manages to walk across the sand toward his car, and the long, circuitous, and risky drive to the city.

Days of Heaven

FROM PLOUGHSHARES

THEIR PLANS were to develop the valley, and my plans were to stop them. I was caretaking this ranch in Montana that the two of them had bought, or were buying. One of them was an alcoholic and the other was a realtor. The alcoholic — the big one — was from New York and did something on the Stock Exchange.

The realtor had narrow, close-together eyes, little pinpoints in his pasty, puffy face, like raisins set in dough. He wore new jeans and a Western shirt with silver buttons and a big metal belt buckle with a horse on it, and he walked in his new cowboy boots in tiny little steps with his toes pointed in. He always walked that way. The realtor — Zim — was from Billings.

The big guy's name was Quentin. He had a big round stomach and a small mustache, and looked like a polar bear.

The feeling I got from the big guy was that he was recovering from some kind of breakdown, is why he was out here. And Zim — grinning, loose-necked, giggling pointy-toe-walking-all-the-time, always walking around as if he were an infant who'd just shit his diapers — Zim, the predator, had just the piece of Big Sky Quentin needed. I'll go ahead and say it right now, so that nobody gets the wrong idea: I didn't like Zim.

It was going fast, the Big Sky was, said Zim. All sorts of famous people — celebrities — were vacationing there. Moving there. "Brooke Shields," he said. "Tom Brokaw. Jim Nabors. Rich people, I mean *really* rich people. You could sell them things. Say you owned the little store in this valley — the mercantile — and say Michael Jackson — well, no, not *him* — say Kirk Douglas lives ten miles down the road. What's he going to do when he's having a party and realizes he doesn't have enough Dom Perignon? Who's he gonna call?

"He'll call your store, if you have such a service. Say the bottle costs $75. You'll sell it to him for $100 — you'll *deliver* it, you'll drive that ten miles up the road to take it to him — and he'll be glad to pay that extra money.

"Bing! Bang! Bim, bam!" Zim said, snapping his fingers and then rubbing them together, his mindless raisin eyes set so far back, glittering. His mouth was small and round and pale, like an anus. "You've made twenty-five dollars," he said, and the mouth broke into a grin.

What's twenty-five dollars, to a stockbroker guy? But I saw that Quentin was listening.

I've lived on this ranch for four years now. The guy who used to own this place before Quentin — he was a predator, too. A rough guy from Australia, he had put his life savings into building this mansion, this fortress deep in the woods, looking out over the big meadow.

The previous owner's name was Beauregard. He had built the mansion three stories tall, rising up into the trees like one of Tarzan's haunts. Beauregard had constructed, all over the property, various buildings and structures related to the dismemberment of his quarry: smokehouses with wire screening to keep the other predators out, and butchering houses (long wooden tables, with sinks, and high-intensity interrogating lamps over the long tables, for night work). There were even huge windmill-type hoists all over the property, which would be used to lift the hoof-sprawling animals — moose, bear, elk, their heads and necks limp in death — up into the sky, so that their hides could first be stripped, leaving the meat revealed . . .

It had been Beauregard's life dream to be a hunting guide, and he wanted to take rich people into the woods, so they could come out dragging behind them a deer, or a bear — some wild creature they could kill and then take home with them — and Beauregard made a go of it for three years, before the business went down and the bad spirits set in and he got divorced and had to put the place up for sale to make the alimony payments. The

divorce settlement would in no way allow either of the parties to
live in the mansion — it had to be both or none — and that's
where I came in: to caretake the place until it sold. They'd sunk
too much money into Beauregard's mansion to just leave it sitting out there in the forest, idle. Beauregard went back to Washington, D.C., where he got a job doing something for the CIA —
tracking fugitives was my guess, or maybe even killing them,
while his wife went to California with the kids.

Beauregard had been a mercenary for a while. He said the bat-
tles were usually fought at dawn and dusk, so sometimes in the
middle of the day he'd been able to get away and go hunting. In
the mansion, the dark, noble heads of long-ago beasts from all
over the world — elephants, and elk, and greater Thomson's ga-
zelles, and giant oryx — lined the walls of all the rooms. There
was a giant gleaming sailfish leaping over the headboard of my
bed upstairs, and there were woodstoves, and fireplaces, but no
electricity. This place is so far into the middle of nowhere. After
I took the caretaking position, the ex-wife would send postcards
saying how much she enjoyed twenty-four-hour electricity and
how she'd get up in the middle of the night — two A.M., four
A.M. — and flick on a light switch, just for the hell of it.

I felt like I was taking advantage of Beauregard, moving into
his castle while he slaved away in D.C. — but I'm a bit of a killer
myself, in some ways, if you get right down to it, and if Beauregard's hard luck was my good luck, well, I tried not to lose any
sleep over it.

If anything, I gained sleep over it, especially in the summer.
I'd get up kind of late — eight, nine o'clock — and fix a big
breakfast, and feed my dogs, and then go out on the porch and
sit in the rocking chair, and look out over the valley or read.

Then about noon I'd pack a lunch and go for a walk. I'd take
the dogs with me, and a book, and we'd start up the trail behind
the house, walking through the centuries-old larch and cedar
forest, following the creek up to the big waterfall — heavy, heavy
timber. Deer moved quietly through that forest, big deer, and
pileated woodpeckers, too, banging away on some of the old
dead trees, going at it like cannons. It was shady back in that old
forest, and the sun rarely made it down to the ground, stopping
instead on all the various levels of leaves. I'd get to the waterfall,

and swim — so cold! — with the dogs, and then they'd nap in some ferns while I sat on a rock and read some more.

In mid-afternoon I'd come home — it would be hot then, in the summer — the fields and meadows all around the ranch smelled of wild strawberries, and I'd stop and pick some when I came out of the forest. By that time of day it would be too hot to do anything but take a nap, so that's what I'd do, upstairs, on the bare mattress with no sheets, with the windows all open, no breeze, and a fly buzzing faintly in one of the other rooms, one of the many empty other rooms.

I would sleep in that sun-filled room upstairs, groggy in the heat — sleeping a pure, happy, dreamless sleep — and then when it cooled down enough — around seven or eight in the evening — I'd wake up and take my fly rod over to the other side of the meadow. It didn't get dark until midnight, in the summer. A spring creek wandered along the edge of that far meadow, and I'd catch a brook trout for supper: I'd keep just one. There were too many fish in the little creek, and they were too easy to catch, so that after an hour or two I'd get tired of catching them, and I'd take the one I'd decided to keep back to the cabin, and fry him for supper.

Then I would have to decide whether to read some more, or go for another walk, or to just sit on the porch with a drink in hand — just one big one — and watch the elk come out into the meadow. Usually I chose that last option — the one about the single big drink — and sometimes, while I was out on the porch, this great gray owl would come flying in from out of the woods. It was always a thrill to see it — that huge, wild, silent creature flying into my front yard.

The great gray owl's a strange creature. It's immense, and so shy that it lives only back in the oldest of the old-growth forests, among giant trees, as if to match its own great size against them. It sits very still for long stretches of time, back in the woods, motionless, watching for prey, until — so say the biologists — *it believes it is invisible,* and a person or a deer can walk right past it — or can even walk right up to it — and so secure is the bird in its invisibility, its psychological cloak of being hidden, that it will not move — even if you're looking straight at it, it's convinced you can't see it, and it won't blink, won't move.

Now *that's* shy.

My job, my only job, was to live in the lodge, and keep intruders out. There had been a "For Sale" sign out front, but I'd taken that down and hidden it in the garage the first day.

After a couple of years, Beauregard, the real killer, did sell the place, and was out of the picture. Pointy-toed Zim got his ten percent, I suppose — ten percent of $350,000, a third of a million for some place with no electricity! — but Quentin, the breaker of stocks, didn't buy it right away. He *said* he was going to buy it, the first day, the first five minutes he saw it — he took me aside and asked if I could stay on, and, like a true predator, I said, Hell yes. I didn't care who owned it, as long as I got to stay there, and as long as the owner lived far away, and wasn't someone who would keep mucking up my life with a lot of visits.

Quentin didn't want to live there, or even visit — he just wanted to *own* it. He wanted to buy the place, but first he wanted to toy with Beauregard for a while, to try and drive the price down five or ten or twenty thousand; he wanted to *flirt* with him, I think.

Myself, I would've been terrified to jack with Beauregard. The man had bullet holes in his arms and legs; he'd been in foreign prisons, and had killed people. A bear had bitten him in the face on one of his hunts, a bear he'd thought was dead.

Quentin and Zim would sometimes come out on "scouting trips," that summer and fall that they were buying the place — Zim's family back in Billings, and Quentin's back in the Big Apple — and they'd show up unannounced, with a bag of stupid groceries — Cheerios, and Pop Tarts, and hot dogs, and a big carton of Marlboro cigarettes — and they'd want to stay for the weekend, to get a better "feel" for the place. I'd have to move my stuff — sleeping bag, and frying pan, and fishing rod — over to the guest house, which was spacious enough. I didn't mind that; I just didn't like the idea of having them in the house.

Once, while Quentin and Zim were walking in the woods behind the house, I looked in one of their dumb little sacks of groceries to see what stupid things they'd brought this time, and a magazine fell out of one of the sacks — a magazine with a picture of naked men on the cover; I mean, drooping penises and all, and the inside of the magazine was worse, with naked little boys, and naked men on motorcycles.

None of the naked men or boys were *doing* anything — they weren't touching each other — but still, the whole magazine, that part of it that I looked at, was nothing but heinies and penises.

Realtors!

I'd see the two old boys out on the front porch, the cabin all ablaze with light — those sapsuckers running *my* generator, *my* propane, far into the night, playing *my* Jimmy Buffett records, sitting out on the front porch and singing at the tops of their lungs — and then finally, they'd turn the lights off, shut the generator down, and go to bed.

Except Quentin would stay up a little longer. I'd sit on the porch of the guest house, at the other end of the meadow, my pups asleep at my feet, and I'd see Quentin moving through the house, lighting the gas lanterns, walking from room to room, like a ghost, and then the son of a bitch would start having one of his fits.

He'd break things — my things, and Beauregard's things — though I suppose they were now *his* things, since the deal was in the works: plates, saucers, and lanterns, and windows . . . I'd listen to the crashing of glass, and watch his big polar-bear whirling shape passing from room to room — sometimes he'd have a pistol (they both carried 9mm Blackhawks on their hips, like little cowboys) — and sometimes Quentin would shoot holes in the ceiling, holes in the walls.

I'd tense, there in the dark. . . . This wasn't good for my peace of mind. My days of heaven — I'd gotten used to them, and I wanted to defend them, and protect them, even if they weren't mine in the first place; even if I'd never owned them.

Then I'd see, in that low lamplight, Zim come into the room. Like some old queen, he'd put his arm around Quentin's big shoulders, and lead him away, lead him to bed.

After they left, the house stank of cigarettes, and I wouldn't sleep in the bed for weeks. I'd sleep in one of the many guest rooms. Once I found some mouthwash spray under the bed, and pictured the two of them lying there in bed, spraying it into each other's mouths in the morning, before kissing . . .

I'm talking like a homophobe here. I don't think it's that at all. I think it was just that realtor. He wasn't in it for the love. He was just turning a trick, was all.

I felt sorry for Quentin. It was strange how shy he was — how he always tried to cover up his destruction — smearing wood putty into the bullet holes in the ceiling and mopping the food off the ceiling — this fractured *stockbroker*, doing domestic work — making lame excuses to me the next day about the broken glass — "I was shooting at a bat," he'd say, "a bat came in the window" — and all the while, Zim, in pursuit of that ten percent, would be sitting out on my porch, looking out at my valley — this *Billings* person, from the hot, dry, dusty eastern part of the state — sitting there with his boots propped up on the railing and smoking the cigarettes that would not kill him quick enough.

Once, as the three of us sat there — Quentin asking me some questions about the valley, about how cold it got, in the winter ("Cold," I said, "very, *very* cold") — we saw a coyote and her three pups go trotting, in the middle of the day, across the meadow.

And Zim jumped up, seized a stick of firewood from the front porch (*my* firewood!) and ran, in his dirty-diaper waddle, out into the field after the mother coyote and pups, running like a madman, waving the club. The mother coyote got two of the pups into the trees, picking them up and carrying them by the scruff of their necks, but Zim, Zim got the third one, and stood over it, pounding, in the hot midday sun.

It's an old story, but it was a new one for me — how narrow the boundary is between invisibility and collusion. If you don't stop it, if you don't single-handedly step up and change things, then aren't you just as guilty?

I didn't say anything — not even when Zim came huffing back up to the porch, walking like a man who had just gone to get the morning paper. There was blood speckled around the cuffs of his pants, and even then I said nothing. I did not want to lose my job. My love for this valley had me trapped.

We all three sat there on the porch like everything was the same — Zim breathing a bit more heavily, was all — and I thought I would be able to keep my allegiances secret, through my silence. But they knew whose side I was on. It had been *re-*

vealed to them. It was as if they had infrared vision, as if they
could see everywhere — and everything.

"Coyotes eat baby deer and livestock," said the raisin-eyed son
of a bitch. "Remember," he said, addressing my silence, "it's not
your ranch anymore. All you do is live here and keep the pipes
from freezing." Zim glanced over at his big soulmate. I thought
how when Quentin had another crack-up and lost this place,
Zim would get the ten percent again, and again and again, each
time.

Quentin's face was hard to read; I couldn't tell if he was angry
with Zim or not. Everything about Quentin seemed hidden at
that moment. How did they do it? How could the sons of bitches
be so good at camouflaging themselves when they had to?

I wanted to trick them. I wanted to hide and see them reveal
their hearts — I wanted to watch them when they did not know I
was watching, and see how they really were — not just listen to
them shooting the shit about their plans for the valley, but
deeper. I wanted to see what was at the *bottom* of their black fucking hearts.

Finally Quentin blinked and turned calmly, still revealing no
emotion, and gave his pronouncement.

"If the coyotes eat the little deers, they should go," he said.
"Hunters should be the only thing out here getting the little
deers."

The woods still felt the same, when I went for my walks after the
two old boys departed. Yellow tanagers still flitted through the
trees, flashing blazes of gold, and the deer were still tame. Ravens
quorked as they passed through the dark woods, as if to reassure
me that they were still on my side, that I was still with nature,
rather than without.

I slept late. I read. I hiked. I fished in the evenings. I saw the
most spectacular sights. Northern lights kept me up until four in
the morning some nights — coiling in red and green spirals
across the sky, exploding in iridescent furls and banners. . . .
The northern lights never displayed themselves while the killers
were there, and for that, I was glad.

In the late mornings and early afternoons, I'd sit by the waterfall and eat my peanut butter and jelly sandwich. I'd see the same
magic sights: bull moose, their shovel antlers still in velvet, step-

ping over fallen, rotting logs; calypso orchids sprouting along
the trail, glistening and nodding — but it felt, too, like the woods
were a vessel, filling up with something of which they could only
hold so much — call it wildness — and when they had absorbed
all they could, when they could hold no more, then things would
change, and that wildness they could not hold would have to spill
out, would have to go somewhere . . .

Zim and Quentin came out only two or three times a year, for
two or three days at a time. The rest of the time, heaven was
mine — all those days of heaven. You wouldn't think they could
hurt anything, coming out so infrequently. But how little of a
thing does it take to change — spoil — another thing?

I'll tell you what I think: The cleaner and emptier a place is,
the less it can take. It's like some crazy kind of paradox.

After a while Zim came up with the idea of bulldozing the
meadow across the way, and building a lake, with sailboats and
docks. He hooked Quentin up into a deal with a log-home man-
ufacturer in the southern part of the state, and was going to put
shiny new "El Supremo" model log homes all around the lake.
He was going to build a small hydro dam on the creek, and bring
electricity into the valley with it, which would automatically double real estate values, Zim said. He was going to run cattle in the
woods, lots of cattle. And set up a little gold mine operation, over
on the north face of Roderick Butte. The two boys had folders
and folders of ideas, plans.

They just needed a little investment capital, was all.

In the South, where I had come from, tenants held the power
of a barnburning if their landlords got out of hand. Even a poor
man or woman can light a match. But not here: a fire in this
country wouldn't ever stop.

There seemed like there was nothing — absolutely nothing —
I could do. Anything I did short of killing Zim and Quentin
would be a token act, a symbol. Before I figured that out, I sacrificed a tree, chopped down a big wind-leaning larch so that it fell
on top of the cabin, doing great damage while Zim and Quentin
were upstairs. I wanted to show them what a money sink the
ranch was, and how dangerous it could be, and I told them how
beavers, forest beavers, had chewed down that tree that had
missed landing in their bedroom by only a few feet.

I know now that those razor-bastards knew everything; they

could *sense* that I'd cut that tree. But for some crazy reason they pretended to go along with my story. Quentin had me spend two days sawing the tree up for firewood, and before he could get the carpenters out to repair the damage, a hard rain blew in and soaked some of my books.

I figured there was nothing I could *do*. Anything I did to harm the land or their property would harm me.

Meanwhile, the valley flowered. Summer came, stretched and yawned, and then it was early fall. Quentin brought his children out, early that second fall — the fall of ownership. Zim didn't make that trip, nor did I spy any of the nekkid magazines. The kids — two teenage girls, and a teenage boy, a younger Quentin — were okay for a day or two (the girls running the generator and watching movies on the VCR the whole day long), but the boy, little Quentin, was going to be trouble, I could tell — the first words out of his mouth when they arrived were "Is it any kind of . . . is there any season for . . . can you *shoot* anything right now? Rabbits? Marmots?"

And sure enough, they made it two days before discovering there were fish — delicate little brook trout, with polka-dotted, flashy, colorful sides, and intelligent little gold-rimmed eyes, spawning on gravel beds in the shallow little creek that ran through the meadow on the other side of the road — and what Quentin's son did, after discovering this fact, was to borrow his dad's shotgun, and he began shooting the fish.

Little Quentin loaded, blasted away, reloaded — it was a pump-action twelve gauge, like the ones used in big-city detective movies, and the motion was like masturbating — jack, jack, *boom,* jack, jack, *boom* — and little Quentin's sisters came running out and rolled up their pants legs and waded out into the stream and began picking up the dead fish, and pieces of fish, and began eating those fish.

Quentin sat up on the porch with his drink in hand, and watched, smiling.

In the first week of November, while out walking — the skies that sweet, dull, purple lead color, and the air frosty, flirting with snow — I heard ravens, and then scented the newly dead smell of a kill, and moved over in that direction.

I saw the ravens' black shapes taking flight up into the trees as I approached; I could see the huge shape of what they'd been feasting on — a body of such immensity that I paused, frightened, even though the huge shape was obviously dead.

It was two bull moose, their antlers locked up from rut-combat — the rut having been over for a month, I knew — and I guessed they'd been locked up for at least that long. One moose was long-ago dead (two weeks?) but the other moose had died so recently (that morning, perhaps) that he still had all his hide on him, and wasn't even stiff. The ravens and coyotes had already done a pretty good job on the first moose, stripping what they could while his partner, his enemy, was thrashing and flailing, I could tell; small trees and brush were leveled all around them, and I could see the swath, the direction from which they had come — locked-up, floundering, fighting — to this final resting spot.

I went and borrowed a neighbor's draft horse. The moose that had died just that morning wasn't so much heavy as he was just big — he'd lost a lot of weight during the month he'd been tied up with the other moose — and the other one was just a ship of bones, mostly empty air.

Their antlers were locked together as if welded. I tied a big rope around the newly dead moose's rear legs and got the draft horse to drag the cargo out of the woods and down through the forest, to the ranch. It was a couple of miles, and I walked next to the old draft horse, soothing him as he sledded, forty feet behind him, his strange load. Ravens flew behind us, cawing at our theft; some of them filtered down through the trees and landed on top of the newly dead moose's brave, humped back and rode along like that, pecking at the hide, trying to find an opening — but the hide was too thick, they'd have to wait for the coyotes to open it — and so they rode with me like gypsies: myself, and the draft horse, and the ravens, and the dead moose (as if they'd come back to life) moving through the woods like a giant serpent, snaking our way through the trees.

I hid the carcasses at the edge of the woods and then, on the other side of a small clearing, built a blind of branches and leaves where I could hide and watch over the carcasses.

I painted my face camouflage green and brown, and settled into my blind, and waited.

The next day, like buffalo wolves from out of the mist, Quentin and Zim reappeared. I'd hidden my truck a couple of miles away and locked up the cabin so they'd think I was gone.

I wanted to watch without being seen. I wanted to see them in the wild — wanted to see what they were like when humans weren't watching them.

"What the *shit!*" Zim cried as he got out of his big mongo-tire Jeep, the one with the electric winch, electric windows, electric sunroof, electric cattle prod. Ravens were swarming my trap, gorging, and coyotes darted in and out, tearing at that other moose's hide, trying to peel the hide back and reveal the new flesh.

"Shit fire!" Zim cried, running across the yard — hopping the buck-and-rail fence, his flabby ass getting caught astraddle the high bar for a moment. He ran out into the woods, shooing the ravens and coyotes. The ravens all screamed and rose into the sky as if caught in a huge tornado, as if *summoned*. Some of the bolder ones came back down and made passes at Zim's head, but he waved them away, and shouted, "Shit fire!" again, and then, examining the newly dead moose, said, "This meat's still good!"

Zim and Quentin worked by lantern light that night: peeling the hide back with butchering and skinning knives, and hacking at the flesh with hatchets. I stayed in the bushes and watched. The hatchets made whacks when they hit the flesh, and cracking sounds when they hit bone. I could hear the two men laughing. Zim reached over and spread a smear of blood, delicately, on Quentin's cheeks, applying it like makeup, or medicine of some sort, and they paused, catching their breath from their mad chopping, and then they went back to work. They ripped and sawed slabs of meat from the carcass and hooted, cheering each time they pulled a leg off the carcass.

They dragged the meat up to the smokehouse — dragging it through the autumn-dead grass — and cut the head and antlers off last, right before daylight.

I hiked over and got my truck, washed my face in a stream, and drove shakily home.

They waved when they saw me come driving up; they were out on the front porch having breakfast, all clean and fresh-scrubbed.

I went up to the porch, where they were talking among themselves as they always had, talking as normal as pie.

Zim was lecturing to Quentin — waving his arm at the meadow and preaching the catechism of development to him.

"You could have a nice hunting camp and send 'em all out into the woods on horses, with a yellow slicker and a gun — boom! They're living the Western Experience. Then in the winter, you could run just a regular guest lodge, like on *Newhart*. Make 'em pay for everything. They want to go cross-country skiing? Rent 'em. They want to race snowmobiles? Rent 'em. Charge 'em for taking a *piss*. Rich people don't mind."

I was just hanging on: shaky. They finished their breakfast and went back inside to plot, or watch VCR movies. I went over to the smokehouse, and peered through the dusty windows. Blood dripped from the gleaming red hindquarters. They'd cut the moose's head off and nailed it, with the antlers, to one of the walls, so that his blue-blind eyes were looking out at his own corpse. There was a baseball cap on his antlers, and a cigar stuck between his big lips.

I went up into the woods.

But I knew I'd come back. I liked living in that cabin, and liked living at the edge of that meadow, and looking out at it.

Later that evening, we were out on the porch again, watching the end of the day come in — the days getting so much shorter — and Quentin and Zim were still pretending to be normal, still pretending that none of the previous night's savagery had happened.

It occurred to me that if they thought I had the power to stop them, they would have put my head in that smokehouse a long time ago. Would have put a baseball cap on my head, stuck a cigar in my mouth.

Quentin, looking especially burned out, had slipped from his chair. He was sitting on the floor with his back to the cabin wall, bottle of rum in hand, looking toward the meadow, where his lake and lots of cabins with lights burning in each of them would someday sit. I was just hanging around to see what was what, to eavesdrop, and to try to slow them down — to talk about those hard winters whenever I got the chance, and to mention how unfriendly the people in the valley were. Which was true, but hard to convince Quentin of, because every time he showed up, they got friendly.

"I'd like that a lot," said Quentin, speaking slowly. Earlier in the day I'd seen a coyote, or possibly a wolf — *sans* pups — trot across the meadow, but I sure hadn't pointed it to anyone. Even as we were sitting on the porch, there was the great gray owl — he'd flown in like a plane, ghostly gray, a four-foot wingspan — perched on the falling-down buck-and-rail fence by the road. I hadn't seen the owl in a couple of weeks, and I felt uneasy. It would be nothing for a man like Zim to walk up to that owl with his cowboy pistol, and put a bullet, point blank, into the big bird's ear — the big bird with his eyes set in his face, looking straight at you, the way all predators do.

"I'd like that so much," Quentin said again — meaning Zim's idea of the lodge as a resort, in winter. He was wearing a gold chain around his neck, with a little gold pistol dangling from it. He'd have to get rid of that necklace if he moved out here. It looked like something he might have gotten from a Cracker Jack box, but was, doubtless, real gold.

"It may sound corny," Quentin said, "but if I owned this valley, I'd let people from New York, from California, from wherever, come out here for Christmas and New Year's. I'd put a big sixty-foot Christmas tree in the middle of the road, up by the mercantile and the saloon, and string it with lights, and we'd all ride up there in a sleigh, Christmas Eve and New Year's Eve, and we'd sing carols, you know? It would be real small-town and homey," Quentin said. "Maybe corny, but that's what I'd do."

Zim nodded. "There's lonely people who would pay through the nose for something like that," he said.

We sat there and just watched the dusk gliding in over the meadow, cooling things off, blanketing the field's dull warmth of the day and making mist and steam rise from the field.

Quentin and Zim were waiting for money, and Quentin, especially, was still waiting for his nerves to calm: almost a year he'd owned the ranch, a full cycle of seasons, and still he wasn't well.

A little something — peace? — would do him good. I could see that Christmas tree all lit up; I could feel that sense of *community*, of new beginnings.

I wouldn't go to such a festivity; I'd stay back in the woods, like the great gray. But I could see the attraction, could see Quentin's need for peace; how he had to have a place to start anew — though soon enough, too, I knew, he would begin taking ten percent from the newness again.

Around midnight, I knew, he'd take to smashing things — and I couldn't blame him. Quentin was wild, and of course he wanted to come to the woods, too.

I didn't know if the woods would have him.

We sat there and watched dusk come sliding in. All I could do was wait. I sat very still, like that owl, and thought about where I could go next, after this place was gone. Maybe, I thought, if I sit very still, they will just go away.

THOMAS BELLER

A Different Kind
of Imperfection

FROM THE NEW YORKER

AND THEN IT was Christmas vacation and he was home. "Welcome home, Alexander!" his mother said when he walked in the door, pressing her warm face against his cold one. She was the only person who used his full name. It sounded odd.

She had bought some flowers and arranged them around the house in the special way she had of making things seem nice and attended to. Having brought him up alone — his father had died when he was ten — his mother was diligent about respecting his privacy, not prying into his life. He always felt guilty about not wanting to tell her things about himself, the few times she asked. After all, he was her son, her only child, and his life would be of interest to her.

"So. Tell me about school," she said now, sitting across from him at the kitchen table. His bags were piled up behind him in the foyer, and he slouched in his chair, which felt too small for him. The whole house seemed oddly small in comparison with the high ceilings of the ancient dorm he lived in at Vassar, where he was now a sophomore.

The scene — his mother and himself in the same chairs, the same look on her face — reminded him of coming home from kindergarten and having his mother and his father ask him how school was, while they sat at the kitchen table. He had always shrugged and said nothing, but he sometimes wondered whether both of his parents had spent their entire day waiting for him at the kitchen table, discussing him. All that attention seemed to demand more from him than anything he could supply with meager details about his fractions or his papier-mâché cow, so he usually said nothing. Eventually, he would shrug and slouch on into his room, down the long dark hallway. But he had always liked the idea that both his parents had been in conference over him all day.

Now here was his mother sitting in the same position at the kitchen table, smiling and asking him the same questions, looking loving and a little daunting, as usual. It was too much love to live up to.

"There's really nothing much to say," he answered, thinking about Sloan, his suddenly ex-girlfriend. She lived in Baltimore. He had never thought about that city, but now that Sloan lived there, was in fact there that very moment, Baltimore seemed like an alluring place. "I seem to be getting the hang of how to be a college student," he said. "It's not too difficult."

"And your studies?"

Alex winced at the word. "Studies" was too dignified for what he was doing. "Well, I'm not going to major in sociology. That's all I can say for sure."

"What's it like?" she asked.

"The dorms are pretty nice, but at night the only place to get food is the candy machine." He paused for a moment. "The classes are good, though," he went on, thinking she would enjoy hearing that.

Sloan was the first girl he had really gone out with in college, and, by extension, the first girl he had really broken up with. She was a vegetarian poet who had her own place off campus, which seemed like a very daring move in sophomore year. Her apartment was just across the road, but the fact that it was technically off campus made it feel illicit. They had gone out together for a few months, but just before vacation Sloan informed him — or "reminded" him, as she pointed out — that she had another boyfriend at home. She told him that she felt she had to give that a chance. It was shaping up to be a miserable Christmas vacation, he thought.

His mother cupped her face in her hands. Her chin rested on the heel of each palm, and her fingers were over her cheeks, framing her face. She was very pretty, and yet even her happiest expression always seemed to have a tinge of sadness. His father had died of cancer ten years earlier, and Alex couldn't remember whether this look of gravity had come into her face after that. Perhaps being happy always reminded her of her loss. She hadn't remarried. She hadn't even painted the apartment. Alex looked into her liquid eyes and smiled. Then he escaped down the hall.

His room seemed different. Freshman year, he had scurried down to New York from Poughkeepsie almost every chance he got, and his first Christmas vacation had seemed like a reprieve. His room had welcomed him. His mother had welcomed him. The whole house had burst into life, as if it had been in suspended animation since the day he left. Coming home this time was different; he couldn't get over how strange it felt to be back. His room was exactly as he had left it, but it just sat there, inanimate, waiting to be occupied by whoever came along.

He went out into the early-evening light and walked over to a bar on Eighty-third and Amsterdam, the Jaunting Car. It was the last bar in his neighborhood with any charm, but today it was almost empty. He ordered a Scotch and looked at himself in the mirror behind the bar. One of the better things he had acquired since going to college was a taste for Scotch. Previously he had drunk only vodka, a habit he had formed at the age of fourteen when he had sampled all the bottles in his parents' liquor cabinet and had decided that vodka was the least unpleasant. His mother didn't drink, and hardly ever had guests, and it had sometimes occurred to him that the bottle of Wolfschmidt he was drinking from had probably been bought by his father. His first cigarette, which he had smoked at about the same age, had come from an ancient pack of Dunhills he had found in a table drawer, in among a collection of broken sunglasses frames, pipe cleaners, loose buttons, and other artifacts of his father's. It was an odd collection of items, the debris that comes together only because there isn't enough of any one thing to require its own drawer. When he came upon it, four years after his father died, the stash itself looked static, stunned with age. That cigarette, Alex recalled now, was rancid. The pack of Dunhills was probably still there. The drawer was always shut.

He spent the first few days back from school mostly alone. He had stopped frantically trying to touch base with friends from high school the way he'd done at this time a year ago. He thought about Sloan, he walked around the streets at midday in the bright high winter sun, and spent hours meandering around his house examining shelves and closets he hadn't looked at in years. The apartment, with its cracked and peeling paint, its rickety wooden chairs with half-broken cane seats, was filled with books, among them many dark green or maroon volumes with titles like *Textbook of Pathology, Clinical Hematology,* and a huge book with the ominous title *Heart.* His father had been a doctor — a psychiatrist. Alex perused the bookshelves with a peculiar interest, as if he were looking for clues. One set of twenty-four books in pale blue dust jackets took up an entire shelf: the complete works of Sigmund Freud. He took out *Totem and Taboo* and looked at the first chapter, "The Horror of Incest." He put the book back with the haste of someone who has opened the door of an occupied bathroom.

Scanning for a lighter topic, he took down *Jokes and Their Relation to the Unconscious.* He opened to a random page and read, "It is remarkable how universally popular a smutty interchange of this kind is among the common people and how it unfailingly produces a cheerful mood."

He returned the book to its place, and listened to the silence of the house. He and his mother lived in an apartment building, but all their neighbors were quiet. While he was growing up, the only noisy person in the building had been himself — he had once bounced a rubber ball so incessantly that the downstairs neighbors had called the police. He then took to throwing water balloons out the window. He was so intrigued by the way the balloons shimmered — like Jell-O, he thought — in their flight that he always forgot to duck his head back in the window in time and soon he got caught. He and his mother were nearly evicted, she told him. Again and again, as he prowled around the house now, he was struck by the evidence of lives lived. It lay on the shelves, along the walls, stacked in piles on the floor.

Alex's college roommate, Milo, called and announced that he was going to be in New York for an afternoon before he went skiing. They met in a coffee shop for lunch.

"You're bored," Milo said over a tuna fish sandwich. "You should get out of New York. Come skiing with me."

"I don't ski," Alex said.

"Come for the scenery."

"There's plenty of scenery here. I can see a little sliver of the Hudson River and part of New Jersey from my window."

Milo gave Alex an appraising look. "Come for the women," he said. "This place is going to be crawling with women. You need a distraction."

"I am distracted," said Alex. "I need to concentrate."

"You're concentrating on your distraction," Milo said. A little piece of food had lodged itself at the corner of his mouth. This completely discredited him in Alex's mind. The guy couldn't swallow properly; he wasn't someone whose advice was going to be helpful.

"All right, all right," Milo went on. "You're concentrating on Sloan, which is depressing you. Tell you what — work on it, and when you've got it perfected give me a call." Then he neatly pinched the tuna speck from the corner of his mouth and flicked it at Alex.

"That was the problem with you and Sloan," he went on, with some satisfaction. "You were just an amateur at being depressed. Sloan was a pro. You couldn't keep up."

The apartment's foreignness had begun to wear off, giving way to something even more disturbing. It was familiarity, but not the kind that makes things disappear into the background. Now every detail jumped out and announced itself as significant, the way banal things became conspicuous whenever there were guests in the apartment. Alex was his own guest now, he decided, a sightseer in his own home.

He began to realize that his apartment was submerged in books — hundreds and hundreds of them, in the corner bookshelf, on the bookshelf against the wall, or stacked in dusty heaps in a corner, spilling over everywhere. He noticed that some of the books held slivers of paper, which projected above the tops of the pages. He opened one such book and discovered faded pencil underlinings on each of the marked pages, with a word or two of comment here and there in the margin. Alex didn't know much about his father's intellectual life, but he had lately noticed that his father's haphazard handwriting bore a conspicuous resemblance to his own. He examined the pages more carefully, and the marginal notes seemed to confirm it. He went from book to book and eventually stopped at one and began to read. It was *To the Lighthouse,* by Virginia Woolf — a book he'd never read.

The volume itself was old; its gray cloth cover was tattered at the corners, but the binding remained stiff and dignified. The pages were only slightly yellow and had a certain weight to them. The book had been published in 1927, five years after his father was born.

When had his father read it? He had arrived in America as a teenager sometime before the Second World War. So if his father had read this in college it would have been the early 1940s, and he would have been almost the same age as Alex was now, reading the same pages. But there was the possibility that his father read the book years later. Maybe even after Alex was born. There were no marks to indicate which, one way or another.

He read on, turning each page in anticipation of another one of his father's marks. On page 99, a strand of pencil underlined a fragment of a sentence: ". . . she had known happiness, exquisite happiness, intense happiness." It was not a line that would have jumped out at Alex, but seeing it underlined by his father disturbed him and moved him. The words "exquisite happiness, intense happiness" resonated above the whispery pencil mark that flowed underneath them. Alex stared at the pencil lines for a moment, as if they were completely separated from the writing. He was waiting for the lines to reveal something. The pencil was neither sharp nor dull. The lines didn't seem to have been drawn with a great deal of pressure, but they weren't too light, either. Had they been made in bed, or at a desk, or in an armchair — or on a bus? He felt a pang of frustration, trying to imagine what his father had been thinking. It was a sharp twinge that made him shudder for a moment.

He was in the kitchen one afternoon, staring into the refrigerator, when his mother came in and sat down at the table expectantly, as if she wanted to have a conversation. He obliged, sitting down across from her.

She smiled, tilted her head a little, and said, "What are you thinking?"

"Nothing," he said. He wanted to say more but he couldn't. It was always this way with his mother — the unwilling retreat.

"You have been walking around with a funny expression, as if something were bothering you."

"Nothing is bothering me. It's just odd to be back. You know, like, when you go away and then come back and it's, like —"

"Stop saying 'like.' "

"It's weird, then."

"I can tell something is on your mind. You have this cloudy look about you. I've been wanting to bring it up for some time now."

"I've only been home for three days."

"But before, even. I've been worried about you." His mother had the rare but unmistakable expression she got when she was preparing to try to exert authority. She wasn't the authoritarian type, but in the absence of his father she had to take the offensive periodically.

"You seem very unfocused," she said. "As if you're drifting. There is a certain urgency lacking."

"What's there to be urgent about, Mom? It's Christmas vacation."

She looked at him some more, with her hazel eyes, which sometimes turned green. Her affection was discomforting, though he had never been without it, or even considered that he might ever be. He felt his cheeks warm up, and watched the corners of her mouth slowly turn into a bittersweet smile, as if she were seeing something that had not yet come into view for him.

Another passage read: "He knew, of course he knew, that she loved him. He could not deny it. And smiling she looked out of the window and said (thinking to herself, Nothing on earth can equal this happiness) —" A dried piece of scraggly orangish paper — a ripped strip of it — had stuck out of the top of the book like a buoy in a channel, and when he got to it he found those words underlined in pencil.

He took out the shred of paper and examined it. He was sitting on the floor in a dusty corner of the study, next to a ragged brown armchair. It was a shred, all right — one of several torn up and placed, perhaps, in a pile, so they could be used over the course of a reading session. This shred was the first of several sprouting up from the top of the book, a grove of markers densely clustered in an area where his father seemed to have found interesting material.

The next marked page contained just one underlined sentence: "It's almost too dark to see." Very enigmatic observation, thought Alex.

Some lines were neatly drawn, but most had been made casually, almost sloppily, though they never ran over the words. They wavered. It was hard for him to gauge how much the pencil marks had faded over time.

The whole issue of time and dates bothered him. How old had his father been when he made these marks? Alex wanted to know. Another underlined segment he came across was itself in quotes and read: " 'And all the lives we ever lived / And all the lives to be, / Are full of trees and changing leaves.' " How old would the man be who had marked that?

Alex walked around his neighborhood in the daytime, looking at people passing, and wondering why they weren't at work. No one in the middle of the day in a residential neighborhood was in a rush, he realized. He scrutinized faces, searching for the anxiety of lateness, but only found people drifting in or out of hardware stores, clothing stores, the corner market. What was their excuse? He had his and it comforted him: he was a student. Such an easy excuse — he wondered how long it would last. At this rate, he thought, an eternity.

He imagined calling Sloan. "I've discovered peeling paint on all the walls and I've walked around the apartment pulling pieces off the ceiling so it won't look as bad," he would say. "The house hasn't been painted since three years before my dad died."

"Maybe you should get the place painted," she would say. She was annoyingly pragmatic when she wanted to keep a distance between them.

"I thought maybe you weren't having a good time with what's-his-name and wanted to come up to New York," he would say. He imagined what she would say to a question like that. He decided he wouldn't want to hear it.

Amid a battalion of small photographs set up on his mother's bedroom bureau there was a small snapshot of his parents. His father and mother were extremely good-looking — particularly his mother, who had high, sharp cheekbones and thin lips, and wore her brown hair in a bun. Her family was from Berlin; her grandfather had been an enormously wealthy banker who shot himself just after the First World War, when he had lost all his money. Alex liked that detail of his family history; the combination of death and money had a certain glamour for him.

His father had been born in Vienna. He was handsome in the photograph, with dark hair and deep grooves in his face, particularly in the forehead. He had a certain monkey quality to him. The picture was a head-and-shoulders shot of the two of them, dressed up nicely, with their shoulders squared to the camera but with their heads turned a little toward each other, each of them gazing at the other's face. His mother looked stunning. She was wearing a black dress that contrasted sharply with the string of pearls around her neck; her smooth skin caught the light and glowed. His father was merely handsome in comparison, and his smile suggested that he felt gleeful at his good luck. But they shared a conspiratorial look, glimmering with hidden knowledge. Was it the secret of beauty? Was it the secret of happiness? Alex imagined the moment as intense.

The picture was small, no more than two inches square. She liked antique things, small things — frames and cameos in particular. The family history had a nineteenth-century ambience, completed by ornate silver embellishments and delicate wood carvings around the frames. The frames were precious, personal. He rarely saw them, though. Because of the sharp rays of the morning sun that flooded his mother's window, the pictures were all turned to face the wall. She had never managed to put up any blinds.

That the sun was fading her photos was a discovery his mother had made somewhat late in the game, and most of the pictures had already lost a good deal of clarity, as if they were undergoing the development process in reverse. In one, he himself was walking on unsteady legs across the grass. He was chubby-cheeked but had a look of great purpose. But the photograph was now nearly a mirage; it had faded so badly.

His parents' good looks interested him, but not as much as their shared expression in the small picture. They had recently married. That was for sure. His father was rugged and dark, and wise-looking, with his lined face. His mother looked like a goddess. Her eyes and his seared into each other's with deep meaning. Or was it just lust?

"Exquisite happiness, intense happiness." He looked at the words and the scrawny pencil lines underneath them. The underlining was no more or less emphatic than elsewhere, but he still stared at it, trying to infer something more. When did his father read this? When did he make these marks? What was the proximity of the time of these marks to that of the small picture? To all the pictures? The day Alex had gone to the bureau and, in a rout of the established order, about-faced the whole group of photographs so he could look at them together, it had dawned on him that all the photographs of his father were taken when he was an adult. He had reached a watershed in life that Alex had yet to get near. He had the look of a man whose twenties had never taken place, or, if they had, were somehow lost. Where had his father been when he was twenty? What secrets had he learned between twenty and the time of the picture? What prompted him to underline those words? What had he figured out?

An impossibility, an immovable wall lay between Alex and the answer. He felt the strain of permanence in the situation and in everything that reminded him of it: the remaining cigarettes, the same paint on the walls, the stain on the headboard on his father's side of the bed. There was a secret in them which had clearly been lost. Gone down, away. It had descended beneath an impenetrable surface. Alex could only run his hands over it, searching for a subtle suggestion, a different kind of imperfection. He didn't feel sentimental about it. Just frustrated, like an archeologist who has hit bedrock — no farther to dig. No more options. Except, perhaps, one. He decided to move laterally.

He began to scavenge the house for things obsolete, unexpected. He took the pack of old, yellowed cigarettes and marched out into the day with it. Broadway glistened in the stunning white light of noon. It had been remarkably clear weather since he got back. Walking down the street with an ancient and unlit cigarette between his fingers, it occurred to him that he wasn't depressed at all. If anything, he was buoyant. He had this thing, this business about his father and the secrets of his happiness, that he couldn't figure out. The challenge was dredging him up out of his self-pity over Sloan, and he took this to be a good sign.

He wasn't depressed — he was merely mystified. He was looking for something between the lines. Enjoying this new state, he lit the cigarette and took a few lung-scorching puffs. Awful. He held the cigarette between his thumb and index finger, felt its warmth. He liked it in his hand. It was his father's cigarette — one of the last few in the pack that he had never had a chance to smoke. They'd been stranded.

Alex went on reading *To the Lighthouse* with a dual diligence. He was watching for his father's markings, but at the same time the book had caught him in its rhythm, like a boat that rocks subtly, and whose rocking sensation persists even after its passengers have disembarked. Then, as he turned page 193, he made a startling discovery. Between the next two pages he found a business card. Clearly meant to be a marker, it had slipped down, so it hadn't been visible. The card was yellowed, and on it was his father's name, "Solomon Fader, M.D." In the lower right-hand corner was his father's office address and telephone number, with the exchange spelled out: "Trafalgar 9-3072." Alex picked up the card and turned it over in his hand for a moment before realizing the significance of the find. His father had been at that office for only the last nine years of his life. This meant that he had probably known he was dying as he read *To the Lighthouse*, for his illness, Alex knew, had lasted more than eight years.

Alex suddenly thought about a spring walk in Central Park that his mother had once told him about. The day was warm and sunny, and his parents had gone out for a stroll at lunchtime. Things were going well for them, by any standard. Except that during that particular walk the man in the picture told his wife that he was dying, and things were no longer going well. By any standard. The words "She had known happiness, exquisite happiness, intense happiness" sprang to Alex's mind again. Then came the image in the photograph — that secret but happy gaze his parents shared.

Did his father read the book just before he found out he was dying of cancer, when things had been going so well? When he had a career and a wife and a baby boy — or just after, when all such perceptions would be influenced by this new knowledge? Or had dying caused some kind of purified state of emotion, something that heightened everything? Was imminent death a magnifying glass through which the heat of life was intensified — enlarged and sharpened into a prism-point of misery or joy?

He went out again and walked down the street, preoccupied with his thoughts. His gaze was fixed on the pavement in front of him. Then he lifted his head and saw his mother just down the block. She was holding a plastic grocery bag, but it was a light load, probably only a carton of milk, maybe some oranges, some bread. His mother, when not in a celebratory mood, lived frugally.

But it was her expression that stopped him. She, too, was engrossed in something and had her head down as she scrutinized the ground in front of her. Her face looked concerned, even old, and it struck him that his mother was aging. Not that the idea was such a shock, but it jarred him to see how different the face he was looking at just then was from the taut, angular, smooth-skinned face that looked so coolly into the smiling monkey face of his father, in the photograph. This face — her face now — wore an expression of mild confusion, as if she were trying to remember where she had left her keys.

He stood still as she approached him on a direct collision course. She was oblivious. The face that had so often warmed his looked a little gray. It came nearer, a visage, and only when she was five or ten feet away did she look up abruptly, as if she had noticed his shoes standing still on the pavement. Alex had been smiling as she came nearer, and he was looking forward to the prospect of surprising her. But when she suddenly looked up she had such an expression of alarm and shock that he felt his own face freeze. Her expression was completely unfamiliar. She was wholly surprised, off guard. Her mouth was slightly ajar, her eyes wide, her face a little slack around the edges. She blinked a moment, composing herself, registering that this was her son in front of her, and then started to smile.

But it was too late; he was upon her, hugging her. Something had come over him at the sight of her disorientation, and he had leaped forward to embrace her, as if he were catching her in midfall. The leap was urgent — desperate, even — and when he got to her he put his arms around her and squeezed her tightly to his chest, as if he were afraid that she might drop something or lose something, or as if some secret that only she knew would slip away.

AMY BLOOM

Silver Water

FROM STORY

MY SISTER'S VOICE was like mountain water in a silver pitcher;
the clear, blue beauty of it cools you and lifts you up beyond your
heat, beyond your body. After we went to see *La Traviata,* when
she was fourteen and I was twelve, she elbowed me in the parking lot and said, "Check this out." And she opened her mouth
unnaturally wide and her voice came out, so crystalline and
bright, that all the departing operagoers stood frozen by their
cars, unable to take out their keys or open their doors until she
had finished and then they cheered like hell.

That's what I like to remember and that's the story I told to all
of her therapists. I wanted them to know her, to know that who
they saw was not all there was to see. That before the constant
tinkling of commercials and fast-food jingles, there had been
Puccini and Mozart and hymns so sweet and mighty, you expected Jesus to come down off his cross and clap. That before
there was a mountain of Thorazined fat, swaying down the halls
in nylon maternity tops and sweatpants, there had been the prettiest girl in Arrandale Elementary School, the belle of Landmark
Junior High. Maybe there were other pretty girls, but I didn't see
them. To me, Rose, my beautiful blond defender, my guide to
Tampax and my mother's moods, was perfect.

She had her first psychotic break when she was fifteen. She
had been coming home moody and tearful, then quietly beam-
ing, then she stopped coming home. She would go out into the
woods behind our house and not come in until my mother would
go out at dusk, and step gently into the briars and saplings and

pull her out, blank-faced, her pale blue pullover covered with crumbled leaves, her white jeans smeared with dirt. After three weeks of this, my mother, who is a musician and widely regarded as eccentric, said to my father, who is a psychiatrist and a kind, sad man, "She's going off."

"What is that, your professional opinion?" He picked up the newspaper and put it down again, sighing. "I'm sorry, I didn't mean to snap at you. I know something's bothering her. Have you talked to her?"

"What's there to say? David, she's going crazy, she doesn't need a heart-to-heart talk with Mom, she needs a hospital."

They went back and forth and my father sat down with Rose for a few hours and she sat there, licking the hairs on her forearm, first one way, then the other. My mother stood in the hallway, dry-eyed and pale, watching the two of them. She had already packed Rose's bag and when three of my father's friends dropped by to offer free consultations and recommendations, my mother and Rose's suitcase were already in the car. My mother hugged me and told me that they would be back that night, but not with Rose. She also said, divining my worst fear, "It won't happen to you, honey. Some people go crazy and some people never do. You never will." She smiled and stroked my hair. "Not even when you want to."

Rose was in hospitals, great and small, for the next ten years. She had lots of terrible therapists and a few good ones. One place had no pictures on the walls, no windows, and the patients all wore slippers with the hospital crest on them. My mother didn't even bother to go to Admissions. She turned Rose around and the two of them marched out, my father, trailing behind them, apologizing to his colleagues. My mother ignored the psychiatrists, the social workers and the nurses and she played Handel and Bessie Smith for the patients on whatever piano was available. At some places, she had a Steinway donated by a grateful, or optimistic, family; at others, she banged out "Gimme a Pigfoot" on an old, scarred box that hadn't been tuned since there'd been English-speaking physicians on the grounds. My father talked in serious, appreciative voices to the administrators and unit chiefs and tried to be friendly with whoever was managing Rose's case. We all hated the family therapists.

The worst family therapist we ever had sat in a pale green room with us, visibly taking stock of my mother's ethereal beauty and her faded blue T-shirt and girl-sized jeans, my father's rumpled suit and stained tie and my own unreadable, sixteen-year-old fashion statement. Rose was beyond fashion that year, in one of her dancing-teddy-bear smocks and extra-extra-large Celtics sweatpants. Mr. Walker read Rose's file in front of us and then watched, in alarm, as Rose began crooning, beautifully, and slowly massaging her breasts. My mother and I started to laugh and even my father started to smile. This was Rose's usual opening salvo for new therapists.

Mr. Walker said, "I wonder why it is that everyone is so entertained by Rose behaving inappropriately."

Rose burped and then we all laughed. This was the seventh family therapist we had seen and none of them had lasted very long. Mr. Walker, unfortunately, was determined to do right by us.

"What do you think of Rose's behavior, Violet?" They did this sometimes. In their manual, it must say, if you think the parents are too weird, try talking to the sister.

"I don't know. Maybe she's trying to get you to stop talking about her in the third person."

"Nicely put," my father said.

"Indeed," my mother said.

"Fuckin' A," Rose said.

"Well, this is something that the whole family agrees upon," Mr. Walker said, trying to act as if he understood, or even liked us.

"That was not a successful intervention, Ferret Face." Rose tended to function better when she was angry. He did look like a blond ferret and we all laughed again. Even my father, who tried to give these people a chance out of some sense of collegiality, had given it up.

Mr. Walker decided, after fourteen minutes, that our time was up and walked out, leaving us grinning at each other. Rose was still nuts, but at least we'd all had a little fun.

Our best family therapist started out almost as badly. We scared off a resident and then scared off her supervisor, who sent us Dr. Thorne. Three hundred pounds of Texas chili, corn-

bread and Lone Star beer, finished off with big black cowboy
boots and a little string tie around the area of his neck.

"Oh, frabjous day, it's Big Nut." Rose was in heaven and
stopped massaging her breasts immediately.

"Hey, Little Nut." You have to understand how big a man
would have to be to call my sister "little." He christened us all,
right away. "And it's the good Doctor Nut, and Madame Hickory
Nut, 'cause they are the hardest damn nuts to crack, and over
here in the overalls and not much else, is No One's Nut" — a
name which summed up both my sanity and my loneliness. We
all relaxed.

Dr. Thorne was good for us. Rose moved into a halfway house,
whose director loved Big Nut so much she kept Rose even when
Rose went through a period of having sex with everyone who
passed her door. She was in a fever for a while, trying to still the
voices by fucking her brains out.

Big Nut said, "Darlin', I can't. I cannot make love to every
beautiful woman I meet and, furthermore, I can't do that and be
your therapist, too. It's a great shame, but I think you might be
able to find a really nice guy, someone who treats you just as
sweet and kind as I would, if I were lucky enough to be your
beau. I don't want you to settle for less." And she stopped prop-
ositioning the crack addicts and the alcoholics and the guys at the
shelter. We loved Dr. Thorne.

My father cut back on seeing rich neurotics and helped out
one day a week at Dr. Thorne's walk-in clinic. My mother finished a record of Mozart concerti and played at fund-raisers for
Rose's halfway house. I went back to college and found a wonderful linebacker from Texas to sleep with. In the dark, I would
make him call me "darlin'." Rose took her meds, lost about fifty
pounds and began singing at the A.M.E. Zion Church, down the
street from the halfway house.

At first, they didn't know what to do with this big, blond lady,
dressed funny and hovering wistfully in the doorway during
their rehearsals, but she gave them a few bars of "Precious Lord"
and the choir director felt God's hand and saw that, with the help
of His sweet child, Rose, the Prospect Street Choir was going all
the way to the Gospel Olympics.

Amidst a sea of beige, umber, cinnamon and espresso faces,
there was Rose, bigger, blonder and pinker than any two white

women could be. And Rose and the choir's contralto, Addie Robicheaux, laid out their gold and silver voices and wove them together in strands as fine as silk, as strong as steel. And we wept as
Rose and Addie, in their billowing garnet robes, swayed together, clasping hands until the last perfect note floated up to
God and then they smiled down at us.

Rose would still go off from time to time and the voices would
tell her to do bad things, but Dr. Thorne or Addie or my mother
could usually bring her back. After five good years, Big Nut died.
Stuffing his face with a chili dog, sitting in his un-air-conditioned
office in the middle of July, he had one big, Texas-sized aneu-
rism and died.

Rose held on tight for seven days; she took her meds, went to
choir practice and rearranged her room about a hundred times.
His funeral was a Lourdes for the mentally ill. If you were psychotic, borderline, bad-off neurotic, or just very hard to get
along with, you were there. People shaking so bad from years of
heavy meds that they fell out of the pews. People holding hands,
crying, moaning, talking to themselves; the crazy and the not-so-
crazy were all huddled together, like puppies at the pound.

Rose stopped taking her meds and the halfway house wouldn't
keep her after she pitched another patient down the stairs. My
father called the insurance company and found out that Rose's
new, improved psychiatric coverage wouldn't begin for forty-five
days. I put all of her stuff in a garbage bag and we walked out of
the halfway house, Rose winking at the poor, drooling boy on the
couch.

"This is going to be difficult — not all bad, but difficult — for
the whole family and I thought we should discuss everybody's
expectations. I know I have some concerns." My father had con-
vened a family meeting as soon as Rose had finished putting each
one of her thirty stuffed bears in its own special place.

"No meds," Rose said, her eyes lowered, her stubby fingers,
those fingers that had braided my hair and painted tulips on my
cheeks, pulling hard on the hem of her dirty smock.

My father looked in despair at my mother.

"Rosie, do you want to drive the new car?" my mother asked.

Rose's face lit up. "I'd love to drive that car. I'd drive to California, I'd go see the bears at the San Diego Zoo. I would take
you, Violet, but you always hated the zoo. Remember how she

cried at the Bronx Zoo when she found out that the animals
didn't get to go home at closing?" Rose put her damp hand on
mine and squeezed it, sympathetically. "Poor Vi."

"If you take your medication, after a while, you'll be able to
drive the car. That's the deal. Meds, car." My mother sounded
accommodating but unenthusiastic, careful not to heat up Rose's
paranoia.

"You got yourself a deal, darlin'."

I was living about an hour away then, teaching English during
the day, writing poetry at night. I went home every few days, for
dinner. I called every night.

My father said, quietly, "It's very hard. We're doing all right, I
think. Rose has been walking in the mornings with your mother
and she watches a lot of TV. She won't go to the day hospital and
she won't go back to the choir. Her friend, Mrs. Robicheaux,
came by a couple of times. What a sweet woman. Rose wouldn't
even talk to her; she just sat there, staring at the wall and humming. We're not doing all that well, actually, but I guess we're
getting by. I'm sorry, sweetheart, I don't mean to depress you."

My mother said, emphatically, "We're doing fine. We've got
our routine and we stick to it and we're fine. You don't need to
come home so often, you know. Wait till Sunday, just come for
the day. Lead your life, Vi. She's leading hers."

I stayed away until Sunday, afraid to pick up my phone, grateful to my mother for her harsh calm and her reticence, the qual-
ities that had enraged me throughout my childhood.

I came on a Sunday, in the early afternoon, to help my father
garden, something we had always enjoyed together. We weeded
and staked tomatoes and killed aphids while my mother and
Rose were down at the lake. I didn't even get into the house until
four, when I needed a glass of water.

Someone had broken the piano bench into five neatly stacked
pieces and placed them where the piano bench usually was.

"We were having such a nice time, I couldn't bear to bring it
up," my father said, standing in the doorway, carefully keeping
his gardening boots out of the kitchen.

"What did Mommy say?"

"She said, 'Better the bench than the piano.' And your sister
lay down on the floor and just wept. Then, your mother took her
down to the lake. This can't go on, Vi. We have twenty-seven

days left, your mother gets no sleep because Rose doesn't sleep and if I could just pay twenty-seven thousand dollars to keep her in the hospital until the insurance takes over, I'd do it."

"All right. Do it. Pay the money and take her back to Hartley-Rees. It was the prettiest place and she liked the art therapy there."

"I would if I could. The policy states that she must be symptom-free for at least forty-five days before her coverage begins. Symptom-free means no hospitalization."

"Jesus, Daddy, how could you get that kind of policy? She hasn't been symptom-free for forty-five minutes."

"It's the only one I could get for long-term psychiatric." He put his hand over his mouth to block whatever he was about to say and went back out to the garden. I couldn't see if he was crying.

He stayed outside and I stayed inside, until Rose and my mother came home from the lake. Rose's soggy sweatpants were rolled up to her knees and she had a bucketful of shells and gray stones, which my mother persuaded her to leave on the back porch. My mother kissed me lightly and told Rose to go up to her room and change out of her wet pants.

Rose's eyes grew very wide. "Never. I will never . . ." she began banging her head with rhythmic intensity, against the kitchen floor, throwing all of her weight behind each attack. My mother put her arms around Rose's waist and tried to hold her back. Rose shook her off, not even looking around to see what was slowing her down. My mother crumpled next to the refrigerator.

"Violet, please . . ."

I threw myself onto the kitchen floor, becoming the spot that Rose was smacking her head against. She stopped a fraction of an inch short of my stomach.

"Oh, Vi, Mommy, I'm sorry. I'm sorry, don't hate me." She staggered to her feet and ran, wailing, to her room.

My mother got up and washed her face, brusquely, rubbing it dry with a dishcloth. My father heard the wailing and came running in, slipping his long bare feet out of his rubber boots.

"Galen, Galen, let me see." He held her head and looked closely for bruises on her pale, small face. "What happened?" My mother looked at me. "Violet, what happened? Where's Rose?"

"Rose got upset and when she went running upstairs, she

pushed Mommy out of the way." I've only told three lies in my life and that was my second.

"She must feel terrible, pushing you, of all people. It would have to be you, but I know she didn't want it to be." He made my mother a cup of tea and all the love he had for her, despite her silent rages and her vague stares, came pouring through the teapot, warming her cup, filling her small, long-fingered hands. He stood by her and she rested her head against his hip. I looked away.

"Let's make dinner, then I'll call her. Or you call her, David, maybe she'd rather see your face first."

Dinner was filled with all of our starts and stops and Rose's desperate efforts to control herself. She could barely eat and hummed the McDonald's theme song over and over again, pausing only to spill her juice down the front of her smock and begin weeping. My father looked at my mother and handed Rose his napkin. She dabbed at herself, listlessly, but the tears stopped.

"I want to go to bed. I want to go to bed and be in my head. I want to go to bed and be in my bed and in my head and just wear red. For red is the color that my baby wore and once more, it's true, yes, it is, it's true. Please don't wear red tonight, ohh, ohh, please don't wear red tonight, for red is the color —"

"Okay, okay, Rose. It's okay. I'll go upstairs with you and you can get ready for bed. Then, Mommy will come up and say good night, too. It's okay, Rose." My father reached out his hand and Rose grasped it and they walked out of the dining room together, his long arm around her middle.

My mother sat at the table for a moment, her face in her hands and then she began clearing the table. We cleared without talking, my mother humming Schubert's "Schlummerlied," a lullaby about the woods and the river calling to the child to go to sleep. She sang it to us every night, when we were small.

My father came back into the kitchen and signaled to my mother. She went upstairs and they came back down together, a few minutes later.

"She's asleep," they said and we went to sit on the porch and listen to the crickets. I don't remember the rest of the evening, but I remember it as quietly sad and I remember the rare sight of my parents holding hands, sitting on the picnic table, watching the sunset.

I woke up at three o'clock in the morning, feeling the cool night air through my sheet. I went down the hall for another blanket and looked into Rose's room, for no reason. She wasn't there. I put on my jeans and a sweater and went downstairs. I could feel her absence. I went outside and saw her wide, draggy footprints darkening the wet grass, into the woods.

"Rosie," I called, too softly, not wanting to wake my parents, not wanting to startle Rose. "Rosie, it's me. Are you here? Are you all right?"

I almost fell over her. Huge and white in the moonlight, her flowered smock bleached in the light and shadow, her sweatpants now completely wet. Her head was flung back, her white, white neck exposed like a lost Greek column.

"Rosie, Rosie —" Her breathing was very slow and her lips were not as pink as they usually were. Her eyelids fluttered.

"Closing time," she whispered. I believe that's what she said.

I sat with her, uncovering the bottle of white pills by her hand, and watched the stars fade.

When the stars were invisible and the sun was warming the air, I went back to the house. My mother was standing on the porch, wrapped in a blanket, watching me. Every step I took overwhelmed me; I could picture my mother slapping me, shooting me for letting her favorite die.

"Warrior queens," she said, wrapping her thin strong arms around me. "I raised warrior queens." She kissed me fiercely and went into the woods by herself.

A little later, she woke my father, who could not go into the woods, and still later she called the police and the funeral parlor. She hung up the phone, lay down, and didn't get back out of bed until the day of the funeral. My father fed us both and called the people who needed to be called and picked out Rose's coffin by himself.

My mother played the piano and Addie sang her pure gold notes and I closed my eyes and saw my sister, fourteen years old, lion's mane thrown back and her eyes tightly closed against the glare of the parking lot lights. That sweet sound held us tight, flowing around us, eddying through our hearts, rising, still rising.

ROBERT OLEN BUTLER

A Good Scent from a Strange Mountain

FROM NEW ENGLAND REVIEW

HO CHI MINH came to me again last night, his hands covered with confectioners' sugar. This was something of a surprise to me, the first time I saw him beside my bed, in the dim light from the open shade. My oldest daughter leaves my shades open, I think so that I will not forget that the sun has risen again in the morning. I am a very old man. She seems to expect that one morning I will simply forget to keep living. This is very foolish. I will one night rise up from my bed and slip into her room and open the shade there. Let *her* see the sun in the morning. She is sixty-four years old and she should worry for herself. I could never die from forgetting.

But the light from the street was enough to let me recognize Ho when I woke, and he said to me, "Dao, my old friend, I have heard it is time to visit you." Already on that first night there was a sweet smell about him, very strong in the dark, even before I could see his hands. I said nothing, but I stretched to the night-stand beside me and I turned on the light to see if he would go away. And he did not. He stood there beside the bed — I could even see him reflected in the window — and I knew it was real because he did not appear as he was when I'd known him but as he was when he'd died. This was Uncle Ho before me, the thin old man with the dewlap beard wearing the dark clothes of a peasant and the rubber sandals, just like in the news pictures I studied with such a strange feeling for all those years. Strange because when I knew him, he was not yet Ho Chi Minh. It was 1917 and he was Nguyen Ai Quoc and we were both young men with clean-shaven faces, the best of friends, and we worked at the Carlton Hotel in London where I was a dishwasher and he was a pastry cook under the great Escoffier. We were the best of friends and we saw snow for the first time together. This was before we began to work at the hotel. We shoveled snow and Ho would stop for a moment and blow his breath out before him and it would make him smile, to see what was inside him, as if it was the casting of bones to tell the future.

On that first night when he came to me in my house in New Orleans, I finally saw what it was that smelled so sweet and I said to him, "Your hands are covered with sugar."

He looked at them with a kind of sadness.

I have received that look myself in the past week. It is time now for me to see my family, and the friends I have made who are still alive. This is our custom from Vietnam. When you are very old, you put aside a week or two to receive the people of your life so that you can tell each other your feelings, or try at last to understand each other, or simply say good-bye. It is a formal leave-taking, and with good luck you can do this before you have your final illness. I have lived almost a century and perhaps I should have called them all to me sooner, but at last I felt a deep weariness and I said to my oldest daughter that it was time.

They look at me with sadness, some of them. Usually the dull-witted ones, or the insincere ones. But Ho's look was, of course, not dull-witted or insincere. He considered his hands and said, "The glaze. Maestro's glaze."

There was the soft edge of yearning in his voice and I had the thought that perhaps he had come to me for some sort of help. I said to him, "I don't remember. I only washed dishes." As soon as the words were out of my mouth, I decided it was foolish for me to think he had come to ask me about the glaze.

But Ho did not treat me as foolish. He looked at me and shook his head. "It's all right," he said, "I remember the temperature now. Two hundred and thirty degrees, when the sugar is between the large thread stage and the small orb stage. The Maestro was very clear about that and I remember." I knew from his eyes, however, that there was much more that still eluded him.

His eyes did not seem to move at all from my face, but there was some little shifting of them, a restlessness that perhaps only I could see, since I was his close friend from the days when the world did not know him.

I am nearly one hundred years old but I can still read a man's face. Perhaps better than I ever have. I sit in the overstuffed chair in my living room and I receive my visitors and I want these people, even the dull-witted and insincere ones — please excuse an old man's ill temper for calling them that — I want them all to be good with each other. A Vietnamese family is extended as far as the bloodline strings us together, like so many paper lanterns around a village square. And we all give off light together. That's the way it has always been in our culture. But these people that come to visit me have been in America for a long time and there are very strange things going on that I can see in their faces.

None stranger than this morning. I was in my overstuffed chair and with me there were four of the many members of my family: my son-in-law Thang, a former colonel in the Army of the Republic of Vietnam and one of the insincere ones, sitting on my Castro Convertible couch; his youngest son Loi, who had come in late, just a few minutes earlier, and had thrown himself down on the couch as well, youngest but a man old enough to have served as a lieutenant under his father as our country fell to the communists more than a decade ago; my daughter Lam, who is Thang's wife, hovering behind the both of them and refusing all invitations to sit down; and my oldest daughter, leaning against the door frame, having no doubt just returned from my room, where she had opened the shade that I had closed when I awoke.

It was Thang who gave me the sad look I have grown accustomed to, and I perhaps seemed to him at that moment a little weak, a little distant. I had stopped listening to the small talk of these people and I had let my eyes half close, though I could still see them clearly and I was very alert. Thang has a steady face and the quick eyes of a man who is ready to come under fire, but I have always read much more there, in spite of his efforts to show nothing. So after he thought I'd faded from the room, it was with slow eyes, not quick, that he moved to his son and began to speak of the killing.

You should understand that Mr. Nguyen Bich Le had been shot dead in our community here in New Orleans just last week. There are many of us Vietnamese living in New Orleans and one man, Mr. Le, published a little newspaper for all of us. He had recently made the fatal error — though it should not be that in America — of writing that it was time to accept the reality of the communist government in Vietnam and begin to talk to them. We had to work now with those who controlled our country. He said that he remained a patriot to the Republic of Vietnam, and I believed him. If anyone had asked an old man's opinion on this whole matter, I would not have been afraid to say that Mr. Le was right.

But he was shot dead last week. He was forty-five years old and he had a wife and three children and he was shot as he sat behind the wheel of his Chevrolet pickup truck. I find a detail like that especially moving, that this man was killed in his Chevrolet, which I understand is a strongly American thing. We know this in Saigon. In Saigon it was very American to own a Chevrolet, just as it was French to own a Citroën.

And Mr. Le had taken one more step in his trusting embrace of this new culture. He had bought not only a Chevrolet but a Chevrolet pickup truck, which made him not only American but a man of Louisiana, where there are many pickup trucks. He did not, however, also purchase a gun rack for the back window, another sign of this place. Perhaps it would have been well if he had, for it was through the back window that the bullet was fired. Someone had hidden in the bed of his truck and had killed him from behind in his Chevrolet and the reason for this act was made very clear in a phone call to the newspaper office by a nameless representative of the Vietnamese Party for the Annihilation of Communism and for the National Restoration.

And Thang my son-in-law said to his youngest son Loi, "There is no murder weapon." What I saw was a faint lift of his eyebrows as he said this, as if he were inviting his son to listen beneath his words. Then he said it again, more slowly, as if it were code. "There is *no weapon*." My grandson nodded his head once, a crisp little snap. Then my daughter Lam said in a very loud voice, with her eyes on me, "That was a terrible thing, the death of Mr. Le." She nudged her husband and son, and both men turned their faces sharply to me and they looked at me squarely and said, also in very loud voices, "Yes, it was terrible."

I am not deaf, and I closed my eyes further, having seen enough and wanting them to think that their loud talk had not only failed to awaken me but had put me more completely to sleep. I did not like to deceive them, however, even though I have already spoken critically of these members of my family. I am a Hoa Hao Buddhist and I believe in harmony among all living things, especially the members of a Vietnamese family.

After Ho had reassured me, on that first visit, about the temperature needed to heat Maestro Escoffier's glaze, he said, "Dao, my old friend, do you still follow the path you chose in Paris?"

He meant by this my religion. It was in Paris that I embraced the Buddha and disappointed Ho. We went to France in early 1918, with the war still on, and we lived in the poorest street of the poorest part of the Seventeenth Arrondissement. Number nine, Impasse Compoint, a blind alley with a few crumbling houses, all but ours rented out for storage. The cobblestones were littered with fallen roof tiles and Quoc and I each had a tiny single room with only an iron bedstead and a crate to sit on. I could see my friend Quoc in the light of the tallow candle and he was dressed in a dark suit and a bowler hat and he looked very foolish. I did not say so, but he knew it himself and he kept seating and reseating the hat and shaking his head very slowly, with a loudly silent anger. This was near the end of our time together, for I was visiting daily with a Buddhist monk and he was drawing me back to the religion of my father. I had run from my father, gone to sea, and that was where I had met Nguyen Ai Quoc and we had gone to London and to Paris and now my father was calling me back, through a Vietnamese monk I met in the Tuileries.

Quoc, on the other hand, was being called not from his past but from his future. He had rented the dark suit and bowler and he would spend the following weeks in Versailles, walking up and down the mirrored corridors of the Palace trying to gain an audience with Woodrow Wilson. Quoc had eight requests for the Western world concerning Indochina. Simple things. Equal rights, freedom of assembly, freedom of the press. The essential things that he knew Wilson would understand, based as they were on Wilson's own Fourteen Points. And Quoc did not even intend to ask for independence. He wanted Vietnamese representatives in the French Parliament. That was all he would ask. But his bowler made him angry. He wrenched out of the puddle of candlelight, both his hands clutching the bowler, and I heard him muttering in the darkness, and I felt that this was a bad sign already, even before he had set foot in Versailles. And as it turned out, he never saw Wilson, or Lloyd George either, or even Clemenceau. But somehow his frustration with his hat was what made me sad, even now, and I reached out from my bedside and said, "Uncle Ho, it's all right."

He was still beside me. This was not an awakening, as you might expect, this was not a dream ending with the bowler in Paris and me awaking to find that Ho was never there. He was still beside my bed, though he was just beyond my outstretched hand and he did not move to me. He smiled on one side of his mouth, a smile full of irony, as if he too were thinking about the night he'd tried on his rented clothes. He said, "Do you remember how I worked in Paris?"

I thought about this and I did remember, with the words of his advertisement in the newspaper *La Vie Ouvrière:* "If you would like a lifelong momento of your family, have your photos retouched at Nguyen Ai Quoc's." This was his work in Paris; he retouched photos with a very delicate hand, the same fine hand that Monsieur Escoffier had admired in London. I said, "Yes, I remember."

Ho nodded gravely. "I painted the blush into the cheeks of Frenchmen."

I said, "A lovely portrait in a lovely frame for forty francs," another phrase from his advertisement.

"Forty-five," Ho said.

I thought now of his question that I had not answered. I motioned to the far corner of the room where the prayer table stood. "I still follow the path."

He looked and said, "At least you became a Hoa Hao."

He could tell this from the simplicity of the table. There was only a red cloth upon it and four Chinese characters: Bao Son Ky Huong. This is the saying of the Hoa Haos. We follow the teachings of a monk who broke away from the fancy rituals of the other Buddhists. We do not need elaborate pagodas or rituals. The Hoa Hao believes that the maintenance of our spirits is very simple, and the mystery of joy is simple too. The four characters mean "A good scent from a strange mountain."

I had always admired the sense of humor of my friend Quoc so I said, "You never did stop painting the blush into the faces of Westerners."

Ho looked back to me but he did not smile. I was surprised at this but more surprised at my little joke seeming to remind him of his hands. He raised them and studied them and said, "After the heating, what was the surface for the glaze?"

"My old friend," I said, "you worry me now."

But Ho did not seem to hear. He turned away and crossed the room and I knew he was real because he did not vanish from my sight but opened the door and went out and closed the door behind him with a loud click.

I rang for my daughter. She had given me a porcelain bell and after allowing Ho enough time to go down the stairs and out the front door, if that was where he was headed, I rang the bell, and my daughter, who is a very light sleeper, soon appeared.

"What is it, father?" she asked with great patience in her voice. She is a good girl. She understands about Vietnamese families and she is a smart girl.

"Please feel the doorknob," I said.

She did so without the slightest hesitation and this was a lovely gesture on her part, a thing that made me wish to rise up and embrace her, though I was very tired and did not move.

"Yes?" she asked after touching the knob.

"Is it sticky?"

She touched it again. "Ever so slightly," she said. "Would you like me to clean it?"

"In the morning," I said.

She smiled and crossed the room and kissed me on the forehead. She smelled of lavender and fresh bedclothes and there are so many who have gone on before me into the world of spirits and I yearn for them all, yearn to find them all together in a village square, my wife there smelling of lavender and our own sweat, like on a night in Saigon soon after the terrible fighting in 1968 when we finally opened the windows onto the night and there were sounds of bombs falling on the horizon and there was

no breeze at all, just the heavy stillness of the time between the
dry season and the wet, and Saigon smelled of tar and motorcy-
cle exhaust and cordite, but when I opened the window and
turned to my wife, the room was full of a wonderful scent, a
sweet smell that made her sit up, for she sensed it too. This was a
smell that had nothing to do with flowers but instead reminded
us that flowers were always ready to fall into dust. This smell was
as if a gemstone had begun to give off a scent, as if a mountain of
emerald had found its own scent. I crossed the room to my wife
and we were already old, we had already buried children and
grandchildren that we prayed waited for us in that village square
at the foot of the strange mountain, but when I came near the
bed she lifted her silk gown and threw it aside and I pressed close
to her and our own sweat smelled sweet on that night. I want to
be with her in that square and with the rest of those we'd buried,
the tiny limbs and the sullen eyes and the gray faces of the puzzled children and the surprised adults and the weary old people
who have gone before us, who know the secrets now. And the
sweet smell of the glaze on Ho's hands reminds me of others that
I would want in the square, the people from the ship, too, the
Vietnamese boy from a village near my own who died of a fever
in the Indian Ocean and the natives in Dakar who were forced
by colonial officials to swim out to our ship in shark-infested
waters to secure the moorings. Two were killed before our eyes
without a French regret. Ho was very moved by this, and I want
those men in our square and I want the Frenchman, too, who
called Ho "monsieur" for the first time. A man on the dock in
Marseilles. Ho spoke of him twice more during our years together and I want that Frenchman there. And, of course, Ho.
Was he in the village square even now, waiting? Heating his glaze
fondant? My daughter was smoothing my covers around me and
the smell of lavender on her was still strong.

"He was in this room," I said to her to explain the sticky doorknob.

"Who was?"

But I was very sleepy and I could say no more, though perhaps
she would not have understood anyway, in spite of being the
smart girl that she is.

The next night I left my light on to watch for Ho's arrival, but

I dozed off and he had to wake me. He was sitting in a chair that he'd brought from across the room. He said to me, "Dao. Wake up, my old friend."

I must have awakened when he pulled the chair near to me, for I heard each of his words. "I am awake," I said. "I was thinking of the poor men who had to swim out to our ship."

"They are already among those I have served," Ho said. "Before I forgot." And he raised his hands and they were still covered with sugar.

I said, "Wasn't it a marble slab?" I had a memory, strangely clear after these many years, as strange as my memory of Ho's Paris business card.

"A marble slab," Ho repeated, puzzled.

"That you poured the heated sugar on."

"Yes." Ho's sweet-smelling hands came forward but they did not quite touch me. I thought to reach out from beneath the covers and take them in my own hands, but Ho leaped up and paced about the room. "The marble slab, moderately oiled. Of course. I am to let the sugar half cool and then use the spatula to move it about in all directions, every bit of it, so that it doesn't harden and form lumps."

I asked, "Have you seen my wife?"

Ho had wandered to the far side of the room, but he turned and crossed back to me at this. "I'm sorry, my friend. I never knew her."

I must have shown some disappointment in my face, for Ho sat down and brought his own face near mine. "I'm sorry," he said. "There are many other people that I must find here."

"Are you very disappointed in me?" I asked. "For not having traveled the road with you?"

"It's very complicated," Ho said softly. "You felt that you'd taken action. I am no longer in a position to question another soul's choice."

"Are you at peace, where you are?" I asked this knowing of his worry over the recipe for the glaze, but I hoped that this was only a minor difficulty in the afterlife, like the natural anticipation of the good cook expecting guests when everything always turns out fine in the end.

But Ho said, "I am not at peace."

"Is Monsieur Escoffier over there?"

"I have not seen him. This has nothing to do with him, directly."

"What is it about?"

"I don't know."

"You won the country. You know that, don't you?"

Ho shrugged. "There are no countries here."

I should have remembered Ho's shrug when I began to see things in the faces of my son-in-law and grandson this morning. But something quickened in me, a suspicion. I kept my eyes shut and laid my head to the side, as if I were fast asleep, encouraging them to talk more.

My daughter said, "This is not the place to speak."

But the men did not regard her. "How?" Loi asked his father, referring to the missing murder weapon.

"It's best not to know too much," Thang said.

Then there was a silence. For all the quickness I'd felt at the first suspicion, I was very slow now. In fact, I did think of Ho from that second night. Not his shrug. He had fallen silent for a long time and I had closed my eyes, for the light seemed very bright. I listened to his silence just as I listened to the silence of these two conspirators before me.

And then Ho said, "They were fools but I can't bring myself to grow angry anymore."

I opened my eyes in the bedroom and the light was off. Ho had turned it off, knowing that it was bothering me. "Who were fools?" I asked.

"We had fought together to throw out the Japanese. I had very good friends among them. I smoked their lovely Salem cigarettes. They had been repressed by colonialists themselves. Did they not know their own history?"

"Do you mean the Americans?"

"There are a million souls here with me, the young men of our country, and they are all dressed in black suits and bowler hats. In the mirrors they are made ten million, a hundred million."

"I chose my path, my dear friend Quoc, so that there might be harmony."

And even with that yearning for harmony I could not overlook what my mind made of what my ears had heard this morning.

Thang was telling Loi that the murder weapon had been disposed of. Thang and Loi both knew the killers, were in sympathy with them, perhaps were part of the killing. The father and son had been airborne rangers and I had several times heard them talk bitterly of the exile of our people. We were fools for trusting the Americans all along, they said. We should have taken matters forward and disposed of the infinitely corrupt Thieu and done what needed to be done. Whenever they spoke like this in front of me there was soon a quick exchange of sideways glances at me and then a turn and an apology. "We're sorry, grandfather. Old times often bring old anger. We are happy our family is living a new life."

I would wave my hand at this, glad to have the peace of the family restored. Glad to turn my face and smell the dogwood tree or even smell the coffee plant across the highway. These things had come to be the new smells of our family. But then a weakness often came upon me. The others would drift away, the men, and perhaps one of my daughters would come to me and stroke my head and not say a word and none of them ever would ask why I was weeping. I would smell the rich blood smells of the afterbirth and I would hold our first son, still slippery in my arms, and there was the smell of dust from the square and the smell of the South China Sea just over the rise of the hill and there was the smell of the blood and of the inner flesh from my wife as my son's own private sea flowed from this woman that I loved, flowed and carried him into the life that would disappear from him so soon. In the afterlife would he stand before me on unsteady child's legs, would I have to bend low to greet him, or would he be a man now?

My grandson said, after the silence had nearly carried me into real sleep, troubled sleep, my grandson Loi said to his father, "I would be a coward not to know."

Thang laughed and said, "You have proved yourself no coward."

And I wished then to sleep, I wished to fall asleep and let go of life somewhere in my dreams and seek my village square. I have lived too long, I thought. My daughter was saying, "Are you both mad?" And then she changed her voice, making the words very precise. "Let grandfather sleep."

So when Ho came tonight for the third time, I wanted to ask his advice. His hands were still covered with sugar and his mind was, as it had been for the past two nights, very much distracted. "There's something still wrong with the glaze," he said to me in the dark and I pulled back the covers and swung my legs around to get up. He did not try to stop me, but he did draw back quietly into the shadows.

"I want to pace the room with you," I said. "As we did in Paris, those tiny rooms of ours. We would talk about Marx and about Buddha and I must pace with you now."

"Very well," he said. "Perhaps it will help me remember."

I slipped on my sandals and I stood up and Ho's shadow moved past me, through the spill of streetlight and into the dark near the door. I followed him, smelling the sugar on his hands, first before me and then moving past me as I went on into the darkness he'd just left. I stopped as I turned and I could see Ho outlined before the window and I said, "I believe my son-in-law and grandson are involved in the killing of a man. A political killing."

Ho stayed where he was, a dark shape against the light, and he said nothing, and I could not smell his hands from across the room. I smelled only the sourness of Loi as he laid his head on my shoulder. He was a baby and my daughter Lam retreated to our balcony window after handing him to me and the boy turned his head and I turned mine to him and I could smell his mother's milk, sour on his breath, he had a sour smell and there was incense burning in the room, jasmine, the smoke of souls, and the boy sighed on my shoulder, and I turned my face away from the smell of him. Thang was across the room and his eyes were quick to find his wife and he was waiting for her to take the child from me.

"You have never done the political thing," Ho said.

"Is this true?"

"Of course."

I asked, "Are there politics where you are now, my friend?"

I did not see him moving toward me but the smell of the sugar on his hands grew stronger, very strong, and I felt Ho Chi Minh very close to me, though I could not see him. He was very close and the smell was strong and sweet and it was filling my lungs as if from the inside, as if Ho was passing through my very body, and I heard the door open behind me and then close softly shut.

I moved across the room to the bed. I turned to sit down but I was facing the window, the scattering of a streetlamp on the window like a nova in some far part of the universe. I stepped to the window and touched the reflected light there, wondering if there was a great smell when a star explodes, a great burning smell of gas and dust. Then I closed the shade and slipped into bed, quite gracefully, I felt, I was quite wonderfully graceful, and I lie here now waiting for sleep. Ho is right, of course. I will never say a word about my grandson. And perhaps I will be as restless as Ho when I join him. But that will be all right. He and I will be together again and perhaps we can help each other. I know now what it is that he has forgotten. He has used confectioners' sugar for his glaze fondant and he should be using granulated sugar. I was only a washer of dishes but I did listen carefully when Monsieur Escoffier spoke. I wanted to understand everything. His kitchen was full of such smells that you knew you had to understand everything or you would be incomplete forever.

MAVIS GALLANT

Across the Bridge

FROM THE NEW YORKER

WE WERE WALKING over the bridge from the Place de la Con-
corde, my mother and I — arm in arm, like two sisters who never
quarrel. She had the invitations to my wedding in a leather shopping bag: I was supposed to be getting married to Arnaud Pons.
My father's first cousin, Gaston Castelli, deputy for a district in
the south, had agreed to frank the envelopes. He was expecting
us at the Palais Bourbon, at the other end of the bridge. His small
office looked out on nothing in particular — a wall and some
windows. A typist who did not seem to work for anyone in particular sat outside his door. He believed she was there to spy on
him, and for that reason had told my mother to keep the invitations out of sight.

I had been taken to see him there once or twice. On the wall
were two photographs of Vincent Auriol, President of the Republic, one of them signed, and a picture of the restaurant where
Jean Jaurès was shot to death; it showed the façade and the wait-
ers standing in the street in their long white aprons. For furniture he had a Louis Philippe armchair, with sticking plaster
around all four legs, a lumpy couch covered with a blanket, and,
for visitors, a pair of shaky varnished chairs filched from another
room. When the Assembly was in session he slept on the couch.
(Deputies were not supposed actually to live on the premises, but
some of those from out of town liked to save on hotel bills.) His
son Julien was fighting in Indochina. My mother had already
cautioned me to ask how Julien was getting along and when he
thought the war would be over. Only a few months earlier she

might have hinted about a wedding when Julien came back, pretending to make a joke of it, but it was too late now for insinuations: I was nearly at the altar with someone else. My marrying Julien was a thought my parents and Cousin Gaston had enjoyed. In some way, we would have remained their children forever.

When Cousin Gaston came to dinner he and Papa discussed their relations in Nice and the decadent state of France. Women were not expected to join in: Maman always found a reason to go off to the kitchen and talk things over with Claudine, a farm girl from Normandy she had trained to cook and wait. Claudine was about my age, but Maman seemed much freer with her than with me; she took it for granted that Claudine was informed about all the roads and corners of life. Having no excuse to leave, I would examine the silver, the pattern on my dinner plate, my own hands. The men, meanwhile, went on about the lowering of morality and the lack of guts of the middle class. They split over what was to be done: our cousin was a Socialist, though not a fierce one. He saw hope in the new postwar managerial generation, who read Marx without becoming dogmatic Marxists, while my father thought the smart postwar men would be swept downhill along with the rest of us.

Once, Cousin Gaston mentioned why his office was so seedily fitted out. It seemed that the government had to spend great sums on rebuilding roads; they had gone to pieces during the war and, of course, were worse today. Squads of German prisoners of war sent to put them right had stuffed the roadbeds with leaves and dead branches. As the underlay began to rot, the surfaces had collapsed. Now repairs were made by French workers — unionized, Communist-led, always on the verge of a national strike. There was no money left over.

"There never has been any money left over," Papa said. "When there is, they keep it quiet."

He felt uneasy about the franking business. The typist in the hall might find out and tell a reporter on one of the opposition weeklies. The reporter would then write a blistering piece on nepotism and the misuse of public funds, naming names. (My mother never worried. She took small favors to be part of the grace of life.)

It was hot on the bridge, July in April. We still wore our heavy coats. Too much good weather was not to be trusted. There were no clouds over the river, but just the kind of firm blue sky I found easy to paint. Halfway across, we stopped to look at a boat with strings of flags, and tourists sitting along the bank. Some of the men had their shirts off. I stared at the water and saw how far below it was and how cold it looked, and I said, "If I weren't a Catholic, I'd throw myself in."

"Sylvie!" — as if she had lost me in a crowd.

"We're going to so much trouble," I said. "Just so I can marry a man I don't love."

"How do you know you don't love him?"

"I'd know if I did."

"You haven't tried," she said. "It takes patience, like practicing scales. Don't you want a husband?"

"Not Arnaud."

"What's wrong with Arnaud?"

"I don't know."

"Well," after a pause, "what *do* you know?"

"I want to marry Bernard Brunelle. He lives in Lille. His father owns a big textile business — the factories, everything. We've been writing. He doesn't know I'm engaged."

"Brunelle? Brunelle? Textiles? From Lille? It sounds like a mistake. In Lille they just marry each other, and textiles marry textiles."

"I've got one thing right," I said. "I want to marry Bernard."

My mother was a born coaxer and wheedler, avoided confrontation, preferring to move to a different terrain and beckon, smiling. One promised nearly anything just to keep the smile on her face. She was slim and quick, like a girl of fourteen. My father liked her in flowered hats, so she still wore the floral bandeaux with their wisps of veil that had been fashionable ten years before. Papa used to tell about a funeral service where Maman had removed her hat so as to drape a mantilla over her hair. An usher, noticing the hat beside her on the pew, had placed it with the other flowers around the coffin. When I repeated the story to Arnaud he said the floral-hat anecdote was one of the world's oldest. He had heard it a dozen times, always about a different funeral. I could not see why Papa would go on telling it if it were not true, or why Maman would let him. Perhaps she was the first woman it had ever happened to.

"You say that Bernard has written to you," she said, in her lightest, prettiest, most teasing manner. "But where did he send the letters? Not to the house. I'd have noticed."

No conspirator gives up a network that easily. Mine consisted of Chantal Nauzan, my trusted friend, the daughter of a general my father greatly admired. Recently Papa had begun saying that if I had been a boy he might have wanted a career in the army for me. As I was a girl, he did not want me to do anything too particular or specific. He did not want to have to say, "My daughter is . . ." or "Sylvie does . . ." because it might make me sound needy or plain.

"Dear Sylvie," my mother went on. "Look at me. Let me see your eyes. Has he written 'marriage' in a letter signed with his name?" I looked away. What a question! "Would you show me the letter — the important one? I promise not to read the whole thing." I shook my head no. I was not sharing Bernard. She moved to new ground, so fast I could barely keep up. "And you would throw yourself off a bridge for him?"

"Just in my thoughts," I said. "I think about it when Arnaud makes me listen to records — all those stories about women dying, Brünhilde and Mimi and Butterfly. I think that for the rest of my life I'll be listening to records and remembering Bernard. It's all I have to look forward to, because it is what you and Papa want."

"No," she said. "It is not at all what we want." She placed the leather bag on the parapet and turned it upside down over the river, using both hands. I watched the envelopes fall in a slow shower and land on the dark water and float apart. Strangers leaned on the parapet and stared, too, but nobody spoke.

"Papa will know what to do next," she said, altogether calmly, giving the bag a final shake. "For the time being, don't write any more letters and don't mention Bernard. Not to anyone."

I could not have defined her tone or expression. She behaved as if we had put something over on life, or on men; but that may be what I have read into it since. I looked for a clue, wondering how she wanted me to react, but she had started to walk on, making up the story we would tell our cousin, still waiting in his office to do us a good turn. (In the end, she said the wedding had to be postponed owing to a death in Arnaud's family.)

"Papa won't be able to have M. Pons as a friend now," she remarked. "He's going to miss him. I hope your M. Brunelle in Lille can make up the loss."

"I have never met him," I said.

I could see white patches just under the surface of the river, quite far along. They could have been candy papers or scraps of rubbish from a barge. Maman seemed to be studying the current, too. She said, "I'm not asking you to tell me how you met him."

"In the Luxembourg Gardens. I was sketching the beehives."

"You made a nice watercolor from that sketch. I'll have it framed. You can hang it in your bedroom."

Did she mean now or after I was married? I was taller than she was: when I turned my head, trying to read her face, my eyes were level with her smooth forehead and the bandeau of daisies she was wearing that day. She said, "My girl," and took my hand — not possessively but as a sort of welcome. I was her kind, she seemed to be telling me, though she had never broken an engagement that I knew. Another of my father's stories was how she had proposed to him, had chased and cornered him and made the incredible offer. He was a young doctor then, new to Paris. Now he was an ear specialist with a large practice. His office and secretary and waiting room were in a separate wing of the apartment. When the windows were open, in warm weather, we could hear him laughing and joking with Melle Coutard, the secretary. She had been with him for years and kept his accounts; he used to say she knew all his bad secrets. My mother's people thought he was too southern, too easily amused, too loud in his laughter. My Castelli great-grandparents had started a wholesale fruit business, across from the old bus terminal at Nice. The whole block was empty now and waiting to be torn down, so that tall buildings could replace the ocher warehouses and stores with their dark red roofs. "Castelli" was still painted over a doorway, in faded blue. My father had worked hard to lose his local accent, which sounded comical in Paris and prevented patients from taking him seriously, but it always returned when he was with Cousin Gaston. Cousin Gaston cherished his own accent, polished and refined it: his voters mistrusted any voice that sounded north of Marseilles.

I cannot say what was taking place in the world that spring; my father did not like to see young women reading newspapers. Echoes from Indochina came to me, and news of our cousin Julien drifted around the family, but the war itself was like the murmur of a radio in a distant room. I know that it was the year of *Imperial Violets*, with Luis Mariano singing the lead. At intermission he came out to the theater lobby, where his records were on sale, and autographed programs and record sleeves. I bought "Love Is a Bouquet of Violets," and my mother and I got in line, but when my turn came I said my name so softly that she had to repeat it for me. After the performance he took six calls and stood for a long time throwing kisses.

My mother said, "Don't start to dream about Mariano, Sylvie. He's an actor. He may not mean a word he says about love."

I was not likely to. He was too old for me, and I supposed that actors were nice to everybody in the same way. I wanted plenty of children and a husband who would always be there, not traveling and rehearsing. I wanted him to like me more than other people. I dreamed about Bernard Brunelle. I was engaged to Arnaud Pons.

Arnaud was the son of another man my father admired, I think more than anyone else. They had got to know each other through one of my father's patients, a M. Tarre. My father had treated him for a chronically abscessed ear — eight appointments — and, at the end, when M. Tarre asked if he wanted a check at once or preferred to send a bill, my father answered that he took cash, and on the nail. M. Tarre inquired if that was his usual custom. My father said it was the custom of every specialist he had ever heard of, on which M. Tarre threatened to drag him before an ethics committee. "And your secretary, too!" he shouted. We could hear him in the other wing. "Your accomplice in felony!" My mother pulled me away from the window and said I was to go on being nice to Melle Coutard.

It turned out that M. Tarre was retired from the Ministry of Health and knew all the rules. Papa calmed him down by agreeing to meet a lawyer M. Tarre knew, called Alexandre Pons. He liked the sound of the name, which had a ring of the south. Even when it turned out that those particular Ponses had been in Paris for generations, my father did not withdraw his good will.

M. Pons arrived a few days later, along with M. Tarre, who seemed to have all the time in the world. He told my father that a reprimand from an ethics committee was nothing compared with a charge of tax fraud. Imagine, M. Pons said, a team of men in English-style suits pawing over your accounts. He turned to his friend Tarre and continued, "Over yours, too. Once they get started."

M. Tarre said that his life was a house of glass, anyone was welcome to look inside, but after more remarks from M. Pons, and a couple of generous suggestions from my father, he agreed to let the thing drop.

As a way of thanking M. Pons, as well as getting to know him better, Papa asked my mother to invite him to dinner. For some reason, M. Pons waited several days before calling to say he had a wife. She turned out to be difficult, I remember, telling how she had fainted six times in eighteen months, and announcing, just as the roast lamb was served, that the smell of meat made her feel sick. However, when my mother discovered there was also a Pons son, aged twenty-six, unmarried, living at home, and working in the legal department of a large maritime-insurance firm, she asked them again, this time with Arnaud.

During the second dinner Maman said, "Sylvie is something of an artist. Everything on the dining room walls is Sylvie's work."

Arnaud looked around, briefly. He was silent, though not shy, with a thin face and brown hair. His mind was somewhere else, perhaps in livelier company. He ate everything on his plate, sometimes frowning; when it was something he seemed to like, his expression cleared. He glanced at me, then back at my depictions of the Roman countryside and the harbor at Naples in 1850. I was sure he could see they were replicas and that he knew the originals, and perhaps despised me.

"They are only copies," I managed to say.

"But full of feeling," said Maman.

He nodded, as if acknowledging a distant and somewhat forward acquaintance — a look neither cold nor quite welcoming. I wondered what his friends were like and if they had to pass a special test before he would consent to conversation.

After dinner, in the parlor, there was the usual difficulty over coffee. Claudine was slow to serve, and particularly slow to collect the empty cups. A chinoiserie table stood just under the chandelier, but Maman made sure nothing ever was placed on it. She found an excuse to call attention to the marble floor, because she took pleasure in the icy look of it, but no one picked up the remark. Mme. Pons was first to sit down. She put her cup on the floor, crossed her legs, and tapped her foot to some tune playing in her head. Perhaps she was recalling an evening before her marriage when she had danced wearing a pleated skirt and ropes of beads: I had seen pictures of my mother dressed that way.

I had settled my own cup predicament by refusing coffee. Now I took a chair at some distance from Mme. Pons: I guessed she would soon snap out of her dream and start to ask personal questions. I looked at my hands and saw they were stained with paint. I sat on them: nobody paid attention.

My mother was showing Arnaud loose sketches and unframed watercolors of mine that she kept in a folder — more views of Italy, copies, and scenes in Paris parks drawn from life.

"Take one! Take one!" she cried.

My father went over to see what kind of taste Arnaud had. He had picked the thing nearest him, a crayon drawing of Vesuvius — not my best work. My father laughed, and said my idea of a volcano in eruption was like a haystack on fire.

Bernard's father did not respond to my father's first approach — a letter that began: "I understand that our two children, Bernard and Sylvie, are anxious to unite their destinies." Probably he was too busy finding out if we were solvent, Papa said.

My mother canceled the wedding dates, civil and church. There were just a few presents that had to be returned to close relatives. The names of the other guests had dissolved in the Seine. "It should be done quickly," she had told my father, once the sudden change had been explained half a dozen times and he was nearly over the shock. He wondered if haste had anything to do with disgrace, though he could hardly believe it of me. No, no, nothing like that, she said. She wanted to see me safe and settled and in good hands. Well, of course, he wanted something like that, too.

As for me, I was sure I had been put on earth to marry Bernard Brunelle and move to Lille and live in a large stone house. ("Brick," my friend Chantal corrected, when I told her. "It's all brick up in Lille.") A whole floor would be given over to my children's nurseries and bedrooms and classrooms. They would learn English, Russian, German, and Italian. There would be tutors and governesses, holidays by the sea, ponies to ride, birthday parties with huge pink cakes, servants wearing white gloves. I had never known anyone who lived exactly that way, but my vision was so precise and highly colored that it had to be prompted from Heaven. I saw the curtains in the children's rooms, and their smooth hair and clear eyes, and their neat schoolbooks. I knew it might rain in Lille, day after day: I would never complain. The weather would be part of my enchanted life.

By this time, of course, Arnaud had been invited by my father to have an important talk. But then my father balked, saying he would undertake nothing unless my mother was there. After all, I had two parents. He thought of inviting Arnaud to lunch in a restaurant — Lipp, say, so noisy and crowded that any shock Arnaud showed would not be noticed. Maman pointed out that one always ended up trying to shout over the noise, so there was a danger of being overheard. In the end, Papa asked him to come round to the apartment, at about five o'clock. He arrived with daffodils for my mother and a smaller bunch for me. He believed Papa was planning a change in the marriage contract: he would buy an apartment for us outright instead of granting a twenty-year loan, adjustable to devaluation or inflation, interest-free.

They received him in the parlor, standing, and Maman handed him the sealed rejection she had helped me compose. If I had written the narrowest kind of exact analysis it would have been: "I have tried to love you, and can't. My feelings toward you are cordial and full of respect. If you don't want me to hate the sight of you, please go away." I think that is the truth about any such failure, but nobody says it. In any case, Maman would not have permitted such a thing. She had dictated roundabout excuses, ending with a wish for his future happiness. What did we mean by happiness for Arnaud? I suppose, peace of mind.

Papa walked over to the window and stood drumming on the pane. He made some unthinking remark — that he could see part of the Church of Saint-Augustin, the air was so clear. In fact, thick, gray, lashing rain obscured everything except the nearest rank of trees.

Arnaud looked up from the letter and said, "I must be dreaming." His clever, melancholy face was the color of the rain. My mother was afraid he would faint, as Mme. Pons so liked doing, and hurt his head on the marble floor. The chill of the marble had worked through everyone's shoes. She tried to edge the men over to a carpet, but Arnaud seemed paralyzed. Filling in silence, she went on about the floor: the marble came from Italy; people had warned her against it; it was hard to keep clean and it held the cold.

Arnaud stared at his own feet, then hers. Finally, he asked where I was.

"Sylvie has withdrawn from worldly life," my mother said. I had mentioned nothing in my letter about marrying another man, so he asked a second, logical question: Was I thinking of becoming a nun?

The rain, dismantling chestnut blossoms outside, sounded like gravel thrown against the windows. I know, because I was in my bedroom, just along the passage. I could not see him then as someone frozen and stunned. He was an obstacle on a railway line. My tender and competent mother had agreed to push him off the track.

That evening I said, "What if his parents turn up here and try to make a fuss?"

"They wouldn't dare," she said. "You were more than they had ever dreamed of."

It was an odd, new way of considering the Ponses. Until then, their education and background and attention to things of the past had made up for an embarrassing lack of foresight: they had never acquired property for their only son to inherit. They lived in the same dim apartment, in a lamentable quarter, which they had first rented in 1926, the year of their marriage. It was on a street filled with uninviting stores and insurance offices, east of the Saint-Lazare station, near the old German church. (Arnaud had taken me to the church for a concert of recorded music. I had never been inside a Protestant church before. It was spare and bare and somehow useful-looking, like a large broom closet. I wondered where they hatched the Protestant plots Cousin Gaston often mentioned, such as the crushing of Mediterranean culture by peaceful means. I remember that I felt lonely and out of place, and took Arnaud's hand. He was wearing his distant, listening-to-music expression, and seemed not to notice. At any rate, he didn't mind.)

Families such as the Ponses had left the area long before, but Arnaud's father said his belongings were too ancient and precious to be bumped down a winding staircase and heaved aboard a van. Papa thought he just wanted to hang on to his renewable lease, which happened to fall under the grace of a haphazard rent-control law: he still paid just about the same rent he had been paying before the war. Whatever he saved had never been squandered on paint or new curtains. His eleven rooms shared the same degree of decay and looked alike: you never knew if you were in a dining room or somebody's bedroom. There were antique tables and bedsteads everywhere. All the mirrors were stained with those dark blotches that resemble maps. Papa often wondered if the Ponses knew what they really looked like, if they actually saw themselves as silvery white, with parts of their faces spotted or missing.

One of the first things Mme. Pons had ever shown me was a mute harpsichord, which she wanted to pass on to Arnaud and me. To get it to look right — never mind the sound — would have required months of expert mending, more than Arnaud could afford. Looking around for something else to talk about, I saw in a far, dim corner a bathtub and washstand, valuable relics, in their way, streaked and stained with age. Someone had used them recently: the towels on a rack nearby looked damp. I had good reason for thinking the family all used the same towels.

What went wrong for M. Pons, the winter of my engagement? Even Papa never managed to find out. He supposed M. Pons had been giving too much taxation advice, on too grand a scale. He took down from his front door the brass plate mentioning office hours and went to work in a firm that did not carry his name. His wife had an uncommon past, at once aristocratic and vaguely bohemian. My parents wondered what it could mean. My children would inherit a quarter share of blue blood, true, but they might also come by a tendency to dance naked in Montmartre. Her fa-

ther had been killed in the First World War, leaving furniture, a
name, and a long tradition of perishing in battle. She was the first
woman in her circle ever to work. Her mother used to cry every
morning as she watched her pinning her hat on and counting
her lunch money. Her name was Marie-Eugènie-Paule-Diane.
Her husband called her Nenanne — I never knew why.

Arnaud had studied law, for the sake of family tradition, but
his true calling was to write opinions about music. He wished he
had been a music critic on a daily newspaper, incorruptible and
feared. He wanted to expose the sham and vulgarity of Paris
taste; so he said. Conductors and sopranos would feel the extra
edge of anxiety that makes for a good performance, knowing the
incorruptible Arnaud Pons was in the house. (Arnaud had no
way of judging whether he was incorruptible, my father said. He
had never tried earning a living by writing criticism in Paris.)

We spent most of our time together listening to records, while
Arnaud told me what was wrong with Toscanini or Bruno Wal-
ter. He would stop the record and play the same part again,
pointing out the mistakes. The music seemed as worn and
shabby as the room. I imagined the musicians in those great or-
chestras of the past to be covered with dust, playing on instruments cracked, split, daubed with fingerprints, held together
with glue and string. My children in Lille had spotless instruments, perfectly tuned. Their music floated into a dark garden
drenched with silent rain. But then my thoughts would be over-
taken by the yells and screams of one of Arnaud's doomed sopranos — a Tosca, a Mimi — and I would shut my eyes and let
myself fall. A still surface of water rose to meet me. I was not
dying but letting go.

Bernard's father answered Papa's second approach, which had
been much like the first. He said that his son was a student, with
no roof or income of his own. It would be a long time before he
could join his destiny to anyone's, and it would not be to mine.
Bernard had no inclination for me; none whatever. He had
taken me to be an attractive and artistic girl, anxious to please,
perhaps a bit lonely. As an ardent writer of letters, with pen
friends as far away as Belgium, Bernard had offered the hand of
epistolary comradeship. I had grabbed the hand and called it a
commitment. Bernard was ready to swear in court (should a law-

suit be among my father's insane intentions) that he had taken no risks and never dropped his guard with an unclaimed young person, encountered in a public park. (My parents were puzzled by "unclaimed." I had to explain that I used to take off my engagement ring and carry it loose in a pocket. They asked why. I could not remember.)

M. Brunelle, the answer went on, hoped M. Castelli would put a stop to my fervent outpourings in the form of letters. Their agitated content and their frequency — as many as three a day — interfered with Bernard's studies and, indeed, kept him from sleeping. Surely my father did not want to see me waste the passion of a young heart on a delusion that led nowhere ("on a chimera that can only run dry in the Sahara of disappointment" was what M. Brunelle actually wrote). He begged my father to accept the word of a gentleman that my effusions had been destroyed. "Gentleman" was in English and underlined.

My parents shut themselves up in their bedroom. From my own room, where I sat at the window, holding Bernard's messages, I could hear my father's shouts. He was blaming Maman. Eventually she came in, and I stood up and handed her the whole packet: three letters and a postcard.

"Just the important one," she said. "The one I should have made you show me last April. I want the letter that mentions marriage."

"It was between the lines," I said, watching her face as she read.

"It was nowhere." She seemed sorry for me, all at once. "Oh, Sylvie, Sylvie. My poor Sylvie. Tear it up. Tear every one of them up. All this because you would not try to love Arnaud."

"I thought he loved me," I said. "Bernard, I mean. He never said he didn't."

The Heaven-sent vision of my future life had already faded: the voices of my angelic children became indistinct. I might, now, have been turning the pages of an old storybook with black-and-white engravings.

I said, "I'll apologize to Papa and ask him to forgive me. I can't explain what happened. I thought he wanted what I wanted. He never said that he didn't. I promise never to paint pictures again."

I had not intended the remark about painting pictures. It said itself. Before I could take it back, Maman said, "Forgive you? You're like a little child. Does forgiveness include sending our most humble excuses to the Brunelle family and our having to explain that our only daughter is a fool? Does it account for behavior no sane person can understand? Parents knew what they were doing when they kept their daughters on a short lead. My mother read every letter I wrote until I was married. We were too loving, too lenient."

Her face looked pinched and shrunken. Her love, her loyalties, whatever was left of her youth and charm pulled away from me to be mustered in favor of Papa. She stood perfectly still, almost at attention. I think we both felt at a loss. I thought she was waiting for a signal so she could leave the room. Finally, my father called her. I heard her mutter, "Please get out of my way," though I was nowhere near the door.

My friend Chantal — my postal station, my go-between — came over as soon as she heard the news. It had been whispered by my mother to Chantal's mother, over the telephone, in a version of events that absolved me entirely and turned the Brunelles into fortune-hunting, come-lately provincial merchants and rogues. Chantal knew better, though she still believed the Brunelles had misrepresented their case and came in for censure. She had brought chocolates to cheer me up; we ate most of a box, sitting in a corner of the salon like two travelers in a hotel lobby. She wore her hair in the newest style, cut short and curled thickly on her forehead. I have forgotten the name of the actress who started the fashion: Chantal told me, but I could not take it in.

Chantal was a good friend, perhaps because she had never taken me seriously as a rival; and perhaps in saying this I misjudge her. At any rate, she lost no time in giving me brisk advice. I ought to cut my hair, change my appearance. It was the first step on the way to a new life. She knew I loved children and might never have any of my own: I had no idea how to go about meeting a man or how to hang on to one if he drifted my way. As the next-best thing, I should enter a training college and learn to teach nursery classes. There wasn't much to it, she said. You encouraged them to draw with crayons and sing and run in circles. You put them on pots after lunch and spread blankets on the floor for their afternoon nap. She knew plenty of girls who had done this after their engagements, for some reason, collapsed.

She had recently got to know a naval lieutenant while on a family holiday in the Alps, and now they were planning a Christmas wedding. Perhaps I could persuade my family to try the same thing; but finding a fiancé in the mountains was a new idea — to my mother chancy and doubtful, while my father imagined swindlers and foreigners trampling snow in pursuit of other men's daughters.

Since the fiasco, as he called it, Papa would not look at me. When he had anything to say he shouted it to Maman. They did not take their annual holiday that year but remained in the shuttered apartment, doing penance for my sins. The whole world was away, except us. From Normandy, Claudine sent my mother a postcard of the basilica at Lisieux and the message "My maman, being a mother, respectfully shares your grief" — as if I had died.

At dinner one night — curtains drawn, no one saying much — Papa suddenly held up his hands, palms out. "How many hands do you count?" he said, straight to me.

"Two?" I made it a question in case it was a trick.

"Right. Two hands. All I needed to pull me to the top of my profession. I gave my wife the life she wanted, and I gave my daughter a royal upbringing."

I could sense my mother's close attention, her wanting me to say whatever Papa expected. He had drunk most of a bottle of Brouilly by himself and seemed bound for headlong action. In the end, his message was a simple one: he had forgiven me. My life was a shambles and our family's reputation gravely injured, but I was not wholly to blame. Look at the young men I'd had to deal with: neutered puppies. No wonder there were so many old maids now. I had missed out on the only virile generation of the twentieth century, the age group that took in M. Pons, Cousin Gaston, and, of course, Papa himself.

"We were a strong rung on the ladder of progress," he said. "After us, the whole ladder broke down." The name of Pons, seldom mentioned, seemed to evoke some faraway catastrophe, recalled by a constant few. He bent his head and I thought, Surely he isn't going to cry. I recalled how my mother had said, "We

were too loving." I saw the storehouse in Nice and our name in
faded blue. There were no more Castellis, except Julien in Indochina. I put my napkin over my face and began to bawl.

Papa cheered up. "Two hands," he said, this time to Maman.
"And no help from any quarter. Isn't that true?"

"Everybody admired you," she said. She was clearing plates,
fetching dessert. I was too overcome to help; besides, she didn't
want me. She missed Claudine. My mother sat down again and
looked at Papa, leaving me out. I was a dreary guest, like Mme.
Pons getting ready to show hysteria at the sight of a veal chop.
They might have preferred her company to mine, given the
choice. She had done them no harm and gave them reasons to
laugh. I refused dessert, though no one cared. They continued
to eat their fresh figs poached in honey, with double cream: too
sugary for Maman, really, but a great favorite of Papa's. "The
sweeter the food, the better the temper" was a general truth she
applied to married life.

My mother dreamed she saw a young woman pushed off the top
of a tall building. The woman plunged headfirst, with her wedding veil streaming. The veil materialized the next day, as details
of the dream returned. At first Maman described the victim as a
man, but the veil confirmed her mistake. She mentioned her
shock and horror at my remark on the bridge. The dream surely
had been sent as a reminder: I was not to be crossed or harshly
contradicted or thrust in the wrong direction. Chantal's plans for
my future had struck her as worse than foolery: they seemed
downright dangerous. I knew nothing about little children. I
would let them swallow coins and crayon stubs, leave a child or
two behind on our excursions to parks and squares, lose their
rain boots and sweaters. Nursery schools were places for nuns
and devoted celibates. More to the point, there were no men to
be found on the premises, save the occasional inspector, already
married, and underpaid. Men earning pittance salaries always
married young. It was not an opinion, my mother said. It was a
statistic.

Because of the dream she began to show her feelings through
hints and silences or by telling anecdotes concerning wretched
and despairing spinster teachers she had known. I had never

heard their names before and wondered when she had come across all those Martines and Georgettes. My father, closed to dreams, in particular the threatening kind, wanted to know why I felt such an urge to wipe the noses and bottoms of children who were no relation of mine. Dealing with one's own offspring was thankless enough. He spoke of the violent selfishness of the young, their mindless questions, their love of dirt. Nothing was more deadening to an adult intellect than a child's cycle of self-centered days and long, shapeless summers.

I began to sleep late. Nothing dragged me awake, not even the sound of Papa calling my mother from room to room. At noon I trailed unwashed to the kitchen and heated leftover coffee. Claudine, having returned to claim all my mother's attention, rinsed lettuce and breaded cutlets for lunch, and walked around me as though I were furniture. One morning Maman brought my breakfast on a tray, sat down on the edge of the bed, and said Julien had been reported missing. He could be a prisoner or he might be dead. Waiting for news, I was to lead a quiet life and to pray. She was dressed to go out, I remember, wearing clothes for the wrong season — all in pale blue, with a bandeau of forget-me-nots and her turquoise earrings and a number of little chains. Her new watch, Papa's latest present, was the size of a coin. She had to bring it up to her eyes.

"It isn't too late, you know," she said. I stared at her. "Too late for Arnaud."

I supposed she meant he could still be killed in Indochina, if he wanted that. To hear Cousin Gaston and Papa, one could imagine it was all any younger man craved. I started to say that Arnaud was twenty-seven now and might be too old for wars, but Maman broke in: Arnaud had left Paris and gone to live in Rennes. Last April, after the meeting in the parlor, he had asked his maritime-insurance firm to move him to a branch office. It had taken months to find him the right place; being Arnaud, he wanted not only a transfer but a promotion. Until just five days ago he had never been on his own. There had always been a woman to take care of him; namely, Mme. Pons. Mme. Pons was sure he had already started looking around in Rennes for someone to marry. He would begin with the girls in his new office, probably, and widen the circle to church and concerts.

"It isn't too late," said Maman.

"Arnaud hates me now," I said. "Besides, I can work. I can take a course in something. Mme. Pons worked."

"We don't know what Mme. Pons did."

"I could mind children, take them for walks in the afternoon."

My double file of charges, hand in hand, stopped at the curb. A policeman held up traffic. We crossed and entered the court of an ancient abbey, now a museum. The children clambered over fragments of statues and broken columns. I showed them medieval angels.

Mme. Pons did not want a strange daughter-in-law from a provincial city, my mother said. She wanted me, as before.

For the first time I understood about the compact of mothers and the conspiracy that never ends. They stand together like trees, shadowing and protecting, shutting out the view if it happens to suit them, letting in just so much light. She started to remove the tray, though I hadn't touched a thing.

"Get up, Sylvie," she said. It would have seemed like an order except for the tone. Her coaxing, teasing manner had come back. I was still wondering about the pale blue dress: was she pretending it was spring, trying to pick up whatever had been dropped in April? "It's time you had your hair cut. Sometimes you look eighteen. It may be part of your trouble. We can lunch at the Trois Quartiers and buy you some clothes. We're lucky to have Papa. He never grumbles about spending."

My mother had never had her own bank account or signed a check. As a married woman she would have needed Papa's consent, and he preferred to hand over wads of cash, on demand. Melle Coutard got the envelopes ready and jotted the amounts in a ledger. Owing to a system invented by M. Pons, the money was deducted from Papa's income tax.

"And then," said Maman, "you can go to the mountains for two weeks." It was no surprise: Chantal and her lieutenant wanted to return to Chamonix on a lovers' pilgrimage, but General Nauzan, Chantal's father, would not hear of it unless I went, too. It was part of my mission to sleep in her room: the Nauzans would not have to rush the wedding or have a large and healthy baby appear seven months after the ceremony, to be passed off as premature. So I would not feel like an odd number — in the daytime, that is — the lieutenant would bring along his brother, a junior tennis champion, aged fifteen.

(We were well into our first week at Chamonix before Chantal began to disappear in the afternoon, leaving me to take a tennis lesson from the champion. I think I have a recollection of her telling me, late at night, in the darkness of our shared room, "To tell you the truth, I could do without all that side of it. Do you want to go with him tomorrow, instead of me? He thinks you're very nice." But that kind of remembering is like trying to read a book with some of the pages torn out. Things are said at intervals and nothing connects.)

I got up and dressed, as my mother wanted, and we took the bus to her hairdresser's. She called herself Ingrid. Pasted to the big wall mirror were about a dozen photographs cut from *Paris Match* of Ingrid Bergman and her little boy. I put on a pink smock that covered my clothes and Ingrid cut my long hair. My mother saved a few locks, one for Papa, the others in case I ever wanted to see what I had once been like, later on. The two women decided I would look silly with curls on my forehead, so Ingrid combed the new style sleek.

What Chantal had said was true: I looked entirely different. I seemed poised, sharp, rather daunting. Ingrid held a looking glass up so I could see the back of my head and my profile. I turned my head slowly. I had a slim neck and perfect ears and my mother's forehead. For a second a thought flared, and then it died: with her blue frock and blue floral hat and numerous trinkets Maman was like a little girl dressed up. I stared and stared, and the women smiled at each other. I saw their eyes meet in the mirror. They thought they were watching emerging pride, the kind that could make me strong. Even vanity would have pleased them; any awakening would do.

I felt nothing but the desire for a life to match my changed appearance. It was a longing more passionate and mysterious than any sort of love. My role could not be played by another person. All I had to do now was wait for my true life to reveal itself and the other players to let me in.

My father took the news from Indochina to be part of a family curse. He had hoped I would marry Julien. He would have had Castelli grandchildren. But Julien and I were too close in age and

forever squabbling. He was more like a brother. "Lover" still
held a small quantity of false knowledge. Perhaps I had always
wanted a stranger. Papa said the best were being taken, as in all
wars. He was sorry he had not been gunned down in the last one.
He was forty-nine and had survived to see his only daughter
washed up, a decent family nearly extinct, the whole nation idle
and soft.

He repeated all these things, and more, as he drove me to the
railway station where I was to meet Chantal, the lieutenant, and
the junior champion. His parting words reproached me for indifference to Julien's fate, and I got on the train in tears.

My mother was home, at the neat little desk where she plotted
so many grave events. For the first time in her life, she delivered
an invitation to dinner by telephone. I still have the letter she
sent me in Chamonix, describing what they had had to eat and
what Mme. Pons had worn: salmon pink, sleeveless, with spike
heels and fake pearls. She had also worn my rejected engagement ring. Mme. Pons could get away with lack of judgment and
taste, now. We were the suppliants.

My father had been warned it would be fish, because of Mme.
Pons, but he forgot and said quite loudly, "Are you trying to tell
me there's nothing after the turbot? Are the butchers on strike?
Is it Good Friday? Has the whole world gone crazy? Poor
France!" he said, turning to M. Pons. "I mean it. These changes
in manners and customs are part of the decline."

The two guests pretended not to hear. They gazed at my
painting of the harbor at Naples — afraid, Papa said later, we
might try to give it to them.

When Papa asked if I'd enjoyed myself in the Alps I said, "There
was a lot of tennis." It had the dampening effect I had hoped for,
and he began to talk about a man who had just deserted from the
army because he was a pacifist, and who ought to be shot. Maman
took me aside as soon as she could and told me her news: Arnaud
was still undecided. His continued license to choose was like a
spell of restless weather. The two mothers studied the sky. How
long could it last? He never mentioned me, but Mme. Pons was
sure he was waiting for a move.

"What move?" I said. "A letter from Papa?"

"You can't expect Papa to write any more letters," she said. "It has to come from you."

Once again, I let my mother dictate a letter for Arnaud. I had no idea what to say; or, rather, of the correct way of saying anything. It was a formal request for an appointment, at Arnaud's convenience, at the venue of his choice. That was all. I signed my full name: Sylvie Mireille Castelli. I had never written to anyone in Rennes before. I could not imagine his street. I wondered if he lived in someone else's house or had found his own apartment. I wondered who made his breakfast and hung up his clothes and changed the towels in the bathroom. I wondered how he would feel when he saw my handwriting; if he would burn the letter, unread.

He waited ten days before saying he did not mind seeing me, and suggested having lunch in a restaurant. He could come to Paris on a Sunday, returning to Rennes the same day. It seemed to me an enormous feat of endurance. The fastest train, in those days, took more than three hours. He said he would let me know more on the matter very soon. The move to Rennes had worn him down and he needed a holiday. He signed "A. Pons." ("That's new," my father said, about the invitation to lunch. He considered Arnaud's approach to money to be conservative, not to say nervous.)

He arrived in Paris on the third Sunday in October, finally, almost a year to the day from our first meeting. I puzzled over the timetable, wondering why he had chosen to get up at dawn to catch a train that stopped everywhere when there was a direct train two hours later. Papa pointed out the extra-fare sign for the express. "And Arnaud . . ." he said, but left it at that.

Papa and I drove to the old Montparnasse station, where the trains came in from the west of France. Hardly anyone remembers it now: a low gray building with a wooden floor. I have a black-and-white postcard that shows the curb where my father parked his Citroën and the station clock we watched and the door I went through to meet Arnaud face to face. We got there early and sat in the car, holding hands sometimes, listening to a Sunday morning program of political satire — songs and poems and imitations of men in power — but Papa soon grew tired of laughing alone and switched it off. He smoked four Gitanes from a pack Uncle Gaston had left behind. When his lighter balked he pretended to throw it away, trying to make me smile. I could see nothing funny about the loss of a beautiful silver lighter, the gift of a patient. It seemed wasteful, not amusing. I ate some expensive chocolates I found in the glove compartment: Melle Coutard's, I think.

He kept leaning forward to read the station clock, in case his watch and my watch and the dashboard clock were slow. When it was time, he kissed me and made me promise to call the minute I knew the time of Arnaud's return train, so he could come and fetch me. He gave me the names of two or three restaurants he liked, pointing in the direction of the Boulevard Raspail — places he had taken me that smelled of cigars and red Burgundy. They looked a bit like station buffets, but were more comfortable and far more expensive. I imagined that Arnaud and I would be walking along the boulevard in the opposite direction, where there were plenty of smaller, cheaper places. Papa and Cousin Gaston smoked Gitanes in memory of their student days. They did, sometimes, visit the restaurants of their youth, where the smells were of boiled beef and fried potatoes and dark tobacco, but they knew the difference between a sentimental excursion and a good meal.

As I turned away, my heart pounding enough to shake me, I heard him say, "Remember, whatever happens, you will always have a home," which was true but also a manner of speaking.

The first passenger off the train was a girl with plastic roses pinned to her curly hair. She ran into the arms of two other girls. They looked alike, in the same long coats with ornamental buttons, the same frothy hair and plastic hair slides. One of the Parisians took the passenger's cardboard suitcase and they went off, still embracing and chattering. Chantal had warned me not to speak to any man in the station, even if he seemed respectable. She had described the sad girls who came from the west, a deeply depressed area, to find work as maids and waitresses, and the gangsters who hung around the train gates. They would pick the girls up and after a short time put them on the street. If a girl got tired of the life and tried to run away, they had her murdered and her body thrown in the Seine. The crimes were never solved; nobody cared.

Actually, most of the men I saw looked like citified Breton farmers. I had a problem that seemed, at the moment, far more acute than the possibility of being led astray and forced into prostitution. I had no idea what to say to Arnaud, how to break the ice. My mother had advised me to talk about Rennes if conversation ran thin. I could mention the great fire of 1720 and the fine houses it had destroyed. Arnaud walked straight past me and suddenly turned back. On his arm he carried a new raincoat with a plaid lining. He was wearing gloves; he took one off to shake hands.

I said, "I've had my hair cut."

"So I see."

That put a stop to 1720, or anything else, for the moment. We crossed the Boulevard du Montparnasse without touching or speaking. He turned, as I had expected, in the direction of the cheaper restaurants. We read and discussed the menus posted outside. He settled on Rougeot. Not only did Rougeot have a long artistic and social history, Arnaud said, but it offered a fixed-price meal with a variety of choice. Erik Satie had eaten here. No one guessed how poor Satie had been until after his death, when Cocteau and others had visited his wretched suburban home and learned the truth. Rilke had eaten here, too. It was around the time when he was discovering Cézanne and writing those letters. I recognized Arnaud's way of mentioning famous people, pausing before the name and dropping his voice.

The window tables were already taken. Arnaud made less fuss than I expected. Actually, I had never been alone at a restaurant with Arnaud; it was my father I was thinking of, and how violently he wanted whatever he wanted. Arnaud would not hang up his coat. He had bought it just the day before and did not want a lot of dirty garments full of fleas in close touch. He folded it on a chair, lining out. It fell on the floor every time a waiter went by.

I memorized the menu so I could describe it to Maman. Our first course was hard-boiled eggs with mayonnaise, then we chose the liver. Liver was something his mother would not have in the house, said Arnaud. As a result, he and his father were chronically lacking in iron. I wanted to ask where he ate his meals now, if he had an obliging landlady who cooked or if he had the daily expense of a restaurant; but it seemed too much like prying.

The red wine, included in the menu, arrived in a thick, stained decanter. Arnaud asked to be shown the original label. The waiter said the label had been thrown away, along with the bottle. There was something of a sneer in his voice, as if we were foreigners, and Arnaud turned away coldly. The potatoes served with the liver had been boiled early and heated up: we both noticed. Arnaud said it did not matter; because of the wine incident, we were never coming back. "We" suggested a common future, but it may have been a slip of the tongue; I pretended I hadn't heard. For dessert I picked custard flan and Arnaud had prunes in wine. Neither of us was hungry by then, but dessert was included, and it would have been a waste of money to skip a course. Arnaud made some reference to this.

I want to say that I never found him mean. He had not come to Paris to charm or impress me; he was here to test his own feelings at the sight of me and to find out if I understood what getting married meant — in particular, to him. His conversation was calm and instructive. He told me about "situations," meaning the entanglements people got into when they were characters in novels and plays. He compared the theatre of Henry de Montherlant with Jean Anouilh's: how they considered the part played by innocent girls in the lives of more worldly men. To Anouilh a girl was a dove, Arnaud said, an innocent dressed in white, ultimately and almost accidentally destroyed. Montherlant saw them as ignorant rather than innocent — more knowing than any man suspected, unlearned and crass.

All at once he said a personal thing: "You aren't eating your dessert."

"There's something strange on it," I said. "Green flakes."

He pulled my plate over and scraped the top of the flan with my spoon. (I had taken one bite and put the spoon down.) "Parsley," he said. "There was a mistake made in the kitchen. They took the flan for a slice of quiche."

"I know it is paid for," I said. "But I can't."

I was close to tears. It occurred to me that I sounded like Mme. Pons. He began to eat the flan, slowly, using my spoon. Each time he put the spoon in his mouth I said to myself, He must love me. Otherwise it would be disgusting. When he had finished, he folded his napkin in the exact way that always annoyed my mother and said he loved me. Oh, not as before, but enough to let him believe he could live with me. I was not to apologize for last spring or to ask for forgiveness. As Cosima had said to Hans von Bülow, after giving birth to Wagner's child, forgiveness was not called for — just understanding. (I knew who Wagner was, but the rest bewildered me utterly.) I had blurted out something innocent, impulsive, Arnaud continued, and my mother — herself a child — had acted as though it were a mature decision. My mother had told his mother about the bridge and the turning point; he understood that, too. He knew all about infatuation. At one time he had actually believed my drawing of Vesuvius could bring him luck, and had carried it around with the legal papers in his briefcase. That was how eaten up by love he had been, at twenty-six. Well, that kind of storm and passion of the soul was behind him. He was twenty-seven, and through with extremes. He blamed my mother, but one had to take into account her infantile nature. He was inclined to be harder on Bernard — speaking the name easily, as if "Bernard Brunelle" were a character in one of the plays he had just mentioned. Brunelle was a vulgar libertine, toying with the feelings of an untried and trustful girl and discarding her when the novelty wore off. He, Arnaud, was prepared to put the clock back to where it had stood exactly a second before my mother wrenched the wedding invitations out of my hands and hurled them into the Seine.

Seated beside a large window that overlooked the terrace and boulevard were the three curly-haired girls I had noticed at the station. They poured wine for each other and leaned into the table, so that their heads almost touched. Above them floated a flat layer of thin blue smoke. Once I was married, I thought, I would smoke. It would give me something to do with my hands when other people talked, and would make me look as if I were enjoying myself. One of the girls caught me looking, and smiled. It was a smile of recognition, but hesitant, too, as if she wondered if I would want to acknowledge her. She turned back, a little disappointed. When I looked again, I had a glimpse of her in profile, and saw why she had seemed familiar and yet diffident: she was the typist who sat outside Cousin Gaston's office, who had caused him and Papa so much anxiety and apprehension. She was just eighteen — nineteen at most. How could they have taken her for a spy? She was one of three kittenish friends, perhaps sisters, from the poorest part of France.

Look at it this way, Arnaud was saying. We had gone through tests and trials, like Tamino and Pamina, and had emerged tempered and strong. I must have looked blank, for he said, a little sharply, "In *The Magic Flute*. We spent a whole Sunday on it. I translated every word for you — six records, twelve sides."

I said, "Does she die?"

"No," said Arnaud. "If she had to die we would not be sitting here." Now, he said, lowering his voice, there was one more thing he needed to know. This was not low curiosity on his part, but a desire to have the whole truth spread out — "like a sheet spread on green grass, drying in sunshine" was the way he put it. My answer would make no difference; his decisions concerning me and our future were final. The question was, had Bernard Brunelle *succeeded* and, if so, to what extent? Was I entirely, or partly, or not at all the same as before? Again, he said the stranger's name as if it were an invention, a name assigned to an imaginary life.

It took a few moments for me to understand what Arnaud was talking about. Then I said, "Bernard Brunelle? Why, I've never even kissed him. I saw him only that once. He lives in Lille."

His return train did not leave for another hour. I asked if he would like to walk around Montparnasse and look at the famous cafés my father liked, but the sidewalk was spotted with rain, and I think he did not want to get his coat wet. As we crossed the boulevard again, he took my arm and remarked that he did not care for Bretons and their way of thinking. He would not spend his life in Rennes. Unfortunately, he had asked for the transfer and the firm had actually created a post for him. It would be some time before he could say he had changed his mind. In the meantime, he would come to Paris every other weekend. Perhaps I could come to Rennes, too, with or without a friend. We had reached the age of common sense and could be trusted. Some of the beaches in Brittany were all right, he said, but you never could be sure of the weather. He preferred the Basque coast, where his mother used to take him when he was a child. He had just spent four weeks there, in fact.

I did not dare ask if he had been alone; in any case, he was here, with me. We sat down on a bench in the station. I could think of nothing more to say. The great fire of 1720 seemed inappropriate as a topic for someone who had just declared an aversion to Bretons and their history. I had a headache, and was just as glad to be quiet. I wondered how long it would take to wean him away from the Pons family habit of drinking low-cost wine. He picked up a newspaper someone had left behind and began to read yesterday's news. There was more about the pacifist deserter; traitors (I supposed they must be that) were forming a defense committee. I thought about Basque beaches, wondering if they were sand or shale, and if my children would be able to build sand castles.

Presently Arnaud folded the paper, in the same careful way he always folded a table napkin, and said I ought to follow Chantal's suggestion and get a job teaching in a nursery school. (So Maman had mentioned that to Mme. Pons, too.) I should teach until I had enough working time behind me to claim a pension. It would be good for me in my old age to have an income of my own. Anything could happen. He could be killed in a train crash or called up for a war. My father could easily be ruined in a lawsuit and die covered with debts. There were advantages to teaching, such as long holidays and reduced train fares.

"How long would it take?" I said. "Before I could stop teaching and get my pension."

"Thirty-five years," said Arnaud. "I'll ask my mother. She had no training, either, but she taught private classes. All you need is a decent background and some recommendations."

Wait till Papa hears this, I thought. He had imagined everything possible, even that she had been the paid mistress of a Romanian royal.

Arnaud said a strange thing then: "You would have all summer long for your art. I would never stand in your way. In fact, I would do everything to help. I would mind the children, take them off your hands."

In those days men did not mind children. I had never in my

life seen a married man carrying a child except to board a train
or at a parade. I was glad my father hadn't heard. I think I was
shocked: I believe that, in my mind, Arnaud climbed down a
notch. More to the point, I had not touched a brush or drawing
pencil since the day my mother had read the letter from Bernard — the important one. Perhaps if I did not paint and draw
and get stains on my hands and clothes Arnaud would be disappointed. Perhaps, like Maman, he wanted to be able to say that
everything hanging on the walls was mine. What he had said
about not standing in my way was unusual, certainly; but it was
kind, too.

We stood up and he shook and then folded his coat, holding
the newspaper under his arm. He pulled his gloves out of his
coat pocket, came to a silent decision, and put them back. He
handed me the newspaper, but changed his mind: he would
work the crossword puzzle on the way back to Rennes. By the
end of the day, I thought, he would have traveled some eight
hours and have missed a Sunday afternoon concert, because of
me. He started to say goodbye at the gate, but I wanted to see
him board the train. A special platform ticket was required: he
hesitated until I said I would buy it myself, and then he bought it
for me.

From the step of the train he leaned down to kiss my cheek.

I said, "Shall I let it grow back?"

"What?"

"My hair. Do you like it short or long?"

He was unable to answer, and seemed to find the question as-
tonishing. I walked along the platform and saw him enter his
compartment. There was a discussion with a lady about the window seat. He would never grab or want anything he had no claim
on, but he would always establish his rights, where they existed.
He sat down in the place he had a right to, having shown his seat
reservation, and opened the paper to the puzzle. I waited until
the train pulled away. He did not look out. In his mind I was on
my way home.

I was not quite sure what to do next, but I was certain of one
thing: I would not call Papa. Arnaud had not called his family,
either. We had behaved like a real couple, in a strange city, where
we knew no one but each other. From the moment of his arrival

until now we had not been separated; not once. I decided I
would walk home. It was a long way, much of it uphill once I
crossed the river, but I would be moving along, as Arnaud was
moving with the train. I would be accompanying him during at
least part of his journey.

I began to walk, under a slight, not a soaking, drizzle, along
the boulevard, alongside the autumn trees. The gray clouds
looked sculptured, the traffic lights unnaturally bright. I was sitting on a sandy beach somewhere along the Basque coast. A red
ribbon held my long hair, kept it from blowing across my face. I
sat in the shade of a white parasol, upon a striped towel. My
knees were drawn up to support my sketch pad. I bent my head
and drew my children as they dug holes in the sand. They wore
white sun hats. Their arms and legs were brown.

By the time I reached the Invalides the rain had stopped. Instead of taking the shortest route home, I had made a wide detour west. The lights gleamed brighter than ever as night came
down. There were yellow streaks low in the sky. I skirted the little
park and saw old soldiers, survivors of wars lovingly recalled by
Cousin Gaston and Papa, sitting on damp benches. They lived in
the veterans' hospital nearby and had nothing else to do. I
turned the corner and started down toward the Seine, walking
slowly. I still had a considerable distance to cover, but it seemed
unfair to arrive home before Arnaud; that was why I had gone
so far out of my way. My parents could think whatever they
liked: that he had taken a later train, that I had got wet finding a
taxi. I would never tell anyone how I had traveled with Arnaud,
not even Arnaud. It was a small secret, insignificant, but it belonged to the true life that was almost ready to let me in. And so
it did; and, yes, it made me happy.

TIM GAUTREAUX

Same Place, Same Things

FROM THE ATLANTIC MONTHLY

THE PUMP REPAIRMAN was cautious. He saw the dry rut in the lane and geared the truck down so he could take it through slow. The thin wheels of his ancient Ford bounced heavily, the road ridge scraping the axles. A few blackbirds charged out of the dead brush along the road and wheeled through the sky like a thrown handful of gravel. He wondered how far down the farm lane the woman lived. When she had called him at the tourist court, she had not been confident about giving directions, seeming unsure where her own house was. On both sides of the road fields of strawberries baked in the sun. It had not rained, the locals told him, for seven weeks.

Leafless branches reached out to snatch away his headlights. Billows of dust flew up behind the truck like a woman's face powder, settling on roadside dewberry bushes that resembled thickened fountains of lava. It was an awful drought.

In a short while he arrived at a weathered farmhouse set behind a leaning barbed-wire fence. He pulled up and got out. No one came from the house, so he slammed the door of the truck and coughed loudly. He had been in this part of the country long enough to know that the farm people did not want you on their porches unless you were a relative or a neighbor. Now, in the Depression, life was so hard for them that they trusted almost nobody.

Finally he blew the truck's horn and was rewarded with a movement at one of the windows. In half a minute a woman in a thin cotton housedress came out.

"You the pump man?" she asked.

"Yes, ma'am. Name's Harry Lintel."

She looked him over as though he were a goat she might or might not buy. Walking to the edge of her porch, she looked back toward the field behind the house. "If you walk this trail here for a while, you'll find my husband trying to fix the pump." He did not like the way she made a face when she said "husband." He was uneasy around women who did not like their men. She walked off the porch and through the fifteen feet of thistle and clover that served as a front lawn, moving carefully toward the pump repairman, who regarded her warily. Poor people made him nervous. He was poor himself, at least as far as money goes, but he was not hangdog and spiritless like many of the people he'd met in this part of the state, beaten down and ruined inside by hard times. She looked at his eyes. "How old you think I am?"

She seemed about forty, four years younger than he was, but with farm women you could never tell. He looked at her sandy hair and gray eyes. She was thin, but something about the way she looked at him suggested toughness. "Lady, I've come to fix a pump. What kind do you have and what's wrong with it?"

"My husband, he'll be back in a minute. He'll know what all you need to find out. What I want to know is where you're from. I ain't heard nobody around here talk like you in a while." She had her hair tied back in a loose knot and reached up to touch it delicately. This motion caught his eye. He guessed she might be closer to thirty-five.

Harry Lintel put a hand in his right front pocket and leaned back against the door of his truck. Taking off his straw hat, he threw it into the front seat over his shoulder. "I'm from Missouri," he said, running a hand through a clump of short, brassy hair.

Her expression was still one of intense evaluation. "Ain't there no pump work in Missouri?" she asked. "Or did your woman run you off?"

"My wife died," he said. "As for pump work, when it's dry and the local pump repairmen can't keep up with their work, or there ain't any pump repairmen, I come around and take up the slack." He looked around her at the peeling house and its broken panes patched with cardboard.

"So why ain't you where you belong, taking up slack?"

He looked at her hard. That last remark showed some wit, something he had not found in a woman for a while. "Where's your husband, lady? I've got cash jobs waiting for me up Highway Fifty-one."

"Keep your pants on. He'll be here, I said." She folded her arms and came a step closer. "I'm just curious why anyone would come to this part of Louisiana from somewheres else."

"I follow the droughts," he said, straightening up and walking along the fence to where it opened into a rutted drive. The woman followed him, sliding her hands down her hips to smooth her dress. "Last week I was in Texas. Was doing a good trade until an all-night rain came in from Mexico and put me out of business. Wasn't much of a pumping situation after that, and the local repairmen could keep things going." He looked down the path as far as he could see along the field of limp plants. "Month before that I was in North Georgia. Before that I fixed pumps over in Alabama. Those people had a time with their green peppers. Where the devil's your old man?"

"I never see anyone but my husband and two or three buyers that come back in here to deal with him." She began to look at his clothes, and this made him uneasy, because he knew she saw that they were clean and not patched. He wore a khaki shirt and trousers. Perhaps no one she knew wore unpatched clothes. Her housedress looked like it had been made from a faded window curtain. "Texas," she said. "I saw your ad in the paper and I figured you were a traveling man."

"No, ma'am," he said. "I'm a man who travels." He saw she did not understand that there was a difference. She seemed desperate and bored, but many people he met were that way. Very few were curious about where he came from, however. They cared only that he was Harry Lintel, who could fix any irrigation pump or engine ever made.

He walked into the field toward the tree line a quarter mile off, and the woman went quickly to the house. He saw a wire strung from the house into a chinaberry tree, and then through a long file of willows edging a ditch, and figured this led to an electric pump. He was almost disappointed that the woman wasn't following him.

As he walked, he looked around at the farm. It was typical of the worst. He came upon a Titan tractor stilted on wood blocks in the weeds, its head cracked. Behind it was a corroded disc harrow, which could still have been useful had it been taken care of. In the empty field to his right stood two cows suffering from the bloat.

He was sweating through his shirt by the time he reached a thin stand of bramble-infested loblolly edging the field. Two hundred feet down the row of trees a man hunched over an electric motor, his back to the repairman. Calling out to him, Lintel walked in that direction, but the other man did not respond — he was absorbed in close inspection of a belt drive, the pump repairman guessed. The farmer was sprawled on a steel grid that hung over an open well. Harry walked up and said hello, but the farmer said nothing. He seemed to be asleep, even though he was out in the sun and his undershirt was as wet as a dishcloth. Harry stooped down and looked over the pump and the way it was installed. He saw that it was bolted to the grid without insulation. Two stray wires dangled into the well. He watched for the rise and fall of the man's body, but the man was not breathing. Kneeling down, Harry touched the back of his knuckles to the steel grid. There was no shock, so he grabbed the man by his arms and pulled him off the motor, turning him over. He was dead, without a doubt: electrocuted. His fingers were burned, and a dark stain ran down his pants leg. Harry felt the man's neck for a pulse and, finding none, sat there for a long time, studying the man's broad, slick face, a face angry and stupid even in death. He looked around at the sorry farm as though it were responsible, got up, and walked back to the farmhouse.

The woman was sitting on the porch in a rocker, staring off into a parched, fallow field. She looked at the repairman and smiled, just barely.

Harry Lintel rubbed his chin. "You got a phone?"

"Nope," she said, smoothing her hair down with her right hand. "There's one at the store out on Fifty-one."

He did not want to tell her, feeling that it would be better for someone else to break the news. "You've got a lady friend lives around here?"

She looked at him sharply, her gray eyes round. "What you want to know that for?"

"I've got my reasons," he said. He began to get into his big dusty truck, trying to act as though nothing had happened. He wanted to put some distance between himself and her coming sorrow.

"The first house where you turned in, there's Mary. But she don't have no phone."

"See you in a few minutes," he said, cranking up the truck.

At the highway he found Mary and told her to go back and tell the woman that her husband was dead out by the pump. The old woman simply nodded, went back into her house, and got her son to go with her. Her lack of concern bothered him. Didn't she care about the death of her neighbor?

At the store he called the sheriff and waited. He rode with the deputies back to the farmhouse and told them what he knew. They stood over the body, looked up at the dry sky, and told the pump repairman to go back to his business, that they would take care of everything.

He and one of the deputies walked out of the field past the farmhouse, and he tried not to look at the porch as he passed, but he could not keep himself from listening. He heard nothing — no crying, no voices heavy with muted passion. The two women were on the porch step talking calmly, as though they were discussing the price of berries. The widow watched him carefully as he got into the police car. He thought he detected a trace of perfume in the air and looked around inside the gritty sedan for its source.

That day he repaired six engines, saving little farms from turning back to sand. The repairs were hard ones that no one else could manage: broken timing gears, worn-out governors, cracked water jackets. At least one person on each farm asked him if he was the one who had found the dead man, and when he admitted that he was, each sullen farmer backed off and let him work alone. Late in the afternoon he was heating an engine head in his portable forge, watching the hue of the metal so that he could judge whether the temperature was right for brazing. He waited for the right color to rise like the blush on a woman's cheek, and when it did, he sealed a complex crack with a clean streak of molten brass. A wizened Italian farmer watched him like a chicken hawk, his arms folded across a washed-out denim shirt. "It's no gonna work," he said.

But when, near dusk, Harry pulled the flywheel, and the engine sprang to life with a heavy, thudding exhaust, turning up a rill of sunset-tinged water into the field, the farmer cracked a faint smile. "If you couldna fixed it, we'da run you out the parish."

Harry began to clean his hands with care. "Why?"

"Stranger find a dead man, that's bad luck."

"It's better I found him than his wife, isn't it?"

The farmer poked a few bills at Harry, turned, and began walking toward his packing shed. "Nothin' surprise that woman," he said.

It was eight-thirty when he got back to the Bell Pepper Tourist Court, a collection of six pink stucco cabins with a large oval window embedded in each. The office, which also contained a small café, was open, but he was too tired to eat. He sat on his jittery bed, staring across the highway to the railroad, where a local passenger train trundled by, its whistle singing for a crossing. Beyond this was yet another truck farm, maybe twelve acres punctuated by a tin-roof shack. He wondered how many other women were stuck back in the woods living without a husband. The widow of the electrocuted man didn't even have children to take her mind off her loneliness. He had that. He had gotten married when he was seventeen and had raised two daughters and a son. He was now forty-four and on his own, his wife having died five years before. The small Missouri town he was raised in couldn't keep him provided with work, so he had struck out, roaming the South and the Southwest, looking for machines that nobody else could repair.

He stared through the oval window at his truck. At least he could move around and meet different people, being either sorry to leave them or glad to get away, depending. He gazed fondly at the Ford, its stake body loaded with blacksmith's tongs, welding tools, a portable forge, and boxes of parts, wrenches, sockets, coal, hardies, gasket material, all covered with a green tarp slung over the wooden sides. It could take him anywhere, and with his tools he could fix anything but the weather.

The next morning at dawn he headed out for the first job of the day, noticing that the early sky was like a piece of sheet metal heated to a blue-gray color. He pulled up to a farmhouse and a small man wearing a ponderous mustache came out from around back, cursing. Harry Lintel threw his hat back into the truck and ran his hands through his hair. He had never seen people who disliked strangers so much. The little farmer spat on the Ford's tire and told him to drive into the field behind the farmhouse. "My McCormick won't throw no spark," he said.

Harry turned to get under way, but over the Ford's hood he saw, two hundred yards off, the back of a woman's head moving above the weeds in an idle field. "Who's that?" he asked, pointing two fields over.

The farmer craned his neck but could not recognize the figure, who disappeared behind a briar patch between two farms. "I don't know," the farmer said, scratching his three-day beard, "but a woman what walk around like that with nothing better to do is thinking up trouble." He pointed to Harry. "When a woman thinks too long, look out! Now, get to work, you."

The day turned as hot as a furnace and his skin rolled with sweat. By noon he had worked on three machines within a half mile of one another. From little farms up and down Highway 51 he could hear the thud and pop of pump engines. He was in a field of berries, finishing up with a balky International, when he saw a woman walking along the railroad embankment with a basket in the crook of her right arm. It was the wife of the dead farmer. He waited until she was several rows off and then looked up at her. She met his look head on, her eyes the color of dull nickel. He admitted to himself then and there that it scared him, the way she looked at him. Harry Lintel could figure out any machine on earth, but with women he wished for an instruction manual.

She walked up to him and set the basket on top of his wrenches. "You ready to eat?" she asked, as though he had expected her.

He wiped his hands on a kerosene-soaked rag. "Where'd you come from?"

"It's not far from my place," she said. He noticed that she was wearing a new cotton dress, which seemed to have been snagged in a few places by briars. She knelt down and opened the basket, pulling out a baby quilt and sandwiches. He sat on the parched grass next to her in a spot of shade thrown by a willow.

"I'm sorry about your man," he said. "I should have told you myself."

Her hands moved busily in the basket. "That woman and I get along all right. You did as good as you could." They ate in silence for a while. From the distance came the deep music of a big Illinois Central freight engine, its whistle filling the afternoon, swaying up and down a scale of frantic notes. The Crimson Flyer thundered north, trailing a hundred refrigerated cars of berries, the work of an entire year for many local farmers. "That train's off its time," she said. "Seems like everything's off schedule lately." She took a bite of ham sandwich and chewed absently.

"I asked the boys that own this engine about your man. They didn't want to talk about him." He took a bite of sandwich and tried not to make a face. It was dry, and the ham tasted like it had been in the icebox too long. He wondered if she had fed her husband any better.

"He was from New Orleans, not from around here. Nobody liked him much, because of his berries. He tried to ship bad Klondykes once, and the men at the loading dock broke his leg."

The pump man shook his head. "Breaking a farmer's leg's kind of rough treatment."

"He deserved it," she said matter-of-factly. "Shipping bad berries give the area farmers a bad name." She looked at her sandwich as though she had seen it for the first time, and threw it into the basket. "He was too damned lazy to pick early enough to ship on time."

He was afraid she was going to cry, but her face remained as dry as the gravel road that ran along the track. He began to wonder what she had done about her husband. "What about the services for your old man?"

"Mary's pickers helped me put him in this morning after the coroner came out and give us the okay."

So that's it, he thought. Half your life working in the sun and then your woman plants you in back of the tool shed like a dog. He was tempted to toss his sandwich, but he was hungrier than he had been in weeks, so he bit at it again. The woman put her eyes all over him, and he knew what she was doing. He began to compare himself with her husband. He was bigger. People told him frequently that he had a pleasant face, which he figured was their way of telling him he wasn't outright ugly.

When she stared away at a noisy crow, he stole a long look at her. The dress fit her pretty well, and if she were another woman, one that hadn't just put her husband in the ground, he might have asked her for a date. A row of pale freckles fell across her nose, and today her hair was untied, hanging down over her shoulders. Something in the back of his mind bothered him.

"What's your name?" he asked.

"Ada," she said quickly, as though she had expected the question.

"I thank you for the sandwich, but I've got to get going up the road."

She looked along the railway. "Must be nice to take off whenever you've a mind to. I bet you travel all over."

"A lot travel more'n I do." He bent down and began to pick up box-end wrenches.

"What you in such a hurry for?" she asked, stretching out her long legs into the dead grass. Harry studied them a moment.

"Lady, people around here wonder what the trees are up to when they lean with the breeze. What you think someone that sees us is going to think?"

He walked over to his truck, placed his tools in the proper boxes, row-hopped over to the engine, slung the flywheel with a cast-iron crank, and backed off to hear the exhausts talk to him. The woman watched his moves, all of them. As he was driving out of the field, he felt her eyes on the back of his neck.

That evening after supper in the Bell Pepper Tourist Court café Harry looked up from his coffee and saw Ada walk in through the screen door. She walked across the hard-scrubbed pine floor as if she came into the place all the time, sat across from him in a booth, and put on the table a bottle of bright-red strawberry wine. She had washed her hair and put on a jasmine perfume.

Harry was embarrassed. A couple of farmers looked at them in hangdog fashion, and Marie, the owner, lifted her chin when she saw the bottle of wine. He was at first grouchy about the visit, not liking to be surprised, but as she asked him questions about his travels, he studied her skin, which was not as rough as he had first thought, her sandy hair, and those eyes that seemed to drink him in. He wondered how she had passed her life so far, stuck

on a mud lane in the most spiritless backwater he'd ever seen. He
was as curious about her static, unmoving world as she was about
his wandering one.

Conversation was not his long suit, but the woman had an
hour's worth of questions about Arkansas and Georgia, listening
to his tales of mountains as though he were telling her of China
or the moon. What he wanted to talk about was Missouri and his
children, but her questions wouldn't let him. At one point in the
conversation she looked over at Marie and said, "There's them
around here that say if you hang around me, there's no telling
what trouble you'll get into." She put her hands together and
placed them in the middle of the green oilcloth.

He looked at them, realizing that she had told him almost
nothing about herself. "You said your husband was from New
Orleans, but you didn't say where you were from."

She took a swallow of wine from a water glass. "Let's just say I
showed up here a few years ago. Nobody knows nothing much
about me except I was kept back in that patch and never came in
to drink or dance or nothing. Where I'm from's not so important, is it?" She took a sip and smiled at him over the rim of her
glass. "You like to dance?" she asked quickly.

"I can glide around some," he said. "But about this afternoon.
Why'd you follow me with them sandwiches out in the field?"

Ada bit her lower lip and thought a moment. "Maybe I want to
move on," she said flatly. Harry looked out the window and whistled.

They took their time finishing off the bottle. She went to the
ladies' room and he walked outside into the dark parking lot. He
stood there stretching the kinks out of his muscles. Ada came out
to him, looked up and down 51 for cars, and threw her arms
around his waist, giving him a hard kiss. Then she backed off,
smiling, and began walking up the dark highway toward her
place.

Oh, my, he thought. Her mouth had tasted of strawberry
wine, hot and sweet. Oh, my.

Later that night he lay in his bed with the window open, listening to the pump engines running out in the fields, which
stretched away on all sides of the tourist court for miles. They
throbbed, as delicate as distant heartbeats. He could tell which

type each was by the sound it made. He heard an International hit-and-miss engine fire once and then coast slower and slower through several cycles before firing again. Woven into that sound was a distant Fairbanks Morse with a bad magneto throbbing steadily, then cutting off, slowing, slowing almost to stillness before the spark built up again and the engine boomed back alive. Across the road a little McCormick muttered in a ditch. In the quiet night the engines fought the drought, popping like the musketry of a losing army. Through the screen of his window drifted the scent of kerosene exhaust.

He thought of the farmer's widow and finally admitted to himself, there in the dark, that she was good-looking. What was she doing right now, he wondered. Reading? For some reason he doubted this. Sewing? What, traveling clothes? Was she planning to sell the patch and move back, as many women had done, to wherever she had come from? If she had any sense, he thought, she'd be asleep, and he turned over and faced the wall, listening to the springs ring under him. He tried to remember what he had done at night when he was at home, when he was twenty-four and had three children and a wife, but nothing at all came to him. Then, slowly, thoughts of rocking sick babies and helping his wife can sweet corn came to him, and before two minutes had passed he was asleep.

The next morning the sky was as hard and expressionless as a pawnbroker's face. At eight o'clock the temperature was ninety-one, and the repairman had already welded a piston rod in Amite and was headed south. When he passed the woman's lane, he forced himself not to look down its rutted surface. He had dreamed of her last night, and that was enough, he thought. Times were so hard he could afford only his dreams. A half mile down the road he began working at pouring new babbit bearings for an old Dan Patch engine. The owners of the farm left him alone so that they could oversee a group of inexperienced pickers, and at nine-thirty, while he was turning the blower for the forge, she came out of the brush to the north carrying a clear-glass jug of lemonade.

"I'll bet you're dry," she said, giving him the jug and a tin cup.

"You're an awful friendly lady," he said, pouring himself a drink and looking at her slim waist, her long hair.

"I can be friendly when I want to be." She rested her hand on his damp shoulder a moment and let it slide off slow.

They talked while he worked the forge. He tried to tell her about his children, but she seemed not to be interested. She wanted to know where he had been and where he was going. She wanted to know how it was living on the road, what people were like in different places. "Do you stay in tourist courts every night?" she asked, wide-eyed.

By the time he had finished his repair, she had told him that she had just buried her third husband, that she had never been a hundred miles from the spot they were standing in, and that she didn't care if she never saw another strawberry for the rest of her days. "Sometimes I think it's staying in the same place, doing the same things, day in, day out, that gets me down. Get up in the morning and look out the window and see that same rusty fence. Look out another window and see that same willow tree. Out another and see that field. Same place, same things, all my life." She heard a distant train whistle and looked off toward it, caught up in the haunting sound.

Harry Lintel was at a loss in dealing with unhappy people. He remembered that putting his big arms around his young wife years ago would stop her from crying, but he had no notion why this worked. Looking at the delicate hollow of Ada's cheek, he felt sorry that he didn't know what to do for her. He wondered if she would take up with him in his truck if he asked her, would just go off with him up the highway to Tennessee or Georgia, wherever the next drought was needing him to fix engines or windmills. Would this heal what was wrong?

After a local freight train racketed by, three men in overalls drove over the track, got out of their pickup, and began telling him about a big engine in a dry field six miles west, and how nobody could get it to run all week. The men ignored the woman, and as the repairman packed his tools and dumped the forge, he saw her walk off. She went south, away from her place, along the dirt lane that sidled up to the railroad, keeping her thin brown shoes out of the heaped-up dust ridge. After he had loaded the truck, he cranked it, and headed not west, along the route given him by the three men, but north. Turning into her lane, he bumped along the ruts down to her farmhouse. He walked to the back of the property and saw her berries blanched by the sun as

if they'd had kettles of boiling water poured over them. Returning to the house, he opened the fuse box nailed to the rear outside wall and saw that one fuse was blown, even though it was a
special heavy-duty type. He used his pocket knife to pry off the
faceplate and saw where a switch wire cut into the circuit and ran
from the bottom of the box through a hole into the house.

He found the front door unlocked. Walking through the
house, he saw there was little furniture: only a set of dark-var-
nished chairs, two small, rough tables, and a rickety, curled-up
sofa. The windows were dirty. In the kitchen he found the wall
switch that activated the pump and, peering close, saw that it had
been turned on. He was sure that many farms with electric
pumps also had inside switches. But surely the man would have
killed the circuit before he went out to work on the thing. And
then he remembered that he hadn't seen any switch out in the
field.

He sat down at the oilcloth-covered kitchen table and squinted
out the front window. He saw a rusty fence. Looking out a side
window, he saw a willow tree. My God, he thought. He turned to
look through the rear window, into a field. Near the broken tractor was a freshly dug mound of dirt. He put his face down into
his hands and shook like a man who had just missed being in a
terrible accident.

The next ten days he worked the whole parish. Wild animals
came out of the woods looking for water. Bottoms of drainage
ditches cracked open and buckled. He saw pickers brought out
of the field with heatstroke. The woman found him only twice,
and he was polite, listening to her tell him about her nights and
what she saw through her windows. She wore the same dress, but
kept it clean and ironed. Once she asked him to come over for
supper, but he said he had work to do past dark.

At the tourist court he avoided the café and went to bed early,
putting himself to sleep thinking of his wife, painfully, deliberately. He remembered the kindness of her meals in their kitchen
and the fondness of her touch, which was on him still, teaching
him.

On a Thursday morning before dawn he was awakened by a
drumming sound to the northwest. At first he thought it was
someone at the door, but when the sound rolled down on the
parish again, he knew it was thunder. By first light the rain had

started in earnest, and at eight he was still in his room, staring out at sheets of wind-tortured spray welling up in puddles along the highway — three inches at least, and more to come by the looks of the sky. It was time to move on.

In the café, for the first time Marie had no repair calls for him. He paid up, gave her a hug, and headed out north in his groaning truck, rainwater spilling off the taut new tarp covering the back.

The highway followed the railroad up through a series of small towns, and he made good time despite a traffic of small truckloads of produce and an occasional horsedrawn farm wagon. He felt lighthearted for the first time in days, and whistled as he steered around slower vehicles navigating the rainy road. There was something good about getting out of this section of the country, he felt, something good about pointing his headlights toward Jackson or Memphis, where he would hole up in a boardinghouse and read a big-city paper until the weather reports told him where he'd find lots of dust, heat, worn-out pumps, and busted windmills.

About noon he pulled over at a café south of McComb. Walking to the back of the truck, he saw that one of the tarp ropes had come undone. When he raised the cloth to check inside, the woman lifted her face toward him, her eyes rusty and dark. "When I heard the rain start on my roof, I knew you'd be pulling out," she said. "You can go somewheres. I can't."

He stared at her for a long time, trying to figure what to say. He looked up and down the red-dirt highway lined with spindly telephone poles and then at the café, which was closed, he realized. Finally he climbed in and sat on a toolbox lid next to her in the oily dark. "You can't come along with me."

"Don't say that," she said, putting her arms loosely around his neck. "You're the only person I ever met can go where he wants to go." She said this not in a pleading voice but as a statement of fact. "I can go with you. I'll be good to you, Mr. Lintel."

He looked at her eyes and guessed that she was desperate for his freedom of movement but not for him. The eyes seemed already to be looking ahead, looking at a whole world passing by a truck window. "Where you want to go," he said at last, "I can't take you."

She pulled her arms away quickly. "What you mean by that?

You just going to toss me off on the side of the road like a worn-out machine? There's something in me what needs to get away with you."

Harry Lintel leaned toward her and took her hands, trying to remember the ways he had once brought solace to his wife. "If I could help you, I'd bring you along for the ride," he said. "But I can't do a thing for you." He half expected her to cry when he said that, but she only shook her head.

"You've got a heart like a rock," she told him.

"No, ma'am," he said. "I loved a good woman once, and I could love another. You can't come with me because you killed your old man."

Her eyes seemed to pulse, and what softness lingered around the corners of her mouth disappeared into a flinty expression of fear and desperation.

He reached for his wallet. "I'm going to buy a ticket and put you on the southbound. You can walk home from the station."

She grabbed a bill from him and then straightened up, throwing an arm in back of her as if she were searching for the handle of her cardboard suitcase. Harry stared at his empty hand for a moment and turned to climb out into the drizzle. He heard the music of a tempered wrench being picked up, and then a bomb went off in his head, and he was down on the floorboards, rolling in cinders and wire, his arms and legs uncontrolled, his eyes letting in a broken vision of the woman standing over him, looking down the way someone might examine a stunned fish. "I've never met a man I could put up with for long," she told him. "I'm glad I got shut of all of mine."

His head roared like a forge, and he tried to rise, his eyes flickering, his arms pushing him toward the woman's upraised fist, where his biggest box-end wrench glimmered like a thunderbolt. The blow was a star-giving ball of pain, and he felt the tailgate in the small of his back, the world going over like a flywheel, his face in collision with gravel and clay, a coppery rill coursing through his nose and mouth. The only thing in his head was the silver ringing sound of a tool, and then the exhaust of a four-cylinder engine pulling away, fading into a clash of gears at the top of a hill, and then, for the longest time, nothing. Somewhere a cow bellowed, or a car passed without stopping, or wind blew through the grass around him like knowledge through an ear.

Near dusk he woke to a dove singing on the phone wires. He idly wondered where she would sell the truck, to what town she would ride on the train. It didn't matter. She was a woman who would never get where she wanted to go. He was always where he was going.

One eye began to work, and he watched clouds, the broken pieces of the world hanging above like tomorrow's big repair job, waiting.

DENIS JOHNSON

Emergency

FROM THE NEW YORKER

I'D BEEN WORKING in the emergency room for about three weeks, I guess. This was in 1973, before the summer ended. With nothing to do on the overnight shift but batch the insurance reports from the daytime shifts, I just started wandering around, over to the coronary-care unit, down to the cafeteria, et cetera, looking for Georgie, the orderly, a pretty good friend of mine. He often stole pills from the cabinets.

He was running over the tiled floor of the operating room with a mop. "Are you still doing that?" I said.

"Jesus, there's a lot of blood here," he complained.

"Where?" The floor looked clean enough to me.

"What the hell were they doing in here?" he asked me.

"They were performing surgery, Georgie," I told him.

"There's so much goop inside of us, man," he said, "and it all wants to get out." He leaned his mop against a cabinet.

"What are you crying for?" I didn't understand.

He stood still, raised both arms slowly behind his head, and tightened his ponytail. Then he grabbed the mop and started making broad random arcs with it, trembling and weeping and moving all around the place really fast. "What am I *crying* for?" he said. "Jesus. Wow, oh boy, perfect."

I was hanging out in the E.R. with fat, quivering Nurse. One of the Family Service doctors that nobody liked came in looking for Georgie to wipe up after him. "Where's Georgie?" this guy asked.

"Georgie's in O.R.," Nurse said.

"Again?"

"No," Nurse said. "Still."

"Still? Doing what?"

"Cleaning the floor."

"Again?"

"No," Nurse said again. "Still."

Back in O.R., Georgie dropped his mop and bent over in the posture of a child soiling its diapers. He stared down with his mouth open in terror.

He said, "What am I going to do about these fucking *shoes,* man?"

"Whatever you stole," I said, "I guess you already ate it all, right?"

"Listen to how they squish," he said, walking around carefully on his heels.

"Let me check your pockets, man."

He stood still a minute, and I found his stash. I left him two of each, whatever they were. "Shift is about half over," I told him.

"Good. Because I really, really, really need a drink," he said. "Will you please help me get this blood mopped *up?*"

Around 3:30 A.M. a guy with a knife in his eye came in, led by Georgie.

"I hope *you* didn't do that to him," Nurse said.

"Me?" Georgie said. "No. He was like this."

"My wife did it," the man said. The blade was buried to the hilt in the outside corner of his left eye. It was a hunting knife kind of thing.

"Who brought you in?" Nurse said.

"Nobody. I just walked down. It's only three blocks," the man said.

Nurse peered at him. "We'd better get you lying down."

"O.K., I'm certainly ready for something like that," the man said.

She peered a bit longer into his face. "Is your other eye," she said, "a glass eye?"

"It's plastic, or something artificial like that," he said.

"And you can see out of *this* eye?" she asked, meaning the wounded one.

"I can see. But I can't make a fist out of my left hand because this knife is doing something to my brain."

"My God," Nurse said.

"I guess I'd better get the doctor," I said.

"There you go," Nurse agreed.

They got him lying down, and Georgie says to the patient, "Name?"

"Terrence Weber."

"Your face is dark. I can't see what you're saying."

"Georgie," I said.

"What are you saying, man? I can't see."

Nurse came over, and Georgie said to her, "His face is dark."

She leaned over the patient. "How long ago did this happen, Terry?" she shouted down into his face.

"Just a while ago. My wife did it. I was asleep," the patient said.

"Do you want the police?"

He thought about it and finally said, "Not unless I die."

Nurse went to the wall intercom and buzzed the doctor on duty, the Family Service person. "Got a surprise for you," she said over the intercom. He took his time getting down the hall to her, because he knew she hated Family Service and her happy tone of voice could only mean something beyond his competence and potentially humiliating.

He peeked into the trauma room and saw the situation: the clerk — that is, me — standing next to the orderly, Georgie, both of us on drugs, looking down at a patient with a knife sticking up out of his face.

"What seems to be the trouble?" he said.

The doctor gathered the three of us around him in the office and said, "Here's the situation. We've got to get a team here, an entire team. I want a good eye man. A great eye man. The best eye man. I want a brain surgeon. And I want a really good gas man, get me a genius. I'm not touching that head. I'm just going to watch this one. I know my limits. We'll just get him prepped and sit tight. Orderly!"

"Do you mean me?" Georgie said. "Should I get him prepped?"

"Is this a hospital?" the doctor asked. "Is this the emergency room? Is that a patient? Are you the orderly?"

I dialed the hospital operator and told her to get me the eye man and the brain man and the gas man.

Georgie could be heard across the hall, washing his hands and singing a Neil Young song that went "Hello cowgirl in the sand. Is this place at your command?"

"That person is not right, not at all, not one bit," the doctor said.

"As long as my instructions are audible to him it doesn't concern me," Nurse insisted, spooning stuff up out of a little Dixie cup. "I've got my own life and the protection of my family to think of."

"Well, O.K., O.K. Don't chew my head off," the doctor said.

The eye man was on vacation or something. While the hospital's operator called around to find someone else just as good, the other specialists were hurrying through the night to join us. I stood around looking at charts and chewing up more of Georgie's pills. Some of them tasted the way urine smells, some of them burned, some of them tasted like chalk. Various nurses, and two physicians who'd been tending somebody in I.C.U., were hanging out down here with us now.

Everybody had a different idea about exactly how to approach the problem of removing the knife from Terrence Weber's brain. But when Georgie came in from prepping the patient — from shaving the patient's eyebrow and disinfecting the area around the wound, and so on — he seemed to be holding the hunting knife in his left hand.

The talk just dropped off a cliff.

"Where," the doctor asked finally, "did you get that?"

Nobody said one thing more, not for quite a long time.

After a while, one of the I.C.U. nurses said, "Your shoelace is untied." Georgie laid the knife on a chart and bent down to fix his shoe.

There were twenty more minutes left to get through.

"How's the guy doing?" I asked.

"Who?" Georgie said.

It turned out that Terrence Weber still had excellent vision in

the one good eye, and acceptable motor and reflex, despite his
earlier motor complaint. "His vitals are normal," Nurse said.
"There's nothing wrong with the guy. It's one of those things."

After a while you forget it's summer. You don't remember what
the morning is. I'd worked two doubles with eight hours off in
between, which I'd spent sleeping on a gurney in the nurses' station. Georgie's pills were making me feel like a giant helium-
filled balloon, but I was wide awake. Georgie and I went out to
the lot, to his orange pickup.

We lay down on a stretch of dusty plywood in the back of the
truck with the daylight knocking against our eyelids and the fragrance of alfalfa thickening on our tongues.

"I want to go to church," Georgie said.

"Let's go to the county fair."

"I'd like to worship. I would."

"They have these injured hawks and eagles there. From the
Humane Society," I said.

"I need a quiet chapel about now."

Georgie and I had a terrific time driving around. For a while the
day was clear and peaceful. It was one of the moments you stay
in, to hell with all the troubles of before and after. The sky is
blue, and the dead are coming back. Later in the afternoon, with
sad resignation, the county fair bares its breasts. A champion of
the drug LSD, a very famous guru of the love generation, is
being interviewed amid a TV crew off to the left of the poultry
cages. His eyeballs look like he bought them in a joke shop. It
doesn't occur to me, as I pity this extraterrestrial, that in my life
I've taken as much acid as he has.

After that, we got lost. We drove for hours, literally hours, but
we couldn't find the road back to town.

Georgie started to complain. "That was the worst fair I've been
to. Where were the rides?"

"They had rides," I said.

"I didn't see one ride."

A jackrabbit scurried out in front of us, and we hit it.

"There was a merry-go-round, a Ferris wheel, and a thing

called the Hammer that people were bent over vomiting from after they got off," I said. "Are you completely blind?"

"What was that?"

"A rabbit."

"Something thumped."

"You hit him. *He* thumped."

Georgie stood on the brake pedal. "Rabbit stew."

He threw the truck in reverse and zigzagged back toward the rabbit. "Where's my hunting knife?" He almost ran over the poor animal a second time.

"We'll camp in the wilderness," he said. "In the morning we'll breakfast on its haunches." He was waving Terrence Weber's hunting knife around in what I was sure was a dangerous way.

In a minute he was standing at the edge of the fields, cutting the scrawny little thing up, tossing away its organs. "I should have been a doctor," he cried.

A family in a big Dodge, the only car we'd seen for a long time, slowed down and gawked out the windows as they passed by. The father said, "What is it, a snake?"

"No, it's not a snake," Georgie said. "It's a rabbit with babies inside it."

"Babies!" the mother said, and the father sped the car forward, over the protests of several little kids in the back.

Georgie came back to my side of the truck with his shirtfront stretched out in front of him as if he were carrying apples in it, or some such, but they were, in fact, slimy miniature bunnies. "No way I'm eating those things," I told him.

"Take them, take them. I gotta drive, take them," he said, dumping them in my lap and getting in on his side of the truck. He started driving along faster and faster, with a look of glory on his face. "We killed the mother and saved the children," he said.

"It's getting late," I said. "Let's get back to town."

"You bet." Sixty, seventy, eighty-five, just topping ninety.

"These rabbits better be kept warm." One at a time I slid the little things in between my shirt buttons and nestled them against my belly. "They're hardly moving," I told Georgie.

"We'll get some milk and sugar and all that, and we'll raise them up ourselves. They'll get as big as gorillas."

The road we were lost on cut straight through the middle of the world. It was still daytime, but the sun had no more power than an ornament or a sponge. In this light the truck's hood, which had been bright orange, had turned a deep blue.

Georgie let us drift to the shoulder of the road, slowly, slowly, as if he'd fallen asleep or given up trying to find his way.

"What is it?"

"We can't go on. I don't have any headlights," Georgie said.

We parked under a strange sky with a faint image of a quarter-moon superimposed on it.

There was a little woods beside us. This day had been dry and hot, the buck pines and what all simmering patiently, but as we sat there smoking cigarettes it started to get very cold.

"The summer's over," I said.

That was the year when arctic clouds moved down over the Midwest, and we had two weeks of winter in September.

"Do you realize it's going to snow?" Georgie asked me.

He was right, a gun-blue storm was shaping up. We got out and walked around idiotically. The beautiful chill! That sudden crispness, and the tang of evergreen stabbing us!

The gusts of snow twisted themselves around our heads while the night fell. I couldn't find the truck. We just kept getting more and more lost. I kept calling, "Georgie, can you see?" and he kept saying, "See what? See what?"

The only light visible was a streak of sunset flickering below the hem of the clouds. We headed that way.

We bumped softly down a hill toward an open field that seemed to be a military graveyard, filled with rows and rows of austere, identical markers over soldiers' graves. I'd never before come across this cemetery. On the farther side of the field, just beyond the curtains of snow, the sky was torn away and the angels were descending out of a brilliant blue summer, their huge faces streaked with light and full of pity. The sight of them cut through my heart and down the knuckles of my spine, and if there'd been anything in my bowels I would have messed my pants from fear.

Georgie opened his arms and cried out, "It's the drive-in, man!"

"The drive-in . . ." I wasn't sure what these words meant.

"They're showing movies in a fucking blizzard!" Georgie screamed.

"I see. I thought it was something else," I said.

We walked carefully down there and climbed through the busted fence and stood in the very back. The speakers, which I'd mistaken for grave markers, muttered in unison. Then there was tinkly music, of which I could very nearly make out the tune. Famous movie stars rode bicycles beside a river, laughing out of their gigantic lovely mouths. If anybody had come to see this show, they'd left when the weather started. Not one car remained, not even a broken-down one from last week, or one left here because it was out of gas. In a couple of minutes, in the middle of a whirling square dance, the screen turned black, the cinematic summer ended, the snow went dark, there was nothing but my breath.

"I'm starting to get my eyes back," Georgie said in another minute.

A general grayness was giving birth to various shapes, it was true. "But which ones are close and which ones are far off?" I begged him to tell me.

By trial and error, with a lot of walking back and forth in wet shoes, we found the truck and sat inside it, shivering.

"Let's get out of here," I said.

"We can't go anywhere without headlights."

"We've gotta get back. We're a long way from home."

"No, we're not."

"We must have come three hundred miles."

"We're right outside town, Fuckhead. We've just been driving around and around."

"This is no place to camp. I hear the interstate over there."

"We'll just stay here till it gets late. We can drive home late. We'll be invisible."

We listened to the big rigs going from San Francisco to Pennsylvania along the interstate, like shudders down a long hacksaw blade, while the snow buried us.

Eventually Georgie said, "We better get some milk for those bunnies."

"We don't have *milk*," I said.

"We'll mix sugar up with it."

"Will you forget about this milk all of a sudden?"

"They're mammals, man."

"Forget about those rabbits."

"Where are they, anyway?"

"You're not listening to me. I said, 'Forget the rabbits.' "

"Where are they?"

The truth was I'd forgotten all about them, and they were dead.

"They slid around behind me and got squashed," I said tearfully.

"They slid around *behind*?"

He watched while I pried them out from behind my back.

I picked them out one at a time and held them in my hands and we looked at them. There were eight. They weren't any bigger than my fingers, but everything was there.

Little feet! Eyelids! Even whiskers! "Deceased," I said.

Georgie asked, "Does everything you touch turn to shit? Does this happen to you every time?"

"No wonder they call me Fuckhead."

"It's a name that's going to stick."

"I realize that."

" 'Fuckhead' is gonna ride you to your grave."

"I just said so. I agreed with you in advance," I said.

Or maybe that wasn't the time it snowed. Maybe it was the time we slept in the truck and I rolled over on the bunnies and flattened them. It doesn't matter. What's important for me to remember now is that early the next morning the snow was melted off the windshield and the daylight woke me up. A mist covered everything and, with the sunshine, was beginning to grow sharp and strange. The bunnies weren't a problem yet, or they'd already been a problem and were already forgotten, and there was nothing on my mind. I felt the beauty of the morning. I could understand how a drowning man might suddenly feel a deep thirst being quenched. Or how the slave might become a friend to his master. Georgie slept with his face right on the steering wheel.

I saw bits of snow resembling an abundance of blossoms on the stems of the drive-in speakers — no, revealing the blossoms that were always there. A bull elk stood still in the pasture beyond the fence giving off an air of authority and stupidity. And a coyote jogged across the pasture and faded away among the saplings.

That afternoon we got back to work in time to resume everything as if it had never stopped happening and we'd never been anywhere else.

"The Lord," the intercom said, "is my shepherd." It did that each evening because this was a Catholic hospital. "Our Father, who art in Heaven," and so on.

"Yeah, yeah," Nurse said.

The man with the knife in his head, Terrence Weber, was released around suppertime. They'd kept him overnight and given him an eyepatch — all for no reason, really.

He stopped off at E.R. to say good-bye. "Well, those pills they gave me make everything taste terrible," he said.

"It could have been worse," Nurse said.

"Even my tongue."

"It's just a miracle you didn't end up sightless or at least dead," she reminded him.

The patient recognized me. He acknowledged me with a smile. "I was peeping on the lady next door while she was out there sunbathing," he said. "My wife decided to blind me."

He shook Georgie's hand. Georgie didn't know him. "Who are you supposed to be?" he asked Terrence Weber.

Some hours before that, Georgie had said something that had suddenly and completely explained the difference between us. We'd been driving back toward town, along the Old Highway, through the flatness. We picked up a hitchhiker, a boy I knew. We stopped the truck and the boy climbed slowly up out of the fields as out of the mouth of a volcano. His name was Hardee. He looked even worse than we probably did.

"We got messed up and slept in the truck all night," I told Hardee.

"I had a feeling," Hardee said. "Either that or, you know, driving a thousand miles."

"That, too," I said.

"Or you're sick or diseased or something."

"Who's this guy?" Georgie asked.

"This is Hardee. He lived with me last summer. I found him on the doorstep. What happened to your dog?" I asked Hardee.

"He's still down there."

"Yeah, I heard you went to Texas."

"I was working on a bee farm," Hardee said.

"Wow. Do those things sting you?"

"Not like you'd think," Hardee said. "You're part of their daily drill. It's all part of a harmony."

Outside, the same identical stretch of ground repeatedly rolled past our faces. The day was cloudless, blinding. But Georgie said, "Look at that," pointing straight ahead of us.

One star was so hot it showed, bright and blue, in the empty sky.

"I recognized you right away," I told Hardee. "But what happened to your hair? Who chopped it off?"

"I hate to say."

"Don't tell me."

"They drafted me."

"Oh no."

"Oh yeah. I'm AWOL. I'm bad AWOL. I got to get to Canada."

"Oh, that's terrible," I said to Hardee.

"Don't worry," Georgie said. "We'll get you there."

"How?"

"Somehow. I think I know some people. Don't worry. You're on your way to Canada."

That world! These days it's all been erased and they've rolled it up like a scroll and put it away somewhere. Yes, I can touch it with my fingers. But where is it?

After a while Hardee asked Georgie, "What do you do for a job?," and Georgie said, "I save lives."

THOM JONES

The Pugilist at Rest

FROM THE NEW YORKER

HEY BABY got caught writing a letter to his girl when he was
supposed to be taking notes on the specs of the M-14 rifle. We
were sitting in a stifling hot Quonset hut during the first weeks
of boot camp, August 1966, at the Marine Corps Recruit Depot
in San Diego. Sergeant Wright snatched the letter out of Hey Baby's hand, and later that night in the squad bay he read the letter
to the Marine recruits of Platoon 263, his voice laden with sar-
casm. "*Hey, Baby!*" he began, and then as he went into the body
of the letter he worked himself into a state of outrage and disgust. It was a letter to *Rosie Rottencrotch*, he said at the end, and
what really mattered, what was really at issue and what was of
utter importance was not *Rosie Rottencrotch* and her steaming-hot
panties but rather the muzzle velocity of the M-14 rifle.

Hey Baby paid for the letter by doing a hundred squat thrusts
on the concrete floor of the squad bay, but the main prize he won
that night was that he became forever known as Hey Baby to the
recruits of Platoon 263 — in addition to being a shitbird, a fag-
got, a turd, a maggot, and other such standard appellations. To
top it all off, shortly after the incident, Hey Baby got a Dear John
from this girl back in Chicago, of whom Sergeant Wright, myself, and seventy-eight other Marine recruits had come to know
just a little.

Hey Baby was not in the Marine Corps for very long. The reason for this was that he started in on my buddy, Jorgeson. Jorgeson was my main man, and Hey Baby started calling him Jorge-
pussy and began harassing him and pushing him around. He

was down on Jorgeson because whenever we were taught some
sort of combat maneuver or tactic, Jorgeson would say, under his
breath, "You could get *killed* if you try that." Or, "Your ass is *had*,
if you do that." You got the feeling that Jorgeson didn't think
loving the American flag and defending democratic ideals in
Southeast Asia were all that important. He told me that what he
really wanted to do was have an artist's loft in the SoHo district
of New York City, wear a beret, eat liver sausage sandwiches
made with stale baguettes, drink Tokay wine, smoke dope, paint
pictures, and listen to the wailing, sorrowful songs of that French
singer Edith Piaf, otherwise known as "The Little Sparrow."

After the first half hour of boot camp most of the other recruits wanted to get out, too, but they nourished dreams of surf-
boards, Corvettes, and blond babes. Jorgeson wanted to be a
beatnik and hang out with Jack Kerouac and Neal Cassady, slam
down burning shots of amber whiskey, and hear Charles Mingus
play real cool jazz on the bass fiddle. He wanted to practice Zen
Buddhism, throw the I Ching, eat couscous, and study astrology
charts. All of this was foreign territory to me. I had grown up in
Aurora, Illinois, and had never heard of such things. Jorgeson
had a sharp tongue and was so supercilious in his remarks that I
didn't know quite how seriously I should take this talk, but I enjoyed his humor and I did believe he had the sensibilities of an
artist. It was not some vague yearning. I believed very much that
he could become a painter of pictures. At that point he wasn't
putting his heart and soul into becoming a Marine. He wasn't a
true believer like me.

Some weeks after Hey Baby began hassling Jorgeson, Sergeant
Wright gave us his best speech: "You men are going off to war,
and it's not a pretty thing," etc. & etc., "and if Luke the Gook
knocks down one of your buddies, a fellow Marine, you are
going to risk your life and go in and get that Marine and you are
going to bring him out. Not because I said so. No! You are going
after that Marine because *you* are a Marine, a member of the
most elite fighting force in the world, and that man out there
who's gone down is a Marine, and he's your *buddy*. He is your
brother! Once you are a Marine, you are *always* a Marine and you
will never let another Marine down." Etc. & etc. "You can take a
Marine out of the Corps but you can't take the Corps out of a

Marine." Etc. & etc. At the time it seemed to me a very good
speech, and it stirred me deeply. Sergeant Wright was no candy
ass. He was one squared-away dude, and he could call cadence.
Man, it puts a lump in my throat when I remember how that man
could sing cadence. Apart from Jorgeson, I think all of the recruits in Platoon 263 were proud of Sergeant Wright. He was the
real thing, the genuine article. He was a crackerjack Marine.

In the course of training, lots of the recruits dropped out of
the original platoon. Some couldn't pass the physical fitness tests
and had to go to a special camp for pussies. This was a particularly shameful shortcoming, the most humiliating apart from
bed-wetting. Other recruits would get pneumonia, strep throat,
infected foot blisters, or whatever, and lose time that way. Some
didn't qualify at the rifle range. One would break a leg. Another
would have a nervous breakdown (and this was also deplorable).
People dropped out right and left. When the recruit corrected
whatever deficiency he had, or when he got better, he would be
picked up by another platoon that was in the stage of basic training that he had been in when his training was interrupted. Platoon 263 picked up dozens of recruits in this fashion. If everything went well, however, you got through with the whole
business in twelve weeks. That's not a long time, but it seemed
like a long time. You did not see a female in all that time. You did
not see a newspaper or a television set. You did not eat a candy
bar. Another thing was the fact that you had someone on top of
you, watching every move you made. When it was time to "shit,
shower, and shave," you were given just ten minutes, and had to
confront lines and so on to complete the entire affair. Head calls
were so infrequent that I spent a lot of time that might otherwise
have been neutral or painless in the eye-watering anxiety that I
was going to piss my pants. We *ran* to chow, where we were faced
with enormous steam vents that spewed out a sickening smell of
rancid, superheated grease. Still, we entered the mess hall with
ravenous appetites, ate a huge tray of food in just a few minutes,
and then *ran* back to our company area in formation, choking
back the burning bile of a meal too big to be eaten so fast. God
forbid that you would lose control and vomit.

If all had gone well in the preceding hours, Sergeant Wright
would permit us to smoke one cigarette after each meal. Jorge-

son had shown me the wisdom of switching from Camels to Pall
Malls — they were much longer, packed a pretty good jolt, and
when we snapped open our brushed-chrome Zippos, torched
up, and inhaled the first few drags, we shared the overmastering
pleasure that tobacco can bring if you use it seldom and judi-
ciously. These were always the best moments of the day — brief
respites from the tyrannical repression of recruit training. As we
got close to the end of it all Jorgeson liked to play a little game.
He used to say to me (with fragrant blue smoke curling out of his
nostrils), "If someone said, 'I'll give you ten thousand dollars to
do all of this again,' what would you say?" "No way, Jack!" He
would keep on upping it until he had John Beresford Tipton,
the guy from "The Millionaire," offering me a check for a million bucks. "Not for any money," I'd say.

While they were all smoldering under various pressures, the
recruits were also getting pretty "salty" — they were beginning
to believe. They were beginning to think of themselves as Marines. If you could make it through this, the reasoning went, you
wouldn't crack in combat. So I remember that I had tears in my
eyes when Sergeant Wright gave us the spiel about how a Marine
would charge a machine-gun nest to save his buddies, dive on a
hand grenade, do whatever it takes — and yet I was ashamed
when Jorgeson caught me wiping them away. All of the recruits
were teary except Jorgeson. He had these very clear cobalt blue
eyes. They were so remarkable that they caused you to notice
Jorgeson in a crowd. There was unusual beauty in these eyes,
and there was an extraordinary power in them. Apart from having a pleasant enough face, Jorgeson was small and unassuming
except for these eyes. Anyhow, when he caught me getting sentimental he gave me this look that penetrated to the core of my
being. It was the icy look of absolute contempt, and it caused me
to doubt myself. I said, "Man! Can't you get into it? For Christ's
sake!"

"I'm not like you," he said. "But I am into it, more than you
could ever know. I never told you this before, but I am Kal-El,
born on the planet Krypton and rocketed to Earth as an infant,
moments before my world exploded. Disguised as a mild-man-
nered Marine, I have resolved to use my powers for the good of
mankind. Whenever danger appears on the scene, truth and jus-

tice will be served as I slip into the green U.S.M.C. utility uniform and become Earth's greatest hero."

I got highly pissed and didn't talk to him for a couple of days after this. Then, about two weeks before boot camp was over, when we were running out to the parade field for drill with our rifles at port arms, all assholes and elbows, I saw Hey Baby give Jorgeson a nasty shove with his M-14. Hey Baby was a large and fairly tough young man who liked to displace his aggressive impulses on Jorgeson, but he wasn't as big or as tough as I.

Jorgeson nearly fell down as the other recruits scrambled out to the parade field, and Hey Baby gave a short, malicious laugh. I ran past Jorgeson and caught up to Hey Baby; he picked me up in his peripheral vision, but by then it was too late. I set my body so that I could put everything into it, and with one deft stroke I hammered him in the temple with the sharp edge of the steel butt plate of my M-14. It was not exactly a premeditated crime, although I had been laying to get him. My idea before this had simply been to lay my hands on him, but now I had blood in my eye. I was a skilled boxer, and I knew the temple was a vulnerable spot; the human skull is otherwise hard and durable, except at its base. There was a sickening crunch, and Hey Baby dropped into the ice plants along the side of the company street.

The entire platoon was out on the parade field when the house mouse screamed at the assistant D.I., who rushed back to the scene of the crime to find Hey Baby crumpled in a fetal position in the ice plants with blood all over the place. There was blood from the scalp wound as well as a froth of blood emitting from his nostrils and his mouth. Blood was leaking from his right ear. Did I see skull fragments and brain tissue? It seemed that I did. To tell you the truth, I wouldn't have cared in the least if I had killed him, but like most criminals I was very much afraid of getting caught. It suddenly occurred to me that I could be headed for the brig for a long time. My heart was pounding out of my chest. Yet the larger part of me didn't care. Jorgeson was my buddy, and I wasn't going to stand still and let someone fuck him over.

The platoon waited at parade rest while Sergeant Wright came out of the duty hut and took command of the situation. An ambulance was called, and it came almost immediately. A number

of corpsmen squatted down alongside the fallen man for what
seemed an eternity. Eventually they took Hey Baby off with a
fractured skull. It would be the last we ever saw of him. Three
evenings later, in the squad bay, the assistant D.I. told us rather
ominously that Hey Baby had recovered consciousness. That's all
he said. What did *that* mean? I was worried, because Hey Baby
had seen me make my move, but, as it turned out, when he came
to he had forgotten the incident and all events of the preceding
two weeks. Retrograde amnesia. Lucky for me. I also knew that
at least three other recruits had seen what I did, but none of
them reported me. Every member of the platoon was called in
and grilled by a team of hard-ass captains and a light colonel
from the Criminal Investigation Detachment. It took a certain
amount of balls to lie to them, yet none of my fellow jarheads
reported me. I was well liked and Hey Baby was not. Indeed,
many felt that he got exactly what was coming to him.

The other day — Memorial Day, as it happened — I was cleaning some stuff out of the attic when I came upon my old dress-
blue uniform. It's a beautiful uniform, easily the most handsome
worn by any of the U.S. armed forces. The rich color recalled
Jorgeson's eyes for me — not that the color matched, but in the
sense that the color of each was so startling. The tunic does not
have lapels, of course, but a high collar with red piping and the
traditional golden eagle, globe, and anchor insignia on either
side of the neck clasp. The tunic buttons are not brassy — although they are in fact made of brass — but are a delicate gold
in color, like Florentine gold. On the sleeves of the tunic my staff
sergeant's chevrons are gold on red. High on the left breast is a
rainbow display of fruit salad representing my various combat
citations. Just below these are my marksmanship badges; I shot
Expert in rifle as well as pistol.

I opened a sandalwood box and took my various medals out of
the large plastic bag I had packed them in to prevent them from
tarnishing. The Navy Cross and the two Silver Stars are the best;
they are such pretty things they dazzle you. I found a couple of
Thai sticks in the sandalwood box as well. I took a whiff of the
box and smelled the smells of Saigon — the whores, the dope,
the saffron, cloves, jasmine, and patchouli oil. I put the Thai

sticks back, recalling the three-day hangover that particular batch of dope had given me more than twenty-three years before. Again I looked at my dress-blue tunic. My most distinctive badge, the crowning glory, and the one of which I am most proud, is the set of Airborne wings. I remember how it was, walking around Oceanside, California — the Airborne wings and the high-and-tight haircut were recognized by all the Marines; they meant you were the crème de la crème, you were a recon Marine.

Recon was all Jorgeson's idea. We had lost touch with each other after boot camp. I was sent to com school in San Diego, where I had to sit in a hot Class A wool uniform all day and learn the Morse code. I deliberately flunked out, and when I was given the perfunctory option for a second shot, I told the colonel, "Hell no, sir. I want to go 003 — infantry. I want to be a ground-pounder. I didn't join the service to sit at a desk all day."

I was on a bus to Camp Pendleton three days later, and when I got there I ran into Jorgeson. I had been thinking of him a lot. He was a clerk in headquarters company. Much to my astonishment, he was fifteen pounds heavier, and had grown two inches, and he told me he was hitting the weight pile every night after running seven miles up and down the foothills of Pendleton in combat boots, carrying a rifle and a full field pack. After the usual what's-been-happening? b.s., he got down to business and said, "They need people in Force Recon, what do you think? Headquarters is one boring motherfucker."

I said, "Recon? Paratrooper? You got to be shittin' me! When did you get so gung-ho, man?"

He said, "Hey, you were the one who *bought* the program. Don't fade on me now, God damn it! Look, we pass the physical fitness test and then they send us to jump school at Benning. If we pass that, we're in. And we'll pass. Those doggies ain't got jack. Semper fi, motherfucker! Let's do it."

There was no more talk of Neal Cassady, Edith Piaf, or the artist's loft in SoHo. I said, "If Sergeant Wright could only see you now!"

We were just three days in country when we got dropped in somewhere in the western highlands of the Quang Tri province. It was a routine reconnaissance patrol. It was not supposed to be

any kind of big deal at all — just acclimation. The morning after
our drop we approached a clear field. I recall that it gave me a
funny feeling, but I was too new to fully trust my instincts. *Everything* was spooky; I was fresh meat, F.N.G. — a Fucking New
Guy.

Before moving into the field, our team leader sent Hanes — a
lance corporal, a short-timer, with only twelve days left before
his rotation was over — across the field as a point man. This was
a bad omen and everyone knew it. Hanes had two Purple Hearts.
He followed the order with no hesitation and crossed the field
without drawing fire. The team leader signaled for us to fan out
and told me to circumvent the field and hump through the jungle to investigate a small mound of loose red dirt that I had
missed completely but that he had picked up with his trained eye.
I remember I kept saying, "Where?" He pointed to a heap of
earth about thirty yards along the tree line and about ten feet
back in the bushes. Most likely it was an anthill, but you never
knew — it could have been an N.V.A. tunnel. "Over there," he
hissed. "God damn it, do I have to draw pictures for you?"

I moved smartly in the direction of the mound while the rest
of the team reconverged to discuss something. As I approached
the mound I saw that it was in fact an anthill, and I looked back
at the team and saw they were already halfway across the field,
moving very fast.

Suddenly there were several loud hollow pops and the cry "In-
coming!" Seconds later the first of a half-dozen mortar rounds
landed in the loose earth surrounding the anthill. For a millisec-
ond, everything went black. I was blown back and lifted up on a
cushion of warm air. At first it was like the thrill of a carnival
ride, but it was quickly followed by that stunned, jangly, electric
feeling you get when you hit your crazy bone. Like that, but not
confined to a small area like the elbow. I felt it shoot through my
spine and into all four limbs. A thick plaster of sand and red clay
plugged up my nostrils and ears. Grit was blown in between my
teeth. If I hadn't been wearing a pair of Ray-Ban aviator shades,
I would certainly have been blinded permanently — as it was, my
eyes were loaded with grit. (I later discovered that fine red earth
was somehow blown in behind the crystal of my pressure-tested
Rolex Submariner, underneath my fingernails and toenails, and

deep into the pores of my skin.) When I was able to, I pulled out a canteen filled with lemon-lime Kool-Aid and tried to flood my eyes clean. This helped a little, but my eyes still felt like they were on fire. I rinsed them again and blinked furiously.

I rolled over on my stomach in the prone position and leveled my field-issue M-16. A company of screaming N.V.A. soldiers ran into the field, firing as they came — I saw their green tracer rounds blanket the position where the team had quickly congregated to lay out a perimeter, but none of our own red tracers were going out. Several of the Marines had been killed outright by the mortar rounds. Jorgeson was all right, and I saw him cast a nervous glance in my direction. Then he turned to the enemy and began to fire his M-16. I clicked my rifle on to automatic and pulled the trigger, but the gun was loaded with dirt and it wouldn't fire.

Apart from Jorgeson, the only other American putting out any fire was Second Lieutenant Milton, also a fairly new guy, a "cherry," who was down on one knee firing his .45, an exercise in almost complete futility. I assumed that Milton's 16 had jammed, like mine, and watched as AK-47 rounds, having penetrated his flak jacket and then his chest, ripped through the back of his field pack and buzzed into the jungle beyond like a deadly swarm of bees. A few seconds later, I heard the swoosh of an R.P.G. rocket, a dud round that dinged the lieutenant's left shoulder before it flew off in the bush behind him. It took off his whole arm, and for an instant I could see the white bone and ligaments of his shoulder, and the red flesh of muscle tissue, looking very much like fresh prime beef, well marbled and encased in a thin layer of yellowish white adipose tissue that quickly became saturated with dark red blood. What a lot of blood there was. Still, Milton continued to fire his .45. When he emptied his clip, I watched him remove a fresh one from his web gear and attempt to load the pistol with one hand. He seemed to fumble with the fresh clip for a long time, until at last he dropped it, along with his .45. The lieutenant's head slowly sagged forward, but he stayed up on one knee with his remaining arm extended out to the enemy, palm upward in the soulful, heartrending gesture of Al Jolson doing a rendition of "Mammy."

A hail of green tracer rounds buzzed past Jorgeson, but he

coolly returned fire in short, controlled bursts. The light, tinny pops from his M-16 did not sound very reassuring, but I saw several N.V.A. go down. AK-47 fire kicked up red dust all around Jorgeson's feet. He was basically out in the open, and if ever a man was totally alone it was Jorgeson. He was dead meat and he had to know it. It was very strange that he wasn't hit immediately.

Jorgeson zigged his way over to the body of a large black Marine who carried an M-60 machine gun. Most of the recon Marines carried grease guns or Swedish Ks; an M-60 was too heavy for traveling light and fast, but this Marine had been big and he had been paranoid. I had known him least of anyone in the squad. In three days he had said nothing to me, I suppose because I was F.N.G., and had spooked him. Indeed, now he was dead. That august seeker of truth, Schopenhauer, was correct: *We are like lambs in a field, disporting themselves under the eye of the butcher, who chooses out first one and then another for his prey. So it is that in our good days we are all unconscious of the evil Fate may have presently in store for us — sickness, poverty, mutilation, loss of sight or reason.*

It was difficult to judge how quickly time was moving. Although my senses had been stunned by the concussion of the mortar rounds, they were, however paradoxical this may seem, more acute than ever before. I watched Jorgeson pick up the machine gun and begin to spread an impressive field of fire back at the enemy. Thuk thuk thuk, thuk thuk thuk, thuk thuk thuk! I saw several more bodies fall, and began to think that things might turn out all right after all. The N.V.A. dropped for cover, and many of them turned back and headed for the tree line. Jorgeson fired off a couple of bandoliers, and after he stopped to load another, he turned back and looked at me with those blue eyes and a smile like "How am I doing?" Then I heard the steel-cork pop of an M-79 launcher and saw a rocket grenade explode through Jorgeson's upper abdomen, causing him to do something like a back flip. His M-60 machine gun flew straight up into the air. The barrel was glowing red like a hot poker, and continued to fire in a "cook off" until the entire bandolier had run through.

In the meantime I had pulled a cleaning rod out of my pack and worked it through the barrel of my M-16. When I next tried to shoot, the Tonka-toy son of a bitch remained jammed, and at last I frantically broke it down to find the source of the problem. I had a dirty bolt. Fucking dirt everywhere. With numbed fingers I removed the firing pin and worked it over with a toothbrush, dropping it in the red dirt, picking it up, cleaning it, and dropping it again. My fingers felt like Novocain, and while I could see far away, I was unable to see up close. I poured some more Kool-Aid over my eyes. It was impossible for me to get my weapon clean. Lucky for me, ultimately.

Suddenly N.V.A. soldiers were running through the field shoving bayonets into the bodies of the downed Marines. It was not until an N.V.A. trooper kicked Lieutenant Milton out of his tripod position that he finally fell to the ground. Then the soldiers started going through the dead Marines' gear. I was still frantically struggling with my weapon when it began to dawn on me that the enemy had forgotten me in the excitement of the firefight. I wondered what had happened to Hanes and if he had gotten clear. I doubted it, and hopped on my survival radio to call in an air strike when finally a canny N.V.A. trooper did remember me and headed in my direction most ricky-tick.

With a tight grip on the spoon, I pulled the pin on a fragmentation grenade and then unsheathed my K-bar. About this time Jorgeson let off a horrendous shriek — a gut shot is worse than anything. Or did Jorgeson scream to save my life? The N.V.A. moving in my direction turned back to him, studied him for a moment, and then thrust a bayonet into his heart. As badly as my own eyes hurt, I was able to see Jorgeson's eyes — a final flash of glorious azure before they faded into the unfocused and glazed gray of death. I repinned the grenade, got up on my knees, and scrambled away until finally I was on my feet with a useless and incomplete handful of M-16 parts, and I was running as fast and as hard as I have ever run in my life. A pair of Phantom F-4s came in very low with delayed-action high-explosive rounds and napalm. I could feel the almost unbearable heat waves of the latter, volley after volley. I can still feel it and smell it to this day.

Concerning Lance Corporal Hanes: they found him later, fried to a crisp by the napalm, but it was nonetheless ascertained that he had been mutilated while alive. He was like the rest of us — eighteen, nineteen, twenty years old. What did we know of

life? Before Vietnam, Hanes didn't think he would ever die. I
mean, yes, he knew that in theory he would die, but he *felt* like he
was going to live forever. I know that I felt that way. Hanes was
down to twelve days and a wake-up. When other Marines saw a
short-timer get greased, it devastated their morale. However,
when I saw them zip up the body bag on Hanes I became in-
censed. Why hadn't Milton sent him back to the rear to burn shit
or something when he got so short? Twelve days to go and then
mutilated. Fucking Milton! Fucking Second Lieutenant!

Theogenes was the greatest of gladiators. He was a boxer who
served under the patronage of a cruel nobleman, a prince who
took great delight in bloody spectacles. Although this was several
hundred years before the times of those most enlightened of
men Socrates, Plato, and Aristotle, and well after the Minoans of
Crete, it still remains a high point in the history of Western civilization and culture. It was the approximate time of Homer, the
greatest poet who ever lived. Then, as now, violence, suffering,
and the cheapness of life were the rule.

The sort of boxing Theogenes practiced was not like modern-
day boxing with those kindergarten Queensberry Rules. The two
contestants were not permitted the freedom of a ring. Instead,
they were strapped to flat stones, facing each other nose-to-nose.
When the signal was given they would begin hammering each
other with fists encased in heavy leather thongs. It was a fight to
the death. Fourteen hundred and twenty-five times Theogenes
was strapped to the stone and fourteen hundred and twenty-five
times he emerged a victor.

Perhaps it is Theogenes who is depicted in the famous Roman
statue (based on the earlier Greek original) of "The Pugilist at
Rest." I keep a grainy black-and-white photograph of it in my
room. The statue depicts a muscular athlete approaching his
middle age. He has a thick beard and a full head of curly hair. In
addition to the telltale broken nose and cauliflower ears of a
boxer, the pugilist has the slanted, drooping brows that bespeak
torn nerves. Also, the forehead is piled with scar tissue. As may
be expected, the pugilist has the musculature of a fighter. His
neck and trapezius muscles are well developed. His shoulders
are enormous; his chest is thick and flat, without the bulging pec-

torals of the bodybuilder. His back, oblique, and abdominal muscles are highly pronounced, and he has that greatest asset of the modern boxer — sturdy legs. The arms are large, particularly the forearms, which are reinforced with the leather wrappings of the cestus. It is the body of a small heavyweight — lithe rather than bulky, but by no means lacking in power: a Jack Johnson or a Dempsey, say. If you see the authentic statue at the Terme Museum, in Rome, you will see that the seated boxer is really not much more than a light heavyweight. People were small in those days. The important thing was that he was perfectly proportioned.

The pugilist is sitting on a rock with his forearms balanced on his thighs. That he is seated and not pacing implies that he has been through all this many times before. It appears that he is conserving his strength. His head is turned as if he were looking over his shoulder — as if someone had just whispered something to him. It is in this that the "art" of the sculpture is conveyed to the viewer. Could it be that someone has just summoned him to the arena? There is a slight look of befuddlement on his face, but there is no trace of fear. There is an air about him that suggests that he is eager to proceed and does not wish to cause anyone any trouble or to create a delay, even though his life will soon be on the line. Besides the deformities on his noble face, there is also the suggestion of weariness and philosophical resignation. *All the world's a stage, and all the men and women merely players.* Exactly! He knew this more than two thousand years before Shakespeare penned the line. How did he come to be at this place in space and time? Would he rather be safely removed to the countryside — an obscure, stinking peasant shoving a plow behind a mule? Would that be better? Or does he revel in his role? Perhaps he once did, but surely not now. Is this the great Theogenes or merely a journeyman fighter, a former slave or criminal bought by one of the many contractors who for months trained the condemned for their brief moment in the arena? I wonder if Marcus Aurelius loved the "Pugilist" as I do, and came to study it and to meditate before it?

I cut and ran from that field in Southeast Asia. I've read that Davy Crockett, hero of the American frontier, was cowering under a bed when Santa Anna and his soldiers stormed into the

Alamo. What is the truth? Jack Dempsey used to get so scared
before his fights that he sometimes wet his pants. But look what
he did to Willard and to Luis Firpo, the Wild Bull of the Pampas!
It was something close to homicide. What is courage? What is
cowardice? The magnificent Roberto Duran gave us *"No más,"*
but who had a greater fighting heart than Duran?

I got over that first scare and saw that I was something quite
other than that which I had known myself to be. Hey Baby
proved only my warm-up act. There was a reservoir of malice,
poison, and vicious sadism in my soul, and it poured forth freely
in the jungles and rice paddies of Vietnam. I pulled three tours.
I wanted some payback for Jorgeson. I grieved for Lance Corporal Hanes. I grieved for myself and what I had lost. I committed unspeakable crimes and got medals for it.

It was only fair that I got a head injury myself. I never got a
scratch in Vietnam, but I got tagged in a boxing smoker at Pendleton. Fought a bad-ass light heavyweight from artillery. Nobody would fight this guy. He could box. He had all the moves.
But mainly he was a puncher — it was said that he could punch
with either hand. It was said that his hand speed was superb. I
had finished off at least a half rack of Hamm's before I went in
with him and started getting hit with head shots I didn't even see
coming. They were right. His hand speed *was* superb.

I was twenty-seven years old, smoked two packs a day, was a
borderline alcoholic. I shouldn't have fought him — I knew
that — but he had been making noise. A very long time before, I
had been the middleweight champion of the First Marine Division. I had been a so-called war hero. I had been a recon Marine.
But now I was a garrison Marine and in no kind of shape.

He put me down almost immediately, and when I got up I was
terribly afraid. I was tight and I could not breathe. It felt like he
was hitting me in the face with a ball peen hammer. It felt like he
was busting light bulbs in my face. Rather than one opponent, I
saw three. I was convinced his gloves were loaded, and a wave of
self-pity ran through me.

I began to move. He made a mistake by expending a lot of energy trying to put me away quickly. I had no intention of going
down again, and I knew I wouldn't. My buddies were watching,

and I had to give them a good show. While I was afraid, I was also exhilarated; I had not felt this alive since Vietnam. I began to score with my left jab, and because of this I was able to withstand his bull charges and divert them. I thought he would throw his bolt, but in the beginning he was tireless. I must have hit him with four hundred left jabs. It got so that I could score at will, with either hand, but he would counter, trap me on the ropes, and pound. He was the better puncher and was truly hurting me, but I was scoring, and as the fight went on the momentum shifted and I took over. I staggered him again and again. The Marines at ringside were screaming for me to put him away, but however much I tried, I could not. Although I could barely stand by the end, I was sorry that the fight was over. Who had won? The referee raised my arm in victory, but I think it was pretty much a draw. Judging a prizefight is a very subjective thing.

About an hour after the bout, when the adrenaline had subsided, I realized I had a terrible headache. It kept getting worse, and I rushed out of the N.C.O. Club, where I had gone with my buddies to get loaded.

I stumbled outside, struggling to breathe, and I headed away from the company area toward Sheepshit Hill, one of the many low brown foothills in the vicinity. Like a dog who wants to die alone, so it was with me. Everything got swirly, and I dropped in the bushes.

I was unconscious for nearly an hour, and for the next two weeks I walked around like I was drunk, with double vision. I had constant headaches and seemed to have grown old overnight. My health was gone.

I became a very timid individual. I became introspective. I wondered what had made me act the way I had acted. Why had I killed my fellowmen in war, without any feeling, remorse, or regret? And when the war was over, why did I continue to drink and swagger around and get into fistfights? Why did I like to dish out pain, and why did I take positive delight in the suffering of others? Was I insane? Was it too much testosterone? Women don't do things like that. The rapacious Will to Power lost its hold on me. Suddenly I began to feel sympathetic to the cares and sufferings of all living creatures. You lose your health and you start thinking this way.

Has man become any better since the times of Theogenes?
The world is replete with badness. I'm not talking about that
old routine where you drag out the Spanish Inquisition, the
Holocaust, Joseph Stalin, the Khmer Rouge, etc. It happens
in our own back yard. Twentieth-century America is one of the
most materially prosperous nations in history. But take a walk
through an American prison, a nursing home, the slums where
the homeless live in cardboard boxes, a cancer ward. Go to a
Vietnam vets' meeting, or an A.A. meeting, or an Overeaters
Anonymous meeting. *How hollow and unreal a thing is life, how de-
ceitful are its pleasures, what horrible aspects it possesses.* Is the world
not rather like a hell, as Schopenhauer, that clearheaded seer —
who has helped me transform my suffering into an object of understanding — was so quick to point out? They called him a pes-
simist and dismissed him with a word, but it is peace and self-
renewal that I have found in his pages.

About a year after my fight with the guy from artillery I started
having seizures. I suffered from a form of left-temporal-lobe seizure which is sometimes called Dostoyevski's epilepsy. It's so rare
as to be almost unknown. Freud, himself a neurologist, specu-
lated that Dostoyevski was a hysterical epileptic, and that his fits
were unrelated to brain damage — psychogenic in origin. Dostoyevski did not have his first attack until the age of twenty-five,
when he was imprisoned in Siberia and received fifty lashes after
complaining about the food. Freud figured that after Dostoyevski's mock execution, the four years' imprisonment in Siberia,
the tormented childhood, the murder of his tyrannical father,
etc. & etc. — he had all the earmarks of hysteria, of grave psychological trauma. And Dostoyevski had displayed the trade-
mark features of the psychomotor epileptic long before his first
attack. These days physicians insist there is no such thing as the
"epileptic personality." I think they say this because they do not
want to add to the burden of the epileptic's suffering with an extra stigma. Privately they do believe in these traits. Dostoyevski
was nervous and depressed, a tormented hypochondriac, a com-
pulsive writer obsessed with religious and philosophic themes.
He was hyperloquacious, raving, etc. & etc. His gambling addic-
tion is well known. By most accounts he was a sick soul.

The peculiar and most distinctive thing about his epilepsy was that in the split second before his fit — in the aura, which is in fact officially a part of the attack — Dostoyevski experienced a sense of felicity, of ecstatic well-being unlike anything an ordinary mortal could hope to imagine. It was the experience of satori. Not the nickel-and-dime satori of Abraham Maslow, but the Supreme. He said that he wouldn't trade ten years of life for this feeling, and I, who have had it, too, would have to agree. I can't explain it, I don't understand it — it becomes slippery and elusive when it gets any distance on you — but I have felt this down to the core of my being. Yes, God exists! But then it slides away and I lose it. I become a doubter. Even Dostoyevski, the fervent Christian, makes an almost airtight case against the possibility of the existence of God in the Grand Inquisitor digression in *The Brothers Karamazov*. It is probably the greatest passage in all of world literature, and it tilts you to the court of the atheist. This is what happens when you approach Him with the intellect.

It is thought that St. Paul had a temporal-lobe fit on the road to Damascus. Paul warns us in First Corinthians that God will confound the intellectuals. It is known that Muhammad composed the Koran after attacks of epilepsy. Black Elk experienced fits before his grand "buffalo" vision. Joan of Arc is thought to have been a left-temporal-lobe epileptic. Each of these in a terrible flash of brain lightning was able to pierce the murky veil of illusion which is spread over all things. Just so did the scales fall from my eyes. It is called the "sacred disease."

But what a price. I rarely leave the house anymore. To avoid falling injuries, I always wear my old boxer's headgear, and I always carry my mouthpiece. Rather more often than the aura where "every common bush is afire with God," I have the typical epileptic aura, which is that of terror and impending doom. If I can keep my head and think of it, and if there is time, I slip the mouthpiece in and thus avoid biting my tongue. I bit it in half once, and when they sewed it back together it swelled enormously, like a huge red-and-black sausage. I was unable to close my mouth for more than two weeks.

The fits are coming more and more. I'm loaded on Depakene, phenobarbital, Tegretol, Dilantin — the whole shitload. A nurse from the V.A. bought a pair of Staffordshire terriers for me and trained them to watch me as I sleep, in case I have a fit and smother face down in my bedding. What delightful companions these dogs are! One of them, Gloria, is especially intrepid and clever. Inevitably, when I come to I find that the dogs have dragged me into the kitchen, away from blankets and pillows, rugs, and objects that might suffocate me, and that they have turned me on my back. There's Gloria, barking in my face. Isn't this incredible?

My sister brought a neurosurgeon over to my place around Christmas — not some V.A. butcher but a guy from the university hospital. He was a slick dude in a nine-hundred-dollar suit. He came down on me hard, like a used-car salesman. He wants to cauterize a small spot in a nerve bundle in my brain. "It's not a lobotomy, it's a *cingulotomy*," he said.

Reckless, desperate, last-ditch psychosurgery is still pretty much unthinkable in the conservative medical establishment. That's why he made a personal visit to my place. A house call. Drumming up some action to make himself a name. "See that bottle of Thorazine?" he said. "You can throw that poison away," he said. "All that amitriptyline. That's garbage, you can toss that, too." He said, "Tell me something. How can you take all of that shit and still walk?" He said, "You take enough drugs to drop an elephant."

He wants to cut me. He said that the feelings of guilt and worthlessness, and the heaviness of a heart blackened by sin, will go away. "It is *not* a lobotomy," he said.

I don't like the guy. I don't trust him. I'm not convinced, but I can't go on like this. If I am not having a panic attack I am engulfed in tedious, unrelenting depression. I am overcome with a deadening sense of languor; I can't *do* anything. I wanted to give my buddies a good show! What a goddam fool. I am a goddam fool!

It has taken me six months to put my thoughts in order, but I wanted to do it in case I am a vegetable after the operation. I know that my buddy Jorgeson was a real American hero. I wish that he had lived to be something else, if not a painter of pictures then even some kind of fuckup with a factory job and four di-

vorces, bankruptcy petitions, in and out of jail. I wish he had
been that. I wish he had been *anything* rather than a real American hero. So, then, if I am to feel somewhat *indifferent* to life after
the operation, all the better. If not, not.

If I had a more conventional sense of morality I would shitcan
those dress blues, and I'd send that Navy Cross to Jorgeson's
brother. Jorgeson was the one who won it, who pulled the John
Wayne number up there near Khe Sanh and saved my life, although I lied and took the credit for all of those dead N.V.A. He
had created a stunning body count — nothing like Theogenes,
but Jorgeson only had something like twelve minutes total in the
theater of war.

The high command almost awarded me the Medal of Honor,
but of course there were no witnesses to what I claimed I had
done, and I had saved no one's life. When I think back on it, my
tale probably did not sound as credible as I thought it had at the
time. I was only nineteen years old and not all that practiced a
liar. I figure if they *had* given me the Medal of Honor, I would
have stood in the ring up at Camp Las Pulgas in Pendleton and
let that light heavyweight from artillery fucking kill me.

Now I'm thinking I might call Hey Baby and ask how he's
doing. No shit, a couple of neuropsyches — we probably have a
lot in common. I could apologize to him. But I learned from my
fits that you don't have to do that. Good and evil are only illu-
sions. Still, I cannot help but wonder sometimes if my vision of
the Supreme Reality was any more real than the demons visited
upon schizophrenics and madmen. Has it all been just a stupid
neurochemical event? Is there no God at all? The human heart
rebels against this.

If they fuck up the operation, I hope I get to keep my dogs
somehow — maybe stay at my sister's place. If they send me to
the nuthouse I lose the dogs for sure.

JunHee

FROM THE NEW YORKER

WE SAID the word "abortion" the day the test came back, when
we were still in shock, but it was only a formality — an option
too familiar for silence but easily crossed off in our excitement.
"JunHee, you're pregnant," Tanner whispered. He kept smiling.
I questioned our decision, of course — I would feel worse now if
I hadn't — especially in the mornings and early evenings during
those two weeks when I was miserable and sick on the bathroom
tile. I wondered if we had thought things out enough. I wondered what would happen to the comfortable isolation that Tanner and I had built — it would be unfair to keep our child to ourselves like that. I felt the weight through my abdomen and into
my thighs, the weight of fear and instinct. I had questions, but
each day they moved closer to being the questions of how to do
this right and further from the question of whether we should
do it at all.

Still, when the child was gone, she left the guilt behind.

My mother came like a thief in the night and took the child
from me. I saw her in a dream. There were Tanner and I, up
above everything, and the tidy oval of cotton blanket in my arms,
the warmth against my chest. Be careful, Tanner said, and we
were. There was the sense of accomplishment and wonder, hung
across our shoulders like a shawl. And then my mother was below us. Yoo-hoo, she called. Her bright tone frightened me because she was a serious and dour person. I leaned out the window, and she stood on the sidewalk in the burgundy dress that
she had worn the last time I saw her. Come down, baby, she

called with a smile. She spoke in Korean. She waved to me, or to the child. The child was there in front of me. There was the small sound of wind in my ears, then my mother: Fall down, baby. Come, come. The child was there in front of me and, though I did not give her up, I did not reach to save her. She fell into my mother's arms; there was only the small wind. That's better, my mother whispered, bent over the child. My mother looked up at me — her face was red and swollen with tears.

I let the doctor provide her own explanation; I didn't tell her about my mother. This kind of thing happened, she told us; there was nothing anyone could have done. She said it was an "isolated tragedy"; there was no reason to think that we couldn't try again and have a perfectly healthy baby. The doctor was sorry. "I'm so sorry," she said.

I understood that the dream was something that belonged to both of us, but I didn't tell Tanner. I knew he wouldn't have accepted it. He would have resorted to medical explanations that he knew nothing about, pretending they required less of his faith. I was afraid he would want to talk me out of the dream, as if doing me a favor. I should have told him, but I didn't.

Tanner's instinct was to reason, to use hindsight to reconstruct the past. For him the past was something that led logically and fluidly into the future, like a river. He decided that what had happened was for the best: we had never wanted a child to begin with and had been too caught up in the excitement and the surprise. He compared it to a couple who fall in love at first sight and decide to marry the same day — they're unprepared for the disappointments and boredom of a lifetime; they just want that first day to go on and on.

In the evenings I was haunted by my dream. Tanner and I would lie together, pretending to sleep. I wondered how the child had left my arms, I wondered what Tanner had known when he warned me to be careful. I didn't like my mother's saying "That's better." I didn't like her tears, as if she had done something she hated but was obliged to do. Most of all, I was troubled by the instant in which I could have reached out and taken the baby back. I couldn't see her small face, but I imagined that if I had seen it, her look would have been of surprise and disappointment. I wondered if this was a test that Tanner and I had failed. I wondered if every woman was tested by her own mother before being allowed her pregnancy, and if most of them remembered passing or only felt it as a tightness in their consciences. We never wished the child any harm, I told myself.

Tanner was in a minor accident on his way to work. He made a wide turn pulling into the driveway at his machine shop, and a woman tried to pass him on the right, slamming into his front end. That night he dramatized her crazy defensiveness for me, her flying out of her car. "I thought you were turning left — I was looking, you started left!"

"I had my signal on," he had told her.

"You didn't have your signal on — I looked. I thought you were turning left. I was looking."

It turned out that the insurance company she told him to call had dropped her four months before, and she actually had no insurance. She was recently divorced, and working for the first time in her life at the age of forty-seven — for five-fifty an hour. The bottom line was that we would either break this woman's back or pay for the damage ourselves. I didn't know whether to be mad at the woman for allowing herself to be so dependent on her former husband or sorry for her as a victim of her dependence. What surprised me, though, was the way it weighed on Tanner. At dinner he furrowed his brow and winced, as if carrying on his own debate. I bit my wineglass to keep from laughing, and finally I asked, "What is it, Tanner?"

He looked surprised to find me still at the table. "Think about it," he said.

He was so serious I couldn't help laughing. "Think about what? Think about a woman screwed by her husband and by a culture that says it's ladylike to be dependent? Come on, Tanner, that's old news."

"That's not what I mean." He shook his head.

I thought maybe my tone had been a little cruel. "I'm sorry," I told him.

He stared vacantly at the table and shook his head. He said, "I was driving down a road I drive every day, a road I've driven for four years, turning in to a driveway I've turned in to a thousand times. Maybe I was worried about the furnace for Honeywell, I don't know. I started my turn without thinking."

He sat back and shrugged his shoulders. "I probably *did* make a wide turn, I probably do every time." Tanner wore the concerned look that I had seen before. It meant only that the logic and order of his world were temporarily being put into question: could it really be that there were unexplainable events? Heavens! I wanted to kiss him.

"Then she slams into me," he continued, gesturing, "and suddenly I'm in the world of things beyond myself. There are traffic noises, and there's a desperate woman begging me to say it wasn't her fault, and it's raining, even."

Tanner shook his head and smiled and I went to him. I knelt on the floor and laid my head and my arms in his lap. He ran his fingers across my back.

"Lots of things have nothing to do with us," he said. I laughed then, and soon he did, too. "You know what I mean." He smiled and shook his head, yet again.

"You're going to wear out your neck," I told him.

I called my father in Seoul, catching him in the morning before he went to work. I had talked to him only twice in the fifteen months since my mother's death, so I asked if he was lonely. First he said, "You should hear yourself, JunHee, you speak your Korean like a foreigner." Then he answered my question. "No, your mother and I talk more now than we did when we were together. She's become more thoughtful in death; she has more to say."

"Where do you speak?" I asked. I heard the front door open and Tanner came in. He was home early from work; he carried a bag of groceries in one arm. I waved to him and tried to look happily surprised.

"What do you mean?" my father said. "We talk wherever she wants to. Sometimes she asks me questions at work, in front of a manager or a clerk. Questions she knows will make me angry and want to answer her there."

Tanner began to unload groceries into the refrigerator and the cabinets. I took the phone out to the porch. "Can't you just *think* back an answer? You don't really have to talk, do you?"

"No, JunHee. I talk. She talks to me; I talk back. It's a conversation."

"Forgive me; I'm not up on all of this." There was a short silence between us.

"She said she's seen you," my father continued.

I felt my stomach turn. "Really?" I asked. "What else did she say about me?"

"She said she took your baby."

I swallowed hard and sat down. "That's true." I kept my back to the kitchen and there was no sound — I guessed that Tanner might have gone to the bedroom to change. "It was a terrible thing for her to do." I knew that he would disagree, that my father believed our future lay in the hands of the dead. Like fate, they could do no wrong or right. There was a low rattle across the phone line. He didn't have to answer me, but in his long silence there seemed an intentional cruelty. "Did she tell you why?" I asked, and I was surprised to find myself crying.

"No." His voice was sad, yet resigned. My father carried a self-control that exerted its presence on anyone near him. With a conscious depth in his voice, he said, "I know why, though. She told me something before she died." He waited. Finally, he said, "She told me she forgives you. She said, 'I have forgiven our JunHee and you will, too. But her children never will. They'll never have America and they'll never have Korea. The voices of their ancestors will be too tangled to hear.'"

I wiped a hand across my face and felt angry at my own ridiculous tears. I was careful to keep them from my voice. "She had no right to say that. You both knew that Tanner and I had no plans for children." I whispered now, I don't know why. "She had no right to take our child, to decide for us."

"Don't argue with me, I'm telling you what she said. Besides, JunHee, children or not, the fact is you've brought the end of our family. It's not your mother's fault."

My head was swimming and I felt suddenly foolish for calling him. Could I have expected anything better than this? I disconnected the line. I sat still a moment and wiped my eyes again. Then I went to the kitchen and hung up the phone. Tanner was out of sight. On the porch I sat in a frayed lawn chair. I wondered if my father was pleased by the phone call, or if he could still feel bad for me. I began to cry again — it felt natural, and I

decided not to be embarrassed. I knew the next time I talked to
him, in a month or a year, there would be no reference to any of
this. We would act as if it hadn't happened and resume our careful roles. And wasn't that the way I wanted it? Wasn't the distance
what I had wanted since leaving Korea?

Tanner came out onto the porch; he had changed into shorts
and a T-shirt. His right hand was taped up and his pinkie was
stiff with a splint. He sat down in the chair across from me, and I
sniffled and leaned forward.

"I got in another accident," he said, smiling and holding the
hand out. "Broke the finger in two places. I may have totaled the
rental car."

He laughed and I did, too. I wiped my eyes. "What happened?" I asked.

"I missed a possum and hit a tree in the process. My pinkie
turned backward when my hand hit the dash."

"Tanner." I sat beside him and he laughed again. "What
should we do with you?"

He said, "I blacked out for a minute, too. They took me to the
hospital, but the doctor decided my head was all right."

"You should have called me."

"The doctor laughed when I told him the whole story."

I smiled and shook my head. "And then you went and got groceries?"

"I called Frank at the shop, and he drove me home. I'm starving."

I went to a Catholic church where I knew two Korean families worshipped. I didn't expect to see either of them; it was
just the only church in the area that I knew anything about. I
picked a Thursday morning — for some reason I didn't want
Tanner to know — and I called the lab to tell Alex I'd be late to
work.

My mother never left the *Buddhasasana,* though she had to face
cruel jokes from my father whenever she voiced her beliefs. He'd
had a Protestant "uncle" from Britain when he was young — actually just a close friend of his father's. There was always his
proud insistence that he was a Protestant, his telling me, often
while angry or drinking, the story of Christ. Later, when I took a

class in college here, I realized how little he really understood Christianity and how his Mahayana Buddhist upbringing had not left him.

I knew the connection to my mother was thin in this church. But I went for my own sake — maybe I would feel closer to her.

It was a new, squat building with white aluminum siding and very few windows — industrial-strength religion, I suppose. The only sign of holiness was a small golden cross, perched at the crown of the roof like a weathervane. I arrived at twenty after eight and the next mass was scheduled for nine, which didn't bother me at all. I didn't feel up to the crowd or the structure of a mass — it was the first time I had been in a church in six years, and the last time had been for our wedding.

I found a pew far enough from the altar not to feel intimidated but close enough to help me work up something like a prayer. I folded my hands in my lap. There was a ceramic figure of the Virgin Mary hanging by the altar, and I found her eyes meeting my own.

When I thought of the baby I pictured the bundle of blanket from the dream. But I knew my child had been little more than a fertilized egg and a lot of blood. There were the films I had seen in college charting the development of the fetus — the tight curl of the back, the odd, oversized head, the arms and hands and dark red fingers. I stared at Mary, at the wrinkled blue of her ceramic gown, at her wide shoulders and small breasts. Finally I asked to speak to my mother. Despite what my father had said, I spoke only in thoughts.

I closed my eyes and that helped me to concentrate, to see her in my memory. "I want to talk to you. What you did to Tanner and me was wrong. I want to know why you did it. I deserve an explanation."

I pictured my mother in her burgundy, Western-style dress, the one she had worn in the dream. I pictured her hearing me and considering an answer. I imagined the weight of wisdom and perspective in her features — the confidence of the dead, the thoughtfulness that my father had mentioned. I wondered what she had done with my daughter, and I wanted to see the child, too, but my imagination had limits.

I waited. When I opened my eyes, the church held a yellow glow from the candlelight and the morning sun through the high windows. There was a clean smell, like varnish.

"I don't understand," I whispered. There was no one close enough to overhear. I rested my chin on my folded hands, on the back of the pew before me. "I don't know, I don't know if this church helps anything or not, for you. I'm very serious, though. I don't think I'm asking too much."

I waited. I thought of my mother in Korea, of the continual shuffle of her slippers and the hollow quiet in her eyes. I imagined her caring for my child in death, a grandmother, and I began to feel the heaviness of self-pity in my stomach. "You owe me this," I whispered, trying not to be bitter or pitiful. I stood to go. At the last minute I decided to cross myself.

At work, Tanner left the power on while he was wiring a control box and gave himself a shock that could have been fatal. When he called me at the lab I could hear a smile in his voice, but he was no longer up to a laugh. "What do you think it is?" I asked. "Can this really be just coincidence?"

"I don't know."

I waited. "Tanner, maybe you should talk to someone who knows something about this."

"Yeah," he said, as if he had already considered this. "Join the analyst generation, huh?"

"No. Just get some help, before you kill yourself."

"I'm not going to kill myself. I just — I don't know. I think it's that my mind's been elsewhere a lot. Both accidents happened while I was doing something routine — I wasn't even thinking. The possum accident I had no control over. Sometimes I wonder if I'm subconsciously punishing myself."

"For what? That's ridiculous."

"Maybe," he laughed, though it was not a pleasant laugh, "but so is wrecking two cars and electrocuting yourself in one week. It's pathetic, JunHee. I haven't felt this clumsy since puberty. I'm like some teenager."

Alex walked by my cubicle and gave the microscope a heavy glance, as if I were invisible unless bent over the eyepiece. He went on into his office without a word. "Well," I said to Tanner,

"I just don't buy the do-it-yourself Freud." I waited for a response, but all he said was "Uh-huh."

"Listen," I said. "I have to go. Alex is on the prowl. I'm coming home soon, though, and we'll heat up some leftovers. I'll bring us a bottle of wine. You *are* old enough to drink, aren't you, my late bloomer?"

Late in the evening, we lay together on the sofa with the lights out and I kissed his smooth chest, both of his tiny pink nipples. We hadn't spoken for some time. When Tanner began, his tone was distant, as if from somewhere in his memory.

"The night before we lost the baby," he said, "I lay beside you in bed and I couldn't sleep. You had been out cold for a while. At some point, I decided to turn the spare room into a nursery, all in my mind."

He paused. I put my ear to his chest and heard the even thump of his heart. He said, "I took down the ridiculous wallpaper first thing. I painted the walls a light blue, with white clouds spread across the ceiling. I went slowly, taking the time to imagine everything until I could see it. You know?"

I nodded against his chest. I touched the curve of his side. "Yes."

"I put in baseboards all the way around, nice stained wood. I stenciled tumbling clowns across them, and yellow tulips. I replaced the bed with a crib made of white painted wicker. Then I hung a mobile above the crib — blue waves and silver dolphins. Every detail, JunHee."

I closed my eyes and imagined the room for myself.

"In place of our dresser I put one made of the same painted wicker, with drawers that smelled like cedar and a cloth top, for changing diapers, that smelled of talcum. In place of the desk went the bassinet and a hamper."

I touched his stomach and I heard his voice from within his chest. He bent one knee and turned close against me.

"On the wall I hung a bright-faced clock with fat numbers and a mouse on the minute hand. Everything. When I was done I looked at the alarm clock in our room and it had taken me two full hours. Just to imagine it and plan it out. I still couldn't sleep, though, so I got out of bed and went down the hall. I walked through the room for a while and I looked out the window, past the crib." He paused. "I imagined the view in the morning."

I touched the deep curve above his hip and I closed my eyes. I thought of where I had been that night, with the child and my mother, while Tanner built his nursery. It seemed to me, here and now, that the accumulation of six years of marriage hadn't closed the distances I had thought it would.

When he spoke again, his voice had come back beside me. "It's the coldest room in the house — I thought about it later. It's on that corner with just the one duct. It never would have worked."

"It could have," I said.

"No, it's too far from our room. We wouldn't have heard the baby when it woke at night and began to cry."

"We would have," I said.

He hit himself on the thumb with a hammer — not a hard thing to do, really. Then he got a sleeve caught in some kind of standup drill, but it only scratched his wrist and ripped the shirt. I told him he should stay in his office more, maybe stick to the telephone and a dull pencil. "Thanks for the confidence," he said. "That's exactly what Frank said — for the sake of the company insurance policy if not for my own good."

The next day he decided we needed a trip. He planned the whole thing out before springing it on me. We would go up to New Hampshire and hike in the White Mountains, a "someday" he'd been talking about for quite a while. We could do two day hikes, and find a cheap motel for the Saturday night between. Friday, on the way up, we would spend with his mother — who was beginning to recover from her stroke — at her house in White River Junction.

It all sounded right to me and we just did it. We both had the vacation day coming, we both knew the break was overdue; we simply decided to take it the very next weekend, and packed.

The day before we left, I got our monthly checking statement in the mail. There were two checks written by Tanner to a Janet Holden, each for a hundred dollars and each written on a payday. It took me a minute to realize that Janet Holden was the woman who had hit Tanner's car, the woman with no insurance. At first there was something like jealousy, but it didn't take long for the feeling to pass. I wondered why he hadn't said any-thing — I was the one who balanced our checkbook, so paying with a check was as good as telling me. I wondered if she had asked for this, and how they decided on exactly a hundred dol-lars for each check. I felt a little angry, too — we already had close to a thousand dollars in repair bills from the two car acci-dents, and I wondered how long he intended to keep up these payments. I didn't want to play the role of the nagging wife, or to give him the role of the good-hearted but misunderstood hus-band, so I decided to let him come and explain it to me. I left the statement out on our desk, so he would know that I had seen it.

That night he said nothing, though I was sure he'd seen the statement. Friday morning we packed up the car and left.

We took the back way, up some beautiful roads, through the Berkshires on Route 7 and into Vermont. Tanner worried about seeing his mother again. It had been four months since a stroke left her virtually paralyzed from the neck down. He had spent a week and a half with her when she got out of the hospital, and we'd been up twice since. She had a full-time nurse and refused to live anywhere but in her own home — a fact that bothered Tanner but that went right along with everything I had admired in her since we'd first met. Besides, I was pretty sure that Tan-ner's real complaint about her stubbornness had nothing to do with her well-being. He wanted either the confident, indepen-dent, and aggressively healthy mother he had always had or a withered and resigned shell that he could remember her in. This in-between stuff scared him — could this person who had to be fed and bathed and changed by a nurse still be the same mother who had raised him? I never would have told Tanner any of this, but I saw that his mother knew it, too. There was a small dis-tance between them since the stroke, and I could tell it hurt them both.

The live-in nurse, whose name was Mrs. Carlis, greeted us from the doorway of his mother's house. "There they are," she called as we stepped out of the car. "Right on time." She was a loud and smothering person, sometimes to the point of being pa-tronizing. The kind of woman who wore no makeup on princi-ple, and was sure to tell you so within an hour of meeting you. She made me laugh.

Tanner's mother was charming and affectionate, clearly excited about our sudden visit. Tanner kissed her cheek and took her folded hands from her lap. He squatted before her wheelchair and whispered something to her; I looked out the window to let them be alone. In a minute his mother said, "Oh, stop it. Get lost now, and let me talk to your wife."

We all sat through the last of the afternoon on her patio. Tanner actually blushed as he went through the list of accidents for his mother, and she smiled with concern and sadness. Occasionally she asked Mrs. Carlis to cross or uncross her legs for her, or to find her sun hat. In the time since our last visit, I had forgotten the stillness with which she listened to people now — her concentration was both flattering and intimidating. But Mrs. Carlis carried the burden of *tsks* and sighs and waved hands for both of them. "Oh, no," Mrs. Carlis said to Tanner. "Oh, that's terrible. My goodness, what you've been through."

His mother said, "Do you expect more damage, or is this it now?"

Tanner shrugged. "If I knew — you know. I don't *expect* anything else; I didn't expect any of it."

"That's good," she said. "Don't lose your confidence, Tanner." She smiled. "Just the same, we'll go with paper plates and plastic knives for dinner, I suppose." We laughed.

In the evening Tanner went out for ice cream and Mrs. Carlis disappeared into her room. "One thing I'll give her," Tanner's mother whispered to me, "she's careful to allow me some privacy."

"That's important," I said.

"Yes. She's O.K. She's better than you might think. Sometimes I like her chatter — it keeps me from feeling lonely. And when I'm tired of her, I say so. She understands."

I nodded. She asked me about Tanner — what I thought was causing all of his accidents. I said I didn't know, but I couldn't believe it was just coincidence anymore. "No," she said, "I think he's expecting things to go wrong. There's something in the way he walks, I think. Maybe the eyes — I'm not sure what." Then she said what we were both really thinking, a talent of hers. "I believe it's his way of dealing with the miscarriage."

She waited for my reaction. I didn't like the word "miscarriage"; I thought it laid the blame on me, as though I had mishandled my own uterus. I instantly felt a powerful urge to tell her my dream, though — to explain what had really happened and to hear her advice.

When I was still quiet she asked, "How about you? Any of your own self-punishment? Any feelings of guilt?" There was empathy in her voice, nothing accusing or patronizing. I had given up comparisons to my own mother a long time ago, but there were still moments of envy.

"I don't know," I said. "There's guilt, sure. Sometimes I wonder how much we really wanted a baby. You know we never planned to have any."

"Yes."

I wanted to tell her; the whole dream was there, and until that moment I hadn't realized quite how heavy it was for me to carry alone. My father had certainly been no help. But the truth was I really didn't know this woman as well as I sometimes pretended to. I was afraid of her reaction, and maybe a little selfish about the dream by now.

I said, "Tanner thinks it was all for the best, that maybe we weren't ready for her."

"It was a girl?"

I was momentarily shocked — I had never thought twice. "I guess so. In my mind it was." We both heard Tanner's car come up the driveway.

She said, "I hope you won't feel I'm butting in if I tell you this: no one is ever ready, JunHee. It's the people who think they're ready who end up in trouble. You should try again. Tanner told me what the doctor said — that it was an isolated thing — and I think the best way for both of you to get over this is to try again. You'll have a perfect child this time."

The front door opened and Tanner came in, wiping his feet on the mat. I was thankful for his timing, because I didn't know what to say. He held up a plastic bag with a quart of ice cream inside. "Mint chocolate chip," he announced — it was my favorite.

That night we slept together in the twin bed that had been Tanner's since childhood. Each time we slept over, we both went through the shifting positions that I remembered from the nights we'd spent together in college: lying close and entangled at first, separating slowly as our limbs became numb and sleep began to feel more important than intimacy, finally dividing the narrow bed into individual spaces, like children in the back seat of a car.

Tonight I found myself unable to sleep. I lay with my back to Tanner and my cold feet tucked beneath his calves. The shades on the windows were pulled, and they gave the darkness of the room a depth and a texture. I imagined that I could see the waves of Tanner's even breath, the way I have sometimes seen the landscape of music. I let myself fall into the ebb and the flow, but there was still the loneliness.

And the distance. I had been in this country for a long time, two years of high school and into college, with the phone calls and my mother weeping and the letters full of affection and guilt, before I understood that the distance was inside me, that it was me. She told me that when I was born she had an idea; she claimed it came to her in the painful moments of my birth, when nothing else could get through: she saw before her each year of my life, each its own instant, a rapid film from birth to death. She saw that I would live long, that I would age well, with a straight back.

The first birthdays I don't remember, of course, though I have seen the photos. They dressed me in a silk kimono — royal blue, a new size each year. My parents were not wealthy when I was young, and this was an unusual extravagance. By my thirteenth birthday, the robes were hanging in their own closet — a rising sea of blue — each worn only once.

In the earliest years that I can recall, when I was five and six, there was expectation and excitement. Before dawn my mother would come with a candle, and the new robe folded over one arm, and a wide smile — a rare gift. Together we dressed me in the thick whispers of the fabric and in our ceremonial silence. Her hands moved continuously — straightening, creasing, cupping, nervous.

My father would have the camera ready on a crude stand — they counted floorboards to be sure of the distance. I stood before the screen that had come from a fisherman in my mother's village, three generations before her. It was a dream: the carp leapt from the river and danced, each tree held its own moon. My shoulders back, arms by my sides, I stared straight into the camera.

When I was positioned, my father and my mother took their places behind the camera and together we waited for dawn. I had been born at dawn — the timing was important. The long window behind them faced east to the bald hills, but they stood with their backs to it, their eyes set on me. I had to watch the camera, but I learned how wide peripheral vision could be. They stood together but never close, my father's hand on the camera, my mother's heavy stare watching for the first rosy light to fall across my cheeks. With each year this stiff wait began to swallow the rest of the ceremony. I learned to dread my birthday. When I was young I thought that it was customary, that everyone went through this. Later I was embarrassed; I stopped telling friends and nagged my mother until she hid the blue kimonos in a box under the bed.

In the photos the progression was clear: the shadings in my face from pride to concentration to boredom and resentment. I knew early that these photos belonged to my mother, that they were her prophecy fulfilled. But for each year I have an image of my own as well. In mine her own progression is the same: from pride to sadness and disappointment. There is the morning, coming through the windows to surround her, and the stillness, the empty promise. Sometimes I flinched at the click of the camera, suddenly remembering that I was posing, that this was a year of my life.

I listened to Tanner's deep breathing. I eased my legs out of the covers and tiptoed to the door. In the living room I found the phone easily — here the shades were up and the night was full of the moon. I dialed my father's number while counting the hours: he would be just home from work.

The connection was bad — pops and clicks, the muffled echo of the ring. It occurred to me that I had nothing to say to him, that he was only a way to her. His phone rang. I struggled for some connection, some way to get to my dream, but eventually I realized that no one would answer. He wasn't home. I hung up the phone and sat back on the couch. The nighttime was pale through the windows.

I waited. Then I reached my arms out and I felt the small weight and warmth, supported in my hands. I lunged forward — in that instant I didn't have to think or decide, because she was falling. I reached out and took her from the air. I took her in and I whispered to her. I held her hard against my chest.

It was really only a drizzle on the road the next morning, and sometimes it stopped completely for a stretch. The sky was all gray, though, with no sign of light. When we were almost there we stopped at a visitors' center and asked a forest ranger about trail conditions. The woman smiled her way through a long list of warnings: trails may be wet and footing slippery, step with care; temperatures can drop thirty degrees in a matter of hours, always pack prepared; conditions above tree line can change in minutes, keep an eye on the sky. She talked us out of Mount Madison — not today — and recommended a peak called Mount Hale instead. She sold us a map and pointed out the most dangerous trails. Her brown uniform was starched and she never bent her back. "Enjoy your stay in the White Mountains," she said.

We drove the few miles to the trailhead, Tanner imitating her perfect posture, and parked our car by the narrow opening through the trees. We checked the map once more, then started up the first trail to the Hale mountain cutoff. There were exposed roots and shallow puddles all over the trail, but we were wearing sneakers and the footing wasn't really so bad. In the distance, whichever way you looked, the trees seemed to mesh with the low sky into a gauzy gray. Occasional branches stretched across the trail and showered us when we cleared the way.

Tanner was bubbly, happy to be here at last. He decided the weather would clear when we were at the top and tomorrow would be a perfect day and we would probably see some deer or moose. I laughed.

We crossed a fast river on a footbridge and soon the trail began to rise more sharply. The rain picked up a little, but we could hardly tell beyond the sound it made on the ceiling of leaves above us. Our breathing picked up as well, and I could feel the sweat run down my back and the insides of my arms. We began to take short breaks, to rest our calves and to take the packs from our shoulders. At one point there was a rocky, exposed outcropping, and the day was full of fog. Below us the trees fell off into a green carpet and were lost.

It happened slowly, but somewhere along the way the mountain became much steeper. We took breaks more often, but we didn't talk much — in a way, it didn't seem necessary. We smiled, though; we were both having fun.

At some point I began to think about the woman with the car who hit Tanner — I couldn't remember her name. I thought of asking him right then about the checks, but the trail zigzagged up a sharp slope, and it just seemed like too much effort. Soon I decided that I wouldn't ask, that he had no right to play this silence game when he knew that I knew. The whole thing reminded me of something my father would do.

Maybe we were both a little lost in thought, but it seemed that suddenly the trees were much shorter and the fog was tight and cool. "We must be close to tree line," Tanner said, and in a few minutes we were there. The trees receded into tough, squat shrubs and we were literally in a cloud. It was fantastic. You could only see maybe a hundred feet in any direction and the mist rolled and tumbled across the rocks and up the mountain. It wasn't really raining now, but the fog was so heavy that it turned into drops on our parkas. In only a minute, there were diamonds sown through Tanner's hair and across his eyebrows and hanging, even, from his lashes.

"This is strange," he said.

"It's amazing." The silence was fuzzy and hollow, as if it would swallow up even a scream. Tanner took my hand, and I realized how wonderfully alone we were. How isolated — we hadn't come upon another hiker all day.

"What time do you think it is?" he asked me. I looked at my watch; it was past twelve-thirty.

"Well," he said, "what do you think?"

He was asking what we should do, and I couldn't believe it. I couldn't believe he could actually consider turning back. "We must be pretty close," I said. "The weather's the same as it's been all day; it's not even raining, really. Where's that map? Let's see where we are."

We looked at the map but we didn't know how to tell how far

we had come. It didn't show any tree line, and on the back it explained that the level varied in different places across the mountain, depending on exposure.

"We can't be too far," I said. "I can't imagine giving up now."

"O.K."

"We can have lunch at the peak. Maybe it'll clear a little and we'll get a view. Who knows?"

"O.K.," he said.

"Tanner. Do you want to do this?"

"Yeah." He nodded and avoided my eyes. Finally he looked at me. "Yes, I do. I really do. Let's just keep an eye on the sky, as our friendly ranger says."

It didn't take long for the shrubs to give way to bare rock, with rock piles stacked a few feet high to show the trail. At first we could see two or three markers ahead, but eventually the fog revealed only one at a time. The cloud moved past us and straight up the mountain, and I imagined that it could carry us, that we could close our eyes and let ourselves be lifted to the peak and across it into the sky.

Just when we were both beginning to lose some confidence (at least I was; Tanner's concerned expression looked set and permanent) we came to a wooden sign knocked in between the rocks. It marked the separation of two trails. One way led down a half mile to a mountain hut, and the other a mile up to the peak of Mount Hale. We took the Hale fork, and for a while it was mostly flat — even downhill in places — and we moved quickly. At one point Tanner made a small jump between rocks, but his foot slid when he landed. He skinned the palm of one hand and tore a small hole in the knee of his jeans.

"Put some antibiotic on your hand," I said.

He shook his head. "I don't want any. I'm fine." He didn't look at me.

Soon the trail turned back uphill, as we both knew it had to, and I began to wonder if our cloud wasn't getting darker. For the first time, the possibility of a thunderstorm occurred to me. I couldn't understand why we hadn't made the peak yet, and I kept looking ahead for the leveling off and the top of the mountain.

Then Tanner just stopped. I sensed everything right away, but when he said, "I don't know where the trail went," I came very close to crying. We looked in all directions for a marker.

"Let's backtrack," I said, but we each had a different idea of the way we'd come. For a few minutes I followed Tanner, but I knew he was going too directly downward — we had come up and across.

"This is wrong," I said. "I think the trail's to the right some." But he kept walking. I stopped. "Tanner. You already got us lost. You don't know where you're going." Now he stopped. He sat down heavily and lay back against his pack. There was something unnatural and afraid in his face.

I knelt beside him. "We can't be far, really. Why don't we look at the map?"

He held his hands interlocked over his closed eyes, the palms outward. One was spotted with thin lines of blood from the scratches. He shook his head. "What good is the map if we're not on a trail? We don't even know how to use the fucking thing."

I felt it all drain out of me — my energy, maybe, my confidence, any last traces of enthusiasm I had for this trip. I said, "When's the last time you remember seeing a marker? How long ago?" He shook his head. "Tanner, what's the matter? Are you sick or something? You're acting strange."

I expected him to open his eyes, to sit up and take my hand or even to smile. But all he did was shake his head again. "You're scaring me," I said. Finally he opened his eyes and sat up with a grunt.

"Let's eat lunch." I took my pack off and opened it. "Let's eat something and have some water and try to think about this without panicking. All right, Tanner?"

Tanner closed his eyes and nodded. I was thankful for a reaction that made sense. He took his pack off.

"I don't know what I was thinking," Tanner said. He bit into a sandwich and stared at the rocks and the fog. "I thought I could tell the trail by the smooth rocks. I forgot about the markers." He laughed. "*All* the rocks are smooth."

We cut straight across the mountain and I kept thinking I saw the vague form of a marker emerging, but it never happened. I kept my watch out now — it was already close to three, and in this weather it would be dark well before eight. I began to lead and Tanner followed me with his head down, watching each step. I got angry. "Tanner, what are you doing? You're not even looking for the trail."

"I don't want to slip again," he said. He held his palm up for me.

"Let's stop a minute and put something on that. Please?"

We got out the first-aid kit and I rubbed antibiotic cream into his cuts. "I figure if we find the trail," I said, just thinking of it then, "we can follow it to that hut. It's not very far, and maybe we could spend the night there." It occurred to me that I was treating him like a child. "You lead," I said.

Tanner seemed to look ahead for the trail now, and I found my mind wandering. I imagined that if the sun burned through for just a minute or two we would see the markers and the shape of the mountain around us. Maybe the trail would be right there, a few yards away. Suddenly, for no reason, the name came to me — Janet Holden. I could see it written across the canceled checks. I felt lonely; I felt lost in a world so far from all of that. I told myself, We woke up this morning in Tanner's tiny bed in White River. Tonight we'll sleep in a lumpy motel bed, or in a sleeping bag at the warm hut. I promised myself that I'd be thankful.

Janet Holden, Janet Holden. It ran through my mind with each step I took, like a drumbeat. I couldn't get rid of it. Janet Holden.

When it was almost five o'clock, my shoulders were burning under the pack and my legs were rubber. I realized, at last, that Tanner had completely given up. I felt that this was the overdue end of a long collapse for him, and I was both sorry and angry. I was angry at the pity I felt, too, and at the fact that he had come to this. I found that there was some small part of me, somewhere behind my ribs, that could hate him. But this wasn't Tanner anymore; I was alone.

At some point I began to cry, and I sat down and let it come. Tanner lay back on the rock beside me, acting as though he couldn't hear me. I got so angry that I punched him hard on the arm. He jumped and glared at me.

"Oh, he lives!" I yelled. "He still feels pain — thank God for that."

Tanner rubbed his arm. I was busy crying and I didn't notice the change, but after a while he spoke. "We should go down," he said softly.

"What?"

"We should go *down*. Straight down. We'd have shelter in the trees. We might be able to find water."

I continued to cry, despite myself. I hugged him and leaned against him, though the anger was still there. "You had no right to leave me alone," I said. "You can't do that — you had no right."

He did hug me back. When I was under some kind of control, he stood and helped me up. He said, "Let's get to the trees, at least," and started down. I watched him a minute. It seemed to me that I would have a hard time forgiving him for this. I had the feeling of some kind of ending — not of our marriage or anything as easy as that. I didn't know what. It was the feeling I had the morning I lost the child.

The way down was steep, and the silence of the fog wrapped thickly around me. I listened for my own breathing, but that sound was gone, too. I imagined that I could let go, just let myself lean over and begin to fall. I would tumble down the long slope; I would land in the wet embrace of a lake.

And then, in no time at all, Tanner saw the sign to the hut. He pointed and said, "There it is," almost casually. It was the same wooden trail marker we had come to hours before. As a celebration, we ate the last of our sandwiches and a good part of our trail mix. We followed the trail down, and neither of us lost sight of the stone markers. In a few minutes, the eerie shape of the hut emerged from the muddy gray.

There was a couple from upstate New York who lent us sweatshirts and pants to wear while we dried our own by a kerosene heater. We had missed dinner, but one of the workers at the hut made us hot soup and coffee. At first she seemed to think I wouldn't understand English; she leaned in to me and spoke slowly. I decided not to be offended, and when I answered her question fluently she seemed to apologize with her gestures and her smile.

Later the thunder came, distant and slow at first, then completely surrounding us. Lightning flashed across the mountain, and the shadows were quick and long. Tanner came to me; he knelt down and laid his head in my lap. He put his arms around my waist. At first I felt the stares and the murmurs from across the room. I touched his hair and his face, and I found that he was crying. I leaned across his back. I missed him, as if we were still apart. I kissed his hair and accepted his apology; it was surprisingly easy.

We slept on a wooden bunk in a borrowed sleeping bag. Tanner was asleep in a minute, and I was surprised to find myself awake. When I closed my eyes I saw an endless pattern of rocks; I felt the stepping up and the stepping down still in my bones. I opened my eyes and listened to the sound of the rain against the roof. I prayed. In Korean I recited one of the meditations I had learned as a child from my mother, the only one I could remember. I asked the bodhisattvas to help me to accept the world of *dukkha* and impermanence, to help me shed my desire to control. The world is change; I am change. Maybe I felt better — I don't know.

My baby was gone and there was really only Tanner and I, as I had once wanted it. My mother had never been with me, not since I left Seoul. The day she died, I had pretended it didn't matter. I went through the whole day at a distance from myself; I decided that it would take a lifetime to get back to her. My father asked me to come for the burial, and I said no.

This night I went back, though; I tried to cover the distance. It was fifteen years since I'd been in Korea, but I knew that she would not come to me, that she had made the reach already, for the last time. Fifteen years is a long way to fall, and I was afraid. I let the silence of the hut calm me.

There in the dark I said to her, I know I gave up my child. I'm sorry I let you down.

I saw her. She stood before me in a black burial gown; she lowered her eyes before her daughter. In the dream I told her, Take care of my baby, and she bowed. The clouds moved around us and across the stones, and she bowed for an eternity. I wanted to touch her skin, but she wouldn't let me. She raised her eyes to me; she saw that I was crying.

Take care of my child, I said.

LORRIE MOORE

Community Life

FROM THE NEW YORKER

WHEN OLENA was a little girl, she had called them lieberries — a
fibbing fruit, a story store — and now she had a job in one. She
had originally wanted to teach English literature, but when she
failed to warm to the graduate study of it, its French-fried theo-
ries — a vocabulary of arson! — she'd transferred to library
school, where everyone was taught to take care of books, ten-
derly, as if they were dishes or dolls.

She had learned to read at an early age. Her parents, newly
settled in Vermont from Tirgu-Mures in Transylvania, were
anxious that their daughter learn to speak English, to blend in
with the community in a way they felt they probably never
would, and so every Saturday they took her to the children's section of the Rutland library and let her spend time with the librarian, who chose books for her and sometimes even read a page or
two out loud, though there was a sign that said PLEASE BE QUIET
BOYS AND GIRLS. No comma.

Which made it seem to Olena that only the boys had to be
quiet. She and the librarian could do whatever they wanted.

She had loved the librarian.

And when Olena's Romanian began to recede altogether, and
in its stead bloomed a slow, rich, English-speaking voice, not unlike the librarian's, too womanly for a little girl, the other children on her street became even more afraid of her. "Dracula!"
they shouted. "Transylvaniess!" they shrieked, and ran.

"You'll have a new name now," her father told her on the first
day of first grade. He had already changed their last name from

Todorescu to Resnick. His shop was called Resnick's Furs. "From here on in, you will no longer be Olena. You will have a nice American name, Nell."

"You make to say the name," her mother said. "When the teacher tell you Olena, you say, 'No, Nell.' Say, 'Nell.' "

"Nell," said Olena. But when she got to school the teacher, sensing something dreamy and outcast in her, clasped her hand and exclaimed, "Olena! What a beautiful name!" Olena's heart filled with gratitude and surprise, and she fell in, adoring and mute, close to the teacher's hip.

From there on in, only her parents, in their throaty Romanian accents, ever called her Nell — her secret, jaunty, American self existing only for them.

"Nell, how are the other children at the school?"

"Nell, please to tell us what you do."

Years later, when they were killed in a car crash on the Farm-to-Market Road, and the Nell who had never lived died with them, Olena, numbly rearranging the letters of her own name on the envelopes of the sympathy cards she received, discovered what the letters spelled. Olena: "Alone." The word was a body walled in the cellar of her, a whiff and forecast of doom like an early, rotten spring — and she longed for the Nell-that-never-lived's return. She wished to start over again, to be someone living coltishly in the world, not someone hidden away behind books, with a carefully learned voice and a sad past.

She missed her mother the most.

The library Olena worked in was one of the most prestigious university libraries in the Midwest. It housed a large collection of rare and foreign books, and she had driven across several states to get there, squinting through the splattered tempera of insects on the windshield, watching for the dark tail of a possible tornado, and getting sick, painfully, in Indiana, along I-80, in the rest rooms of the service plazas named for dead Hoosiers. The ladies' rooms there had had electric eyes for the toilets, the sinks, the hand dryers, and she'd set them all off by staggering in and out of the stalls or leaning into the sinks. "You the only one in here?" asked a cleaning woman. "You the only one in here making this racket?" Olena had smiled, a dog's smile; in the yellowish light everything seemed tragic and ridiculous and unable to stop. The flatness of the terrain gave her vertigo, she decided: that was it. The land was windswept; there were no smells. In Vermont she had felt cradled by mountains. Now, here, she would have to be brave.

But she had no memory of how to be brave. Here, it seemed she had no memories at all. Nothing triggered them. And once in a while, when she gave voice to the fleeting edge of one, it seemed like something she was making up.

Olena first met Nick at the library in May. She was temporarily positioned at the reference desk, hauled out from her ordinary task as the supervisor of foreign cataloguing, to replace someone who was ill. Nick was researching statistics on municipal-campaign spending in the state. "Haven't stepped into a library since I was eighteen," he said. He looked at least forty.

She showed him where he might look. "Try looking here," she said, writing down the names of indexes, but he kept looking at *her*. "Or here."

"I'm managing a county-board-seat campaign," he said. "The election's not until the fall, but I'm trying to get a jump on things."

His hair was a coppery brown, threaded through with silver. There was something animated in his eyes, like pond life. "I just wanted to get some comparison figures. Will you have a cup of coffee with me?"

"I don't think so," she said.

But he came back the next day and asked her again.

The coffee shop near campus was hot and noisy, crowded with students, and Nick loudly ordered espresso for both himself and Olena. She usually didn't like espresso — its gritty, cigarish taste. But a kind of distortion was in the air, something that bent you a little; it caused your usual self to grow slippery, to wander off and shop, to get blurry, bleed, bevel with possibility. She drank fast, with determination and a sense of adventure. "I guess I'll have a second," she said, and wiped her mouth with a napkin.

"I'll get it," said Nick, and when he came back he told her some more about the campaign he was running. "It's important to get the endorsements of the neighborhood associations," he said. He ran a bratwurst and frozen yogurt stand called Please Squeeze & Bratwursts. He had got to know a lot of people that way. "I feel alive and relevant, living my life like this," he said. "I don't feel like I've sold out."

"Sold out to what?" she asked.

He smiled. "I can tell you're not from around here," he said. He raked his hand through the various metals of his hair. *"Selling out.* Like, doing something you really never wanted to do, and getting paid too much for it."

"Oh," she said.

"When I was a kid, my father said to me, 'Sometimes in life, son, you're going to find you have to do things you don't want to do,' and I looked him right in the eye and said, 'No fucking way.' " Olena laughed. "I mean, you probably always wanted to be a librarian, right?"

She looked at all the crooked diagonals of his face and couldn't tell whether he was serious. "Me?" she said. "I first went to graduate school to be an English professor." She sighed, switched elbows, sinking her chin into her other hand. "I did try," she said. "I read Derrida. I read Lacan. I read 'Reading Lacan.' I read 'Reading "Reading Lacan" ' — and that's when I applied to library school."

"I don't know who Lacan is," he said.

"He's, well . . . You see, that's why I like libraries: No whats or whys. Just 'Where is it?' "

"And *where* are you from?" he asked, his face briefly animated by his own clever change of subject. "Originally?" There was, it seemed, a way of spotting those not native to the town. It was a college town, attractive and dull, and it hurried the transients along — the students, gypsies, visiting scholars and comics — with a motion not unlike peristalsis.

"Vermont," she said.

"Vermont!" Nick exclaimed, as if it were exotic, which made her glad she hadn't said something like Transylvania. He leaned toward her, confidentially. "I have to tell you: I own one chair from Ethan Allen."

"You do?" She smiled. "I won't tell anyone."

"Before that, however, I was in prison, and didn't own a stick."

"Really?" she asked. She sat back. Was he telling the truth? As a girl she'd been very gullible, but she had always learned more that way.

"I went to school here," he said. "In the sixties. I bombed a warehouse where the military was storing research supplies. I got twelve years." He paused, searching her eyes to see how she was doing, how *he* was doing. Then he fetched back his gaze, like a piece of jewelry he'd merely wanted to show her, quick. "There wasn't supposed to be anyone there. We'd checked it all out in advance, but this poor asshole named Lawrence Sperry — Larry Sperry! Christ, can you imagine having a name like that?"

"Sure," said Olena.

Nick looked at her suspiciously. "He was in there, working late. He lost a leg and an eye in the explosion. I got the federal pen in Winford. Attempted murder."

The thick coffee coated his lips. He had been looking steadily at her, but now he looked away.

"Would you like a bun?" asked Olena. "I'm going to go get a bun." She stood, but he turned and gazed up at her with such disbelief that she sat back down again, sloppily, sidesaddle. She twisted forward, leaned into the table. "I'm sorry. Is that all true, what you just said? Did that really happen to you?"

"*What?*" His mouth fell open. "You think I'd make that up?"

"It's just that, well, I work around a lot of literature," she said.

"Literature," he repeated.

She touched his hand. She didn't know what else to do. "Can I cook dinner for you some night? Tonight?"

There was a blaze in his eye, a concentrated seeing. He seemed for a moment able to look right into her, to know her in a way that was uncluttered by actually knowing her. He seemed to have no information or misinformation, only a kind of photography, factless but true.

"Yes," he said, "you can."

Which was how he came to spend the evening beneath the cheap stained-glass lamp of her dining room, its barroom red, its Schlitz-Tiffany light, and then to spend the night, and not leave.

Olena had never lived with a man before. "Except my father," she said, and Nick studied her eyes, the streak of blankness in them, when she said it. Though she had dated two different boys in college, they were the kind who liked to leave early, to eat breakfast without her, at smoky greasy spoons, to sit at the counter with large men in blue windbreakers, read the paper, get their cups refilled.

She had never been with anyone who had stayed. Anyone who had moved in his box of tapes, his Ethan Allen chair.

Anyone who had had lease problems at his old place.

"I'm trying to bring this thing together," he said, holding her in the middle of the afternoon. "My life, the campaign, my thing with you — I'm trying to get all my birds to land in the same yard." Out the window there was an afternoon moon like a golf ball, pocked and stuck. She looked at the calcified egg of it, its coin face, its blue neighborhood of nothing. Then she looked at him. There was the pond life again in his eyes, and in the rest of his face a hesitant, warm stillness.

"Do you like making love to me?" she asked, at night during a thunderstorm.

"Of course. Why do you ask?"

"Are you satisfied with me?"

He turned toward her, kissed her. "Yes," he said. "I don't need a show."

She was quiet for a long time. "People are giving shows?"

The rain and wind rushed down the gutters, snapped the branches of the weak trees in the side yard.

He had her inexperience and self-esteem in mind. At the movies, at the beginning, he whispered, "Twentieth Century Fox. Baby, that's you." During a slapstick part, in a library where card catalogues were upended and scattered wildly through the air, she broke into a pale, cold sweat, and he moved toward her, hid her head in his chest, saying, "Don't look, don't look." At the end they would sit through the long credits — gaffer, best boy, key grip. "That's what *we* need to get," he said. "A grip."

"Yes," she said. "And a negative cutter."

Other times he encouraged her to walk around the house naked. "If you got it, do it." He smiled, paused, feigned confusion. "If you do it, have it. If you flaunt it, do it."

"If you have it, got it," she added.

"If you say it, mean it." And he pulled her toward him like a dancing partner with soft shoes and the smiling mouth of love.

But too often she lay awake, wondering. There was something missing. Something wasn't happening to her — or was it to him? — while, all through the summer, thunderstorms set the sky on fire as she lay awake listening for the train sound of a tornado that never came, although the lightning ripped open the night and the trees were lit like things too suddenly remembered, then left indecipherable again in the dark.

"You're not feeling anything, are you?" he finally said. "What's wrong?"

"I'm not sure," she said cryptically. "The rainstorms are so loud in this part of the world." The wind from a storm blew through the screens and caused the door to the bedroom to slam shut. "I don't like a door to slam," she whispered. "It makes me think someone is mad."

At the library there were Romanian books coming in — Olena was to skim them, read them just enough to proffer a brief description for the catalogue listing. It dismayed her that her Romanian was so weak, that it had seemed almost to vanish, a mere handkerchief in a stairwell, and that daily now another book arrived to reprimand her.

She missed her mother the most.

On her lunch break she went to Nick's stand for a frozen yogurt. He looked tired, bedraggled, his hair like sprockets. "You want the Sperry Cherry or the Lemon Bomber?" he asked. These were his joke names, the ones he threatened really to use someday.

"How about apple?" she said.

He cut up an apple and arranged it in a paper dish. He squeezed yogurt from a chrome machine. "There's a fund-raiser tonight for the Teetlebaum campaign."

"Oh," she said. She had been to these fund-raisers before. At first she had liked them, glimpsing corners of the town she would never have seen otherwise, Nick leading her out into them, Nick knowing everyone, so her life seemed filled with possibility, with hopefulness. But finally she felt the events were too full of dreary, glad-handing people talking incessantly of their camping trips out West. They never really spoke to you. They spoke toward you. They spoke at you. They spoke on you, near you. They believed themselves crucial to the welfare of the community. They didn't read books. "At least they're *contributors to the community*," said Nick. "At least they're not sucking the blood of it —"

"Lapping," she said.

"What?"

"Gnashing and lapping. Not sucking."

He looked at her in a doubtful, worried way. "I looked it up once," she said.

"Whatever." He scowled. "At least they care. At least they're trying to give something back."

"I'd rather live in Russia," she said.

"I'll be back around ten or so," he said.

"You don't want me to come?" In truth, she wasn't very impressed with Ken Teetlebaum. Perhaps Nick had figured this out. Though Ken had the support of the local leftover left, there was something fatuous and vain about him. He tended to do little isometric leg exercises while you were talking to him. Often he took out a Woolworth's photo of himself and showed it to people. "Look at this," he'd say. "This was back when I had long hair. Can you believe it?" And people would look and see a handsome, teenaged boy who bore only a slight resemblance to the puffy Ken Teetlebaum of today. "Don't I look like Eric Clapton?"

"Eric Clapton would never have sat in a Woolworth's photo booth like some high school girl," Olena said, in the caustic blurt that sometimes afflicts the shy. Ken looked at her in a laughing, hurt sort of way, and after that he stopped showing the photo around.

"You can come if you want to." Nick reached up, smoothed his hair, and looked handsome again. "Meet me there."

The fund-raiser was in the upstairs room of a local restaurant called Dutch's. She paid ten dollars, went in, and ate a lot of raw cauliflower and hummus before she saw Nick back in a far corner talking to a woman in jeans and a brown blazer. She was the sort of woman that Nick might twist around to look at in restaurants: her fiery auburn hair cut bluntly in a pageboy. She had a pretty face, but the hair was too severe, too separate and tended-to. Olena herself had long, disorganized hair, and she wore it pulled back messily in a clip. When she reached up to wave to Nick, and he looked away without acknowledging her, back toward the auburn pageboy, she kept her hand up and moved it back, to fuss with the clip. She would never fit in here, she thought. Not among these jolly, activist-clerk types. She preferred the quiet poet-clerks of the library. They were delicate and territorial, intellectual, and physically unwell. They sat around at work, thinking up Tom Swifties: *I have to go to the hardware store, he said wrenchingly.*

Would you like a soda? he asked spritely.

They spent weekends at the Mayo Clinic. "An amusement park for hypochondriacs," said a cataloguer named Sarah. "A cross between Lourdes and 'The New Price Is Right,'" said someone else named George. These were the people she liked: the kind you couldn't really live with.

She turned to head toward the ladies' room and bumped into Ken. He gave her a hug hello, and then whispered in her ear, "You live with Nick. Help us think of an issue. I need another issue."

"I'll get you one at the issue store," she said, and pulled away as someone approached him with a heartily extended hand and a false, booming "Here's the man of the hour." In the bathroom she stared at her own reflection. In an attempt at extroversion, she had worn a tunic with large slices of watermelon depicted on the front. What had she been thinking of?

She went into the stall and slid the bolt shut. She read the graffiti on the back of the door: "Anita loves David S." "Christ + Diane W." It was good to see that even in a town like this people could love each other.

"Who were you talking to?" Olena asked Nick later, at home.

"Who? What do you mean?"

"The one with the plasticine hair."

"Oh, Erin? She does look like she does something to her hair. It looks like she hennas it."

"It looks like she tacks it against the wall and stands underneath it."

"She's head of the Bayre Corners Neighborhood Association. Come September we're really going to need her endorsement."

Olena sighed, looked away.

"It's the democratic process," said Nick.

"I'd rather have a king and queen," she said.

The following Friday, the night of the Fish-Fry Fund-Raiser at the Labor Temple, was the night Nick slept with Erin of the Bayre Corners Neighborhood Association. He arrived back home at seven in the morning and confessed to Olena, who, when Nick hadn't come home, had downed half a packet of Dramamine to get to sleep.

"I'm sorry," he said, his head in his hands. "It's a sixties thing."

"A sixties thing?" Olena was fuzzy, zonked from the Dramamine.

"You get all involved in a political event, and you find yourselves sleeping together. She's from that era, too. It's also that, I don't know, she just seems to really care about her community. She's got this reaching, expressive side to her. I got caught up in that." He was sitting down, leaning forward on his knees, talking to his shoes. The electric fan was blowing on him; his hair was moving gently, like weeds in water.

"A sixties thing?" Olena repeated. "A sixties thing, what is that — like 'Easy to Be Hard'?" It was the song she remembered best. But now something switched off in her. The bones in her chest hurt. Even the room seemed changed — brighter and awful. Everything had fled her, run away to become something else. She started to perspire under her arms, and her face grew hot. "You're a murderer," she said. "That's finally what you are. That's finally what you'll always be." She began to weep so loudly that Nick got up, closed the windows. Then he came back and held her — who else was there to hold her? — and she held him, too.

Nick bought Olena a large garnet ring, a cough drop set in brass. He did the dishes ten days in a row. She had a tendency to go to bed right after supper and sleep, heavily, needing the escape. She had become afraid of going out — restaurants, stores, the tension in her shoulders, the fear gripping her face when she was there, as if people knew she was a foreigner and a fool — and for fifteen additional days he did the cooking and shopping. His car was always parked on the outside of the driveway, and hers was always in first, close, blocked off, as if to indicate who most belonged to the community, to the world, and who most belonged tucked away from it, in a house. Perhaps in bed. Perhaps asleep.

"You need more life around you," said Nick, cradling her, though she'd gone stiff and still. His face was plaintive and suntanned, the notes and varnish of a violin. "You need a greater sense of life around you." Outside there was the old-rot smell of rain coming.

"How have you managed to get a suntan when there's been so much rain?" she asked.

"It's summer," he said. "I work outside, remember?"

"There are no sleeve marks," she said. "Where are you going?"

She had become afraid of the community. It was her enemy. Other people, other women.

She had, without realizing it at the time, learned to follow his gaze, learned to know his lust, and when she did go out, to work at least, his desires remained memorized within her. She looked at the attractive women he would look at. She turned to inspect the face that went with every pageboy haircut she saw from behind and passed in her car. She looked at them furtively or squarely — it didn't matter. She appraised their eyes and mouths and wondered about their bodies. She had become him: she longed for these women. But she was also herself, and so she despised them. She lusted after them, but she also wanted to beat them up.

A rapist.

She had become a rapist, driving to work in a car. But for a while it was the only way she could be.

She began to wear his clothes — a shirt, a pair of socks — to keep him next to her, to try to understand why he had done what he'd done. And in this new empathy, in this pants role, as if in an opera, she thought she understood what it was to make love to a woman, to open the hidden underside of her, a secret food, to thrust yourself up in her, to feel her arching and thrashing like a puppet, to watch her later when she got up and walked around without you, oblivious of the injury you'd done her (you'd surely done her). How could you not love her, gratefully, marveling?

She was so mysterious, so recovered, an unshared thought enli-
vening her eyes; you wanted to follow her forever.

A man in love. That was a man in love. So different from a
woman.

A woman cleaned up the kitchen. A woman gave and hid, gave
and hid, like someone with a May basket.

Olena made an appointment with a doctor. Her insurance covered her only if she went to the university hospital, so she made
an appointment there.

"I've made a doctor's appointment," she said to Nick, but he
had the water running in the tub and didn't hear her. "To find
out if there's anything wrong with me."

When he got out, he approached her with nothing on but a
towel. He pulled her close to his chest and lowered her to the
floor, right there in the hall by the bathroom door. Something
was swooping back and forth in an arc above her. Mayday, Mayday. She froze.

"What was that?" She pushed him away.

"What?" He rolled over on his back and looked.

Something was flying around in the stairwell — a bird.

"A bat," he said.

"Oh, my God!" cried Olena.

"The heat can bring them out in these old rental houses," he
said, standing and rewrapping his towel. "Do you have a tennis
racket?"

She showed him where it was. "I've only played tennis once,"
she said. "Do you want to play tennis sometime?" But he pro-
ceeded to stalk the bat in the dark stairwell.

"Now, don't get hysterical," he said.

"I'm already hysterical."

"Don't get — There!" he shouted, and she heard the *thwack* of
the racket against the wall, and the soft drop of the bat to the
landing.

She suddenly felt sick. "Did you have to kill it?" she said.

"What did you want me to do?"

"I don't know. Capture it. Rough it up a little." She felt guilty,
as if her own loathing had brought about its death. "What kind
of bat is it?" She tiptoed up to look, to try to glimpse its monkey

face, its cat teeth, its pterodactyl wings, like beet leaves. "What kind? Is it a fruit bat?"

"Looks pretty straight to me," said Nick. With his fist he tapped Olena's arm lightly, teasingly.

"Will you stop? Maybe it's a brown bat. It's not a vampire bat, is it?"

"I think you have to go to South America for those," he said. "Take your platform shoes!"

She sank down on the steps, pulled her robe tighter. She felt for the light switch and flicked it on. The bat, she could now see, was small and light-colored, its wings folded in like a packed tent — a mouse with backpacking equipment. It had a sweet face, like a deer's, though blood drizzled from its head. It reminded her of a cat she'd seen once as a child, shot in the eye with a BB.

"I can't look anymore," she said, and went back upstairs.

He appeared a half hour later, standing in the doorway. She was in bed, a book propped in her lap — a biography of a French feminist, which she was reading for the hairdo information.

"I had lunch with Erin today," he said.

Olena stared at the page. Snoods. Turbans and snoods. You could go for days in a snood. "Why?"

"A lot of different reasons. For Ken, mostly. Erin's still head of the neighborhood association, and he needs her endorsement. I just wanted to let you know. Listen, you've gotta cut me some slack."

Olena grew hot in the face again. "I've cut you some slack," she said. "I've cut you a whole forest of slack. The whole global slack forest has been cut for you." She closed the book. "I don't know why you cavort with these people. They're nothing but a bunch of clerks."

He'd been trying to look pleasant, but now he winced a little. "Oh, I see," he said. "Miss High-Minded. You whose father made his living off furs. Furs!" He took two steps toward her, then turned and paced back again. "I can't believe I'm living with someone who grew up on the proceeds of tortured animals!"

She was quiet. This lunge at moral fastidiousness was something she'd noticed a lot in the people around here. They were not good people. They were not kind. They played around and lied to their spouses. But they recycled their newspapers!

"Don't drag my father into this."

"Look, I've spent years of my life working for peace and free expression. I've been in prison already. I've lived in a cage! I don't need to live in another one."

"You and your free expression! You who can't listen to me for two minutes!"

"Listen to you what?"

"Listen to me when I" — here she bit her lip a little — "when I tell you that these people you care about, this hateful Erin What's-her-name, they're just small, awful, nothing people."

"So they don't read enough books," he said slowly. "Who the fuck cares?"

The next day Nick was off to a meeting with Ken at the Senior Citizens Association. The host from "Jeopardy!" was going to be there, and Ken wanted to shake a few hands, sign up volunteers. The host from "Jeopardy!" was going to give a talk.

"I don't get it," Olena said.

"I know." Nick sighed, the pond life treading water in his eyes. "But, well — it's the American way." He grabbed his keys, and the look that quickly passed over his face told her this: she wasn't pretty enough.

"I hate America," she said.

Nonetheless, he called her at the library during a break. She'd been sitting in the back with Sarah, thinking up Tom Swifties, her brain ready to bleed through her ears, when the phone rang. "You should see this," he said. "Some old geezer raises his hand, I call on him, and he stands up and the first thing he says is, 'I had my hand raised for ten whole minutes, and you kept passing over me. I don't like to be passed over. You can't just pass over a guy like me, not at my age.' "

Olena laughed, as Nick wanted her to.

This hot dog's awful, she said frankly.

"We've got all these signs up that say 'Teetlebaum for Tort Reform.' "

"Sounds like a Wallace Stevens poem," she said.

"Yeah. I don't know what I expected. But the swirl of this whole event has not felt right."

She's a real dog, he said cattily.

She was quiet, deciding to let him do the work of this call.

"Do you realize that Ken's entire softball team just wrote a letter to the *Star*, calling him a loudmouth and a cheat?"

"Well," she said, "what can you expect from a bunch of grown men who pitch underhand?"

There was some silence. "I care about us," he said finally. "I just want you to know that."

"O.K.," she said.

"I know I'm a pain in the ass to you," he said. "But you're an inspiration to me, you are."

I like a good sled dog, she said huskily.

"Thank you for just — for saying that," she said.

"I just sometimes wish you'd get involved in the community, help out with the campaign. Give of yourself. Connect a little with something."

At the hospital, Olena got up on the table and pulled the paper gown tight around her, her feet in the stirrups. The doctor took a plastic speculum out of a drawer. "Anything particular seem to be the problem today?" asked the doctor.

"I just want you to look and tell me if there's anything wrong," said Olena.

The doctor studied her carefully. "There's a class of medical students outside. Do you mind if they come in?"

"Excuse me?"

"You know this is a teaching hospital," she said. "We hope that our patients won't mind contributing to the education of our medical students by allowing them in during an examination. It's a way of contributing to the larger medical community, if you will. But it's totally up to you. You can say no."

Olena clutched at her paper gown. *There's never been an accident, she said recklessly.* "How many of them are there?"

The doctor smiled quickly. "Seven," she said. "Like dwarfs."

"They'll come in and do what?"

The doctor was growing impatient, looked at her watch. "They'll participate in the examination. It's a learning visit."

Olena sank back down on the table. She didn't feel that she could offer herself up this way. *You're only average, he said meanly.*

"All right," she said. "O.K."

Take a bow, he said sternly.

The doctor opened the door and called down the corridor. "Class?"

They were young, more than half of them men, and they gathered around the examination table in a horseshoe shape, looking slightly ashamed, sorry for her, no doubt, the way art students sometimes felt sorry for the shivering model they were about to draw. The doctor pulled up a stool between Olena's feet and inserted the plastic speculum — the stiff, widening arms of it uncomfortable, embarrassing. "Today we will be doing a routine pelvic examination," the doctor announced loudly, and then she got up again, went to a drawer, and passed out rubber gloves to everyone.

Olena went a little blind. A white light, starting at the center, spread to the black edges of her sight. One by one, the hands of the students entered her or pressed on her abdomen, felt hungrily, innocently, for something to learn from her, in her.

She missed her mother the most.

"Next," the doctor was saying. And then again. "All right. Next?"

Olena missed her mother the most.

But it was her father's face that suddenly loomed before her now; his face at night in the doorway of her bedroom, coming to check on her before he went to bed; his bewildered face, horrified to find her lying there beneath the covers, touching herself and gasping; his whispered "Nell? Are you O.K.?" and then his vanishing, closing the door loudly, to leave her there, finally forever — to die and leave her there feeling only her own sorrow and disgrace, which she would live in as if it were a coat.

There were rubber fingers in her, moving, wriggling around, but not like the others. She sat up abruptly, and the young student withdrew his hand, moved away. "He didn't do it right," she said to the doctor. She pointed at the student. "He didn't do it correctly!"

"All right, then," said the doctor, looking at Olena with concern and alarm. "All right. You may all leave," she said to the students.

The doctor herself found nothing. "You are perfectly normal," she said. But she suggested that Olena take Vitamin B and listen quietly to music in the evenings.

Olena staggered out through the hospital parking lot, not finding her car at first, and then, when she found it, strapping herself in tightly, as if she were something wild.

She went back to the library and sat at her desk. Everyone had gone home already. In the margins of her notepad she wrote, "alone as a book, alone as a desk, alone as a library, alone as a pencil, alone as a catalogue, alone as a number, alone as a notepad." Then she, too, left, went home, made herself tea. She felt separate from her body, felt herself dragging it up the stairs as if it were a big handbag, its leathery hollowness something you could cut up and give away, stick things in. She lay between the sheets of her bed, sweating, perhaps from the tea. The world felt over to her, used up, off to one side. There were no more names to live by.

One should live closer. She had lost her place, as in a book.

One should live closer to where one's parents were buried.

Waiting for Nick's return, she felt herself grow dizzy, float up toward the ceiling, and look down on the handbag. Tomorrow she would get an organ donor's card, an eye donor's card, as many cards as she could get. She would show them all to Nick. "Nick! Look at my cards!"

And, when he didn't come home, she remained awake through the long night, through the muffled thud of a bird's hurling itself against the window, through the thunder approaching and leaving like a voice, through the Frankenstein light of the storm. Over her house, in lieu of stars, she felt the bright heads of her mother and father, searching for her, their eyes beamed down from the sky.

"Oh, there you are," they said. "Oh, there you are."

But then they went away again, and she lay waiting, fist in her spine, for the grace and fatigue that would come — surely it must come — of having given so much to the world.

ALICE MUNRO

Carried Away

FROM THE NEW YORKER

Letters

IN THE DINING ROOM of the Commercial Hotel, Louisa opened
the letter that had arrived that day from overseas. She ate steak
and potatoes, her usual meal, and drank a glass of wine. There
were a few travelers in the room, and the dentist who ate there
every night because he was a widower. He had shown an interest
in her in the beginning but had told her he had never before
seen a woman touch wine or spirits.
"It is for my health," said Louisa gravely.
The white tablecloths were changed every week and in the
meantime were protected by oilcloth mats. In winter, the dining
room smelled of these mats wiped by a kitchen rag, and of coal
fumes from the furnace, and beef gravy and dried potatoes and
onions — a smell not unpleasant to anybody coming in hungry
from the cold. On each table was a little cruet stand with the bottle of brown sauce, the bottle of tomato sauce, and the pot of
horseradish.
The letter was addressed to "The Librarian, Carstairs Public
Library, Carstairs, Ontario." It was dated six weeks before —
January 4, 1917.
*Perhaps you will be surprised to hear from a person you don't know
and that doesn't remember your name. I hope you are still the same Librarian though enough time has gone by that you could have moved on.*
*What has landed me here in Hospital is not too serious. I see worse all
around me and get my mind off of all that by picturing things and won-*

*dering for instance if you are still there in the Library. If you are the one
I mean, you are about of medium size or perhaps not quite, with light
brownish hair. You came a few months before it was time for me to go in
the Army following on Miss Tamblyn who had been there since I first
became a user aged nine or ten. In her time the books were pretty much
every which way, and it was as much as your life was worth to ask her for
the least help or anything since she was quite a dragon. Then when you
came what a change, it was all put into sections of Fiction and Non-
Fiction and History and Travel and you got the magazines arranged in
order and put out as soon as they arrived, not left to molder away till
everything in them was stale. I felt gratitude but did not know how to
say so. Also I wondered what brought you there, you were an educated
person.*

*My name is Jack Agnew and my card is in the drawer. The last book I
took out was very good — H. G. Wells, Mankind in the Making. My
education was to Second Form in High School, then I went into Douds as
many did. I didn't join up right away when I was eighteen so you will not
see me as a Brave Man. I am a person tending to have my own ideas
always. My only relative in Carstairs, or anyplace, is my father Patrick
Agnew. He works for Douds not at the factory but at the house doing the
gardening. He is a lone wolf even more than me and goes out to the country fishing every chance he gets. I write him a letter sometimes but I doubt
if he reads it.*

After supper Louisa went up to the Ladies' Parlor on the second
floor, and sat down at the desk to write her reply.

*I am very glad to hear that you appreciated what I did in the Library,
though it was just the normal organization, nothing special.*

*I am sure you would like to hear news of home, but I am a poor person
for the job, being an outsider here. I do talk to people in the Library and
in the Hotel. The travelers in the Hotel mostly talk about how business is
(it is brisk if you can get the goods) and a little about sickness, and a lot
about the War. There are rumors on rumors and opinions galore, which
I'm sure would make you laugh if they didn't make you angry. I will not
bother to write them down because I am sure there is a Censor reading
this who would cut my letter to ribbons.*

*You ask how I came here. There is no interesting story. My parents are
both dead. My father worked for Eaton's in Toronto in the Furniture
Department, and after his death my mother worked there too in Linens.*

And I also worked there for a while in Books. Perhaps you could say Eaton's was our Douds'. I graduated from Jarvis Collegiate. I had some sickness which put me in hospital for a long time, but I am quite well now. I had a great deal of time to read, and my favorite authors are Thomas Hardy — who is accused of being gloomy but I think is very true to life — and Willa Cather. I just happened to be in this town when I heard the Librarian had died and I thought, perhaps that is the job for me.

•

A good thing your letter reached me today as I am about to be discharged from here and don't know if it would have been sent on to where I am going. I am glad you did not think my letter was too foolish.

If you run into my father or anybody you do not need to say anything about the fact we are writing to each other. It is nobody's business and I know there are plenty of people would laugh at me writing to the Librarian as they did at me going to the Library even, why give them the satisfaction?

I am glad to be getting out of here. So much luckier than some I see that will never walk or have their sight and will have to hide themselves away from the world.

You asked where did I live in Carstairs. Well, it was not anyplace to be proud of. If you know where Vinegar Hill is and you turned off on Flowers Road it is the last house on the right, yellow paint once upon a time. My father grows potatoes, or did. I used to take them around town with my wagon, and got five cents to keep for every load I sold.

You mention favorite authors. At one time I was fond of Zane Grey, but I drifted away from reading Fiction stories to reading History or Travel. I sometimes read books away over my head, I know, but I do get something out of them. H. G. Wells I mentioned is one and Robert Ingersoll who writes about religion. They have given me a lot to think about. If you are very religious I hope I have not offended you.

One day when I got to the Library it was a Saturday afternoon and you had just unlocked the door and were putting the lights on as it was dark and raining out. You had been caught out with no hat or umbrella and your hair had got wet. You took the pins out of it and let it come down. Is it too personal a thing to ask if you have it long still or have you cut it? You went over and stood by the radiator and shook your hair on it and the water sizzled like grease in the frying pan. I was sitting reading in the

Illustrated London News about the War. We exchanged a smile. (I didn't mean to say your hair was greasy when I wrote that!)

•

I have not cut my hair though I often think about it. I do not know if it is vanity or laziness that prevents me.
  I am not very religious.
  I walked up Vinegar Hill and found your house. The potatoes are looking healthy. A Police Dog disputed with me, is he yours?
  The weather is getting quite warm. We have had the flood on the river, which I gather is an annual Spring event. The water got into the Hotel basement and somehow contaminated our drinking supply so that we were given free beer or ginger ale. But only if we lived or were staying there. You can imagine there were plenty of jokes.
  I should ask if there is anything that I could send you.

•

I am not in need of anything particular. I get the tobacco and other bits of things the ladies in Carstairs do up for us. I would like to read some books by the authors you have mentioned but I doubt whether I would get the chance here.
  The other day there was a man died of a heart attack. It was the News of all time. Did you hear about the man who died of a heart attack? That was all you heard about day and night here. Then everybody would laugh which seems hard-hearted but it just seemed so strange. It was not even a hot time so you couldn't say maybe he was scared. (As a matter of fact he was writing a letter at the time so I had better look out.) Before and after him others have died being shot up or blown up but he is the famous one, to die of a heart attack. Everybody is saying what a long way to come and a lot of expense for the Army to go to, for that.

•

The summer has been so dry the watering tank has been doing the streets every day, trying to lay the dust. The children would dance along behind it. There was also a new thing in town — a cart with a little bell that went along selling ice cream, and the children were pretty attentive to this as well. It was pushed by the man who had an accident at the factory — you know who I mean, though I can't recall his name. He lost his arm to the elbow. My room at the Hotel, being on the third floor, was like an

*oven, and I often walked about till after midnight. So did many other
people, sometimes in pajamas. It was like a dream. There was still a little
water in the river, enough so that you could go out in a rowboat, and the
Methodist minister did that on a Sunday in August. He was praying for
rain in a public service. But there was a small leak in the boat and the
water came in and wet his feet, and eventually the boat sank and left him
standing in the water, which did not nearly reach his waist. Was it an
accident or a malicious trick? The talk was all that his prayers were answered but from the wrong direction.*

*I often pass the Douds' place on my walks. Your father keeps the lawns
and hedges looking beautiful. I like the house, so original and airy-look-
ing. But it may not have been cool even there, because I heard the voice
of the mother and little girl late at night as if they were out on the lawn.*

•

*Though I told you there is nothing I need, there is one thing I would like.
That is a photograph of you. I hope you will not think I am overstepping
the bounds to ask for it. Maybe you are engaged to somebody or have a
sweetheart over here you are writing to as well as me. You are a cut above
the ordinary and it would not surprise me if some Officer had spoken for
you. But now that I have asked I cannot take it back and will just leave it
up to you to think what you like of me.*

Louisa was twenty-five years old and had been in love once, with
a doctor she had known in the sanatorium. Her love was returned, eventually, costing the doctor his job. There was some
harsh doubt in her mind about whether he had been told to leave
the sanatorium or had left of his own accord, being weary of the
entanglement. He was married, he had children. Letters had
played a part that time, too. After he left, they were still writing
to one another. And they wrote once or twice after she was released. Then she asked him not to write anymore, and he didn't.
But the failure of his letters to arrive drove her out of Toronto
and made her take a traveling job. Then there would be only the
one disappointment in the week, when she got back on Friday or
Saturday night. Her last letter had been firm and stoical, and
some consciousness of herself as a heroine of love's tragedy went
with her around the country, as she hauled her display cases up
and down the stairs of small hotels, and talked about Paris styles

and said that her sample hats were bewitching, and drank her solitary glass of wine. If she'd had anybody to tell, though, she would have laughed at just that notion. She would have said love was all hocus-pocus, a deception, and she believed that. But at the prospect she still felt a hush, a flutter along the nerves, a bowing down of sense, a flagrant prostration.

She had a picture taken. She knew how she wanted it to be. She would have liked to wear a simple white blouse, a peasant girl's smock with the string open at the neck. She did not own a blouse of that description and in fact had seen them only in pictures. And she would have liked to let her hair down. Or if it had to be up, she would have liked it piled very loosely and bound with strings of pearls.

Instead she wore her blue silk shirtwaist and bound her hair as usual. She thought the picture made her look rather pale, hollow-eyed. Her expression was sterner and more forbidding than she had intended. She sent it anyway.

I am not engaged, and do not have a sweetheart. I was in love once and it had to be broken off. I was upset at the time but I knew I must bear it, and now I believe that it was all for the best.

She had racked her brains, of course, to remember him. She could not remember shaking out her hair, as he said she had done, or smiling at any young man when the raindrops fell on the radiator. He might as well have dreamed all that, and perhaps he had.

She began to follow the war in a more detailed way than she had done previously. She did not try to ignore it anymore. She went along the street with a sense that her head was filled with the same exciting and troubling information as everybody else's. Saint-Quentin, Arras, Montdidier, Amiens, and then there was a battle going on at the Somme River, where surely there had been one before? She spread open on her desk the maps of the war that appeared in the centerfolds of magazines. She saw in colored lines the German drive to the Marne, the first thrust of the Americans at Château-Thierry. She looked at the artist's brown pictures of a horse rearing up during an air attack, of some soldiers in East Africa drinking out of coconuts, and of a line of

German prisoners with bandaged heads or limbs and bleak, sullen expressions. Now she felt what everybody else did — a constant fear and misgiving and at the same time this addictive excitement. You could look up from your life of the moment and feel the world crackling beyond the walls.

I am glad to hear you do not have a sweetheart though I know that is selfish of me. I do not think you and I will ever meet again. I don't say that because I've had a dream about what will happen or am a gloomy person always looking for the worst. It just seems to me it is the most probable thing to happen, though I don't dwell on it and go along every day doing the best I can to stay alive. I am not trying to worry you or get your sympathy either but just explain how the idea I won't ever see Carstairs again makes me think I can say anything I want. I guess it's like being sick with a fever. So I will say I love you. I think of you up on a stool at the Library reaching to put a book away and I come up and put my hands on your waist and lift you down, and you turning around inside my arms as if we agreed about everything.

Every Tuesday afternoon the ladies and girls of the Red Cross met in the council chambers, which were just down the hall from the library. When the library was empty for a few moments Louisa went down the hall and entered the room full of women. She had decided to knit a scarf. At the sanatorium she had learned how to knit a basic stitch, but she had never learned, or had forgotten, how to cast on or off.

The older women were all busy packing boxes or cutting up and folding bandages from sheets of heavy cotton which were spread on the tables. But a lot of girls near the door were eating buns and drinking tea. One was holding a skein of wool on her arms for another to wind.

Louisa told them what she needed to know.

"So what do you want to knit, then?" said one of the girls, with some bun still in her mouth.

Louisa said, "A muffler. For a soldier."

"Oh, you'll want the regulation wool," another said, more politely, and jumped off the table. She came back with some balls of brown wool, and fished a spare pair of needles out of her bag, telling Louisa they could be hers.

"I'll just get you started," she said. "It's a regulation width, too."

Other girls gathered around and teased this girl, whose name was Corrie. They told her she was doing it all wrong.

"Oh, I am, am I?" said Corrie. "How would you like a knitting needle in your eye?" Then she said solicitously to Louisa, "Is it for a friend? A friend overseas?"

"Yes," said Louisa. Of course they would think of her as an old maid, they would laugh at her or feel sorry for her, according to which show they put on — of being brazen or kind.

"So knit up good and tight," said the one who had been eating a bun. "Knit up good and tight to keep him warm!"

One of the girls in this group was Grace Horne. She did not say anything. She was a shy but resolute-looking girl, nineteen years old, with a broad face, thin lips often pressed together, brown hair cut in a straight bang, and an attractively mature body. She had become engaged to Jack Agnew before he went overseas, but they had agreed not to say anything about it.

Spanish Flu

Louisa had made friends with some of the travelers who stayed regularly at the hotel. One of these was Jim Frarey, who sold typewriters and office equipment and books and all sorts of stationery supplies. He was a fair-haired, rather round-shouldered but strongly built man in his middle forties. You would think by the look of him that he sold something heavier and more important in the masculine world, like farm implements.

Jim Frarey kept traveling all through the Spanish flu epidemic, though you never knew then if stores would be open for business or not. Occasionally the hotels, too, would be closed, like the schools and movie houses and even — Jim Frarey thought this a scandal — the churches.

"They ought to be ashamed of themselves, the cowards," he said to Louisa. "What good does it do anybody to lurk around home and wait for it to strike? Now, you never closed the library, did you?"

Louisa said only when she herself had been sick. A mild case, hardly lasting a week, but of course she had to go to the hospital. They wouldn't let her stay in the hotel.

"Cowards," he said. "If you're going to be taken you'll be taken. Don't you agree?"

They discussed the crush in the hospitals, the deaths of doctors and nurses, the unceasing dreary spectacle of the funerals. Jim Frarey lived down the street from an undertaking establishment in Toronto. He said they still got out the black horses, the black carriage, the works, to bury such personages as warranted a fuss.

"Day and night they went on," he said. "Day and night." He raised his glass and said, "Here's to health, then. You look well yourself."

He thought that in fact Louisa was looking better than she used to. Maybe she had started putting on rouge. She had a pale olive skin, and it seemed to him that her cheeks used to be without color. She dressed with more dash, too, and took more trouble to be friendly. She used to be very on-again, off-again, just as she chose. She was drinking whiskey now, too, though she would not try it without drowning it in water. It used to be only a glass of wine. He wondered if it was a boyfriend that had made the difference. But a boyfriend might perk up her looks without increasing her interest in all and sundry, which was what he was pretty sure had happened. It was more likely time running out and the husband prospects being thinned out so dreadfully by the war. That could set a woman stirring. She was smarter and better company and better-looking, too, than most of the married ones. What happened with a woman like that? Sometimes just bad luck. Or bad judgment at a time when it mattered. A little too sharp and self-assured, in the old days, making the men uneasy?

"Life can't be brought to a standstill all the same," he said. "You did the right thing, keeping the library open."

This was in the early winter of 1919, when there had been a fresh outbreak of flu after the danger was supposed to be past. They seemed to be all alone in the hotel. It was only about nine o'clock but the hotelkeeper had gone to bed. His wife was in the hospital with the flu. Jim Frarey had brought the bottle of whiskey from the bar, which was closed for fear of contagion — and they sat at a table beside the window, in the dining room. A winter fog had collected outside and was pressing against the window. You could barely see the streetlights or the few cars that trundled cautiously over the bridge.

"Oh, it was not a matter of principle," Louisa said, "that I kept the library open. It was a more personal reason than you think."

Then she laughed and promised him a peculiar story. "Oh, the whiskey must have loosened my tongue," she said.

"I am not a gossip," said Jim Frarey.

She gave him a hard, laughing look and said that when people announced they weren't gossips, they almost invariably were. The same when they promised never to tell a soul.

"You can tell this where and when you like just as long as you leave out the real names and don't tell it around here," she said. "That I hope I can trust you not to do. Though at the moment I don't feel as if I cared. I'll probably feel otherwise when the drink wears off. It's a lesson, this story. It's a lesson in what fools women can make of themselves. 'So,' you say, 'what's new about that? You can learn it every day!' "

She began to tell him about a soldier who had started writing letters to her from overseas. The soldier remembered her from when he used to go into the library. But she didn't remember him. However, she replied in a friendly way to his first letter, and a correspondence sprang up between them. He told her where he had lived in the town and she walked past the house so that she could tell him how things looked there. He told her what books he'd read and she gave some of the same kind of information. In short, they both revealed something of themselves, and feelings warmed up on either side. On his side first, as far as any declarations went. She was not one to rush in like a fool. At first she thought she was simply being kind. Even later, she didn't want to reject and embarrass him. He asked for a picture. She had one taken; it was not to her liking, but she sent it. He asked if she had a sweetheart and she replied truthfully that she did not. He did not send any picture of himself nor did she ask for one, though of course she was curious as to what he looked like. It would be no easy matter for him to have a picture taken in the middle of a war. Furthermore, she did not want to seem like the sort of woman who would withdraw kindness if looks did not come up to scratch.

He wrote that he did not expect to come home. He said he was not so afraid of dying as he was of ending up like some of the men he had seen when he was in the hospital, wounded. He did not elaborate, but she supposed he meant the cases they were just getting to know about now — the stumps of men, the blinded, the ones made monstrous with burns. He was not whining about his fate, she did not mean to imply that. It was just that he expected to die and picked death over some other options, and he thought about her, and wrote to her as men do to a sweetheart in such a situation.

When the war ended, it was a while since she had heard from him. She went on expecting a letter every day, and nothing came. Nothing came. She was afraid that he might have been one of those unluckiest of soldiers — one of those killed in the last week, or on the last day, or even in the last hour. She searched the local paper every week, and the names of new casualties were still being printed there till after New Year's, but his was not among them. Now the paper began to list, as well, the names of those returning home, often printing a photo with the name, and a little account of rejoicing. When the soldiers were returning thick and fast there was less room for these additions. And then she saw his name, another name on the list. He had not been killed, he had not been wounded, he was coming home to Carstairs, perhaps he was already here.

It was then that she decided to keep the library open, though the flu was raging. Every day she was sure he would come, every day she was prepared for him. Sundays were a torment. When she entered the town hall she always felt he might be there before her, leaning up against the wall awaiting her arrival. She felt this so strongly that sometimes she mistook a shadow for a man. She understood now how people believed they had seen ghosts. Whenever the door opened she expected to look up into his face. Sometimes she made a pact with herself not to look up till she had counted to ten. Few people came in, because of the flu. She set herself jobs of rearranging things, else she would have gone mad. She never locked up until five or ten minutes after closing time. And then she fancied that he might be across the street on the post office steps, watching her, being too shy to make a move. She worried of course that he might be ill; she always sought in conversation for news of the latest cases. No one spoke his name.

It was at this time that she entirely gave up on reading. The covers of books looked like coffins to her, either shabby or ornate, and what was inside them might as well have been dust.

She had to be forgiven, didn't she — she had to be forgiven for thinking, after such letters, that the one thing that could never happen was that he wouldn't approach her, wouldn't get in touch with her at all? Never cross her threshold, after such avowals? Funerals passed by her window and she gave no thought to them, because they were not his. Even when she was sick in the hospital her only thought was that she must get back, she must get out of bed, the door must not stay locked against him. She staggered to her feet and back to work. On a hot afternoon she was arranging fresh newspapers on the racks, and his name jumped out at her like something in her feverish dreams.

She read a short notice of his marriage to a Miss Grace Horne. Not a girl she knew. Not a library user.

The bride wore fawn silk crepe with brown-and-cream piping, and a beige straw hat with brown velvet streamers.

There was no picture. Brown-and-cream piping. Such was the end, and had to be, to her romance.

But on her desk at the library, a matter of a few weeks ago, on a Saturday night after everybody had gone and she had locked the door and was turning out the lights, she discovered a scrap of paper. A few words written on it. *I was engaged before I went overseas.* No name, not his or hers. And there was her photograph, partly shoved under the blotter.

He had been in the library that very evening. It had been a busy time, she had often left the desk to find a book for somebody or to straighten up the papers or to put some books on the shelves. He had been in the same room with her, watched her, and taken his chance. But never made himself known.

I was engaged before I went overseas.

"Do you think it was all a joke on me?" Louisa said. "Do you think a man could be so diabolical?"

"In my experience, tricks like that are far more often indulged in by the women. No, no. Don't you think such a thing. Far more likely he was sincere. He got a little carried away. It's all just the way it looks on the surface. He was engaged before he went overseas, he never expected to get back in one piece but he did. And when he did, there is the fiancée waiting, what else could he do?"

"What indeed?" said Louisa.

"He bit off more than he could chew."

"Ah, that's so, that's so!" Louisa said. "And what was it in my case but vanity, which deserves to get slapped down!" Her eyes were glassy and her expression was roguish. "You don't think he'd had a good look at me any one time and thought the original was even worse than that poor picture, so he backed off?"

"I do not!" said Jim Frarey. "And don't you so belittle yourself."

"I don't want you to think I am stupid," she said. "I am not so stupid and inexperienced as that story makes me sound."

"Indeed, I don't think you are stupid at all."

"But perhaps you think I am inexperienced?"

This was it, he thought — the usual. Women after they have told one story on themselves cannot keep from telling another. Drink upsets them in a radical way, prudence is out the window.

She had confided in him once before that she had been a patient in a sanatorium. Now she told about being in love with a doctor there. The sanatorium was on beautiful grounds up on Hamilton Mountain, and they used to meet there along the hedged walks. Shelves of limestone formed the steps and in sheltered spots there were such plants as you do not commonly see in Ontario — azaleas, rhododendrons, magnolias. The doctor knew something about botany and he told her this was the Carolinian vegetation. Very different from here, lusher, and there were little bits of woodland, too, wonderful trees, paths worn under the trees. Tulip trees.

"Tulips!" said Jim Frarey. "Tulips on the trees!"

"No, no, it is the shape of their leaves!"

She laughed at him challengingly, then bit her lip. He saw fit to continue the dialogue, saying, "Tulips on the trees!" while she said, No, it is the leaves that are shaped like tulips, no, I never said that, stop! So they passed into a state of gingerly evaluation — which he knew well and could only hope she did — full of small, pleasant surprises, half-sardonic signals, a welling up of impudent hopes, and a fateful sort of kindness.

"All to ourselves," Jim Frarey said. "Never happened before, did it? Maybe it never will again."

She let him take her hands, half lift her from her chair. He turned out the dining room lights as they went out. Up the stairs

they went, that they had so often climbed separately. Past the picture of the dog on his master's grave, and Highland Mary singing in the field, and the old king with his bulgy eyes, his look of
indulgence and repletion.

"It's a foggy, foggy night, and my heart is in a fright," Jim
Frarey was half singing, half humming, as they climbed. He kept
an assured hand on Louisa's back. "All's well, all's well," he said
as he steered her round the turn of the stairs. And when they
took the narrow flight of steps to the third floor he said, "Never
climbed so close to heaven in this place before!"

But later in the night Jim Frarey gave a concluding groan and
roused himself to deliver a sleepy scolding. "Louisa, Louisa, why
didn't you tell me that was the way it was?"

"I told you everything," said Louisa in a faint and drifting
voice.

"I got a wrong impression, then," he said. "I never intended
for this to make a difference to you."

She said that it hadn't. Now, without him pinning her down
and steadying her, she felt herself whirling around in an irresist-
ible way, as if the mattress had turned into a child's top and were
carrying her off. She tried to explain that the traces of blood on
the sheets could be credited to her period, but her words came
out with a luxurious nonchalance and could not be fitted together.

Accidents

When Arthur came home from the factory, a little before noon,
he shouted, "Stay out of my way till I wash! There's been an accident over at the works!" Nobody answered. Mrs. Groves, the
housekeeper, was in the kitchen talking on the telephone so
loudly that she could not hear him, and his daughter was, of
course, at school. He washed, and stuffed everything he had
been wearing into the hamper, and scrubbed up the bathroom,
like a murderer. He started out clean, with even his hair slicked
and patted, to drive to the man's house. He had had to ask where
it was. He thought it was up Vinegar Hill but they said no, that
was the father — the young fellow and his wife live on the other

side of town, past where the Apple Evaporator used to be, before the war.

He found the two brick cottages side by side, and picked the left-hand one, as he'd been told. It wouldn't have been hard to pick which house, anyway. News had come before him. The door to the house was open, and children too young to be in school yet hung about in the yard. A small girl sat on a kiddie car, not going anywhere, just blocking his path. He stepped around her. As he did so an older girl spoke to him in a formal way — a warning. "Her dad's dead. Hers!"

A young woman came out of the front room carrying an armload of curtains, which she gave to another woman standing in the hall. The woman who received the curtains was gray-haired, with a pleading face. She had no upper teeth. She probably took her plate out, for comfort, at home. The woman who passed the curtains to her was stout but young, with fresh skin.

"You tell her not to get up on that stepladder," the gray-haired woman said to Arthur. "She's going to break her neck taking down curtains. She thinks we need to get everything washed. Are you the undertaker? Oh, no, excuse me! You're Mr. Doud. Grace, come out here! Grace! It's Mr. Doud!"

"Don't trouble her," Arthur said.

"She thinks she's going to get the curtains all down and washed and up again by tomorrow, because he's going to have to go in the front room. She's my daughter. I can't tell her anything."

"She'll quiet down presently," said a somber but comfortable-looking man in a clerical collar, coming through from the back of the house. Their minister. But not from one of the churches Arthur knew. Baptist? Pentecostal? Plymouth Brethren? He was drinking tea.

Some other woman came and briskly removed the curtains. "We got the machine filled and going," she said. "A day like this, they'll dry like nobody's business. Just keep the kids out of here."

The minister had to stand aside and lift his teacup high, to avoid her and her bundle. He said, "Aren't any of you ladies going to offer Mr. Doud a cup of tea?"

Arthur said, "No, no, don't trouble."

"The funeral expenses," he said to the gray-haired woman. "If you could let her know —"

"Lillian wet her pants!" said a triumphant child at the door. "Mrs. Agnew! Lillian peed her pants!"

"Yes," said the minister. "Yes, they will be very grateful."

"The plot and the stone, everything," Arthur said. "You'll make sure they understand that. Whatever they want on the stone."

The gray-haired woman had gone out into the yard. She came back with a squalling child in her arms. "Poor lamb," she said. "They told her she wasn't supposed to come in the house, so where could she go? What could she do but have an accident!"

The young woman came out of the front room dragging a rug. "I want this put on the line and beat," she said.

"Grace, here is Mr. Doud come to offer his condolences," the minister said.

"And to ask if there is anything I can do," said Arthur.

The gray-haired woman started upstairs with the wet child in her arms and a couple of others following.

Grace spotted them. "Oh, no, you don't! You get back outside!"

"My mom's in here."

"Yes, and your mom's good and busy, she don't need to be bothered with you. She's here helping me out. Don't you know Lillian's dad's dead?"

"Is there anything I can do for you?" Arthur said, meaning to clear out.

Grace stared at him with her mouth open. Sounds of the washing machine filled the house.

"Yes, there is," she said. "You wait here."

"She's overwhelmed," the minister said. "It's not that she means to be rude."

Grace came back with a load of books. "These here," she said. "He had them out of the library. I don't want to have to pay fines on them. He went every Saturday night, so I guess they are due back tomorrow. I don't want to get in trouble about them."

"I'll look after them," Arthur said. "I'd be glad to."

"I just don't want to get in any trouble about them."

"Mr. Doud was saying about taking care of the funeral," the minister said to her, gently admonishing. "Everything including the stone. Whatever you want on the stone."

"Oh, I don't want anything fancy," Grace said.

*

"On Friday morning last there occurred in the sawmill operation of Douds' Factory a particularly ghastly and tragic accident. Mr. Jack Agnew, in reaching under the main shaft, had the misfortune to have his sleeve caught by a setscrew in an adjoining flunge, so that his arm and shoulder were drawn under the shaft. His head in consequence was brought in contact with the circular saw, that saw being about one foot in diameter. In an instant the unfortunate young man's head was separated from his body, being severed at an angle below the left ear and through the neck. His death is believed to have been instantaneous. He never spoke or uttered a cry so it was not by any sound of his but by the spurt and shower of his blood that his fellow workers were horribly alerted to the disaster."

This account was reprinted in the paper a week later, for those who might have missed it or who wished to have an extra copy to send to friends or relations out of town (particularly to people who used to live in Carstairs and did not anymore). The misspelling of "flange" was corrected the next week. There was a note apologizing for the mistake. There was also a description of a very large funeral, attended even by people from neighboring towns and as far away as Walley. They came by car and train, and some by horse and buggy. They had not known Jack Agnew when he was alive, but, as the paper said, they wished to pay tribute to the sensational and tragic manner of his death. All the stores in Carstairs were closed for two hours that afternoon. The hotel did not close its doors, but that was because all the visitors needed somewhere to eat and drink.

The survivors were a wife, Grace, and a four-year-old daughter, Lillian. The victim had fought bravely in the Great War and had been wounded only once, not seriously. Many had commented on this irony.

The paper's failure to mention a surviving father was not deliberate. The editor of the paper was not a native of Carstairs, and people forgot to tell him about the father until it was too late.

The father himself did not complain about the omission. The day of the funeral was very fine, and he headed out of town as he would have done ordinarily on a day he had decided not to spend at Douds'. He was wearing a felt hat and a long coat that would do for a rug if he wanted to take a nap. His overshoes were neatly held on his feet with the rubber rings from sealing jars. He was going out to fish for suckers. The season hadn't opened yet, but he always managed to be a bit ahead of it. He fished through the spring and early summer and cooked and ate what he caught. He had a frying pan and a pot hidden out on the riverbank. The pot was for boiling corn that he snatched out of the fields later in the year, when he was also eating the fruit of wild apple trees and grapevines. He was quite sane but abhorred conversation. He could not altogether avoid it in the weeks following his son's death, but he had a way of cutting it short.

"Should've watched out what he was doing."

Walking in the country that day, he met another person who was not at the funeral. A woman. She did not try to start any conversation and in fact seemed as fierce in her solitude as himself, whipping the air past her with long fervent strides.

The factory stretched along the west side of town, like a medieval town wall. There were two long buildings like the inner and outer ramparts, with a closed-in bridge between them where the main offices were. And reaching up into the town and the streets of workers' houses were the kilns and the sawmill and the lumberyard and storage sheds. The factory whistle dictated the time for many to get up, blowing at six o'clock in the morning. It blew again for work to start, at seven, and at twelve for dinnertime, and at one in the afternoon for work to recommence, and then at five-thirty for the men to lay down their tools and go home.

Rules were posted beside the time clock, under glass. The first two rules were:

ONE MINUTE LATE IS FIFTEEN MINUTES PAY. BE PROMPT.

DON'T TAKE SAFETY FOR GRANTED. WATCH OUT FOR YOURSELF AND THE NEXT MAN.

There had been accidents in the factory and, in fact, a man had been killed when a load of lumber fell on him. That had happened before Arthur's time. And once, during the war, a man had lost an arm, or part of an arm. On the day that happened Arthur was away in Toronto. So he had never seen an accident — nothing serious, anyway. But it was often at the back of his mind now, that something might happen.

Perhaps he no longer felt so sure that trouble wouldn't come near him as he had before his wife died. She had died in 1919, in the last flurry of the Spanish flu, when everyone had got over being frightened. Even she had not been frightened. That was nearly five years ago and it still seemed to Arthur like the end of a carefree time in his life. But to other people he had always seemed very responsible and serious — nobody had noticed much difference in him.

In his dreams of an accident there was a spreading silence, everything was shut down. Every machine in the place stopped making its customary noise and every man's voice was removed, and when Arthur looked out of the office window he understood that doom had fallen. He never could remember any particular thing that he saw that told him this. It was just the space, the dust in the factory yard, that said to him *now*.

The books stayed on the floor of his car for a week or so. His daughter, Bea, said, "What are those books doing here?" And then he remembered.

Bea read out the titles and the authors. *Sir John Franklin and the Romance of the Northwest Passage,* by G. B. Smith. *What's Wrong with the World,* G. K. Chesterton. *The Taking of Quebec,* Archibald Hendry. *The Practice and Theory of Bolshevism,* by Lord Bertrand Russell.

"Bol-*shev*-ism," Bea said, and Arthur told her how to pronounce it correctly. She asked what it was, and he said, "It's something they've got in Russia that I don't understand so well myself. But from what I hear of it, it's a disgrace."

Bea was thirteen at this time. She had heard about the Russian ballet and also about dervishes. She believed for the next couple of years that Bolshevism was some sort of diabolical and maybe indecent dance. At least this was the story she told when she was grown up.

She did not mention that the books were connected with the man who had had the accident. That would have made the story less amusing. Perhaps she had really forgotten.

The librarian was perturbed. The books still had their cards in them, which meant they had never been checked out, just removed from the shelves and taken away.

"The one by Lord Russell has been missing a long time."

Arthur was not used to such reproofs, but he said, mildly, "I am returning them on behalf of somebody else. The chap who was killed. In the accident at the factory."

The librarian had the Franklin book open. She was looking at a picture of the boat trapped in the ice.

"His wife asked me to," Arthur said.

She picked up each book separately, and shook it, as if she expected something to fall out. She ran her fingers between the pages. The bottom part of her face was working in an unsightly way, as if she was chewing at the inside of her cheeks.

"I guess he just took them home as he felt like it," Arthur said.

"I'm sorry?" she said in a minute. "What did you say? I'm sorry."

It was the accident, he thought. The idea that the man who had died in such a way had been the last person to open these books, turn these pages. The thought that he might have left a bit of his life in them, a scrap of paper or a pipe cleaner as a marker, or even a few shreds of tobacco. That unhinged her.

"No matter," he said. "I just dropped by to bring them back."

He turned away from her desk but did not immediately leave the library. He had not been in it for years. There was his father's picture between the two front windows, where it would always be.

"A. V. Doud, Founder of the Doud Organ Factory and Patron of This Library. A Believer in Progress, Culture, and Education. A True Friend of the Town of Carstairs and of the Working Man."

The librarian's desk was in the archway between the front and back rooms. The books were on shelves set in rows in the back room. Green-shaded lamps, with long pull cords, dangled down in the aisles between. Arthur remembered years ago some matter brought up at the council meeting about buying sixty-watt bulbs instead of forty. This librarian was the one who had requested that, and they had done it.

In the front room, there were newspapers and magazines on wooden racks, and some round heavy tables, with chairs, so that people could sit and read, and rows of thick, dark books behind glass. Dictionaries, probably, and atlases and encyclopedias. Two handsome high windows looking out on the main street, with Arthur's father hanging between them. Other pictures around the room hung too high, and were too dim and crowded with figures for the person down below to interpret them easily. (Later, when Arthur had spent many hours in the library and had discussed these pictures with the librarian, he knew that one of them represented the Battle of Flodden Field, with the King of Scotland charging down the hill into a pall of smoke, one the funeral of the Boy King of Rome, and one the Quarrel of Oberon and Titania, from *A Midsummer Night's Dream*.)

He sat down at a reading table, where he could look out the window. He picked up an old copy of *The National Geographic* which was lying there. He had his back to the librarian. He thought this the tactful thing to do, since she seemed somewhat wrought up. Other people came in, and he heard her speak to them. Her voice sounded normal enough now. He kept thinking he would leave, but did not.

He liked the high bare window full of the light of the spring evening, and he liked the dignity and order of these rooms. He was pleasantly mystified by the thought of grown people coming and going here, steadily reading books. Week after week, one book after another, a whole life long. He himself read a book once in a while, when somebody recommended it, and usually he enjoyed it, and then he read magazines, to keep up with things, and never thought about reading a book until another one came along, in this almost accidental way. There would be little spells when nobody was in the library but himself and the librarian.

During one of these she came over and stood near him, replacing some newspapers on the rack. When she finished doing this she spoke to him, with a controlled urgency.

"The account of the accident that was printed in the paper — I take it that was more or less accurate?"

Arthur said that it was possibly too accurate.

"Why? Why do you say that?"

He mentioned the public's endless appetite for horrific details. Ought the paper to pander to that?

"Oh, I think it's natural," the librarian said. "I think it's natural, to want to know the worst. People do want to picture it. I do myself. I am very ignorant of machinery. It's hard for me to imagine what happened. Even with the paper's help. Did the machine do something unexpected?"

"No," Arthur said. "It wasn't the machine grabbing him and

pulling him in, like an animal. He made a wrong move or at any rate a careless move. Then he was done for."

She said nothing but did not move away.

"You have to keep your wits about you," Arthur said. "Never let up for a second. A machine is your servant and it is an excellent servant, but it makes an imbecile master."

He wondered if he had read that somewhere or had thought it up himself.

"And I suppose there are no ways of protecting people?" the librarian said. "But you must know all about that."

She left him then. Somebody had come in.

The accident was followed by a rush of warm weather. The length of the evenings and the heat of the balmy days seemed sudden and surprising, as if this were not the way winter finally ended in that part of the country, almost every year. The sheets of floodwater shrank magically back into the bogs and the leaves shot out of the reddened branches and barnyard smells drifted into town and were wrapped in the smell of lilacs.

Instead of wanting to be outdoors on such evenings, Arthur found himself thinking of the library, and he would often end up there, sitting in the spot he had chosen on his first visit. He would sit for half an hour, or an hour. He looked at the *Illustrated London News*, or *The National Geographic*, or *Saturday Night*, or *Collier's*. All of these magazines arrived at his own house, and he could have been sitting there, in the den, looking out at his hedged lawns, which old Agnew kept in tolerable condition, and the flower beds now full of tulips of every vivid color and combination. It seemed that he preferred the view of the main street, where the occasional brisk-looking new Ford went by, or some stuttering older model car with a dusty cloth top. He preferred the post office, with its clock tower telling four different times in four different directions — and, as people liked to say, all wrong. Also the passing and loitering on the sidewalk. People trying to get the drinking fountain to work, although it wasn't turned on till the first of July.

It was not that he felt the need of sociability. He was not there for chat, though he would greet people if he knew them by name, and he did know most. And he might exchange a few words with the librarian, though often it was only "Good evening" when he came in, and "Good night" when he went out. He made no demands on anybody. He felt his presence to be genial, reassuring, and, above all, natural. By sitting here, reading and reflecting, here instead of at home, he seemed to himself to be providing something. People could count on it.

There was an expression he liked. *Public servant.* His father, who looked out at him here with tinted baby pink cheeks and glassy blue eyes and an old man's petulant mouth, had never thought of himself so. He had thought of himself more as a public character and benefactor. He had operated by whims and decrees, and he had got away with it. He would go around the factory when business was slow, and say to one man and another, "Go home. Go on home now. Go home and stay there till I can use you again." And they would go. They would work in their gardens or go out shooting rabbits and run up bills for whatever they had to buy, and accept that it couldn't be otherwise. It was still a joke with them, to imitate his bark. *Go on home!* He was their hero more than Arthur could ever be, but they were not prepared to take the same treatment today. During the war they had got used to the good wages and to being always in demand. They never thought of the glut of labor the soldiers had created when they came home, never thought about how a business like this was kept going by luck and ingenuity from one year to the next, even from one season to the next. They didn't like changes — they were not happy about the switch now to player pianos, which Arthur believed were the hope of the future. But Arthur would do what he had to, though his way of proceeding was quite the opposite of his father's. Think everything over and then think it over again. Stay in the background except when you have to come forward. Keep your dignity. Try always to be fair.

They expected all to be provided. The whole town expected it. Work would be provided just as the sun would rise in the mornings. And the taxes on the factory were raised, too, and rates were charged for the water that used to come free. Maintenance of the access roads was now the factory's responsibility instead of the town's. The Methodist church requesting a hefty sum to build the new Sunday school. The town hockey team needing new uniforms. The stone gateposts for the War Memorial Park. And every year the smartest boy in the senior class to be sent to university, courtesy of Douds'.

Ask, and ye shall receive.

Expectations at home were not lacking, either. Bea was agitating to go away to private school and Mrs. Groves had her eye on some new mixing apparatus for the kitchen, also a new washing machine. All the trim on the house was due to be painted this year. All that wedding-cake decoration that consumed paint by the gallon. And in the midst of this what had Arthur done but order himself a new car — a Chrysler sedan.

It was necessary, he had to drive a new car. He had to drive a new car, Bea had to go away to school, Mrs. Groves had to have the latest, and the trim had to be as fresh as Christmas snow. Else they would lose respect, they would lose confidence, they would start to wonder if things were going downhill. And it could be managed — with luck it could all be managed.

For years after his father's death, he had felt like an impostor. Not steadily, but from time to time, he had felt that. And now the feeling was gone. It was gone. He could sit here and feel that it was gone.

He had been in the office when the accident happened, consulting with a veneer salesman. Some change in noise registered with him, but it was more of an increase than a hush. It was nothing that alerted him — just an irritation. Because it happened in the sawmill, nobody knew about the accident immediately in the shops or in the kilns or in the yard, and work in some places continued for several minutes. In fact Arthur, bending over the veneer samples on his desk, might have been one of the last people to understand that there had been an intervention. He asked the salesman a question, and the salesman did not answer. Arthur looked up and saw the man's mouth open, his face frightened, his salesman's assurance wiped away.

Then he heard his own name being called — both "Mr. Doud!," as was customary, and "Arthur, Arthur!" by such of the older men as had known him as a boy. Also he heard "saw" and "head" and "Jesus, Jesus, Jesus!"

Arthur could have wished for the silence, the sounds and objects drawing back in that dreadful but releasing way to give him room. It was nothing like that. Yelling and questioning and running around, himself in the midst being propelled to the sawmill. One man had fainted, falling in such a way that if they had not got the saw turned off a moment before, it would have got him, too. It was his body, fallen but entire, that Arthur briefly mistook for the body of the victim. Oh no, no. They pushed him on. The sawdust was scarlet. It was drenched, brilliant. The pile of lumber here was all merrily spattered, and the blades. A heap of work clothes soaked in blood lay in the sawdust, and Arthur realized that it was the body, the trunk with limbs attached. So much blood had flowed as to make its shape not plain at first — to soften it, like a pudding.

The first thing he thought of was to cover that. He took off his jacket and did so. He had to step up close, his shoes squished in it. The reason no one else had done that was simply that no one else was wearing a jacket.

"Have they gone a-get the doctor?" somebody was yelling. "Gone a-get the doctor!" a man quite close to Arthur said. "Can't sew his head back on, doctor. Can he?"

But Arthur gave the order to get the doctor — he imagined it was necessary. You can't have a death without a doctor. That set the rest in motion. Doctor, undertaker, coffin, flowers, preacher. Get started on all that, give them something to do. Shovel up the sawdust, clean up the saw. Send the men who had been close by to wash themselves. Carry the man who had fainted to the lunchroom. Is he all right? Tell the office girl to make tea.

Brandy was what was needed, or whiskey. But he had a rule against it, on the premises.

Something still lacking. Where was it? There, they said. Over there, Arthur heard the sound of vomiting, not far away. All right. Either pick it up or tell somebody to pick it up. The sound of vomiting saved him, steadied him, gave him an almost lighthearted determination. He picked it up. He carried it delicately and securely as you might carry an awkward but valuable jug. Pressing the face out of sight, as if comforting it, against his chest. Blood seeped through his shirt and stuck the material to his skin. Warm. He felt like a wounded man. He was aware of them watching him, and he was aware of himself as an actor must be, or a priest. What to do with it, now that he had it against his chest? The answer to that came, too. Set it down, put it back where it belongs, not, of course, fitted with exactness, not as if a seam could be closed. Just more or less in place, and lift the jacket and tug it into a new position.

He couldn't now ask the man's name. He would have to get it

in some other way. After the intimacy of his services here, such ignorance would be an offense.

But he found he did know it, it came to him. As he edged the corner of his jacket over the ear that had lain and still lay upward, and so looked quite fresh and usable, he received a name. Son of the fellow who came and did the garden, who was not always reliable. A young man taken on again when he came back from the war. Married? He thought so. He would have to go and see her. As soon as possible. Clean clothes.

The librarian often wore a dark red blouse. Her lips were reddened to match, and her hair was bobbed. She was not a young woman anymore, but she maintained an eye-catching style. He remembered that when they had hired her, years ago, he had thought that she got herself up very soberly. Her hair was not bobbed in those days — it was wound around her head, in the old style. It was still the same color — a warm and pleasant color, like leaves — oak leaves, say — in the fall. He tried to think how much she was paid. Not much, certainly. She kept herself looking well on it. And where did she live? In one of the boarding houses — the one with the schoolteachers? No, not there. She lived in the Commercial Hotel.

And now something else was coming to mind. No definite story that he could remember. You could not say with any assurance that she had a bad reputation. But it was not quite a spotless reputation, either. She was said to take a drink with the travelers. Perhaps she had a boyfriend among them. A boyfriend or two.

Well, she was old enough to do as she liked. It wasn't quite the same as it was with a teacher — hired partly to set an example. As long as she did her job well — and anybody could see that she did. She had her life to live, like everyone else. Wouldn't you rather have a nice-looking woman in here than a crabby old affair like Mary Tamblyn? Strangers might drop in, they judge a town by what they see, you want a nice-looking woman with a nice manner.

Stop that. Who said you didn't? He was arguing in his head on her behalf just as if somebody had come along who wanted her chucked out, and he had no intimation at all that that was the case.

What about her question, on the first evening, regarding the machine? What did she mean by that? Was it a sly way of bringing blame?

He had talked to her about the pictures and the lighting and even told her how his father had sent his own workmen over here, paid them to build the library shelves, but he had never again spoken of the man who had taken the books out without letting her know. One at a time, probably. Under his coat? Brought back the same way. He must have brought them back, or else he'd have had a houseful, and his wife would never stand for that. Not stealing, except temporarily. Harmless behavior, but peculiar. Was there any connection? Between thinking you could do things a little differently that way, and thinking you could get away with a careless move, which might catch your sleeve, and bring the saw down on your neck?

There might be, there might be some connection. A matter of attitude.

"That chap — you know the one — the accident —" he said to the librarian one evening. "The way he took off with the books he wanted. Why do you think he did that?"

"People do things," the librarian said. "They tear out pages. On account of something they don't like or something they do. They just do things. I don't know."

"Did he ever tear out some pages? Did you ever give him a lecture? Ever make him scared to face you?"

He meant to tease her a little, implying that she would not be likely to scare anybody, but she did not take it that way.

"How could I when I never spoke to him?" she said. "I never saw him. I never saw him, to know who he was."

She moved away, putting an end to the conversation. So, she did not like to be teased. Was she one of those people full of mended cracks that you could see only close up? Some old misery troubling her, some secret? Maybe a sweetheart had been lost in the war.

On a later evening, a Saturday in the summer, she brought the subject up herself, that he would never have mentioned again.

"Do you remember our talking once about the man who had the accident?"

Arthur said he did.

"I have something to ask you, and you may think it strange."

He nodded.

"And my asking it — I want you to — It is confidential."

"Yes, indeed," he said.

"What did he look like?"

Look like? Arthur was puzzled. He was puzzled by her making such a fuss and secret about it — surely it was natural to be interested in what a man might look like who had been coming in and making off with her books without her knowing about it — and because he could not help her he shook his head. He could not bring any picture of Jack Agnew to mind.

"Tall," he said. "I believe he was on the tall side. Otherwise I cannot tell you. I am really not such a good person to ask. I can recognize a man easily, but I can't ever give much of a physical description of them, even when it's someone I see on a daily basis."

"But I thought you were the one — I heard you were the one —" she said. "Who picked him up. His head."

Arthur said, stiffly, "I didn't think that you could just leave it lying there." He felt disappointed in the woman, uneasy and ashamed for her. But he tried to speak matter-of-factly, keeping reproach out of his voice. "I could not even tell you the color of his hair. It was all — all pretty much obliterated, by that time."

She said nothing for a moment or two and he did not look at her. Then she said, "It must seem as if I am one of those people — one of those people who are fascinated by these sorts of things."

Arthur made a protesting noise, but it did, of course, seem to him that she must be like that.

"I should not have asked you," she said. "I should not have mentioned it. I can never explain to you why I did. I would like just to ask you, if you can help it, never to think that that is the kind of person I am."

Arthur heard the word *never*. She could never explain to him. He was never to think. In the midst of his disappointment he picked up this suggestion, that their conversations were to continue, and perhaps on a less haphazard basis. He heard a humility in her voice, but it was a humility that was based on some kind of assurance. Surely that was sexual.

Or did he think so only because this was the evening it was? It was the Saturday evening in the month when he usually went to Walley. He was going there tonight, he had only dropped in here on his way, he had not meant to stay as long as he had done. It was the night when he went to visit a woman whose name was Jane MacFarlane. Jane MacFarlane lived apart from her husband, but she was not thinking of getting a divorce. She had no children. She earned her living as a dressmaker. Arthur had first met her when she came to his house to make clothes for his wife. Nothing had gone on at that time, and neither of them had thought of it. In some ways Jane MacFarlane was a woman like the librarian — good-looking, though not so young; plucky and stylish and good at her work. In other ways, not so like. He could not imagine Jane ever presenting a man with a mystery and following that up with the information that it would never be solved. Jane was a woman to give a man peace. The submerged dialogue he had with her — sensual, limited, kind — was very like the one he had had with his wife.

The librarian went to the switch by the door, and turned out the main light. She locked the door. She disappeared among the shelves, turning out the lights there, too, in a leisurely way. The town clock was striking nine. She must think that it was right. His own watch said three minutes to.

It was time to get up, time for him to leave, time to go to Walley.

When she had finished dealing with the lights she came and sat down at the table beside him.

He said, "I would never think of you in any way that would make you unhappy."

Turning out the lights shouldn't have made it so dark. They were in the middle of summer. But it seemed that heavy rain clouds had moved in. When Arthur had last paid attention to the street he had seen plenty of daylight left; country people shopping; boys squirting each other at the drinking fountain; and young girls walking up and down in their soft, cheap, flowery summer dresses, letting the young men watch them from wherever the young men congregated — the post office steps, the front of the feedstore. And now that he looked again he saw the street in an uproar from the loud wind that already carried a few drops of rain. The girls were shrieking and laughing and hold-

ing their purses over their heads as they ran to shelter; store
clerks were rolling up awnings and hauling in the baskets of
fruit, the racks of summer shoes, the garden implements that
had been displayed on the sidewalks. The doors of the town hall
banged as the farm women ran inside, grabbing on to packages
and children, to cram themselves into the ladies' rest room.
Somebody tried the library door. The librarian looked over at it
but did not move. And soon the rain was sweeping down like curtains across the street, and the wind battered the town hall roof,
and tore at the treetops. That roaring and danger lasted a few
minutes, while the power of the wind went by. Then the sound
left was the sound of the rain, which was now falling vertically
and so heavily that they might have been under a waterfall.

If the same thing was happening at Walley, he thought, Jane
would know enough not to expect him. This was the last thought
he had of her for a long while.

"Mrs. Groves wouldn't wash my clothes," he said, to his own
surprise. "She was afraid to touch them."

The librarian said in a peculiarly quivering, shamed, and determined voice, "I think what you did — I think that was a remarkable thing to do."

The rain made such a constant noise that he was released from
answering. He found it easy then to turn and look at her. Her
profile was dimly lit by the wash of rain down the windows. Her
expression was calm and reckless. Or so it seemed to him. He
realized that he knew hardly anything about her — what kind of
person she really was or what kind of secrets she could have. He
could not even estimate his own value to her. He knew only that
he had some, and it wasn't the usual.

He could no more describe the feeling he got from her than
you can describe a smell. It's like the scorch of electricity. It's like
burnt kernels of wheat. No, it's like a bitter orange. I give up.

He had never imagined that he would find himself in a situation like this, visited by such a clear compulsion. But it seemed
he was not unprepared. Without thinking twice or even once
what he was letting himself in for he said, "I wish —"

He had spoken too quietly, she did not hear him.

He raised his voice. He said, "I wish we could get married."

Then she looked at him. She laughed but controlled herself.

"I'm sorry," she said. "I'm sorry. It's just what went through
my mind."

"What was that?" he said.

"I thought, That's the last I'll see of him."

Arthur said, "You're mistaken."

Tolpuddle Martyrs

The passenger trains from Carstairs had stopped running during the Second World War and even the rails were taken up. People said it was for the War Effort. When Louisa went to the city,
to see the heart specialist, in the mid-fifties, she had to take the
bus. She was not supposed to drive anymore.

The doctor, the heart specialist, said that her heart was a little
wonky and her pulse inclined to be jumpy. She thought that
made her heart sound like a comedian and her pulse like a
puppy on a leash. She had not come fifty-seven miles to be
treated with such playfulness, but she let it pass, because she was
already distracted by something she had been reading in the doctor's waiting room. Perhaps it was what she had been reading
that had made her pulse jumpy.

On an inside page of the local paper she had seen the headline,
"Local Martyrs Honored," and simply to pass the time she had
read further. She read that there was to be some sort of ceremony that afternoon at Victoria Park. It was a ceremony to
honor the Tolpuddle Martyrs. The paper said that few people
had heard of the Tolpuddle Martyrs, and certainly Louisa had
not. They were six men who had been tried and found guilty for
administering illegal oaths. This peculiar offense, committed
over one hundred years ago in the village of Tolpuddle, in Dor-
set, England, had got them transported to Australia, and later on
some of them had ended up in Ontario, here in London, where
they lived out the rest of their days and were buried without any
special notice or commemoration. They were considered now to
be among the earliest founders of the trade-union movement,
and the Trade Unions Council, along with representatives of the
Canadian Congress of Labour and the ministers of some local
churches, had organized a ceremony that would take place to-

day, the occasion of the hundred-and-twentieth anniversary of their arrest.

"Martyrs" is laying it on somewhat, thought Louisa. They were not executed, after all.

The ceremony was to take place at three o'clock, and the chief speakers were to be one of the local ministers and Mr. John (Jack) Agnew, a union spokesman from Toronto.

It was a quarter after two when Louisa came out of the doctor's office. The bus to Carstairs did not leave until six o'clock. She had thought she would go and have tea and something to eat on the top floor of Simpsons, then shop for a wedding present at Birks, or if the time fitted go to an afternoon movie. Victoria Park lay between the doctor's office and Simpsons, and she decided to cut across it. The day was hot and the shade of the trees pleasant. She could not avoid seeing where the chairs had been set up and a small speakers' platform draped in yellow cloth, with a Canadian flag on one side and what she supposed must be a labor union flag on the other. A group of people had collected, and she found herself changing course in order to get a look at them. Some were old people, very plainly but decently dressed, the women with kerchiefs around their heads on the hot day. Europeans, she thought. Others were factory workers, men in clean short-sleeved shirts and women in fresh blouses and slacks, let out early. A few women must have come from home, because they were wearing summer dresses and sandals and trying to keep track of small children. Louisa thought that they would not care at all for the way she was dressed — fashionably, as always, in beige shantung with a crimson silk tam — but she noticed, just then, a woman more elegantly got up than she was, in green silk with her dark hair drawn tightly back, tied with a green and gold scarf. She might have been forty — her face was worn, but beautiful. She came over to Louisa at once, smiling, and showed her a chair, and gave her a mimeographed paper. Louisa could not read the purple printing. She tried to get a look at some men who were talking beside the platform. Were the speakers among them?

The coincidence of the name was hardly even interesting. Neither the first name nor the last was all that unusual.

She did not know why she had sat down, or why she had come over here in the first place. She was beginning to feel a faintly

sickening, familiar agitation. But once it got going, telling herself
that it was over nothing did no good. The only thing to do was to
get up and get away from here, before any more people sat down
and hemmed her in.

The green woman intercepted her, asked if she was all right.

"I have to catch a bus," said Louisa in a croaky voice. She
cleared her throat. "An out-of-town bus," she said with better
control, and marched away, not in the right direction for Simpsons. She thought in fact that she wouldn't go there, she wouldn't
go to Birks for the wedding present or to a movie, either. She
would just go and sit in the bus depot until it was time for her to
go home.

Half a block from the bus depot she remembered that the bus
had not taken her there that morning. The depot was being torn
down and rebuilt — there was a temporary depot several blocks
away. She had not paid quite enough attention to which street it
was on — York Street, east of the real depot, or King? At any
rate, she had to detour, because both of these streets were being
torn up, and she had almost decided she was lost when she realized she had been lucky enough to come upon the temporary
depot by the back way. It was an old house — one of those tall,
yellow-gray brick houses dating from the time when this was a
residential district. This was probably the last use it would be put
to before being torn down. Houses all around it must have been
torn down to make the large gravel lot where the buses pulled in.
There were still some trees at the edge of the lot and under them
a few rows of chairs that she had not noticed when she got off
the bus before noon. Two men were sitting on what used to be
the veranda of the house, on old car seats. They wore brown
shirts with the bus company's insignia, but they seemed to be
halfhearted about their work, not getting up when she asked if
the bus to Carstairs was leaving at six o'clock as scheduled and
where could she get a soft drink.

Six o'clock, far as they knew.

Coffee shop down the street.

Cooler inside but only Coke and orange left.

She got herself a Coca-Cola out of the cooler in a dirty little
indoor waiting room that smelled of a bad toilet. Moving the depot to this dilapidated house must have thrown everyone into a

state of indolence and fecklessness. There was a fan set up in the room they used as an office, and as she went by on her way outside she saw some papers blow off the desk. "Oh, shit," said the office girl, and stamped her heel on them.

Coming out, Louisa saw that the chairs set up in the shade of the dusty city trees were straight-backed old wooden ones originally painted different colors — they looked as if they had come from various kitchens. Strips of old carpet and rubber bathroom mats were laid down in front of them, to keep your feet off the gravel. On the ground a little way off slept a white calf, which Louisa would not accept, so she squinted at it until it stirred and roused itself and turned into a dingy dog. It trotted over and looked at her for a moment in a grave, semiofficial way, gave a brief sniff at her shoes, and trotted away.

She had not noticed if there were any drinking straws and did not feel like going back to look. She drank Coke from the bottle, tilting back her head and closing her eyes.

When she opened them, a man was sitting one chair away and was speaking to her.

"I got here as soon as I could," he said. "Nancy said you were going to catch a bus. As soon as I finished with the speech I took off. But the bus depot is all torn up."

"Temporarily," she said.

"I knew you right away," he said. "In spite of — well, many years. When I saw you, I was talking to somebody. Then I looked again and you'd disappeared."

"I don't recognize you," said Louisa.

"Well, no," he said. "I guess not. Of course. You wouldn't."

He was wearing tan slacks, a pale yellow short-sleeved shirt, a cream and yellow ascot. A bit of a dandy, for a union man. His hair was white but thick and wavy, the sort of springy hair that goes in ripples, up and back from the forehead. His skin was flushed and his face was deeply wrinkled from the efforts of speechmaking — and from talking to people privately, she supposed, with much of the fervor and persuasiveness of his public speeches. He wore tinted glasses, which he took off now, as if willing that she should see him better. His eyes were a light blue, slightly bloodshot and apprehensive. A good-looking man, trim except for a little authoritative bulge over the belt, but she did not find these serviceable, good looks — the careful, sporty

clothes, the display of ripply hair, the effective expressions —
very attractive. She preferred the kind of looks Arthur had had.
The restraint, the dark-suited dignity that some people could call
pompous but that seemed to her admirable and innocent.

"I always meant to break the ice," he said. "I meant to speak to
you. I should have gone in and said goodbye at least. The oppor-
tunity to leave came up so suddenly."

Louisa did not have any idea what to say to this.

He sighed. He said, "You must have been mad at me. Are you
still?"

"No," she said, and fell back, ridiculously, on the usual courte-
sies. "How is Grace? How is your daughter? Lillian?"

"Grace is not so well. She had some arthritis. Her weight
doesn't help it. Lillian is all right. She's married but she still
teaches high school. Mathematics. Not too usual for a woman."

How could Louisa begin to correct him? Could she say, No,
your wife, Grace, got married again during the war, she married
a farmer, a widower? Before that she used to come in and clean
our house once a week. Mrs. Groves had got too old. And Lillian
never finished high school, how could she be a high school
teacher? She married young, she had some children, she works
in the drugstore. She has your height and your hair, dyed blond.
I used to look at her and think she must be like you. When she
was growing up I used to give her my stepdaughter's outgrown
clothes.

Instead of this, she said, "Then the woman in the green
dress — that was not Lillian?"

"Nancy? Oh no! Nancy is my guardian angel. She keeps track
of where I'm going, and when, and have I got my speech, and
what I drink and eat and have I taken my pills. I tend toward
high blood pressure. Nothing too serious. But my way of life's no
good. I'm on the go constantly. Tonight I've got to fly out of here
to Ottawa, tomorrow I've got a tough meeting, tomorrow night
I've got some fool banquet."

Louisa felt it necessary to say, "You knew that I got married? I
married Arthur Doud."

She thought he showed some surprise. But he said, "Yes, I
heard that. Yes."

"We worked hard, too," said Louisa sturdily. "Arthur died six
years ago. We kept the factory going all through the thirties,

even though at times we were down to three men. We had no money for repairs, and I remember cutting up the office awnings so that Arthur could carry them up on a ladder and patch the roof. We tried making everything we could think of. Even outdoor bowling alleys for those amusement places. Then the war came, and we couldn't keep up with the work. We could sell all the pianos we could make, but we were also making radar cases for the navy. I stayed in the office all through."

"It must have been a change," he said, in what seemed a tactful voice. "A change from the library."

"Work is work," she said. "I still work. My stepdaughter, Bea, is divorced, she keeps house for me after a fashion. My son has finally finished university. He is supposed to be learning about the business, but he has some excuse to go off in the middle of every afternoon. When I come home at suppertime, so tired I could drop, I hear the ice tinkling in their glasses and them laughing behind the hedge. Oh, Mud, they say when they see me — oh, poor Mud, sit down here. Get her a drink! They call me Mud because that was my son's name for me when he was a baby. But they are neither of them babies now. The house is cool when I come home. It's a lovely house if you remember, built in three tiers like a wedding cake. Mosaic tiles in the entrance hall, and wooden trim that looks like lace edges and drinks up the paint. But I am always thinking about the factory — that is what fills my mind. What should we do to stay afloat? There are only five factories in Canada making pianos now, and three of them are in Quebec, with the low cost of labor. No doubt you know all about that. When I talk to Arthur in my head it is always about the same thing. I am very close to him still but it is hardly in a mystical way. You would think that as you get older your mind would fill up with what they call the spiritual side of things, but mine just seems to get more and more practical, trying to get something settled. What a thing to talk to a dead man about."

She stopped, she was embarrassed. But she was not sure that he had listened to all of this and, in fact, she was not sure that she had said all of it.

"What started me off —" he said. "What got me going in the first place, with whatever I have managed to do, was the library. So I owe you a great deal."

He put his hands on his knees and looked down.

"Ah, rubbish," he said.

He groaned, and ended up with a laugh.

"My father," he said. "You wouldn't remember my father?"

"Oh, yes," Louisa said.

"Well. Sometimes I think he had the right idea."

Then he lifted his eyes and made a pronouncement.

"Love never dies."

At first, she felt impatient to the point of taking offense. This is what all the speechmaking turns you into, she thought — a person who can say things like that. Love dies all the time, or at any rate it becomes distracted, overlaid — it might as well be dead.

"Arthur used to come and sit in the library," she said. "In the beginning I was very provoked with him. I used to look at the back of his neck and think, Ha, what if something should hit you there! None of that would make sense to you. It wouldn't make sense. And it turned out to be something else entirely that I wanted. I wanted to marry him and get into a normal life."

"A normal life," she repeated — and a giddiness seemed to be taking over, an airy solemnity and widespread forgiveness, a tender notion of understanding between him and herself. "What do you think I mean by that?"

Across the gravel yard came a group of oddly dressed folk. They moved all together, a clump of black. The women did not show their hair — they had black shawls or bonnets covering their heads. The men wore broad hats and black braces. The children were dressed just like their elders, even to the bonnets and hats. How hot they all looked in those clothes — how hot and dusty and wary and shy.

"The Tolpuddle Martyrs," he said, in a faintly joking, resigned, and compassionate voice. "Ah, I guess I'd better go over. I'd better go over there and have a word with them."

That edge of a joke, the uneasy kindness, made her think of somebody else. Who was it? When she saw the breadth of his shoulders from behind, and the broad flat buttocks, she knew who.

Jim Frarey.

Oh, what kind of a trick was being played on her, or what kind of trick was she playing on herself! She would not have it. She pulled herself up tightly, she saw all those black clothes blotted together. She was dizzy and humiliated. She would not have it.

But not all black, now that they were getting closer. She could see dark blue — those were the men's shirts — and dark blue and purple in some of the women's dresses. She could see faces — the men's behind beards, the women's in their deep-brimmed bonnets. And now she knew who they were. They were Mennonites.

Mennonites were living in this part of the country, where they never used to be. There were some of them around Bondy, a village north of Carstairs. They would be going home on the same bus she was taking.

He was not with them, or anywhere in sight.

A traitor, helplessly. A traveler.

Once she knew that these were Mennonites and not some lost unidentifiable strangers, they did not look so shy or dejected. In fact they seemed quite cheerful, passing around a bag of candy, the adults eating candy with the children. They settled on the chairs all around her.

No wonder she was feeling clammy. She had gone under a wave, which nobody else had noticed. You could say anything you liked about what had happened — but what it amounted to was going under a wave. She had gone under and through it and was left with a cold sheen on her skin, a beating in her ears, a cavity in her chest and revolt in her stomach. It was anarchy she was up against — a devouring muddle. Sudden holes and impromptu tricks and radiant vanishing consolations.

But these settlings of Mennonites, all around her, are a blessing. The plop of behinds on chairs, the crackling of the candy bag, the meditative sucking and soft conversations. Without looking at Louisa, a little girl holds out the bag, and Louisa accepts a butterscotch mint. She is surprised to be able to hold it in her hand, to have her lips shape "Thank you," then to discover in her mouth just the taste that she expected. She sucks on it as they do on theirs, not in any hurry, and allows that taste to promise her some reasonable continuance.

Lights have come on, though it isn't yet evening. In the trees above the wooden chairs someone has strung lines of little colored bulbs that she did not notice until now. They make her think of festivities. Carnivals. Boats of singers on the lake.

"What place is this?" she said to the woman beside her.

*

On the day of Miss Tamblyn's death it happened that Louisa was staying in the Commercial Hotel. She was a traveler then, for a company that sold hats, ribbons, handkerchiefs, trimmings, and ladies' underwear to retail stores. She heard the talk in the hotel, and it occurred to her that the town would soon need a new librarian. She was getting very tired of lugging her sample cases on and off trains, and showing her wares in hotels, packing and unpacking. She went at once and talked to the people in charge of the library. A Mr. Doud and a Mr. Macleod. They sounded like a vaudeville team but did not look it. The pay was poor, but she had not been doing so well on commission, either. She told them that she had finished high school, in Toronto, and had worked in Eaton's Book Department before she switched to traveling. She did not think it necessary to tell them that she had worked there only five months when she was discovered to have TB, and that she had then spent four years in a sanatorium. The TB was cured, anyway — her spots were dry.

The hotel moved her to one of the rooms for permanent guests, on the third floor. She could see the snow-covered hills over the rooftops. The town of Carstairs was in a river valley. It had three or four thousand people and a long main street that ran downhill, over the river, and uphill again. There was a piano and organ factory.

The houses were built for lifetimes and the yards were wide and the streets were lined with mature elm and maple trees. She had never been here when the leaves were on the trees. It must make a great difference. So much that lay open now would be concealed.

She was glad of a fresh start, her spirits were hushed and grateful. She had made fresh starts before and things had not turned out as she had hoped, but she believed in the swift decision, the unforeseen intervention, the uniqueness of her fate.

The town was full of the smell of horses. As evening came on, big blinkered horses with feathered hooves pulled the sleighs across the bridge, past the hotel, beyond the street lights, down the dark side roads. Somewhere out in the country they would lose the sound of each other's bells.

JOYCE CAROL OATES

Is Laughter Contagious?

FROM HARPER'S MAGAZINE

IS LAUGHTER CONTAGIOUS? Driving on North Pearl Street, Franklin Village, Mrs. D. began suddenly to hear laughter on all sides, a wash of laughter gold-spangled like coins, just perceptibly louder issuing from the rear of her car, and she found herself smiling, her brooding thoughtful expression erased as if by force, on the verge of spontaneous laughter herself, for isn't there a natural buoyancy to the heart when we hear laughter? even, or particularly, the laughter of strangers? even an unexpected, inexplicable, mysterious laughter? — though Mrs. D. understood that the laughter surrounding her was in no way mysterious, at least its source was in no way mysterious, for, evidently, she had forgotten to switch off the car radio the last time she had driven the car, and the laughter was issuing from the radio's speakers, the most powerful of which was in the rear of the Mercedes.

What were they laughing about, these phantom radio-people?

Men's laughter? — and, here and there, the isolated sound of a woman's higher-pitched laughter? — delicious, cascading, like a sound of icicles touching?

Though laughing by this time herself, Mrs. D., who was a serious person, with a good deal on her mind — and most of it private, secret, not to be shared even with Mr. D. — switched the radio off, preferring silence.

There.

Christine Delahunt. Thirty-nine years old. Wife, mother. Recently returned to work — a "career." A woman of moral scru-

ples, but not prim, puritanical, dogmatic. Isn't that how Mrs. D.
has defined herself to herself? Isn't Mrs. D., in so defining herself, one of us? — determined, for no reason we can understand,
to define ourselves to — ourselves?

As if we doubt that anyone else is concerned?

Mrs. D. was to tell us, certain of her friendly acquaintances.
Last Thursday it seemed to begin. Did others in Franklin Village
notice — that afternoon, sometime before six o'clock? The time
of suburban car errands, family tasks, last-minute shopping, and
pickups at the dry cleaners and drugstore, the pace of the wan-
ing day quickening, yes and Thursday is the day-preceding-Fri-
day, when the week itself notoriously quickens, a panic sensation
to it, as a river seemingly placid and navigable begins to acceler-
ate, visibly, as it approaches a cataract — though there is, yet, no
clear sign of danger? no reason for alarm?

Outbursts of laughter. Gay infectious laughter. In the Franklin Food Mart, our "quality" grocery store, at one of the checkout
counters when the deaf and dumb packer wearing the badge
FRITZ (pasty-skinned, in his fifties; the Franklin Food Mart is
one of several area businesses that have "made it a policy" to em-
ploy the handicapped) spilled a bag of fresh produce onto the
floor, and Washington State winesaps, bright-dyed Florida navel
oranges, hairy-pungent little kiwifruit, several pygmy heads of
Boston lettuce, a dozen Idaho red potatoes, a single California
melon — all went tumbling, rolling, startling yet comical as the
deaf and dumb packer gaped and blinked, standing frozen in a
kind of terror that for all its public expression seemed to us, wit-
nessing, to be private, thus somehow funnier, and the very cus-
tomer who had paid extravagant prices for these items laughed,
if a bit angrily; and other customers, seeing, burst into laughter,
too; and the checkout cashier, and other cashiers, and employees
of the store, peering over, craning their necks to see what the
commotion is, their laughter tentative at first since the look in
poor Fritz's eyes *was* terror, wasn't it? — then exploding forth,
an honest, candid, gut-laughter, not malicious surely, but, yes,
loud?

Mrs. D. was at an adjacent checkout counter, methodically
making out a check to the Franklin Food Mart, a weekly custom
this is, perhaps it might better be called a blood sacrifice, this
week's check for — how can it be? $328.98 for an unexceptional

week's shopping? for a family of four? no supplies for a dinner party? no beer, wine, liquor? not even any seafood? making out the check with resigned fingers when she heard the strange laughter rising around her, rising, erupting, childlike raucous laughter, and turning, smiling, wanting to join in, Mrs. D. saw the cause — a bag of groceries had overturned, things were rolling on the floor, and that look on that poor man's face, it *was* amusing, but Mrs. D. suppressed laughter for, oh dear, really it *wasn't* amusing, not at all, that poor man backing off and staring at the produce on the floor, paralyzed as everyone laughed so cruelly, what are people thinking of? how can it be? in the Franklin Food Mart of all places?

Are the Delahunts neighbors of ours? Not exactly.

We don't have "neighbors," in the old sense of that word, in Franklin Village. Our houses are constructed on three- and four-acre lots, which means considerable distance between houses, and with our elaborate landscaping (trees of all varieties, shrubs, twelve-foot redwood fences, electrically charged wire-mesh "deer-deterrent" fences) it's possible for the residents of one house to be unable to glimpse even the facade of the house next door, certainly it's possible to go for years without glimpsing the faces of the people who live next door, unless, of course, and this is frequently the case, we encounter one another socially — on neutral territory, you might say. Nor have we sidewalks in residential Franklin Village. Nor have we streets, in the old sense of that word — we have "lanes," we have "drives," we have "passes," "circles," "courts," even "ways," but we do not have "streets."

Are Mr. and Mrs. Delahunt friends of ours? Not exactly.

We don't have "friends," in the old sense of that word, in Franklin Village. Most of us are relatively new here, and a number of us are scheduled to move soon. Spring is the busiest time for moving! (Of course there are residents in this area who are known as "old-time." Who can recall, for instance, when the Franklin Hills Shopping Mall was nothing but an immense tract of open, wild, useless land, and when Main Street in the Village was residential from Pearl Street onward, and when Route 26 was a mere country highway!) Thus the majority of us make no claims to have (or to be) "friends" — but we *are* "friendly acquaintances" of one another and we *are* social. Very!

The Delahunts, Mr. and Mrs., became friendly acquaintances of ours within days of their arrival. They are highly respected, warmly regarded, attractive, energetic, invited almost immediately to join the Franklin Hills Golf Club and the yet more prestigious Franklin Hills Tennis Club. Mr. D. moved his family here three years ago from Greenwich, Connecticut — or was it Grosse Pointe, Michigan? — when he became sales director at W.W.C. & M., and Mrs. D. has recently begun public relations work part-time, for our Republican congressman, Gordon Frayne — Gordon's the man whom the papers so frequently chide, urging him to "upscale" his image. The Delahunts live in a six-bedroom French Normandy house on Fairway Circle, their fourteen-year-old daughter, Tracey, and their eleven-year-old son, Jamey, both attend Franklin Hills Day School. Mrs. D., like many of us, tries to participate in parent-teacher activities at the school, but — when on earth is there *time*?

"Upscaling" Gordon Frayne's image is a challenge, Mrs. D. laughingly, if somewhat worriedly, confesses. But Gordy Frayne — some folks even call him Gordo — wins elections. He's a big-hearted ruddy-faced shooting-from-the-hip character, often in the headlines and on television, one or another controversy, last year he was interviewed on network television and made a statement warning that "ethnic minorities" had better man their own oars "or the venerable Ship of State's gonna capsize and sink" — which naturally led to protests from certain quarters but a good deal of support from other quarters. Mrs. D., like other associates and friendly acquaintances of Gordon Frayne's, has learned to frown as she smiles at his witticisms, just slightly reprovingly, as Franklin Village women often do, she has unconsciously mastered this response, this facial expression, as adroitly as any professional actress — "Oh Gordy! Oh *really!*" It was at a party on Saturday night (the Saturday following the Thursday) that Gordy launched into one of his comical diatribes, the guy could have been a stand-up comedian for sure, cruel but ingenious mimicry of Jesse Jackson (an old routine, but a favorite), and the latest of his AIDS jokes . . . and most, though not all, of the company laughed, Mrs. D. among them, shocked, yes, but not wanting to be a prude, or to seem a prude; but smiling, shaking her head, avoiding the others' eyes as in a communal complicity, but thinking why, why, why, and what will come of this?

Five girls from the Franklin Hills Day School jogging on Park Ridge Road, Monday after school, pumping legs and arms, high-held heads, shorts and loose-fitting school T-shirts and identical expensive jogging shoes, and according to the girls' testimonies after the "vehicular assault" they were running single file, they were keeping to the left side of the road, facing oncoming traffic, careful to keep off the road itself and to run on the asphalt-paved shoulder. As usual one of the girls was falling behind, there were three girls running close together, then, a few yards behind them, the fourth, and approximately twenty feet behind her the fifth, poor Bonnie, Bonnie S., fourteen years old, second year in the "upper form" at the Day School. Bonnie S. is a few pounds overweight, not fat, the most accurate word would be plump but who wants to be plump? who can bear to be plump? fourteen years old and plump in Franklin Village, New York? — poor Bonnie S., whom the other girls like well enough, feel sort of sorry for, she's sweet she tries so hard she's so generous but it's pathetic, Bonnie trying to keep up with the tall thin girls, the girls she envies, letting it be known at school that her problem isn't overeating it's glandular it's "genetic — like fate," and maybe that's true since none of Bonnie's classmates ever sees her eating anything other than apples, carrot sticks, narrow slices of honeydew melon, she'll devour fleshy fruit and rind both — poor Bonnie S.! (But *is* her weight problem "glandular"? Maybe she binges? — in secret? — tries to stick her finger down her throat and vomit it up? — but can't quite *succeed*? — enough to make a difference?) In any case, there was Bonnie S. running fifth in the line of girls, breathless, clumsy, a sweaty sheen to her round flushed face, a glazed look to her damp brown eyes, and the carload of boys swerved around the curve, that curve just beyond Grouse Hill Lane, six older students from the Day School jammed together in a newly purchased white Acura. The girls could hear the radio blasting heavy metal rock even before the car came into sight, they could hear the boys yelling and laughing as the car bore down upon them, they saw the faces of the boys in the front seat clearly, wide grins, gleeful-malicious eyes, a raised beer can or two, then the girls were screaming, scattering. It was Bonnie S. who was the target, poor Bonnie arousing male derision pumping away there twenty feet behind the others, poor plump sweaty Bonnie S. with her expression of incredulous shock and terror as the white car aimed for her, boyish-prankish braying laughter, she threw herself desperately to the left, the car skidded by, missing the screaming girl by perhaps a single inch, then righted itself, regained the road, on shrieking tires it sped away and there was Bonnie S., lying insensible in the shallow concrete drainage ditch like something tossed down, bleeding so profusely from a gash in her forehead that the first of her friends to reach her nearly fainted.

Tracey Delahunt tells her mother afterward, she'll confess to her mother solely, knowing her mother will understand, or, failing to understand — for who after all *can* understand? — will sympathize with the hungry wish to understand. "It happened so fast — oh God! — we looked back and there was Bonnie sort of *flying* off the road like something in a kid's cartoon — and it was horrible — it was just, just horrible, but" — lowering her teary eyes, thick-lashed tawny-green eyes Mrs. D. thinks are far more beautiful than her own, though closely resembling her own — "sort of, in a way — oh God! — *comical* too."

Pressing her fingertips hard against her lips but unable to keep from bursting into a peal of hysterical laughter.

Three days later, the most upsetting incident of all.

Not that Mrs. D. allowed herself to think of it very much afterward. Certainly not obsessively. She isn't that type of mother — the obsessive-neurotic mother. Fantasizing about her children, worrying, suspicious.

She'd entered the house from the rear, as usual. About to step into the kitchen when she'd overheard, coming up from the basement, the "family room" in the basement, the sound of juvenile laughter, boys' laughter, and ordinarily she would not have paused for a moment since Jamey and his friends often took over that room after school to watch videos, yes some of the videos the boys watched were questionable, yes Mrs. D. knew and, yes, she'd tried to exercise some restraint while at the same time she'd tried not to be, nor even to appear to be, censorious and interfering, but that day there was something chilling about the tone of the boys' laughter, and wasn't there, beneath it, another sound? — as of a creature *bleating*? — a queer high-pitched sound that worried Mrs. D. so she went to the door of the family room (which was shut) and pressed her ear against it, hearing the laughter, the giggling, more distinctly, and the other sound too, and carefully, almost timidly — she, Christine Delahunt, nearly forty years old, wife, mother, self-respecting surely? — self-determined surely? — opening a door timidly in her own house? — and saw there a sight that froze her in her tracks even as, in that instant, she was already shoving it from her, banishing it from her consciousness, denying its power to qualify her love for her son: for there were Jamey and several of his boy friends, eighth-graders at the Day School whose faces Mrs. D. knew well, Evan, Allen, Terry, red-haired impish Terry, and who was there with them? a girl? a stranger? and *strange*? — slightly older than the boys, with dull coarse features, eyes puckered at the corners, wet-dribbly mouth, no one Mrs. D. knew or had ever glimpsed before, and this girl was sprawled on her back on the braided "colonial"-style carpet in front of the fireplace, in the Delahunts' family room, her plump knees raised, and spread, naked from the waist down, and what was red-haired Terry doing? — poking something (too large to be a pencil, an object plastic and chunky, was it a child's play baseball bat?), or trying to poke something, into the girl's vagina? — while the other boys, as if transfixed, crouched in a circle, staring, blinking, grinning, giggling.

Mrs. D. cried, without thinking, "Oh what are you doing! Boys! Jamey! And you — you filthy, disgusting *girl*!"

Her voice was unlike any voice she'd ever heard springing from her. Breathless, disbelieving, angry, wounded.

She slammed the door upon the children's startled-guilty-grinning faces and fled. Upstairs.

That evening, at dinner, not a word! not a word! not a word! to Jamey, who, frightened, subdued, ate his food almost shyly, and cast looks of appeal to Mrs. D., who behaved as — as usual? — knowing that the child *knew*.

*

"I'm so afraid."

Mrs. D. was sitting, yes in the family room, which Mr. D. preferred to call the "recreation" room, with a drink in her hand. Her voice was quiet, apologetic.

Mr. D. sipped his drink. Peered at the newspaper. Said, vague, but polite, "Yes?"

"Harry. I'm so afraid."

"Well, all right."

Mr. D. was scanning the paper with increasing impatience. "Christ, it's always the same! AIDS, crack, crime! 'Ghetto!' " He squinted at a photograph of several black youths being herded into a police van, he laughed harshly. "*I'm* a subscriber, for Christ's sake, d'you think these punks subscribe? Why the hell am I always reading about *them?*"

Upstairs a telephone rang. Tracey's private number.

Mrs. D. raised her glass to her lips but did not sip from it. She feared the taste of it — that first slip-sliding taste. She pressed her fingertips to her eyes and sat very still.

After a few minutes Mr. D. inquired, glancing in her direction even as his attention remained on the newspaper, "Chris — are you all right?"

"I'm so afraid."

"Cramps, eh? Migraine?"

"I'm *afraid.*"

Mr. D. was scanning the editorial page. A sudden smile illuminated his face. He nodded, then, suddenly bored, let the newspaper fall. "Everyone has an *opinion.* 'Put your money where your mouth is' my father used to say."

Mr. D. rose — majestically. A solid figure, ham-thighed, with a faintly flushed face, quick eyes. At its edges Mr. D.'s face appeared to have eroded but his mouth was still that "sculpted" mouth which Mrs. D., a very long time ago, so long ago now as to seem laughable, like a scene in a low-budget science-fiction film, had once avidly, ravenously, *insatiably* kissed.

Mr. D. said, walking away, "Two Bufferin. That'll do it."

After dinner, rinsing dishes and setting them carefully into the dishwasher, Mrs. D. smiled tentatively at her reflection in the window above the sink. Why was she afraid? Wasn't she being a bit silly? Where, so often recently, she was thinking of what she was *not* thinking of, now, abruptly, she was *not* thinking of what she was *not* thinking of.

Elsewhere in the house, issuing from the family room, and from Tracey's room upstairs, laughter rippled, peaked — television laughter by the sound of it.

Simple boredom with the subject, maybe.

Which subject?

Mr. H., father of one of the girls who had been jogging on Park Ridge Road on the day of the infamous "vehicular assault," telephoned Mr. D. another time, and, another time, Mr. D. took the call in private, the door to his study firmly shut; and, as they were undressing for bed that night, when Mrs. D. asked cautiously what had been decided, Mr. D. replied affably, "We don't get involved."

Mrs. D. had understood from the very first, even as Tracey was sobbing in her arms, that, given the litigious character of Franklin Hills, this would be the wisest, as it was the most practical, course of action; she gathered too, as things developed, despite Tracey's protestations and bouts of tears, temper, and hysteria, that Tracey concurred, as her girlfriends, apart from Bonnie, concurred, perhaps even before their worried parents advised them, yet she heard herself saying weakly, "Oh Harry — if Tracey *saw* those boys' faces, Tracey wants to *say*," and Mr. D., yawning, stretching, on his way into his bathroom, nodded vaguely in her direction and said, "Set the alarm for six-fifteen, hon, will you? — the limo's picking me up at six-forty-five."

Tracey no longer discusses the incident with Mr. and Mrs. D. *Ugly! — horrible! — nightmare! — never never forget!* — she restricts all discussions of it to her girlfriends, as they restrict their discussions of it too.

That is, the girls who were witnesses to the incident, not Bonnie S., to whom it happened. Not pathetic Bonnie S., to whom they no longer speak, much, at all.

For weeks, red-haired Terry was banished from the Delahunts' house. Not that Mrs. D. spoke of such a banishment, or even suggested it to Jamey, who watched her cautiously, one might

say shrewdly, his gaze shifting from her if she chanced to look
at him.

No need to chastise and embarrass the poor child, Mrs. D. has
begun to think. He's a good decent sensitive civilized child, he
knows how much he has upset me.

Poor Mrs. K.! — poor "Vivvie"!

Since the start of her problem eighteen months ago, the first
mastectomy, and the second mastectomy, and then the chemo-
therapy treatments, her circle of friendly acquaintances has
shrunken; and those who visit her, primarily women, have had
difficulties.

Yes it's so sad it's *so* sad.

Vivvie Kern of all women.

A few of us visited her at the hospital, some of us waited to visit
her at home, it's awkward not knowing what to do or to say, it
sometimes seems there isn't anything *to* do or to say, and there's
the extra burden of having to exchange greetings with Mr. K.,
who appears almost resentful, reproachful, that's how men are
sometimes in such cases, husbands of ex-prom-queen-type
women, and Mrs. K. was, a bit boastfully, one of these. Of course
it's wisest to avoid *the subject,* but how can you avoid *the subject* with
that poor man staring at you unsmiling? — just *staring?*

But it's lovely in their new solarium, at least. So much to look
at, outside and in, and you aren't forced to look at *her,* I mean
exclusively at *her,* poor thing! chattering away so bravely! — and
that gorgeous red-blond hair she'd been so vain about mostly
fallen out now, the wig just sort of *perches* there on her head, and
her eyebrows are drawn on so crudely, and with her eyelashes
gone it's *naked eyes* you have to look at if you can't avoid it, but in
such close quarters and with the woman leaning toward you
sometimes even gripping your arm as if for dear life how can you
avoid it? — except by not visiting poor Mrs. K. at all?

(Of course, some in our circle have stopped seeing her, and it's
embarrassing, how painful, Mrs. K. joking to disguise her bitterness. Saying, "My God, it isn't as if I have AIDS after all, this isn't
contagious, you know!")

Visiting Mrs. K. in late June, having procrastinated for weeks,
Mrs. D. was nervously admiring the numerous hanging plants in

the solarium, listening to Mrs. K. speaking animatedly of mu-
tual acquaintances, complaining good-naturedly of the Hispanic
cleaning woman she and Mrs. D. shared, perhaps half listening
was more accurate, not thinking of what she was not thinking but
she *was* thinking of the ceremonies of grief, death, mourning,
how brave of human beings yet how futile, how futile yet how
brave, for here was a terminally ill woman now speaking aggressively of regaining her lost weight — "muscle tone" she called
it — and returning to the tennis club, and Mrs. D. smiled at the
woman's wide smiling mouth, a thin mouth now and the lips gar-
ishly crimson, yes but you must keep up the pretense, yes but you
must be brave, and smile, and nod, and agree, for isn't it too terrible otherwise?

Sharp-eyed, Mrs. K. has noticed that Mrs. D. has another time
glanced surreptitiously at her wristwatch, as a starving animal
can sense the presence of food, however inaccessible, or even ab-
stract, so does Mrs. K. sense her visitor's yearning to escape, thus
she leans abruptly forward across the glass-topped table, nearly
upsetting both their glasses of white wine, she seems about to
bare her heart, *oh why does Vivvie do such things! with each of us, as
if for the first and only time!* seizing Mrs. D.'s hand in her skeletal
but strong fingers and speaking rapidly, intensely, naked bright-
druggy eyes fixed upon Mrs. D.'s, thus holding her captive.

". . . *can't* bear to think of leaving them . . . abandoning them
. . . poor Gene! poor Robbie! . . . devastated . . . unmoored . . .
already Robbie's been having . . . only thirteen . . . the counselor
he's been seeing . . . specializes in adolescent boys . . . says it's a
particularly sensitive age . . . traumatic . . . for a boy to lose . . . a
mother."

Mrs. D., though giving the impression of having been listening
closely, and being deeply moved, has, in fact, not been listening
to Mrs. K.'s passionate outburst very closely. She has been thinking of, no she has *not* been thinking of. What?

With a startled, gentle little laugh, Mrs. D. says, "Oh — do you
really think so? *Really?*"

Frightened, Mrs. K. says, "Do I really think — what?"

Calmly and unflinching, Mrs. D. looks the doomed woman in
the face for the first time.

"That your husband and son will be 'devastated' when you die?

That they will even miss you, much? I mean, after the initial
shock — the upset to their routines?"
    A long moment.
    A *very* long moment.
    Mrs. K. is staring incredulously at Mrs. D. Slowly, her fingers
relax their death grip on Mrs. D.'s fingers. Her bright lips move,
tremble — but no sound emerges.
    It's as if, in this instant, the oxygen in the solarium is being
sucked out. There's a sense of something, an invisible flame, a
radiance, about to go *out.*
    "Oh, my goodness!" Mrs. D. exclaims, rising. "I must leave, I
still have shopping to do, it's after *six.*"

She would tell us, confide in us, yes we'd had similar experiences
lately, unsettling experiences, sudden laughter like sneezes, giggles like carbonated bubbles breaking the surface of something
you'd believed was firm, solid, permanent, unbreakable, the way
in her car that day, fleeing Mrs. K., Mrs. D. found herself driving
like a drunken woman, dizzy-drunk, scary-drunk, but also *happy-*
drunk as she never is in real life, she was hearing laughter in the
Mercedes, washing tickling over her, so funny! so wild! you
should have seen that woman's face! that bully! that bore! how
dare she! intimidating us! touching us! like that! how dare! as if
I wasn't, for once, telling the truth!
    Hardly a five-minute drive from the Kerns' house on Juniper
Way to the Delahunts' house on Fairway Circle, but Mrs. D.
switched on the radio to keep her company.
    There.

REYNOLDS PRICE

The Fare to the Moon

FROM THE SOUTHERN REVIEW

1

AS EVER, she woke sometime before light. In the fall of the year, and with war savings–time, that meant it was just before five o'clock. The only timepiece in the house was his watch; and that was under his pillow still, still on his wrist. His brother would be here in half an hour; his overnight satchel was already packed — a clean pair of drawers, his toothbrush and razor, a Hershey bar she hid in a pair of his mended socks. There was nothing for her to do here now but make the coffee and watch him walk through the door, down the slope to his brother's car and then away.

She had halfway dreaded the news all summer; but when the letter came three weeks ago and he said "Well" and left it open on the table to read, she knew this morning would be the last. No way the army would turn down a man as strong as he — not scarce as men were, this late in the war. When he had seen her pick up the letter, he stood at the screen door, watching the woods, and told her the ways you could beat the draft — all the foolish dodges he'd heard from scared boys. His favorite seemed to be vinegar and prune pits. The night before your physical exam, you drank a tall glass of white cider vinegar and swallowed three prune pits. Then you told the army you had stomach ulcers; they x-rayed your belly, saw the dark shadows and shriveled lining and sent you home with a sympathetic wave.

Without a word, she had bought the prunes and left them out on the shelf by the stove; the vinegar was always there in plain view. But he never mentioned the plan again, and last night she knew not to bring it up. Every bone in her body guessed he meant to leave. It made good sense, though it hurt like barbed wire raked down her face. She even guessed it hurt him as bad, but he never said it. And she wouldn't force it from him, not that last night. That was up to him.

After she brushed her teeth on the stoop and peed in the bushes, she came back in, damped the woodstove down, then shucked her sweater and dungarees, put on the flannel nightshirt and crawled in beside him. She had lain there flat, saying her few prayers quick before he touched her. But he never did, not with his hands. Their hipbones touched and parts of their legs; but somehow the warm space built up between them till she felt gone already, that near him.

After five minutes he said "Remember, I set the alarm." He knew how much she hated the bell; it was one more way to say *You do it. You wake up and spare us.*

She had said "All right" and then "I'm thinking you'll live through it, Kayes." He had said many times that he knew, if they took him, he'd die overseas; and most of the times, he would laugh or sing a few lines of some hymn. But she knew he meant it; she said it to help him face the night, not because she was sure. And as far as she could tell, he had slept like a baby. She thought *I slept like a baby too, a mighty sick child;* but she also knew she had not dreamed once. That froze her as much as the cold dawn air — *If I didn't dream last night,* I'm *the corpse* — and she calculated they had the minutes to hitch up, one more farewell time. Her hand went toward him under the cover.

For the only time in the months he had known her, he stopped the hand with his own and held it. In another minute he said "Much obliged," then threw back his side of the cover and sat up.

It was still too dark to see him move; so before he could strike a match to the lamp, she thought "Except for this war, we'd stay right here. He don't give a goddamn for nothing but me." Even without the sight of his face, she almost half believed it was true. And early as it was in a chilly week, she was more than half right. It had been nearly true for six quick months. He had never admitted as much by day; but he proved it at dusk by turning back up at this door here, living her life beside her in private and

sometimes in town and telling her things with his body by dark
that, she almost knew, were meant to last.

When he finished the coffee, he poured hot water in the big tin
pan, lit the lamp by the mirror and slowly shaved.

She sat at the table and watched every move. All her life, she
envied men those minutes each morning, staring at a face they
seemed not to notice, not trying to make it thinner or lighter, just
taking it in.

Then he put on the first necktie he had worn since moving here; it had waited on a nail in the old pie safe. He took
his change and knife from the shelf and portioned them out
into several pockets. He took up the long narrow wallet and
searched it.

She thought "Oh Jesus, now here it comes. Like every other
white man God ever made, he thinks we can cross this out with
money."

But he managed it altogether differently. He came the whole
way to the table and sat again, in a fresh cold chair. He said
"Please look right here at my eyes." When she looked, he said
"You have been too good to me, every day. I will know that fact
from here to my grave, wherever I find it. If I don't come back
alive in time, remember I said I love you *true*. I was sober when I
said it, and I meant every word." He had still not smiled, but he
leaned well forward. "Now give me both hands."

She had no choice but to spread both palms between them on
the table, though she watched him still. He laid two fifty-dollar
bills down first; then he took off his watch and laid it on them.
He had sometimes let her wear it on days when she doubted his
promise to be here by dark.

She said "The money will help me a lot; thank you kindly. But
you're going to need that watch overseas."

He understood she didn't mean that; she meant she thought it
belonged to his wife, had been her gift to him years ago. So he
closed both her hands now, money and watch, and said "I bought
that watch myself. It's yours till the day I walk back in here,
claiming it again."

She had to nod, dry-eyed as a boy.

He stood up and, before he got both arms in his coat, a car
horn blew way down by the road. He stepped to the door.

She stood where she was.

With a hand in the air, he kept her in place. "Don't let me see you in the cold," he said. Then some way he melted, silent, and was gone.

It was then that she knew the room was hot and dry as a kiln. She thought she was free to howl like a dog, and she sat there and waited for a moan to rise. But the car door slammed; and she heard it leave and fade completely away toward Raleigh with still no tears in her eyes, no moan. She said his name *Kayes* and waited again. But no, nothing came. So she stood and rinsed out both their cups and set them upside down on the shelf where they sat before he ever came here. Beyond her even, they had been her grandmother's and had sat unbroken in this same room long before she was born to meet this man that hurt her like this.

2

You could call me anything — I used to answer. But from way before I remember good, every soul I knew but my mother called me Blackie. *That was because my skin wasn't black. Mama was medium dark, a good walnut. And Red, Mama's aunt that mostly raised me, said my gone daddy was what they called* blue gum *that long ago, with skin so black his gums were blue. Most Negro babies are born real pale; but even with the kin I had behind me, everybody said I was born nearly white and stayed that way when most children shade on off, tan or dark. So somebody called me* Blackie *early, the way they called my fat friend Skinny Minnie; and* Blackie *hung onto my life like a burr —* Blackster, Black, Blackheart. *I answered.*

Even Kayes sometimes called me Black but just if he got mad or hungry — "Black, get your butt to the stove and start frying." *Mostly he called me Leah or Lee, Leeana, since Leah is my given name. Mama always said it came from the Bible. But when I got old enough to read for myself, the Bible said Leah was what Jacob got for his first wife when what he worked so long for was Rachel. It even said he hated Leah, and that set me back — I was meeting stiff winds from a good many sides, without adding that. So I waited till Mama was gone one night, and then I asked Red. She said* "Your mama can't read a soap box, much less the Good Book. What you think she knew about some dead Leah? She just heard a preacher calling that name and liked the sound. Your mama* *would crawl to the moon for a sound — music in her* bones; *her daddy could* sing."

There have been many people that took me for white. And they didn't think my name was a joke, or maybe it came from my straight hair. Red said I come here, a nappy-haired baby; but it straightened out natural when my bosoms came. Half the men I know — any color you name — have tried to touch my hair, just for luck if no more, no serious fun. I been a clean person; I mean my skin. *Even before I could hardly talk, in this cold house, Red said I would scrub in icy well water before she had time to boil the first kettle — said "Black, you would flat-out* polish *your hide."*

I would. And it paid. I don't mean I've yet took one penny for it. I'm way too proud and, till this spring, I never saw a man I wanted to have it. I mean my skin is the finest I've seen; and I've been up and down the land since 1919, when Mama lit out of here with me by the hand. First stop was Wilmington, Delaware. She stayed a few years; then came on back, too sick to take that winter they have. Watching her cough blood, I began to see I'd die someday. So I traveled a lot while I had strength.

Harlem, Springfield, Pittsburgh — you name it. And nobody, white or green, can match me, nobody I've seen; and I've seen a heap of shows. It's made me good friends, all up the line. Friends, *I'm saying, not tomcats prowling — they'll eat any* meat. *Monied ladies in Packard cars, old men at clubs where I served meals, they told me time and again "You're splendid. Can I touch you for luck?" I tell 'em I'll touch* them *and then touch their hand or the back of their wrist. That does the trick.*

It puts them at ease, almost every time, and I pass on. I've met little meanness, wherever I went; and the little I meet, I dodge in the road or slap up side the head bad, *then run. So I was up North from eighteen to thirty, from the year Mama died down here with TB till fifteen months ago when Red broke her hip and sent for me. I hauled my precious skin on home, this ramshackle room, and kept watch with her till she passed on.*

If I do say so, I did more than watch. Red got far more worse off than a baby, *couldn't hold her water nor none of her mess. She thought I was my own mama most nights. She would lay me out for bringing men close as her Cape jasmine bush, under that window facing the road, and humping on the* ground *where Red could hear.*

I heard more of it than anybody knew. And God's my witness, till I got Red laid out in a casket in white satin pleats and deep in the grave, no

man nor boy — not to mention hot women, and several have tried —
ever laid more skin on me than a finger. I was one brown girl that had
heard enough from two tails pumping. I'd take any music on Earth to
that, any wreck or scream.

All through Red's last weeks alive, men would walk in here with hot
fish dinners, chicken salad, peach pie. I'd thank them "profusely," as Red
used to say, and ask had they heard any war news today? That *would*
throw 'em for a loop! They were all 4-Fers with pus in their blood or,
worse, they were hiding out from the army. Till this war's over, I won't
take that; I feel right patriotic someway. Back at first, I even had dreams
of being an army nurse and going to England when they were so bad off,
bombs every night. I was still fool enough to think they could train you
fast and ship you out. Every Negro I told said "Get your head tested,
child. It ain't your fight. They don't want you." So I stopped telling my
hopes and dreams. But my mind never changed, which is why I couldn't
tell Kayes to shirk, even with that box of prunes I bought.

He came to Red's funeral with Riley his brother. When Kayes walks in,
nobody sees Riley; but he's all right or used to be. Red had been their
grandmother's cook many years; and they were so welcome that one of my
cousins, the big head usher, set Kayes on the front row next to the aisle.
When they led me in behind the casket, the only pew vacant was that same
pew. So I nodded to Kayes, that was next to me, and sat two or three yards'
distance from him.

Make a long story short — he came on with us to the grave out back
and saw Red covered. It near killed me and, swear to God, I thought he
filled up. See, he had loved his grandmother much as I loved Red. She
had raised him when his own mother left, run off with her own first
cousin — a drunk — and left Kayes's daddy, Kayes himself who had just
started talking good and Riley, an even younger baby. She left *them,*
clean as a bat leaves Hell every evening at dusk. And Kayes's old grand-
mother, Miss Marianne, she took the whole crowd in and raised him
right. Or at least the best she knew how to do, with my Red cooking every
crumb they ate and washing and pressing every thread they wore. So sure,
he ought *to have cried at her grave.*

What he did after that was walk halfway through the grove to his
Chevy with Riley beside him. Then he stopped in his tracks like my eyes
had shot him. I hadn't been watching him all that close — I was bent with
the hardest grief I'd known, till this week now — but he spoke to Riley,
who kept on going, and then he came back. When I saw him turn, I said

*in my heart "He's coming to me." I was dead-out wrong. It was still too
early in the spring for flowers. But somehow, somewhere Kayes found a
bloom — a white carnation that had seen better days. It was in his left
hand. No other carnations were anywhere near, no wreath he could have
stolen it from. I know I told myself "Black, he's* grown *it." I must have
thought it bloomed that minute in his fist — big fist that had already
bruised it some.*

*Anyhow not looking to me one time, he came right back to the edge of
the grave, where Red's coffin sat with clods on the lid — two boys were
standing there, waiting for me to move out of sight so they could finish —
and he reached far down as his arm would go and let that one bloom fall
on the dirt, where I knew Red's face was still looking up. I'd never been
partial to grown white people. Red and Mama both said you could trust
them if you'd known them long.*

*I'd known Kayes Paschal since I was maybe four years old — Red
bringing me to work some days when Mama was too sick to watch me and
then was dead. I never had paid him that much notice. There at the grave
though, I thought he looked good. Everybody but Kayes thought that and
still thinks it. But sad as I was, he got no deeper into my mind or bosom
than any tan man, not to mention the dark. I knew he married the banker's daughter that Red once said "could frost the sun," and she didn't
mean with sugar.*

*But once I heard that flower hit Red's dirt, something snapped inside
me in the midst of my chest. It takes a lot more than a white carnation to
catch* my *eye. I didn't forget we were separate people, Kayes and me. I
never once thought he'd speak to me, and I didn't dream I'd want it. But
for some strange reason, I had help up good, right to that moment. You'd
have thought I was some neat-dressed great-niece of Red's. But with
Kayes coming back, giving Red that much, I said in my heart "Live
through this, Leah, and you're* guaranteed.*" I don't know what my fool
mind meant.*

*I sure didn't think how hard his family had worked poor Red and for
what slim pay, or how they'd drive her out every night to this piece of a
shed, saying "See you tomorrow," when for all they knew she'd die in the
night of cold or snakebite. All I understand, even today, is I took the first
step forward to meet him. Kayes saw me moving and stepped on toward
me. It wasn't till he put out his big hand that I saw the wide gold ring on
his left; he was still married to her. But it meant no more to me that day
than a callus or a mole on his finger would.*

Four days later though, as I was thinking I might better get my butt back North, I had stepped out into Red's yard to wash my hair in the sun. It was almost dry when something made me look toward the road. And here came Kayes again, walking the way he had to Red's grave, with his chin tucked down and leaning a little forward on the air, like a wind was trying to send him home. I said to myself "It's nothing but Kayes."

But once he got through the blackberry vines and spoke to the dog — they were friends, way back — I felt my eyes go straight to his hands. Big as they were that day by the grave, they had grown again. The right hand carried a brown paper sack (turned out it was three of the Hershey bars that Red used to want); the left hand that day was naked as mine. My mind said "Blackster, here it comes. Say no. You're too good for this." Even if no two people alive would believe a woman named Blackie was a virgin at thirty-one, I meant not to change, not for this white man I'd known all my life — gold ring or no. Turned out I was wrong.

3

Kayes's only brother was driving — Riley, three years younger but badly nearsighted and safe from the draft. He had married young, a plain girl tall as Riley and patient with all his shyness and fears. And they had two daughters, both smart and so lovely you might have looked at their pleasant parents and thought each girl was bought or adopted from a line of beauties or personally sent as a gift by God. As Kayes sat quiet in the car beside him, he thought "You're plain as boiled potatoes, but you sure got the luck."

It was not self-pity, just the visible truth — look at Riley's wife, their girls, his money. Kayes and Riley had split their father's land with an amicable coin toss. Kayes got the better half and a hardworking tenant but lost money most years. Riley coined gold on sandy soil with a string of tenants no better than thieves. Look at his homely wife, not a penny to call her own and from poor country stock but a certified saint. Kayes's wife Daphne had money to spare from her banker daddy and blood so blue it could pass for ink; but her mind had shut when the son was born, named Curtis after her dead father.

Good as Curtis was, the boy drew all her care onto him. Kayes had guessed that things would balance out as the boy got older.

But now he was fourteen, and still Daphne watched him like the first angel landed. So for that many years, except on unpredictable nights when her gate swung open with no complaint, Kayes was lonesome as the last tree standing on the moon itself. And full though he was of love and need, until he saw Leah that day at Red's funeral, he had touched no more than three other women. And all were white, all big young country girls that laughed at the end and went back to work with barely a word to prove he'd known them.

The Negro part had concerned him at once. When he turned away from Red's graveside, and Leah there behind him, he told himself "Forget her *now*." And he nearly succeeded. Despite the fresh sight of Leah's good face and his older memory of tales his friends told, long years back about colored girls, Kayes's mind soon turned to the things he must order for his tenant at the Feed and Seed — a load of cottonseed meal, one of lime, a case of formula powder for the baby (the tenant had four, none old enough to work).

It wasn't until he climbed the steps of his house an hour later and heard Daphne calling to Curtis — "Baby, *run*" — that Leah rose again in his mind, exactly as fine a face and bones as anybody left in the county, any woman. And before his hand touched the front-door knob, Kayes thought "I've known her since before she could talk." It was simply true but it meant a great deal, much more than he planned, from that week on till now today.

Riley cleared his throat to break the long silence. "You think they'll want you?"

Kayes was so far off, it came at him strangely. "Want me? The army? They'd want *you*, Bud, if you weren't blind."

Riley took both hands off the wheel and bent to the windshield to search out the road, a blind driver. Dawn was in progress, a dull tin color, and the windows were still transmitting cold. "You used to have your old heart murmur. What happened to that?"

Kayes said "My heart ain't spoke for years." He did not mean anything deep or sad; but once it was out, he thought it through. It was wrong; he had spoke out to Leah, just now, in the room. Knowing they had less chance in the world than a baby left all night in the snow, Kayes had finally told her the weight she had in his mind and heart. He turned to the side of his brother's thin face. They had not shared secrets for twenty-odd years; but they'd never broke faith, never lied when pressed or failed one another's unending trust. So Kayes said something he had planned for days, "Riley, if I get killed over —"

Riley didn't look but his right hand came out accurately and brushed Kayes's mouth.

"No, old Bud, this has to be. If I come back in less than top-shape, you'll be my executor; so you need to know. Daphne has got her own money, a plenty. Anyhow the law gives her a widow's share. Most of the rest goes to Curtis of course, but I put down five thousand dollars for you. Please give half of that to Leah."

"Leah?"

"Lee — Blackie — you know. Don't fail me, Bud."

Riley said "Absolutely." And when Kayes stayed quiet, he said, "You really want to leave, don't you, Kay?"

Kayes nodded. "Yes, God — *leave* now awhile but not *die*, I guess." Then he chuckled.

Riley said "I'll be here to meet you, be sure. But where will you live?"

Kayes looked to his right. The sun, in climbing, had turned the pines from a near-black green to a color that made him think "Emerald." As a boy Kayes collected the *most,* the *best,* the *scarcest* things; and somewhere he read that perfect emeralds were rarer than diamonds and cost more money. Though he was the least poetic of souls and cared less for money than a year-old infant, he looked at the pines now and thought "Countless billions." Then he wondered what in the world he meant. Well, surely he was trying to dodge Riley's question. So he kept on looking, counting pine trunks now.

Riley said "You understand Blackie will need to leave, if the army takes you?"

Kayes said "Why's that?" He still faced outward.

"Assuming some white trash doesn't burn her house down, what will she eat? Nobody that knows about you and Daphne will give Black a job."

Kayes saw that was right. But he played the words again in his mind — was Riley hateful at all, out to hurt him? Did he mean to harm Leah? But in memory, the words played back straight and

true. As ever, Riley had no grain of spite. So Kayes felt safe to
look around — Riley met his eyes for as long as was safe — and
said "O.K., I'll authorize you to pay her a wage to stay at old
Red's house and fix it up. Paint the walls, mend the windows —
Lee's smart with a hammer; she says she's worked, painting
rooms up North."

Riley said "I don't doubt it. But Kay, that's not your house to
fix. Nor mine, don't forget. Grandmother gave it to Red, long
since, and the half acre round it."

It was news to Kayes; he thought the house was on Riley's half
of the family land. All through his time out there with Leah,
when his mind backslid, he told himself "My family's owned this
house forever. Let any fool tell me to leave." He gave a little
shake and tried to laugh. But Riley's profile was solemn again. So
Kayes said "You might should have told me that, months ago."

Riley said "You're a grown man. You chose your path."

Kayes waited a good while. "How lost did I get?"

"Beg your pardon?"

Kayes saw Riley now as he was in childhood, a serious boy who
would answer you true — anything you asked. "How much have
I broke?"

Riley knew they were in deep water now; he gave the question
the thought it required. Then again he looked over, for the time
he could spare. "Maybe nothing. Daphne's strong as an iron
stake." He tried to end there.

Kayes pushed him on. "I've got a son —"

Riley nodded. "I'm his godfather. You forget that?"

"Have you talked to Curtis in all these months?"

Riley said "Every Sunday but Easter — he was busy."

"How much does he hate me?"

Riley said "A good deal. He's protecting his mother. You know
how that is."

"Any chance he could ever feel better about me?"

To both their surprise, Riley suddenly laughed. "If you died a
big hero, scaling the breastworks, shot in the brow, Curt might
recover."

Kayes managed to smile. "I may oblige him."

"They don't have breastworks these days, Kay."

By now they had passed all the good things to see, the useful sights — trees and fields and low white houses in bare oak groves, the big hollow rock where a family was buried upright in a shaft, a mother and father and three young boys. Now they were coming to the fringe of Raleigh, where the town swelled out and killed the land from bedrock upward. Even the vacant ground was blighted, unwilling to yield. Kayes told himself "They are all better off, with me out of sight." He meant all the people who thought they needed to lean on him; he hoped they knew better.

Riley spoke as if each word cost thousands. "I guess this here is your best bet, a piece of the war. But I want you to know — I'll miss you terrible. You're a lot to me, Kayes, and nothing's changed that."

Kayes knew not to look; it would break them both. But he said "I guarantee I feel the same." And from there till they parked in front of the place where he and assorted men and boys would be examined for nothing but strength and the sense — if called upon — to die decent, Kayes thought about Leah.

Forget about Hitler and the wide Pacific, I could die this minute in full possession of all I hoped to find in life, whoever I hurt — and I stand ready to pay for them, two of the faces — (I can't help Leah). One smart grown woman wanted *me. Just me in a room, no money, no stunts, no lifetime deal. No mention of what any blind man could see — we were different animals, her and me, not meant to plow in a double yoke, not here nor now.*

But we made it last for six whole months. Any hour on the clock, I could slide my car in off that road, below Red's pitiful piece of a house, and set my foot to the ground to climb those last hundred yards; and Lee would know *it. Some piece of her mind would know I was back and would raise her whole fine shape to meet me. Not a time, no single time I recall, did I climb all the way to the house without her walking to meet me or waiting in the yard with a cup of water or, if it was cold, in the window at least with oil light behind her and both eyes ready to smile me in.*

My skin. *She evermore used my skin. She was like a sensible squaw in the winter, kids starving around her and then her man kills one last deer — Leah took my body and used every* part *to save us both, not a particle wasted. It was all food and* easement. *That's a word I'd never used but in farming, giving somebody an easement on land, to haul his crop across some corner of your woods or fields. But toward the end of the first whole week I stayed at Red's, I woke in the night and could hear Leah breathing like she was awake. She didn't speak though. The few other women I've known, deep in, would need to speak at a time like that, just to prove it was real. Lee was calm as ever. So a word just came to my lips, and I said it — "Easement" — and Lee said "True." I still think she understood all I meant, though we never discussed it by daylight. Never.*

Have I wrecked her too? Bud's right; some trash boys might try to scare her — the Cagles or some of the moron Coggins. But once I finally told her, last night, the possible mess I might leave her in, didn't she say "Where you think I been? I didn't turn nigger this afternoon. All my life I lived for trouble — and child, trouble came — so I take my chances, like I took on you. Look what that got me." When I asked her what?, she said "Some time, a piece of time to think about in my old age, if I live to keep thinking and figuring out." Then she broke out smiling in the dim oil light, the smile that could give me all I lost. And when I tried to say what to do tonight, if the army kept me, she put both hands to her ears and frowned — a grown woman's frown, knowing all she knows. And speaking of pain, she out-knows me.

Riley found a parking place in sight of the warehouse and killed the engine. He looked to Kayes and said "Can I come in?"

Kayes said "Thank you, no. They'd ship you straight to Japan by noon." It didn't mean anything but "Clear out please; let me do this right."

"But what if they fail your stiff old joints? — you've got to ride home."

The fact had really not dawned on Kayes; he was so sure of leaving. He thought it out, chose to skip the word *home* (where on Earth was that?) and then said "The bus'll stop right by Red's, if I ask it to. I won't need it though." He leaned over slowly and amazed his brother with a silent hug. When Kayes sat back, he looked to the panel clock; it was almost seven — he was in good time. He opened his door and said the last thing. "If you don't hear from me by dusk, please drive out to Red's and tell Lee I'm gone. If she needs to go on somewhere safe — maybe one of her cousins — I'll pay for your gas." He handed Riley the keys to his car.

Riley took them and nodded.

And Kayes loped away. Within three yards, he told himself "I

will never see that boy's face again." The boy was Riley, as ever in
his mind. Sad as he knew he ought to feel, Kayes was light on his
feet; and when a kid stood back to let him enter the building first,
Kayes said "We're in the same rowboat, son. You first. After you."

The boy said "Yes sir" and took the lead with all the joy of a
Judas goat at the slaughter pen.

For an instant as the boy moved, the side of his face looked like
young Curtis — young as Curt anyhow, smart and distrustful.
But still Kayes could laugh.

4

Since it was Saturday, Curtis had planned to sleep till ten, maybe
closer to noon. Then he meant to find Cally, his friend with the
rifle, and go squirrel hunting. But at eight o'clock, Daphne came
to the shut door, waited a minute, creaked it open and said
"Please, Curt. I need you today."

He could always wake on a dime, that fast; but he lay on and
thought "You need somebody but I'm not the man." Beneath
him, his dick was hard as a spike; he thought "I'll never get it
down in time." But he said "What for?"

"What time did your father say he was leaving?"

Kayes had been at the west-side door of school yesterday afternoon as Curtis came out. The boy had seen the car, first thing,
and was split between a taste for running straight to it with pleasure and the colder sense of his mother's pride — what she was
still bearing and would need from him. He had seen his father
only four short times in the past six months, and each time was
harder than the one before. So Curtis walked over slowly now,
opened the door and leaned in gravely. Kayes asked him to sit
for a minute and talk. The boy obeyed but the talk came mostly
from Kayes — he had already given Riley instructions to pay for
anything Curt really needed. If the army took him, he'd write
letters weekly; please write to him.

All Curtis could do was nod "Yes sir" and wish it would stop.
He loved this man so much and so deeply, so faraway back in the
fourteen years that felt long to him. Bitterness poured up into
his mouth now and nearly choked him. Curtis kept saying, time
and again to himself, "If he just won't say that woman's name" —

the only name Curtis knew was Blackie; and he heard that at
school, not once from his mother. She'd die before speaking it.

When Kayes let up, the boy looked at him for the first full time
and said "I've thought this through a lot. I hope they take you, I
hope you come back, I hope it's *you* when you get here though."
Kayes waited awhile, looking ahead, and then said "I thank you.
And I'll work on it, son. But this may *be* me, right here and now."
Then he gave Curt an envelope that, back home, turned out to
be two fifties — new as if printed that morning. At the supper
table when the boy's mother asked if Kayes had seen him, Curtis
told her all of the truth he could risk, "Yes ma'm. He looked
ready." She started the growling edge of a sneer; but Curt faced
her down — no word, wide-eyed.

Now as he lay still, praying she would vanish, she held her
ground and repeated "What time?"

"Ask Riley," Curtis said.

"*Uncle* Riley —"

"You know who I mean; he's got a phone."

"Don't be impudent, son — I slept at least two minutes last
night. Anyhow I know Riley's driving him to Raleigh."

"Then you know more than me. I was sleeping fine."

"Curt, where is his car?"

"In Raleigh, I guess."

Daphne said "Surely not; he'd ride with Riley."

Curtis sat up suddenly and faced his mother. Her face, the
face he served every day, was strung tight now and scarily pale.
Still he said "Then I guess the damned car is at Blackie's place.
He gave it to her." Curtis had never seen Blackie, not close at
hand. But once her name was loose in the room, it threatened to
stand her between them now, tall and stern and smelling like
Kayes.

Daphne swallowed hard but concealed the shock. Finally she
said "Is that a known fact, or are you just dealing in meanness
today?"

Curtis said to himself "One more bull's-eye," and his face
flushed red.

He turned to the wall, but he said "What now?"

She said "I've thought all night. By decent rights, that car is
ours —"

"He's not dead, Mother."

"*Hush.* But you know full well the army will take him."

"I don't, no ma'm."

Daphne waited. "Not a blemish on him, not to the eye."

Curtis said "His ear, that strawberry mark."

Before she thought, Daphne said "*No,* that used to be lovely."
Then she heard herself and took a step to leave.

But Curtis said "We could drive out and get it."

"You and me? But who would drive it back? Baby, you aren't
legal at the wheel, not yet."

"You got your key? I can drive as good as any two men; nobody'll stop us."

Daphne said "What if she's there? And what if Riley brings
him back?"

Curtis's dick was calm for the moment. He knew he must take
that chance to dress. As he threw back the cover, he said "I'll tell
my father it was my idea; he still likes me. You can let me out on
the road and head back. I'll handle the rest." As his mother
turned to get herself ready, Curtis made his voice easy; but what
he said was "My father's name is *Kayes* — remember? — not just
he."

Daphne said "I can't say it." It was only a fact, not a plea for
pity.

But all the way into deeper country, with Curtis sullen on the seat
beside her, she gripped the wheel and thought little else. *Kayes,
Kayes. I want it all back, those short first years we were good to each other.
You can't want this; surely you're crazy. But none of your people have lost
their minds; God knows, none of mine. And I can't blame liquor, which
both of my sisters can blame in good faith — I doubt you've had three
drinks in ten years — so here I've stood with no explanation to give the
world, except to say you've lost your mind.*

*All the women I know say that much already, when I'm not present —
though ten days ago in this same car, Roe Boyd said, out of the absolute
blue, 'Daph, the fact that the girl's light-skinned as you makes it all the
worse.' I pretended I missed it and Roe shut up. But I understood her —
Kayes, if you'd gone to a coal black girl, we'd have had this over long
months ago and be back together, on the old right rails. Tell that to any
three doctors south of Baltimore, and they'd sign an order in a New York
minute to straitjacket you and cool you off till reason prevails.*

But you picked a woman no darker than I get, after two or three clear

*days at the beach. And stayed beside her in a house the wind can walk
right through. I've been there with you, far more than once, to see old Red
at Christmas and Easter. Remember I told you her roof was bad and you
sent a man out with brand-new tin, and Red sent me two big dressed
chickens, ready to fry? Red would die all over again, if she knew — you
preying on a child she raised, a Negro that naturally thinks you're God
or, if she doesn't, can't help herself; can't make you leave; may even die
for knowing you, if you leave today and the trash get at her.*

*I'd pray to die, if Curtis didn't need me. I've asked the Lord if I can
pray for you to die in battle soon, in some brave act that cancels this and
lets us lift our heads and move on. But I get no more from God than from
you — not a word, not a look. I go to church and sit there waiting. It
might as well be one dim coffin with me nailed down, alive and stifling
and beating the lid; but nobody hears and no help comes.*

*The nights I've lain awake and watched your pistol on the table, beg-
ging me to pick it up and drive the six miles out to Red's and blow you
and her to deepest Hell, some days at least before God does it. I've cursed
the marksman lesson you gave me. Remember that? Remember anything
we liked to do or pledged to keep on doing forever — like trusting, honoring, serving each other, come sun or storm?*

*We were not back from the honeymoon for more than a month when
you took me out that bright cold Sunday. I thought we were riding
around, just looking. We passed the farm and waved at the tenants. I
thought you'd stop and give the children the Tootsie Rolls we bought in
town. But you pushed on, not saying a word and finally took a sandy trail
that sloped so steep downhill I thought we'd be in water any minute, deep
in. I remember quoting St. Paul to myself, "Love hopes all things, en-
dures all things."*

*I thought I was joking, whistling in the dark. And the sand did deepen
till we nearly got trapped and you stopped cold in a thick bank of briars.
I said "You want me to try to push?" You met my eyes like some rank
stranger. And that was the time I first had to think I'd married a boy I'd
never met, much less really knew.*

*Finally you said "I want you to learn something useful for once." You
always laughed at my fund of knowledge. Remember telling my father
that Christmas "Daph knows everything but how to breathe"? You
reached down under your edge of the seat and pulled out the pistol in a
clean white rag. It looked as big as a cannon to me. Till then I hadn't
seen it — you'd bought it that week. Strange as you looked, I didn't feel*

scared, just puzzled as always. You got out then and beckoned me on.
And what did I do but follow behind you in two-inch heels for what
seemed a mile of ruts and briars? Then the brush stopped dead, we were
in a wide clearing — the light was murky.

But you stood still, not looking at me, and fired six shots at a helpless
pine. Then you reloaded and — still not meeting my eyes or speaking —
you held it my way.

No choice but to take it. Well, I learned to shoot, at the same old tree.
We must have killed it — maybe sixty rounds, most of them mine. Not a
single miss. I could find the pine right now, if it's there.

Were we on Mars? *Has any of this, these sixteen years, really* happened, *Kayes, or am I asleep? I thought I'd love you till both of us died.*
I thought it meant — the one weird day you taught me to shoot — that
you had *to love me. You wanted me, above all, to be* protected *in a world*
you already claimed was wild, *though I didn't believe you yet awhile.*

Even now, this close to Blackie's face, *I beg you to live and come on in.*
I can say your name. I can even say hers; but here and now, in my private
mind, I can barely say home. *Come back to where you promised to stay.*
Everybody will know it was nothing but a nightmare. Wake on up,
Kayes. *There may be time.*

5

The car was there, parked just off the road in a patch of young
cedars. The path to Red's ran uphill from it; and by the time
Daphne pulled to the shoulder, smoke was pouring from the
chimney up there. For an instant she thought "They've burnt it."
Then she thought "She's burning up things of his." But she knew
both were wrong. And Curtis was reaching to open his door. So
she said "I'll drive on down to that sycamore, turn and then follow you on home. Drive slow and easy; and if a patrolman stops
you, I'll explain you're helping your mother out."

Curtis had got his door wide open, and one leg was out.
"Mother, I'm a lot better driver than you. You better hope I'm
near if *you* get stopped." He finally looked back and halfway
grinned.

But Daphne had seen a flash of green. The door of Red's
house had swung back silently; and somebody wearing a bright
green coat was standing there, at the top of the steps. A long

brown skirt, tall, a lot of black hair. That moment, for some entirely strange reason, Daphne wanted to wave, to lean out the
window and say "Step here please." The idea scared her but still,
to her wonderment, she felt no shock. She had not seen Blackie
for twenty years maybe; but now the memory of her face in
childhood came to Daphne — such a pale child, more than normally serious with lovely hair, coarse and strong as an Indian's.

By then Black had come down two of her steps. Two more and
she'd be in the yard, by the path.

Daphne said "Curt, don't say a word. She'll know who you are.
Just unlock the car and be ready when I turn. You take the lead."

Curtis shut the door gently and moved to the car. As he bent
to unlock the door, Blackie gave a wide slow wave, took the last
two steps and started toward him.

Then Daphne was scared but also angry. Curt must get out of
this, with no more hurt or shame on his head. So she opened her
door to meet what came. Blackie was no more than twenty yards
off, looking down but still moving.

Curtis looked back with a heavy scowl. "I'm serious, Mother.
Go turn around and wait down there." He pointed ahead to the
white sycamore. And when his mother paused, he said again
"*Go!* Go straight home now. If anything's wrong. I'll hitchhike
in."

His power was so new that Daphne obeyed it. She went to the
huge tree, backed around slowly; and though the woman had
got down to Curtis and they were standing as still as horses,
Daphne passed on by.

When the sound of her car had vanished, Leah said "You got to
be Curtis."

"Yes ma'm, I —" He felt his face burn and pointed to where
his mother had gone. "I guess I'm supposed to drive this home."

Leah said "Was it his idea, your father's?"

"No ma'm, she —" He pointed toward Daphne again.

Leah smiled a little and raised a hushing finger to her lips. "No
need to call me *ma'm* now, Curtis. I may be pale but I live with the
niggers."

He laughed, then flushed again — this was all wrong; he was
falling all over himself like a child. Finally he said "If this car's

yours, or anything in it, I'll hitch right back. It don't really matter." Not thinking, he had switched to the voice he used with Negroes.

Leah corrected him — "*Doesn't* matter" — but renewed her
smile. "I been to school, Curtis; I did right well." She leaned to
see inside the car. The back seat was littered with Kayes's farm
papers, old catalogs, a pair of gray socks. "Not a thing of mine,
nowhere in *sight*." Her smile hung on. "You might be standing
there, two or three days. This road is lonesome."

Curtis nodded. "I know it. My father and I, we hunt out here."
They had not hunted for nearly two years.

Leah said "You know how much you look like him?" Her hand
came up and touched her own face.

Curtis said "Exactly, before he changed."

"How much has he changed?" She asked sincerely, truly not
knowing.

Somehow the boy felt stronger now, older and honest. He said
"I didn't mean you and — all this." He pointed to the house. "I
mean all the years I've known him, fourteen."

Leah said "I knew him longer. My grandmother cooked for
your grandmother. I was in her kitchen when he was a boy."

Curtis said "I didn't know that." It was only the truth, though
even as he said it, he knew he could barely hear himself think.
Nobody had dealt with him like this, in his whole life till now —
this clean dead-level eye-to-eye truth. He knew he was being
rammed forward through time. Any second now, he would be a
grown man, tall enough to do what was right. But though they
both stood waiting for a long time, nothing right or wrong came
to his mind.

At last Leah said "What if they say no and he comes back?"

"Fine by me —"

"The car, I mean. What'll he have to drive, if you take the car?"

Curtis said "He can hitch into town and get it. You don't have
a car?"

Leah looked around as though she might. The only other machine in view was a dead old cookstove, flung in a ditch. She
turned back to Curtis. "I don't have good sense, much less a car."
She wanted to laugh but a hoarse bark came. She wiped her lips
slowly with the back of her hand.

So Curtis said "Did he live here?" He pointed uphill.

"Who?"

"Mr. Kayes Paschal, the man we mentioned."

Leah also looked behind, to the house, as if she had waked in another life and sought landmarks. And she spoke uphill, away from the boy. "He spent most nights for the past six months, ate a good many suppers, drank a whole world of coffee —"

"Hope the army has coffee or he'll desert."

She said "They got it."

Curtis said "Don't think I came out here to be mean, but tell me one thing please — what was this *for*?"

At first Leah thought "He can't be a child." Then she knew nobody but a child could have aimed it, that dead-eye straight. She said "You trying to kill me, fast?"

"No, I'm hoping to find my father. See, I'm the one missed him all this time."

Leah's hand went out again — stop please now. Thank Jesus she'd spent no time around children. "I wish I could answer, son. Did we hurt you bad?"

"Bad. Yes. And I'm *his* son." He tried to ease it with a partial smile.

She took it full-face but had to wait. "Did me being colored make it worse on you?"

Curtis knew at once and shook his head firmly. "It was you being in this world, out here."

As calmly as if she asked for the time, Leah said "You want me to die right now?"

He said "No. Not now — years ago, before I was born."

"What about your mother?"

He said "What about her?" He had already noticed they hadn't mentioned her.

"You don't fault her for any of this?"

Curtis said "Not more than fifty percent."

Calm as she looked, this meeting had struck Leah harder than anything yet, anything her mind had bothered to store. She said "How would you be different now, if this hadn't been?" She also pointed back at Red's house.

He tried to think. But all he could find was "At least I wouldn't be praying my father would head out to war and be shot dead."

Her hand went up to her own open mouth.

Curtis nodded.

"Say no." She took the steps forward and reached for his wrist. Then she shook it between them in the strong new light — the sky had cleared all through their talk. "Tell God right now you don't mean that."

Curtis said "I don't. I meant to hurt you."

Leah said "You did, man. Don't worry, you did." But he looked so much like her memory of Kayes — Kayes way back when — that she had to say "You hate me this much?"

Curtis had heard her call him *man*. He all but smiled. "I'd probably like you. I'm an outgoing fellow."

"But the way things happened put bad blood between us —" She read it as if it was printed plain on the hood of the car.

Curtis said "I guess." He did not know yet, but his face was sliding back in time. He looked like a child again, tired and hungry.

Leah said "You eat your breakfast yet?"

"No, I came out here too fast."

"I'll cook you some eggs."

He meant to say yes; he could learn so much. But now he was young, he said "My mother is waiting for me."

Leah said "If Kayes comes back, I'll tell him you drove it." She looked at him closely, the first time since they grappled so close. He looked even younger than he had at the start. "You sure you got a driver's license?"

Curtis said "No but that won't matter. All the young patrolmen are off killing Japs. These poor old fellows won't even see me."

Leah nodded and walked a long five steps on the uphill path. Then she turned and said "*I* see you, Curtis. I wish I'd seen you sooner than this."

He said "No you don't. I'd have ruined your time." He didn't know everything he meant. He did know he wanted to smile once more but his mouth refused.

Back in the house, Leah went to the mirror and faced herself. No change, same eyes, same clean tight skin. She thought *I'm going to pack my duds and walk out of here*, whoever *comes back. I didn't set up to be this harmful.* But the thought alone hurt as much as any words said this whole long day, that had only just started. In the glass she could also see behind her the neat-made bed where her grandmother died and she and Kayes had spent their nights.

In that empty space, above those pillows, they said things neither one had said elsewhere — Kayes promised her that. And where were they now? The words anyhow were gone past hearing; they had hurt as many people as they helped — she must get them out of her mind right now. Before she could turn away to pack, Leah faced herself a final moment. "Leave it all here, Black. Leave it and go."

And all through his peaceful ride back home, Curtis knew he had learned some large true thing that would lead him into a better life than he'd known till now — less mess, less meanness, fewer people draining his life for blood. He tried to name his hard new knowledge; he wanted to say it out loud in the car so he'd never forget it. And he dug to find it but got no further than the words "I must —"

He pounded the wheel with both clenched hands and rode for more than a mile, feeling bad. But then he noticed how the sky had opened. The sun was strong as he eased into town; and when he paused at the first stoplight, two country girls from his grade in school crossed the street before him — Willie and Flay. They were both already grown up front and had known, for months, things that still baffled him. So he knocked on the windshield and leaned his face well forward in the sun, with eyes half shut.

Both of them saw him, shrieked; then waved and skipped faster, though they looked back, time and again, and talked a clear blue streak till he turned left and moved away — *Curt Paschal's driving, like he's got good sense when we know he* ain't.

6

Kayes walked through the morning like a man still dreaming. When he entered the draft induction center, he found exactly the room he expected — a dim tall space, two-tone gray walls with benches and maybe a hundred men. Mostly boys, as he'd imagined, all smoking like chimneys and nervous as squirrels.

The obvious cause for worry was a sergeant, built like a concrete bunker and seated on a low platform in a kind of pulpit. Everybody tried not to notice him, Kayes included. So Kayes stopped inside the door, leaned on the wall and searched all the faces. Some of the boys looked younger than Curtis and were digging at their crotches, trying to laugh. Only when he hunted a place to sit did he find a friend.

A deep voice called his first two names, "Wilton Kayes." An arm went up, a man half stood; and Lord, it was Brutus Bickford from grade school.

Kayes stepped over to him. "Brutus, they caught us."

Brutus had grinned but now his face sobered. When Kayes was safely down beside him, he said "They ain't catching *me*, I tell you." He fumbled in his watch pocket, drew out a capsule not much bigger than a grain of rice, revealed it to Kayes, checked to see that the sergeant was turned away and then gulped it.

Kayes said "What will that do?"

"You remember I had high blood pressure, don't you?"

High blood pressure in the third damned grade? Still Kayes said "Sure, I forgot for a minute." Wide as Brutus was, and dazed in the eyes, he looked like a calm rock bathed in the sun.

"I've already had what they call strokettes. A friend of mine claims this pill *guarantees* me freedom today."

Kayes thought "Well, death may amount to freedom — good luck, old son." But he said "We'll know in an hour, I guess."

Brutus said "Kayes, Christ, when have I seen you?"

To his surprise, Kayes knew, to the day. "The morning your mama pulled you out of Miss Allen's class and left. The sixth grade, right after Easter Monday. Y'all moved up here, if memory serves."

Brutus took it for granted that his past was remembered. He merely nodded and said "That bastard, Calvin Pepper — Mama said they were married, her third or fourth husband; I still think they were just shacked up. Anyhow some scoundrel meaner than Cal took umbrage one Saturday night that summer and drilled Cal's pea brain with one clean shot, smack-dab right *here*." Brutus tapped a huge finger between his blue eyes, then broke up laughing. "Her and me bought a case of Pepsis with his cash and two bus tickets to Carolina Beach."

"You still live there?"

"Oh no. She may; I come on back up here and been working. I got a young wife, and she's got kids of her own to feed, so I'm a plasterer and good at it too — let me lay you some walls." Then he locked an unblinking stare on Kayes. "Where you been, Bo?"

Kayes suddenly knew he would tell the truth, and it felt like a fruitful island discovered after months at sea. "I been living in the country with a Negro woman named Leah Birch, Red Birch's niece. You remember old Red, mean as a snake?"

Brutus said "I've known very few niggers, Kayes. We couldn't afford 'em and now I don't care."

Kayes took it peacefully, telling himself *That's a novel approach. In a million years, I'd have never guessed that.* There was nothing to say.

But after a wait, Brutus said "You love her?"

Here was a whole new level of surprise. It seemed as unlikely as an angel visit. And a need to tell the truth was still strong. So Kayes said "I doubt I know what love amounts to."

Brutus laughed. "Sure you do. You used to be smart."

Kayes suddenly saw a new part of the afternoon when Brutus's mother took him away. It was right after lunch; and they were into rest time, hearing Miss Allen read *Bob, Son of Battle.* No warning at all, the hall door opened. And there stood a tall woman, dark purple dress, like a country girl with a big open face but confused in the eyes and with caked-on rouge. She didn't even speak to Miss Allen but looked round wildly and said "Where you *at?*" Brutus sat two seats from Kayes; and at that, he stood like a child agreeing to die at dawn. She said "Hey, boy. We're leaving *out.*" By then Miss Allen had summoned her wits and was asking questions. But all the woman would say was "No, he's mine and we're going."

When Brutus had got his jacket from the cloakroom — his books were still inside his desk — he went to his mother but looked back at Kayes. And when Kayes half waved, Brutus had to pretend he couldn't see. His eyes flinched hard but then firmed up and never blinked, from then till the time she turned him and vanished. Kayes had thought before that the worst thing would be to have your father come to school drunk and call your name. But to have your mother come like this, a raucous gypsy — it shocked Kayes, even now, to see it. So he said to this big man beside him, "I hope I do." In the midst of the words, Kayes wondered what in the world they meant.

"You still married to the Mitchell girl?"

How would Brutus know that? "Legally, yes."

Brutus laughed again, not mocking but in sympathy. "That's what matters, ain't it? — that thin piece of paper. They can slice you with that worse than any bullwhip."

Kayes tried to smile and skate on through it. "They got you over miles of barrels, all right." He wondered how many wives Brutus had left, but he knew not to ask. The sergeant had picked up a clipboard and was standing.

Brutus said "You're praying he takes *you*, I bet." By then his face was a new shade of red; the pill was working.

The sergeant said "Alphabetize yourselves." The alphabet was strung round the walls on dingy cards. A lot of the boys were baffled by the order, and Kayes was trying to smile at that.

Brutus spotted the *B* and pointed to it, but he said to Kayes "I never saw much wrong with niggers that money wouldn't fix. How dark is she, Bo?"

Kayes said "Light as me."

Brutus said "Then you're waist-deep in cow pies, ain't you?" But he didn't explain and before Kayes could ask, he whispered "Look, I'm not feeling so good. If I stroke out here, tell the doc what happened and send my regrets."

Kayes said "Be glad to."

Brutus laughed and went.

Half an hour later when Kayes got upstairs, naked as a newt in a line of men in similar trouble, huddled there in a corner was a ring of doctors around a cot. As Kayes worked through a set of chores for medics — kneeling, bending, exposing his ass and throat and coughing — he came near enough to see the cot. Brutus was laid out naked too, pink as a shrimp with a blood-pressure sleeve on and two doctors, each one holding a wrist. Brutus's eyes were shut and Kayes wondered if he had killed himself with that one pill. He figured the doctors didn't know names, so he said "Brutus" firmly.

Brutus looked up and found Kayes near. Hot as he was, for a

long moment Brutus tried to look solemn. But then he checked
on the doctors — they were busy — so he winked at Kayes.

Kayes lifted a finger and smiled. But through the rest of the
next half hour, in other rooms, he went on seeing Brutus two
ways — the boy leaving school and the clown on the cot, swollen
with blood, gambling with death. And when he had done all the
shameful stunts they forced on his body and another sergeant
had looked down a list and said "So Paschal, you're found fit to
serve," Kayes walked away with a stinging surge of raw grief in
his eyes and mind. Over and over, he told himself what he
thought was the truth. With all the pain he had on his own — the
people he had crushed and a war to face — this sadness now was
for no one or nothing but Brutus Bickford years ago, a twelve-
year-old boy run like a windup doll by a whore.

7

Twenty minutes later, dressed and calm, Kayes got his turn in a
dark phone booth. He paid for the first call, to Riley's house. Riley would hardly be home yet; and though his wife had let Kayes
know she despised his face, he could tell her at least that now he
was boarding a bus to Fort Jackson and basic training. That
should satisfy her so much she might unbend enough to say his
name, which had not crossed her lips since the night he left
home.

But Riley answered on the second ring with a slow "Riley Paschal."

Kayes seized up again but cleared his throat. "Sir, this is Dog
Soldier Paschal, reporting."

Riley said "Oh God —"

"They're herding us onto a bus any minute now, for South
Carolina. I passed, flying colors, which is all I know. I'll write you
from down there, soon as I can."

Riley said "Kay, *call* me, night or day. And call collect; that'll
make it go faster." He needed a long pause. "You bearing up?"

"I plan to live."

Riley said "Don't say it."

"Why?"

"Just don't make claims. This is one show run by others now."

Kayes chuckled. "I recently got that impression."

"What can I send you? You're bound to need something."

Kayes said "I've got my shaving kit. They throw in the clothes at camp, I guess."

"Sure, you'll have a full khaki wardrobe, down to the handkerchiefs. I just meant — what? — snacks, playing cards, writing paper, a Bible with one of those bulletproof covers."

Kayes said "Could you ship me a live new brain?"

"Beg your pardon?"

"A head, in good working order. I could bolt it right on."

Riley said "Got a headache?"

The joke had failed. Kayes paused to say it right. "You remember I asked for one more favor."

"I do indeed."

"Will you please do it soon?"

Riley said "You think she'll still be there?"

"I guarantee it."

"Then what do I say? I don't want to tell her too much, good or bad." Riley might have been contemplating trade with the stars; he was that far out of his element.

But Kayes stayed calm. "Just tell her the news — I'm gone; I've already told her the rest. Then see if she wants you to drive her somewhere, in reason, today. She'd never use mine and you scared me a little there, mentioning trouble. I guess I was fool enough not to expect it. You know Red's got those peculiar nieces on the Alston farm, the ones with orange hair. They'd take Leah in, for a few days at least. She'll run it from there."

Riley said "Red's house is Black's now, don't forget. I can't make her leave. Far as we're concerned, she can stay on there till the roof falls in or she's dead — one."

Kayes said "That may be any day now." He knew he was suddenly past understanding himself.

"You want her to stay?" Riley spoke with the cool authority of a good secretary, taking dictation.

Kayes had never asked his brother's advice in this before. But the desolation of an airless phone booth forced him on. "What if I say yes, keep her there till I'm back; set her up in style?"

Riley knew at once. "I'd say you were cruel."

Kayes suddenly saw why he hadn't asked sooner — Riley

would never volunteer a judgment; but ask him and you got it, full blast, both barrels in the mouth. "Bud, is that all I've been up to now?"

Riley said "I prize you too much, Kay, to answer that. I think you did what you wanted to. I know you watched where you put your feet. You saw who you crushed. And I doubt you pressed anybody too weak to bear your weight."

Kayes said "Curtis."

Riley said "Well, Curt —" and he paused too.

Kayes knew he could not take up the slack yet. And in that instant, the smell of boys' feet and the scurf of this old phone's mouthpiece hit his empty gut. He swallowed hard at a gob that rose to his tongue and teeth.

Riley said "You and Daphne have swamped that boy. You owe him and me a careful war, Kay. Get your ass back here in one piece soon, and make him a father for a few more years."

"Perfect," Kayes thought. "Thank Jesus for Riley." But all he said was "Bud, my ass comes in halves like yours."

Riley said "I wore my ass off years ago, dragging after you."

Kayes said "I love you."

Riley said *"Ditto."*

Kayes took ten seconds to crack the door, draw a deep breath and ask the next boy in line for two minutes. Then he dialed the operator and placed a call, collect to Curtis Paschal. The ring went on till he almost quit, though he couldn't imagine the maid at least wasn't home to answer.

Then it stopped, a long wait — Kayes thought it was dead — and Daphne spoke. When the operator asked for Curtis, she said "Curtis Paschal isn't here. I'll accept the charges if your party has a message."

Kayes had not heard Daphne speak in four months; and through that prologue, he could barely listen for the shock he felt in hearing a voice he had all but forgot, a voice he had once loved near to distraction — what? — two or three seconds ago in his life. Time felt that short; his whole sorry life felt five minutes long. So he said "Operator, I'll talk with the lady, if she accepts."

Daphne said "Surely" and the operator vanished.

"Daphne, it looks like I'm in the army."

"I'm sorry, Kayes." She meant it, though she had not thought of the ways.

"Curt's gone, you say?"

"Right now," she said. "He's out at old Red's place, getting the car."

Blood flooded into Kayes's eyes and mind but he knew to wait. Then he said "That can't have been Curt's idea."

"It was mine. Your son and I are your family, nobody else yet." Her voice was level, no glint of meanness, just the facts to date.

Kayes said "But what if I'd got back tonight?"

"The car would have been yours the instant you asked."

He waited again.

So Daphne said "I'm sorry you're mad."

"Oh Jesus, I'm not. I'm standing here though, trying not to break."

Daphne said "I know. Think how I'd have felt if that girl drove your car up here and knocked on the door or left it in the yard."

Kayes said "She's a full-grown woman, Daph, with manners the equal of any I've known. Red raised her, remember, the same as me."

"Your manners — yes, well." Then she heard that they'd come, one more sad time, to the place where every speech was a blade they forced each other to walk, barefoot. "You want to leave some word for Curt?"

"Just the news — the government wants his dad for a while. I'll be in South Carolina by dark and will write him a letter as soon as they let me."

"I'll tell him, Kayes." She seemed to be writing the actual words. "Will you go overseas?"

"May well. This war is far from won."

"We'll both pray for you."

"Can you do that?"

Daphne thought, to be certain. "I haven't stopped yet. I married you — yesterday, it feels like now." Then she almost laughed. "It's hardly likely I'd cease to care."

"Can you say how much?" He amazed himself.

"No, not here, not down a phone wire."

Riley was right; he hadn't broke Daphne. So he honored her

pride and said "I'll try to write to you, hear? I'm a rotten — no — I'm the youngest boy in this whole building, and that's a big claim. It's a poor damned excuse, but I swear it feels true." He knew nothing else.

She said "I'm so old, I knew *Elijah.*" And she thought "Where in God's name did that come from?" She found herself laughing.

Kayes joined in, glad for the first time in days.

But before he could say a decent good-bye, she was gone, hung up.

He spoke her name twice to the dead receiver, then hung up also, clamped his eyes to flush the pain and opened the booth. To the tall young Negro patiently waiting, he said "I wish you better luck, friend."

The solemn black face nodded but said "If I get it, be the first time *I* smelled luck."

Kayes wanted to stand, like a steer in the road, and bellow, *bellow.* Very likely nobody here would notice. But he looked for the bus door and soon found a sign for LOADING DOCK. Those wide red double doors had to be it. Three boys that looked a bare fifteen were pushing through, grinning. For a long moment, Kayes saw their skulls and how they looked in the graves they would find, no time from now.

8

By four that afternoon, Curtis and Cally, his only real friend, had shot three squirrels and a rabbit between them. They would head on in by dark, skin the catch and take it to the freezer-locker plant where they were storing the fall and winter meat for a stew to serve their grade at school on an early-spring picnic. But while the light was as good as this, they sat on a broad flat rock by the creek and watched the creatures they had spared for now.

Cally watched anyhow; he suspected Curt was not seeing much. Beyond the water was a chattering flock of starlings that a full cyclone could hardly scatter, much less a rifle. They flung their bodies through the woods like handfuls of fat black seed; then walked around like important Negroes, casing the leaves.

Cally knew that today was touchy for Curt, and Curt had not

met his eyes for hours, so he finally took the risk and spoke. "You see your pa off?"

Curtis nodded. "Yesterday."

"Will he let you know if they draft his ass?"

"No, Cal. He'll just vanish off like a ghost. He don't give a shit."

The voice was so hard, and the fury behind it, that Cally thought Curt meant all he said — he hated his father for living with a nigger and was glad to lose him. They'd said very little about this, through these past six months; but with Curt not caring now, maybe he could ask. Cal said "You ever get a look at that girl?"

"What girl?"

"Blackie, I guess they call her — you know."

Curtis faced around with eyes blank as washers. And he waited about a month to speak — it felt that long anyhow to both boys. "I spent a good part of this morning with her."

"*No.*"

Curtis swore in silence, with his hand up between them.

Cally had known Curt all his life. Even with rifles beneath their hands, he knew he was safe. "You feel like telling?"

Curtis looked off again, back toward the starlings but still blank-eyed. Then he passed his left hand over all he saw. "I feel like wiping out everything but me." His right hand dug in the dead rabbit's fur, as if for gold.

Cally said "You'd wipe out *everything* — the WACs and nurses and General MacArthur?" He had always served as Curt's private jokester.

But Curt nodded fiercely.

"Present company included?"

Curtis stood up suddenly; the starlings lifted, then settled again. Cal's rifle was still at his feet on the rock. Throughout what came, he kept on hurling rocks at the birds, who hardly noticed. "I flat-out liked her. I saw the damned point."

"In him living with her? Leaving you and your mother to live with a nigger in a one-room shack?"

"Your mother didn't tell you that word was trash?"

Cally said "Sure but I figure she's earned it — that Blackie girl."

"She's old enough to be your mother."

"Thank Christ she ain't." When Curt said nothing, Cal tried again. "You're bound to know what people are saying."

"People are what I'm wiping out, when my time comes."

Cally said "*Halt,* when's that going to be?"

"Me and God only know."

"You think any white girls will go with you now — down the road, I mean, you know, dates and screwing?"

Curtis said "I screw my own right hand. It's free and it's safe, never hurt *nobody.*"

"How about your friend God? He claims it's a sin."

Curtis said "Friend God has said He loves my ass, right down to the ground. I bet He forgives me."

"I won't stand by you on Judgment Day though; I might get singed."

"Cally, you were jacking off four times a day, when I thought dicks were plumbing fixtures."

"You know better now."

Curtis said "I know they've caused more trouble than Adolf Hitler and the Japanese navy."

Cally said "Not mine. Mine's good to me."

"You wait." Curtis put both hands to his mouth and threw a long shout to the trees beyond them. It was not a word; but it seemed to have meaning, though not one bird paid the slightest notice. He took the cool bodies of all they'd killed and, one by one, pitched each one gently toward the deepest pool of the creek below them. Then he bent for Cal's rifle and stood a long moment. He thought *Pray Jesus don't let him speak. I might go wild.*

But Cally sat still as the rock beneath them, still watching the pool where the squirrels had sunk. For some weird reason the rabbit's head was floating still.

When it finally sank, Curtis started back to a home he'd rather have died, here now, than see again.

Cally spoke out strong enough to carry. "I'm still what I've always been to you, hear?"

Curtis never looked back.

"That's my damned rifle."

Curt said "Come get it." But he thought "*Die,* fool" and kept on going, hoping he would see, sometime between this minute and the grave, one narrow path in the thicket ahead that darkened now with every step.

9

Riley turned off the road just before five. He saw at once that the car was missing, and he naturally thought that Blackie was gone. But smoke was rising from the chimney still; and since the house might burn if the stove was lit, he got out and headed up the hill. Before he had gone six feet, up there the door opened; and Blackie was standing — it had to be her, right age and color, though Riley hadn't seen her since Red's funeral day and then just a glimpse, when her eyes were down.

She watched him come another three steps, then put a hand to her mouth, turned back and shut the door.

Riley saw a good stick beside the path and leaned to get it, in case of dogs. Since childhood Riley had dreaded dogs; and Red kept a rough old mongrel that could be here. Dogs hated strange skin color worse than people did. But he got to the front steps with no mishap and stood to wait. Surely she would come to the window at least. When a quiet minute passed, he called out "Hey?" No answer, nothing. So he climbed the rickety steps and knocked. Absolute silence, a far-off crow, cars on the highway two miles west. He tried the china doorknob — open. So he entered slowly.

The room was dark but he stood on the sill and let his eyes open. Then sitting there on Red's old bed was a woman, fine hair and skin, with eyes big as saucers. He said "Is it Blackie? It's been a long time."

"Leah Birch," she said. "You called me Blackie when we used to play."

Riley covered the distance and held out his hand.

She stood and met it — her own palm was cold. Then she went past him and stood by the stove. "I know they took him."

Riley could hear she was sealing a fact, not asking for news. But he gave her a fair account of the trip to Raleigh that morning and Kayes's phone call — no mention of the will.

She heard him out, with hardly a move, both her hands flat down on the stove as if it was cool or she was iron. But even when

Riley said that Kayes had asked him to drive her to her cousins'
for safety, she never budged, shed a tear or spoke. Even as the
stillness grew in the room, she stayed there upright frozen inside.

Riley saw Kayes's watch on her wrist. What else? How much
more of his brother would walk out of here, if she left now? He
didn't mean theft, just sad curiosity. Like others, he noticed
when Kayes stopped wearing his wedding ring. Where was that
for instance — in his shaving kit? What chance did it have when
this all ended, Blackie up North and the war truly won? He told
himself he was wasting time. And at last he spoke to Blackie
again, "I'm as sorry as you." He had not said what he was sorry
for — that Kayes was gone with four people hurt, that this here
was ended or that Black must scuttle in the cold dusk now like a
wanted thing. That far, Riley was truthful with himself and
her — he did not know what he meant and might never.

Still no move from Blackie; was she drunk or doped? So he
said "Kayes is gone, to parts mysterious. That much we know. He
and I talked about you as kind as we could. We think you may be
in trouble here, if you try to stay on — all the mean old boys
aren't dead yet, Leah. So I'll be glad to drive you on to your cousins' place or even the bus station now, while it's light. But listen,
it's over. This time here at least."

Of all wild things, she broke out smiling; and her lips came
open but still no words. She pointed to the left of Riley, toward
the bed.

He looked behind him and there on the floor was a cardboard
suitcase, a green umbrella, a bright green coat and a mannish
hat. "Good. I'll take these down to the car. But first let's see if the
stove is safe."

"Safe. I looked."

Why had that broke her loose? Whyever, Riley knew he must
trust her. If the place burned down, and the brush all round it,
he must not doubt her now. He saw into Leah's clenched mind
that far. He took up the suitcase and said "I guess you'll wear that
hat." Then he thought of the dog. "Red's old dog — is he still
alive?"

"He was way too old, and nobody round here to take care of
him. I killed him, this morning. Buried out back." She pointed
through the wall.

"Killed him? How?"

"Red's pistol. One shot." She reached up and tapped the crown of her skull.

"Red never had a gun."

Leah nodded. "*Did.* Your grandmother gave it to her, week before your grandma died."

"Where is it now, Black?"

"In your hand. In that suitcase."

"Is it loaded still?"

She nodded. "Five shots."

"Can I open the bag and take out the bullets? You keep them on you, just not in the gun."

"I'll do it." She stayed there but held out her hand.

So Riley stepped over and gave her the suitcase.

She took it with both hands and looked hard at him. "Riley, please go on down and wait. I won't keep you."

At first he thought she wanted the privacy to open her things; so he stepped out and was halfway down before he thought *Oh God, this is it.* He walked on slower, awaiting the shot. If it came, he knew the sheriff would believe him — no risk for him. But for everybody's sake, he hoped she'd live. The sight of her hair came now to his eyes, in beautiful waves. He actually spoke, "No, Black. Go easy."

By the time he reached the car, there had been no sound. So he stood on the far side there and waited. The light was leaking away fast now, and a chill was rising. By then he was thinking it might be fate — he believed more nearly in fate than God, some blind hand liable to thrust in the dark. And nothing behind him, in all his life, told Riley who to blame. He thought they had each done the natural thing, every soul involved. Nobody had set out to strew blood and pain. Nobody was wrong but he knew who lost — everybody in sight, Black and Curtis the most. What was taking so long? He thought *I'll call her name again.* It would break whatever spell they were under, that barred them apart while each one waited for life or death. With both hands up to his mouth, Riley called out "Leah?" twice.

And at once she was there in the door, climbing down. Even this late, the green coat looked like spring on the way. The hat was far on the back of her head, and it made her look tall as the nearest pine. She had left the umbrella but clutched the suitcase.

Whatever he believed, Riley said "Thank *you*." Then he went to help her, the little he could.

When he met her halfway down the path, she held out the bag; and when he took it, his hand brushed hers. To himself Riley said "It was simple as that" — he meant the tie between her and Kayes. What else was it for but two human skins, together awhile? It was not a mean or scornful thought; it was really what he guessed had been here. Now it was over. In all his years, Riley had touched no woman but his homely wife. And though his mind, even now, could drift in warm spring weather, no one yet had drawn him toward her — God knew, none here. This pitiful soul with no home to take her and skin that was four strikes against her, wherever. Again he thought "Just let the pain fade." He mostly found that was all you could hope for.

They reached the car. Riley opened the trunk and put in her suitcase. It didn't weigh six pounds; was this all she owned? Surely she had things stored up North. He knew he had a twenty-dollar bill; he'd give her that much.

By the time he got to the driver's door, Leah had seated herself in back, the usual seat for Negro women bound home from work.

Riley almost asked her to sit up front, no harm in it now. But when he looked in the rearview mirror, he thought he could see that her eyes were closed. He cranked the engine and looked again. By then the eyes were open but fixed; so he said in the gentlest voice he could manage "Which is it — the bus or your cousins' place?"

She waited. "Riley, I just don't —" She stopped, dug into a pocket of her coat and brought out a quarter. She cupped both hands to make a tumbler and shook the coin for a long ten seconds, saying "Heads is the bus." Then she opened her hands and looked. "Heads it is."

"The bus station then?"

"That'll be a first step." She still looked down, talking to the coin.

Riley said "To Wilmington, Delaware?"

"Or North Hell, Arkansas. I'll know when I get there." She suddenly laughed.

He tried to join her. "You sure you got the fare for that distance? I could help you a little."

Leah said "I'm richer than you know, Riley. I could buy me a ticket from here to the moon, if the notion struck me."

"Let it *strike*. Shoot fire! — that's a fine idea." He turned back, grinning at the change of tone.

And Leah nodded to him but said "Easy, child. We're all too sad. Let's show some respect."

Riley also nodded, then backed out slowly. By the time they stopped at the first crossroads, it was pitch-black night, that soon and final, the dark of the moon.

10

At that same time a long way south, Kayes woke in a dim bus among boys, mostly asleep and dreaming. He checked the watch of the gaunt lad beside him and saw that somehow he had slept two hours. Then he checked his mind — no dreams he recalled, no blameful faces. But then the stifling pall of grief he had borne all day fell on him again. He shut his eyes and, for the first time, asked to know what he could do to heal some part of the lives he'd crushed — his wife and son and Leah Birch.

Curtis and Daphne at least stood together and shared the weight. But the sight in his mind of Leah alone hurt too bad to watch, even here far off. So he silently asked her face for pardon; no sound came. Why in God's name should it? He knew there was no least hope of pardon till Riley could write and say she was gone, was safe again working and fed somewhere up North where people, at worst, would just ignore her.

It could be a long wait. How could he last through it? — well, minute by minute like all the pain a grown man causes. How could *she*? Kayes tried to imagine her mind, a thing he had never attempted before. Even as a young boy, he thought he had understood his mother when she left them all. He knew he could read all Daphne's thoughts; it was part of why he had to leave — she ached too much every time he touched her.

But part of Leah had stayed shut to him, the part of her mind that planned for him. He was almost sure it had nothing to do with her color; he had known old Red like an easy book. (Among what Kayes could not know here was that, trusting him with her actual life, Leah was forced against her will to hide and damp her hope and dread.) So now he cleared his mind, leaned back again

and asked for strength to wait in patience, for the grace to recognize and make all due amends as time cooled down. He sat for
a long dry spell in the dark. But no help landed, no word, no clue
but the moaning breath of the boy beside him.

In the orange shine of the aisle light, Kayes reached to his own
feet, found his shaving kit and felt through it slowly, a blind beggar. Finally, under a damp washrag, he found the ring that
Daphne gave him, before God and man, the day they were married fifteen years ago. He knew it would be wrong to wear it now,
wrong to all concerned, a sorry joke. But vain as all his prayers
had been, this empty circle might hold inside it his only chance
of coming back whole from this new danger and starting over in
decency.

He knew the notion was maybe childish, maybe wild as Brutus
risking his life on a dynamite pill. Still he checked to see that no
one watched. Then he brought the gold to his lips and slid it under his tongue. For all the last miles to this next place, it stayed
there, hard and bitter but hot. He hoped there would be a place
at the camp, some vault or locker, to hide it.

But what Kayes knew — all he knew tonight — was a harder
fact than a golden ring or even this night that hid the world (they
might be parts of a riding dream). This much was true — he had
spent from eight to twenty-four hours a day, these six months,
beside a kind intelligent person who fit against his mind and
body, and *chose* to fit, in every way a sane human being would
pray to find this side of death. She was one real woman named
Leah Birch — whatever her color or the size of her house — who
had finally cared so deep and steady as to all but fill the gully cut
in him by his beautiful mother when she heard his prayers one
December night and kissed his cheek and then left him forever
by morning. Now Lee was gone too. He had run them both off.
Who else on Earth will ever risk Kayes Paschal again?

11

Five hours later, home from the picture show and asleep, Curtis
told himself the night's first story, a dream to mend as much as
he could in his own cut mind. *This boy and I are standing on a hill at
the end of what looks like a big picnic — plates on all sides, chicken
bones. All but us have gone on home, but we stand here and face the*

sunset. I tell him we ought to watch till it's gone, completely night. He says well no, then we'll never get down. But I can see he's not really scared; he just may not want to scramble in the dark. I think it's because he's older than me, more dignified. At least he's taller and his eyes blink less. I want his company so I fall in with him as he leaves too.

He was right. Before we're halfway down, the light is too thin to see the rocks and gullies beneath us. I can't even see him clear ahead. Pretty soon I'm scared but I feel my way by listening to where he puts his feet. Before long though, even they fade off. I'm feeling my way with bleeding hands, from root to root on the steep dry ground. Finally I'm so deep gone in the dark, and losing blood, that I think "I'm going to yell. He's bound to come." But Lord, I can't remember his name; so I do stop there in the miserable dirt and call my own name, more than once.

Then something pulls my messed-up hands. I can't even see them, but I feel the tug. And then there seems to be a new light, way above me. I'm not even sure which way up is, but I take a chance. And yes, my friend — is he still my friend? — is flying there in a kind of fire that he seems to throw as he moves, like a falling star. But he rises. He rises in slow perfect circles — he knows the way or is climbing to find it — and after a while, I can barely see. I think he goes that far to catch the last daylight, and I try to wait.

That's when the line really hurts my hands. My friend is moving now like a kite, and I've got the string. It's a thick plaited line and is almost gone, so I grab at it while I still have time. And recalling kites and how not to lose them, I reel him toward me turn by turn till, sure, he's back on the ground in reach. But his back is turned. By now I'm guessing it's Kayes somehow. Once he moves though, he's dark again and I can't know. Still I feel the line draw tight once more, and I guess he's tugging me on back down. Without even knowing his face or voice, I try to bet he's taking me home.

Even as the dream threaded Curt's mind and drew him on, in a whole cool room of his understanding, he saw he was dreaming, saw he was easing himself ahead with childish hope. Yet in that same room, he had watched Kayes soar and wished him luck. From the ground Curt even shouted his thanks to the arms that worked in pure dark now — or so he trusted. At the least, that sight of a useful father let Curt sleep till Sunday daylight, clear and dry with slow church bells, the first whole day of his grown man's life.

ANNICK SMITH

It's Come to This

FROM STORY

NO HORSES. That's how it always starts. I am coming down the meadow, the first snow of September whipping around my boots, and there are no horses to greet me. The first thing I did after Caleb died was get rid of the horses.

"I don't care how much," I told the auctioneer at the Missoula Livestock Company. He looked at me slant-eyed from under his Stetson. "Just don't let the canneries take them." Then I walked away.

What I did not tell him was I couldn't stand the sight of those horses on our meadow, so heedless, grown fat and untended. They reminded me of days when Montana seemed open as the sky.

Now that the horses are gone I am more desolate than ever. If you add one loss to another, what you have is double zip. I am wet to the waist, water sloshing ankle-deep inside my irrigating boots. My toes are numb, my chapped hands are burning from the cold, and down by the gate my dogs are barking at a strange man in a red log truck.

That's how I meet Frank. He is hauling logs down from the Champion timberlands above my place, across the right-of-way I sold to the company after my husband's death. The taxes were piling up. I sold the right-of-way because I would not sell my land. Kids will grow up and leave you, but land is something a woman can hold onto.

I don't like those log trucks rumbling by my house, scattering chickens, tempting my dogs to chase behind their wheels, kicking clouds of dust so thick the grass looks brown and dead. There's nothing I like about logging. It breaks my heart to walk among newly cut limbs, to be enveloped in the sharp odor of sap running like blood. After twenty years on this place, I still cringe at the snap and crash of five-hundred-year-old pines and the far-off screaming of saws.

Anyway, Frank pulls his gyppo logging rig to a stop just past my house in order to open the blue metal gate that separates our outbuildings from the pasture, and while he is at it, he adjusts the chains holding his load. My three mutts take after him as if they are real watchdogs and he stands at the door of the battered red cab holding his hands to his face and pretending to be scared.

"I would surely appreciate it if you'd call off them dogs," says Frank, as if those puppies weren't wagging their tails and jumping up to be patted.

He can see I am shivering and soaked. And I am mad. If I had a gun, I might shoot him.

"You ought to be ashamed . . . a man like you."

"Frank Bowman," he says, grinning and holding out his large thick hand. "From Bowman Corners." Bowman Corners is just down the road.

"What happened to you?" he grins. "Take a shower in your boots?"

How can you stay mad at that man? A man who looks at you and makes you look at yourself. I should have known better. I should have waited for my boys to come home from football practice and help me lift the heavy wet boards in our diversion dam. But my old wooden flume was running full and I was determined to do what had to be done before dark, to be a true country woman like the pioneers I read about as a daydreaming child in Chicago, so long ago it seems another person's life.

"I had to shut off the water," I say. "Before it freezes." Frank nods, as if this explanation explains everything.

Months later I would tell him about Caleb. How he took care of the wooden flume, which was built almost one hundred years ago by his Swedish ancestors. The snaking plank trough crawls up and around a steep slope of igneous rock. It has been patched and rebuilt by generations of hard-handed, blue-eyed Petersons until it reached its present state of tenuous mortality. We open the floodgate in June when Bear Creek is high with snowmelt, and the flume runs full all summer, irrigating our hay meadow of timothy and wild mountain grasses. Each fall, before the first hard freeze, we close the diversion gates and the creek flows in its natural bed down to the Big Blackfoot River.

That's why I'd been standing in the icy creek, hefting six-foot two-by-twelves into the slotted brace that forms the dam. The bottom board was waterlogged and coated with green slime. It slipped in my bare hands and I sat down with a splash, the plank in my lap and the creek surging around me.

"Goddamn it to fucking hell!" I yelled. I was astonished to find tears streaming down my face, for I have always prided myself on my ability to bear hardship. Here is a lesson I've learned. There is no glory in pure backbreaking labor.

Frank would agree. He is wide like his log truck and thick-skinned as a yellow pine, and believes neighbors should be friendly. At five o'clock sharp each workday, on his last run, he would stop at my blue gate and yell, "Call off your beasts," and I would stop whatever I was doing and go down for our friendly chat.

"How can you stand it?" I'd say, referring to the cutting of trees.

"It's a pinprick on the skin of the earth," replies Frank. "God doesn't know the difference."

"Well, I'm not God," I say. "Not on my place. Never."

So Frank would switch to safer topics such as new people moving in like knapweed, or where to find morels, or how the junior high basketball team was doing. One day in October, when red-tails screamed and hoarfrost tipped the meadow grass, the world gone crystal and glowing, he asked could I use some firewood.

"A person can always use firewood," I snapped.

The next day, when I came home from teaching, there was a pickup load by the woodshed — larch and fir, cut to stove size and split.

"Taking care of the widow." Frank grinned when I tried to thank him. I laughed, but that is exactly what he was up to. In this part of the country, a man still takes pains.

When I first came to Montana I was slim as a fashion model and my hair was black and curly. I had met my husband, Caleb, at the

University of Chicago, where a city girl and a raw ranch boy could be equally enthralled by Gothic halls, the great libraries, and gray old Nobel laureates who gathered in the Faculty Club, where no student dared enter.

But after our first two sons were born, after the disillusionments of Vietnam and the cloistered grind of academic life, we decided to break away from Chicago and a life of mind preeminent, and we came to live on the quarter section of land Caleb had inherited from his Swedish grandmother. We would make a new start by raising purebred quarter horses.

For Caleb it was coming home. He had grown up in Sunset, forty miles northeast of Missoula, on his family's homestead ranch. For me it was romance. Caleb had carried the romance of the West for me in the way he walked on high-heeled cowboy boots, and the world he told stories about. It was a world I had imagined from books and movies, a paradise of the shining mountains, clean rivers, and running horses.

I loved the idea of horses. In grade school, I sketched black stallions, white mares, rainbow-spotted appaloosas. My bedroom was hung with horses running, horses jumping, horses rolling in clover. At thirteen I hung around the stables in Lincoln Park and flirted with the stable boys, hoping to charm them into riding lessons my mother could not afford. Sometimes it worked, and I would bounce down the bridle path, free as a princess, never thinking of the payoff that would come at dusk. Pimply-faced boys. Groping and French kisses behind the dark barn that reeked of manure.

For Caleb horses meant honorable outdoor work and a way to make money, work being the prime factor. Horses were history to be reclaimed, identity. It was my turn to bring in the monthly check, so I began teaching at the Sunset school as a stopgap measure to keep our family solvent until the horse-business dream paid off. I am still filling that gap.

We rebuilt the log barn and the corrals, and cross-fenced our one-hundred acres of cleared meadowland. I loved my upland meadow from the first day. As I walked through tall grasses heavy with seed, they moved to the wind, and the undulations were not like water. Now, when I look down from our cliffs, I see the meadow as a handmade thing — a rolling swatch of green hemmed with a stitchery of rocks and trees. The old Swedes who

were Caleb's ancestors cleared that meadow with axes and cross-
cut saws, and I still trip over sawed-off stumps of virgin larch,
sawed level to the ground, too large to pull out with a team of
horses — decaying, but not yet dirt.

We knew land was a way to save your life. Leave the city and
city ambitions, and get back to basics. Roots and dirt and horse
pucky (Caleb's word for horseshit). Bob Dylan and the rest were
all singing about the land, and every stoned, long-haired mother's child was heading for country.

My poor mother, with her Hungarian dreams and Hebrew upbringing, would turn in her grave to know I'm still teaching in a
three-room school with no library or gymnasium, Caleb ten years
dead, our youngest boy packed off to the state university, the
ranch not even paying its taxes, and me, her only child, keeping
company with a two-hundred-and-thirty-pound logger who lives
in a trailer.

"Marry a doctor," she used to say, "or better, a concert pianist,"
and she was not joking. She invented middle-class stories for me
from our walk-up flat on the South Side of Chicago: I would live
in a white house in the suburbs like she had always wanted; my
neighbors would be rich and cultured; the air itself, fragrant
with lilacs in May and heady with burning oak leaves in October,
could lift us out of the city's grime right into her American
dream. My mother would smile with secret intentions. "You will
send your children to Harvard."

Frank's been married twice. "Twice-burned" is how he names it,
and there are Bowman kids scattered up and down the Blackfoot
Valley. Some of them are his. I met his first wife, Fay Dell, before
I ever met Frank. That was eighteen years ago. It was Easter vacation, and I had taken two hundred dollars out of our meager
savings to buy a horse for our brand-new herd. I remember the
day clear as any picture. I remember mud and Blackfoot clay.

Fay Dell is standing in a pasture above Monture Creek. She
wears faded brown Carhartt coveralls, as they do up here in the
winters, and her irrigating boots are crusted with yellow mud.
March runoff has every patch of bare ground spitting streams,
trickles, and puddles of brackish water. Two dozen horses circle
around her. Their ears are laid back and they eye me, ready for

flight. She calls them by name, her voice low, sugary as the car-
rots she holds in her rough hands.

"Take your pick," she says.

I stroke the velvet muzzle of a two-year-old sorrel, a purebred
quarter horse with a white blaze on her forehead.

"Sweet Baby," she says. "You got an eye for the good ones."

"How much?"

"Sorry. That baby is promised."

I walk over to a long-legged bay. There's a smile on Fay Dell's
lips, but her eyes give another message.

"Marigold," she says, rubbing the mare's swollen belly. "She's
in foal. Can't sell my brood mare."

So I try my luck on a pint-sized roan with a high-flying tail. A
good kids' horse. A dandy.

"You can't have Lollipop neither. I'm breaking her for my own
little gal."

I can see we're not getting anywhere when she heads me in the
direction of a pair of wild-eyed geldings.

"Twins," says Fay Dell proudly. "Ruckus and Buckus."

You can tell by the name of a thing if it's any good. These two
were out of the question, coming four and never halter broke.

"Come on back in May." We walk toward the ranch house and
a hot cup of coffee. "I'll have 'em tamed good as any sheepdog.
Two for the price of one. Can't say that ain't a bargain!"

Her two-story frame house sat high above the creek, some
Iowa farmer's dream of the West. The ground, brown with stubble of last year's grass, was littered with old tennis shoes, broken
windshields, rusting cars, shards of aluminum siding. Cast-iron
tractor parts emerged like mushrooms from soot-crusted heaps
of melting snow. I wondered why Fay Dell had posted that ad on
the Sunset school bulletin board: "Good horses for sale. Real
cheap." Why did she bother with such make-believe?

Eighteen years later I am sleeping with her ex-husband, and
the question is answered.

"All my wages gone for hay," says Frank. "The kids in hand-
me-downs . . . the house a goddamn mess. I'll tell you I had a
bellyfull!"

Frank had issued an ultimatum on Easter Sunday, determined
never to be ashamed again of his bedraggled wife and chil-

dren among the slicked-up families in the Blackfoot Community
Church.

"Get rid of them two-year-olds," he warned, "or . . ."

No wonder it took Fay Dell so long to tell me no. What she was
doing that runoff afternoon, seesawing back and forth, was making a choice between her horses and her husband. If Fay Dell
had confessed to me that day, I would not have believed such
choices are possible. Horses, no matter how well you loved them,
seemed mere animal possessions to be bought and sold. I was so
young then, a city girl with no roots at all, and I had grown up
Jewish, where family seemed the only choice.

"Horse poor," Frank says. "That woman wouldn't get rid of
her horses. Not for God, Himself."

March in Montana is a desperate season. You have to know
what you want, and hang on.

Frank's second wife was tall, blond, and young. He won't talk
about her much, just shakes his head when her name comes up
and says, "Guess she couldn't stand the winters." I heard she ran
away to San Luis Obispo with a long-haired carpenter named
Ralph.

"Cleaned me out," Frank says, referring to his brand-new stereo and the golden retriever. She left the double-wide empty,
and the only evidence she had been there at all was the white
picket fence Frank built to make her feel safe. And a heap of
green tomatoes in the weed thicket he calls a garden.

"I told her," he says with a wistful look, "I told that woman you
can't grow red tomatoes in this climate."

As for me, I love winter. Maybe that's why Frank and I can
stand each other. Maybe that's how come we've been keeping
company for five years and marriage is a subject that has never
crossed our lips except once. He's got his place near the highway,
and I've got mine at the end of the dirt road, where the sign
reads, COUNTY MAINTENANCE ENDS HERE. To all eyes but our
own, we have always been a queer, mismatched pair.

After we began neighboring, I would ask Frank in for a cup of
coffee. Before long, it was a beer or two. Soon, my boys were
taking the old McCulloch chain saw to Frank's to be sharpened,
or he was teaching them how to tune up Caleb's ancient Case

tractor. We kept our distance until one thirty-below evening in January when my Blazer wouldn't start, even though its oil-pan heater was plugged in. Frank came up to jump it.

The index finger on my right hand was frostbit from trying to turn the metal ignition key bare-handed. Frostbite is like getting burned, extreme cold acting like fire, and my finger was swollen along the third joint, just below its tip, growing the biggest blister I had ever seen.

"Dumb," Frank says, holding my hand between his large mitts and blowing on the blister. "Don't you have gloves?"

"Couldn't feel the key to turn it with gloves on."

He lifts my egg-size finger to his face and bows down, like a chevalier, to kiss it. I learn the meaning of dumbfounded. I feel the warmth of his lips tracing from my hand down through my privates. I like it. A widow begins to forget how good a man's warmth can be.

"I would like to take you dancing," says Frank.

"It's too damn cold."

"Tomorrow," he says, "the Big Sky Boys are playing at the Awful Burger Bar."

I suck at my finger.

"You're a fine dancer."

"How in God's name would you know?"

"Easy," Frank smiles. "I been watching your moves."

I admit I was scared. I felt like the little girl I had been, so long ago. A thumb-sucker. If I said yes, I knew there would be no saying no.

The Awful Burger Bar is like the Red Cross, you can go there for first aid. It is as great an institution as the Sunset school. The white bungalow sits alone just off the two-lane on a jack-pine flat facing south across irrigated hay meadows to where what's left of the town of Sunset clusters around the school. Friday evenings after Caleb passed away, when I felt too weary to cook and too jumpy to stand the silence of another Blackfoot night, I'd haul the boys up those five miles of asphalt and we'd eat Molly Fry's awful burgers, stacked high with Bermuda onions, lettuce and tomato, hot jo-jos on the side, Millers for me, root beer for them. That's how those kids came to be experts at shooting pool.

The ranching and logging families in this valley had no difficulty understanding why their schoolteacher hung out in a bar and passed the time with hired hands and old-timers. We were all alike in this one thing. Each was drawn from starvation farms in the rock and clay foothills or grassland ranches on the floodplain, down some winding dirt road to the red neon and yellow lights glowing at the dark edge of chance. You could call it home, as they do in the country-and-western songs on the jukebox.

I came to know those songs like a second language. Most, it seemed, written just for me. I longed to sing them out loud, but God or genes or whatever determines what you can be never gave me a singing voice. In my second life I will be a white Billie Holiday with a gardenia stuck behind my ear, belting out songs to make you dance and cry at the same time.

My husband, Caleb, could sing like the choirboy he had been before he went off to Chicago on a scholarship and lost his religion. He taught himself to play harmonica and wrote songs about lost lives. There's one I can't forget:

> *Scattered pieces, scattered pieces,*
> *Come apart for all the world to see.*
>
> *Scattered pieces, lonely pieces,*
> *That's how yours truly came to be.*

When he sang that song, my eyes filled with tears.

"How can you feel that way, and never tell me except in a song?"

"There's lots I don't tell you," he said.

We didn't go to bars much, Caleb and me. First of all we were poor. Then too busy building our log house, taking care of the boys, tending horses. And finally, when the angina pains struck, and the shortness of breath, and we knew that at the age of thirty-seven Caleb had come down with an inherited disease that would choke his arteries and starve his heart, it was too sad, you know, having to sit out the jitterbugs and dance only to slow music. But even then, in those worst of bad times, when the Big Sky Boys came through, we'd hire a sitter and put on our good boots and head for the Awful Burger.

There was one Fourth of July. All the regulars were there, and families from the valley. Frank says he was there, but I didn't know him. Kids were running in and out like they do in Montana, where a country bar is your local community center. Fire-crackers exploded in the gravel parking lot. Show-off college stu-dents from town were dancing cowboy boogie as if they knew what they were doing, and sunburned tourists exuding auras of camp fires and native cutthroat trout kept coming in from motor homes. This was a far way from Connecticut.

We were sitting up close to the band. Caleb was showing our boys how he could juggle peanuts in time to the music. The boys tried to copy him, and peanuts fell like confetti to be crunched under the boots of sweating dancers. The sun streamed in through open doors and windows, even though it was nine at night, and we were flushed from too many beers, too much sun and music.

"Stand up, Caleb. Stand up so's the rest of us can see."

That was our neighbor Melvin Godfrey calling from the next table. Then his wife, Stella, takes up the chant.

"Come on, Caleb. Give us the old one-two-three."

The next thing, Molly Fry is passing lemons from the kitchen where she cooks the awful burgers, and Caleb is standing in front of the Big Sky Boys, the dancers all stopped and watching. Caleb is juggling those lemons to the tune of "Mommas, Don't Let Your Babies Grow Up to Be Cowboys," and he does not miss a beat.

It is a picture in my mind — framed in gold leaf — Caleb on that bandstand, legs straddled, deep-set eyes looking out at no one or nothing, the tip of his tongue between clenched teeth in some kind of frozen smile, his faded blue shirt stained in half-moons under the arms, and three bright yellow lemons rising and falling in perfect synchronicity. I see the picture in stop-ac-tion, like the end of a movie. Two shiny lemons in midair, the third in his palm. Caleb juggling.

It's been a long time coming, the crying. You think there's no pity left, but the sadness is waiting, like a barrel gathering rain, until one sunny day, out of the blue, it just boils over and you've got a flood on your hands. That's what happened one Saturday last January, when Frank took me to celebrate the fifth anniversary of our first night together. The Big Sky Boys were back, and we were at the Awful Burger Bar.

"Look," I say, first thing. "The lead guitar has lost his hair. Those boys are boys no longer."

Frank laughs and points to the bass man. Damned if he isn't wearing a corset to hold his beer belly inside those slick red-satin cowboy shirts the boys have worn all these years.

And Indian Willie is gone. He played steel guitar so blue it broke your heart. Gone back to Oklahoma.

"Heard Willie found Jesus in Tulsa," says Melvin Godfrey, who has joined us at the bar.

"They've replaced him with a child," I say, referring to the pimply, long-legged kid who must be someone's son. "He hits all the right keys, but he'll never break your heart."

We're sitting on high stools, and I'm all dressed up in the long burgundy skirt Frank gave me for Christmas. My frizzy gray hair is swept back in a chignon, and Mother's amethyst earrings catch the light from the revolving Budweiser clock. It is a new me, matronly and going to fat, a stranger I turn away from in the mirror above the bar.

When the band played "Waltz Across Texas" early in the night, Frank led me to the dance floor and we waltzed through to the end, swaying and dipping, laughing in each other's ears. But now he is downing his third Beam ditch and pays no attention to my tapping feet.

I watch the young people boogie. A plain fat girl with long red hair is dressed in worn denim overalls, but she moves like a queen among frogs. In the dim, multicolored light, she is delicate, delicious.

"Who is that girl?" I ask Frank.

"What girl?"

"The redhead."

"How should I know?" he says. "Besides, she's fat."

"Want to dance?"

Frank looks at me as if I were crazy. "You know I can't dance to this fast stuff. I'm too old to jump around and make a fool of myself. You want to dance, you got to find yourself another cowboy."

The attractive men have girls of their own or are looking to nab some hot young dish. Melvin is dancing with Stella, "showing off" as Frank would say, but to me they are a fine-tuned duo who know each move before they take it, like a team of matched circus ponies, or those fancy ice skaters in the Olympics. They dance only with each other, and they dance all night long.

I'm getting bored, tired of whiskey and talk about cows and spotted owls and who's gone broke this week. I can hear all that on the five o'clock news. I'm beginning to feel like a wallflower at a high school sock hop (feelings I don't relish reliving). I'm making plans about going home when a tall, narrow-hipped old geezer in a flowered rayon cowboy shirt taps me on the shoulder.

"May I have this dance, ma'am?"

I look over to Frank, who is deep in conversation with Ed Snow, a logger from Seeley Lake.

"If your husband objects . . ."

"He's not my husband."

The old man is clearly drunk, but he has the courtly manner of an old-time cowboy, and he is a live and willing body.

"Sure," I say. As we head for the dance floor, I see Frank turn his head. He is watching me with a bemused and superior smile. "I'll show that bastard," I say to myself.

The loudspeaker crackles as the lead guitarist announces a medley — "A tribute to our old buddy, Ernest Tubb." The Big Sky Boys launch into "I'm Walking the Floor Over You," and the old man grabs me around the waist.

Our hands meet for the first time. I could die on the spot. If I hadn't been so mad, I would have run back to Frank because that old man's left hand was not a hand, but a claw — all shriveled up from a stroke or some birth defect, the bones dry and brittle, frozen half-shut, the skin white, flaky, and surprisingly soft, like a baby's.

His good right arm is around my waist, guiding me light but firm, and I respond as if it doesn't matter who's in the saddle. But my mind is on that hand. It twirls me and pulls me. We glide. We swing. He draws me close, and I come willingly. His whiskey breath tickles at my ear in a gasping wheeze. We spin one last time, and dip. I wonder if he will die on the spot, like Caleb. Die in mid-motion, alive one minute, dead the next.

I see Caleb in the kitchen that sunstruck evening in May, come in from irrigating the east meadow and washing his hands at the kitchen sink. Stew simmers on the stove, the littlest boys play with English toy soldiers, Mozart on the stereo, a soft breeze blowing through open windows, Caleb turns to me. I will always see him turning. A shadow crosses his face. "Oh dear," he says. And Caleb falls to the maple floor, in one motion a tree cut down. He

does not put out his hands to break his fall. Gone. Blood dribbles
from his broken nose.

There is no going back now. We dance two numbers, the old
cowboy and me, each step smoother and more carefree. We are
breathing hard, beginning to sweat. The claw-hand holds me in
fear and love. This high-stepping old boy is surely alive. He asks
my name.

"Mady."

"Bob," he says. "Bob Beamer. They call me Old Beam." He
laughs like this is a good joke. "Never knowed a Mady before.
That's a new one on me."

"Hungarian," I say, wishing the subject had not come up, not
mentioning the Jewish part for fear of complications. And I talk
to Mother, as I do when feelings get too deep.

"Are you watching me now?" I say to the ghost of her. "It's
come to this, Momushka. Are you watching me now?"

It's odd how you can talk to the ghost of someone more casually and honestly than you ever communicated when they were
alive. When I talk to Caleb's ghost it is usually about work or the
boys or a glimpse of beauty in nature or books. I'll spot a blue-
bird hovering, or young elk playing tag where our meadow joins
the woods, or horses running (I always talk to Caleb about any
experience I have with horses), and the words leap from my
mouth, simple as pie. But when I think of my deep ecology, as
the environmentalists describe it, I speak only to Mother.

I never converse with my father. He is a faded memory of
heavy eyebrows, Chesterfield straights, whiskery kisses. He was a
sculptor and died when I was six. Mother was five feet one, compact and full of energy as a firecracker. Every morning, in our
Chicago apartment lined with books, she wove my tangled bush
of black hair into French braids that pulled so tight my eyes
seemed slanted. Every morning she tried to yank me into shape,
and every morning I screamed so loud Mother was embarrassed
to look our downstairs neighbors in the eyes.

"Be quiet," she commanded. "They will think I am a Nazi."

And there was Grandma, who lived with us and wouldn't learn
English because it was a barbaric language. She would polish
our upright Steinway until the piano shone like ebony. I remember endless piano lessons, Bach and Liszt. "A woman of cul-

ture," Mother said, sure of this one thing. "You will have everything."

"You sure dance American," the old cowboy says, and we are
waltzing to the last dance, a song even older than my memories.

"I was in that war," he says. "Old Tubb must of been on the
same troopship. We was steaming into New York and it was raining in front of us and full moon behind and I saw a rainbow at
midnight like the song says, 'Out on the ocean blue!' "

Frank has moved to the edge of the floor. I see him out the
corner of my eye. We should be dancing this last one, I think, me
and Frank and Old Beam. I close my eyes and all of us are dancing, like in the end of a Fellini movie — Stella and Marvin, the
slick young men and blue-eyed girls, the fat redhead in her overalls, Mother, Caleb. Like Indians in a circle. Like Swede farmers,
Hungarian gypsies.

Tears gather behind my closed lids. I open my eyes and rain is
falling. The song goes on, sentimental and pointless. But the
tears don't stop.

"It's not your fault," I say, trying to smile, choking and sputter-
ing, laughing at the confounded way both these men are looking
at me. "Thank you for a very nice dance."

I cried for months, off and on. The school board made me take
sick leave and see a psychiatrist in Missoula. He gave me drugs.
The pills put me to sleep and I could not think straight, just
walked around like a zombie. I told the shrink I'd rather cry. "It's
good for you," I said. "Cleans out the system."

I would think the spell was done and over, and then I'd see the
first red-winged blackbird in February or snow melting off the
meadow, or a silly tulip coming up before its time, and the water
level in my head would rise, and I'd be at it again.

"Runoff fever" is what Frank calls it. The junk of your life is
laid bare, locked in ice and muck, just where you left it before the
first blizzard buried the whole damned mess under three feet of
pure white. I can't tell you why the crying ended, but I can tell
you precisely when. Perhaps one grief replaces another and the
second grief is something you can fix. Or maybe it's just a change
of internal weather.

Frank and I are walking along Bear Creek on a fine breezy day
in April, grass coming green and thousands of the yellow glacier

lilies we call dogtooth violets lighting the woods. I am picking a
bouquet and bend to smell the flowers. Their scent is elusive, not
sweet as roses or rank as marigolds, but a fine freshness you
might want to drink. I breathe in the pleasure and suddenly I am
weeping. A flash flood of tears.

Frank looks at me bewildered. He reaches for my hand. I pull
away blindly, walking as fast as I can. He grabs my elbow.

"What the hell?" he says. I don't look at him.

"Would you like to get married?" He is almost shouting. "Is
that what you want? Would that cure this goddamned crying?"

What can I say? I am amazed. Unaccountably frightened.
"No," I blurt, shaking free of his grasp and preparing to run.
"It's not you." I am sobbing now, gasping for breath.

Then he has hold of both my arms and is shaking me — a
good-sized woman — as if I were a child. And that is how I feel,
like a naughty girl. The yellow lilies fly from my hands.

"Stop it!" he yells. "Stop that damned bawling!"

Frank's eyes are wild. This is no proposal. I see my fear in his
eyes and I am ashamed. Shame always makes me angry. I try to
slap his face. He catches my hand and pulls me to his belly. It is
warm. Big enough for the both of us. The anger has stopped my
tears. The warmth has stopped my anger. When I raise my head
to kiss Frank's mouth, I see his eyes brimming with salt.

I don't know why, but I am beginning to laugh through my
tears. Laughing at last at myself.

"Will you marry me?" I stutter. "Will that cure you?"

Frank lets go of my arms. He is breathing hard and his face is
flushed a deep red. He sits down on a log and wipes his eyes with
the back of his sleeve. I rub at my arms.

"They're going to be black and blue."

"Sorry," he says.

I go over to Frank's log and sit at his feet, my head against his
knees. He strokes my undone hair. "What about you?" he replies, question for question. "Do you want to do it?"

We are back to a form of discourse we both understand.

"I'm not sure."

"Me neither."

May has come to Montana with a high-intensity green so rich you
can't believe it is natural. I've burned the trash pile and I am

done with crying. I'm back with my fifth-graders and struggling through aerobics classes three nights a week. I stand in the locker room naked and exhausted, my hips splayed wide and belly sagging as if to proclaim, Yes, I've borne four children.

A pubescent girl, thin as a knife, studies me as if I were a creature from another planet, but I don't care because one of these winters Frank and I are going to Hawaii. When I step out on those white beaches I want to look good in my bathing suit.

Fay Dell still lives up on Monture Creek. I see her out in her horse pasture winter and summer as I drive over the pass to Great Falls for a teachers' meeting or ride the school bus to basketball games in the one-room school in Ovando. Her ranch house is gone to hell, unpainted, weathered gray, patched with tar paper. Her second husband left her, and the daughter she broke horses for is a beauty operator in Spokane. Still, there are over a dozen horses in the meadow and Fay Dell gone thin and unkempt in coveralls, tossing hay in February or fixing fence in May or just standing in the herd.

I imagine her low, sugary voice as if I were standing right by her. She is calling those horses by name. Names a child might invent.

"Sweet Baby."

"Marigold."

"Lollipop."

I want my meadow to be running with horses, as it was in the beginning — horses rolling in new grass, tails swatting at summer flies, huddled into a blizzard. I don't have to ride them. I just want their pea-brained beauty around me. I'm in the market for a quarter horse stallion and a couple of mares. I'll need to repair my fences and build a new corral with poles cut from the woods.

My stallion will be named Rainbow at Midnight. Frank laughs and says I should name him Beam, after my cowboy. For a minute I don't know what he's talking about, and then I remember the old man in the Awful Burger Bar. I think of Fay Dell and say, "Maybe I'll name him Frank."

Frank thinks Fay Dell is crazy as a loon. But Fay Dell knows our lives are delicate. Grief will come. Fay Dell knows you don't have to give in. Life is motion. Choose love. A person can fall in love with horses.

CHRISTOPHER TILGHMAN

The Way People Run

FROM THE NEW YORKER

OFF THE ROAD, at least a hundred yards into the yellow scrub, Barry thinks he sees an animal, maybe an antelope, nuzzling the arid brush. He's surprised that it has wandered so far out into the open alone. About a mile ahead he sees the town, or what's left of it — a few blanched hackberry skeletons above a small gathering of houses centered on a two-story brick block. Even from this distance, he can tell that the wooden cornices and pediments of this building, the Commerce Building, are rotting. He has been seeing buildings like these and towns like this one for days; the only way he has of knowing that there are any people left is the sizzling rays of neon beer signs from one or two windows in an otherwise shuttered façade. He glances at his speedometer, and then back at the antelope, but what he first saw as an animal in the brush has broken apart, exploded limb by limb into children, six or seven of them suddenly scattering from their clustered spot. They are all different sizes, and as they run one of the big ones tugs along the littlest, a girl three or four years old, not much smaller than his younger daughter, if the distance, and the shafts of morning light through rain heads, and Barry's tired eyes can be trusted.

The café in town is still called the Virginian. Barry walks into the darkness, not sure he should trust the floor. The place smells of cigarettes and beer — not such a bad combination if left to age on its own, but the air is heavy with air freshener. Lilac, maybe it is, or Mountain Meadow. Someone is keeping a business going in here, perhaps because the county road crew stops three times a week, or because the motor vehicle department keeps a branch open every Tuesday. The tables around the edges of the room are dull black squares rimmed with the semicircles of Windsor chairs. The lamplight is bloodied by red shades at the tables and the bar, but in the center of the room, dominating the territory encompassed by its brilliant processed fluorescence, there is a circular pie cabinet. It is steel and glass, and looks so new that Barry wonders if it is for sale. On the third of six carousel shelves there is an apple pie, scarred by the removal of a single triangle, revolving in solitary repetition.

Barry assumes that the Virginian survives partly on the whims of strangers, but the waitress greets him with a surprised look anyway. He looks for a name tag, or a hint that she might be a relative of some sort. She's about his age, forties, sharp-jawed, and very thin, so thin in her tight bluejeans that she looks almost sexless. She shows him to a table and sets up the silverware in front of him. He sees the pie revolving, watches it several times, and then moves to face the wall. When the waitress comes back with his menu she stares hard enough at his emptied place to force him to explain.

"That pie thing," Barry says. "It's sort of distracting." It's possible that she will find this funny.

The waitress looks at him neutrally, which seems almost a favor. She's not going to knock the establishment; it's clear she's got the only job in town.

"Why is this place called the Virginian?" he asks, looking up from his menu. He has always wondered if the café was named after the book.

She shrugs. "Can't say. Is that where you're from?"

He shakes his head. He hopes she won't ask him "Where, then?" because the true answer is "New York." He hopes she won't ask "So what line are you in?" because these days he's not in any line at all, just sort of looking for work.

"Tourists don't stop in here much," she offers. She hands him this thought.

"Well, no. But . . ."

But what? Coming out West hadn't made a whole lot of sense from the beginning. Barry started this trip with interviews in Los Angeles — fund management, trading, stockbroking, anything with money — even though no one suggested there were any jobs there. He had a briefcase full of recommendations, résumés that came flooding out of copiers and laser printers by the ream in the last days of his firm on Wall Street. At first he called home every night to report. At each stop in California he kept hearing of the boom in Washington — Boeing and Microsoft — and he became part of a wave of suppliants heading north, pilgrims in business suits trying not to recognize each other. He began to want anything that wasn't his: someone's job, someone's car, someone's family. He hit bottom one night in a Seattle hotel that was shabbier than he ought to have risked, considering his mood. He canceled his last interview and headed back over the Cascades toward home, but in the desert he began to lose his way. He was not entirely sure how many days he had been gone. The hundred-dollar bills that he had watched closely and had broken with anxiety suddenly seemed endless, sufficient forever. An obscure elation began to take the place of schedule and plan. And then, as if planted in his mind like a signpost, came the image of this town, and he turned south for it even as his wife, Polly, wailed on the telephone, as she demanded to know what this detour could possibly do to resolve their plight.

The waitress loses interest during this pause and backs off; she's not going to hazard any piece of herself with him, and there's no reason for her to. "What can I get you?" she asks.

Barry looks at his watch and tries to recall the last three or four times he has eaten, decides it's time for a full midday meal, and orders a strip steak. "Our mashed potatoes are real," says the menu. It has begun to seem almost miraculous that he can stop in these ruined Western towns and find food; it's been days since he's seen cattle, or fields of corn, or vegetable gardens; he doesn't even see delivery trucks on the road. He's been asking waitresses "Do you still have any bacon?" or "What have you got?" as if menus were just memories of the times before a civil war out there cut off supplies. He feels the same way about gas; he's begun to think that way about women.

Barry hears the voices of two men behind him — he saw them under their feed-store caps at the bar when he walked in — and suddenly he regrets turning his back to the room. Each time he overhears a conversation he feels he has made a connection; in the same way, it reassures him to read notices for upcoming county fairs and church events. The waitress is going to think he's crazy, he knows, but he moves to a third side of the table.

"Maybe I should put it here and wait for you to catch up to it," she says when she returns, holding his plate above the fourth place. She gives him a smile somewhere between exasperation and interest.

"No. I'm settled now," says Barry. He says this straight, unthinkingly, as part of this conversation, but the statement taken in his own slender context is ridiculous, so ridiculous that he finishes it with a kind of bleating laugh on the "now."

A little off, the waitress seems to decide; he's O.K. but just a little off. She puts down his plate and does not wait to ask him how everything is. He thinks it might be funny to ask her for fresh-ground pepper.

The food is quite good, and he relaxes as he eats. The café's rusting tin ceiling is high above him. Above that ceiling, on the second floor, there were once rooms to let, and in one of those rooms his mother spent a week or two just after the war. Barry can imagine the sounds from other rooms, lovemaking and the beribboned serenade of a Bakelite Motorola. The country was flooding then, filling with expectation, and she had gone to the plains to find her father, who had, so long ago, lost heart. The story of their meeting and the final hurt it had caused her had become over the years, for Barry and his sisters, the text for a sort of catechism: What is the nature of man? How does sin have power over us? What is meant by betrayal? Barry pictures his mother, her clothes neatly placed in the dresser, her pearls and her aspirin arranged on a stained white table furrowed with cigarette burns.

The waitress is sitting behind the cash register, reading a fashion magazine in the light of the pie cabinet. He beckons to her for another beer. She knows it's an Oly, and he feels recognized through it, and when she brings it she lingers for a second or two. The men at the bar have left.

"When I was coming in I thought I saw children out on the plain."

"I expect you did," she says. "Probably dropping cherry bombs down gopher holes."

"Isn't there a school here?" he asks, thinking of Polly's checklist for evaluating a town: good schools, health care, Episcopal or Presbyterian church, pretty streets, Victorian houses, a Toyota dealership.

"In Rylla. But the bus has been broke for a couple of days."
She picks up his plate and asks, "You want a piece of pie?"

Barry asks her for the check instead. He's ready to find out if
she had known his grandfather, but the bartender gives her a
call, and she leaves him with no apology. Back on the street he
blinks in the sun; the clouds have passed, and now there's no
color at all to the light, just illumination, just the searing pressure
of day on these powdery buildings. He opens a road map on the
hood of his car and then stares over it. There is a white church
building with a yard bounded by rusty sheep fencing; the church
had once been repainted up to about five feet high all around,
and it looks as if it's sinking. Beside the church is a brown house
trailer with two bicycles in front, and then a low green ranch with
flowers in the yard, and finally an old gas station with an enigmatic hand-painted sign, running like bunting across the windows and door, saying WELCOME TO ELEVEN-MILE RODEO. The
old man had been happy here; that was his chief offense, the ir-
reparable rebuke carried home with his daughter, and the prin-
cipal evidence of his madness.

"You lost?"

Barry looks up and sees the waitress blinking at him. He thinks
for a moment that she is making a joke. "Which way to Broadway?" he asks.

"You ain't there," she says, but she doesn't laugh. Place, her
place, isn't funny to her.

He thinks of the biggest city around and tells her that's where
he's going.

"I go up there to the dentist," she says.

He folds up his map and he sees her noticing the pile of maps,
maybe a hundred of them, which are spilled out onto the passenger seat of his car. This is how it has been lately: catching a
glimpse of himself through other eyes. He can't help what they
perceive, but he has been careful to shave regularly.

"You know," Barry says, "I've been wanting to ask you. I had
some relatives who lived here once."

"Is that so?" She's at least somewhat interested in this unexpected fact, but not enough to ask who, as Barry thought she certainly would.

"Actually, it was my grandfather. Gordon Fox." Barry does
not want to admit to her that he does not know when or how the

old man died. Barry's mother must have killed her father off in a hundred different speculations, all of them deserved, asked for: drunken staggerings into danger, truculent exposures to the rage of others.

"You're kidding," the waitress says. She whistles. "Old Gordon!"

Barry looks at her carefully to gauge the reaction; claiming kinship with this maligned man could yield unpredictable results.

"Well, I'll be damned," she says, affectionately. She's smiling, at last, and it is quite a nice smile; it fills out her thin face and makes her softer. "He was a funny old prairie dog. He sort of collected cars. You ought to see his place." She gives him quick directions; out here, all directions are quick, even if the distances are long.

He shrugs as if this whole matter were actually not why he came, as if he had business to get on with, and she walks away. He watches her disappear around the church toward the edge of town. He gets in his car and backs out between a dusty Ford pickup and a Subaru; he thinks for a moment that they aren't real vehicles, just junkers without engines that have been left there by the owner of the Virginian to make the place seem popular. He gets back to the main road, and then turns in the direction she told him, back the way he came. He makes a few notations for his journal on the dashboard notepad. These days the journal is nothing but weather; he had recently kept pace with a front, going seventy to remain in the wind and black light, for hundreds of miles. It had left him breathless and exhilarated, as if he had been sailing in a gale.

Back on the prairie the children are one again; Barry imagines the pattern of their clusters and star-shaped explosions across the flats as fireworks. He keeps glancing over at them, and suddenly one of them breaks off and seems to be dancing madly around — a kind of Indian game, maybe. He looks again, and this time it seems that what is happening is that the child is waving at him, that they are all waving at him now. He stops the car and peers over; they are yelling at him. He gets out and begins walking toward them: the soil and the dry fuzz of undergrowth are brittle; his footsteps crunch like broken glass. A little way out

he recognizes that he has underestimated the distance. It gets
hot, and he slips off his shetland sweater.

When Barry begins to close on the children they turn back
away from him, all looking at something at their feet. Now that
he is drawing within several yards he realizes that it is a child on
the ground. The boy has both his hands pressed white against
his left eye socket. There is a little blood on his cheek and forehead and even some coming through his fingers. When Barry
sees this he leaps forward. "What happened? What happened?"
he says. "Is he all right?"

There are mumbles, but no one answers, not even the biggest,
who must be at least sixteen. Instead, they just stare down at the
damaged creature curled at their feet. There's a white dusting of
soil on his hair and clothes. Barry kneels and says to the boy,
"What's hurt? Are you O.K.?"

"My eye," the boy says, scared but not crying. The little girl,
the one Barry noticed from the car, is whimpering, but the rest
are silent.

"Jesus," says Barry. "Let me see." He reaches out and takes
hold of one of the skinny wrists. The boy fights him, and Barry
isn't sure what he's doing is right, because maybe the boy is really
holding the eye in his head like this; maybe, all things considered, keeping pressure on it is best for the moment.

"What happened?" Barry says one more time, this time direct-
ing the question at the oldest.

"Firecracker must of lifted a rock or something. Didn't see it
hit."

Barry looks at the firecrackers on the ground, and they seem
big enough to be dynamite; they aren't what he would have
called cherry bombs.

"Has someone gone to get help?" No one says anything; they
are helpless and hopeless. Barry lets go of the boy's wrist, gently
pressing his hand to tell him that he has changed his mind, that
he doesn't want to see the wound, that it will be best to keep the
pressure on. Barry steadies himself on his knees and then picks
the boy up in his arms. The load is lighter than he expected, but
they're a long way out; his car seems very distant. "Go ahead and
tell someone to get a doctor," he shouts angrily at the others.
They leave in a pack and head toward the town.

Barry is alone with the injured child. "What's your name?" he asks, trying not to sound winded.

The boy snuffles. Barry has to stop for a moment to take the weight off his arms by crouching over his knees. "You're hurting me," says the boy.

The boy smells musty, almost sour, nothing like the limpid fragrance of Barry's girls. The child's hair is coarse and spiky, and his twin cowlicks rub raw on Barry's bare arm; the boy's mouth is open, and Barry can see a gray spot of decay on one of the child's crooked teeth. The boy is becoming almost repellent to him, with these unexpressed needs and sullenly accepted favors, as if what the others knew was that this child deserved this missile in his eye, that it was his fault. He wishes the boy would cry or whimper or call out; this wounded silence, as if life and sight did not matter, is perhaps the worst of it.

"Just a little way to go now," says Barry. He's hoping that by the time he gets back to the road someone from the town will come; he doesn't want to get blood on Polly's Camry, though that's not going to keep him from doing the right thing. But no one is there, so he bats away the pile of maps on the passenger seat and lays the boy there. He goes out into the grasses and tries to rub some of the hardening blood off his hands.

Barry looks out for a car coming the other way, but there is nothing on the road; he's driving carefully to keep the boy from dropping his head onto the door upholstery. He has begun to fear that the boy and his dripping eye have been ceded to him for good, no take-backs. But there is, finally, some activity in town: a woman comes streaming out of the green ranch as he rounds the corner, and another woman and a younger man are climbing into a truck, a cherry red Ford pickup with chrome pipes and reflective windows. The truck is so immaculate that Barry wonders how it got here; it's like an ocean liner on a lake. Barry expects to see the waitress; for some reason he has assumed all along that she will be the first person he greets, that the boy might even be hers.

"Wendall," yells the woman in the truck. She's a sight for this town — almost punk, with lots of makeup and a black leather jacket.

The boy still doesn't cry. What's wrong with him? Barry thinks.

The woman pulls the car door open and helps the boy out. "Can you see out of it, honey?"

"I dunno," the child says.

This single answer from the boy changes the woman's tone. "You know to stand clear," she says harshly, giving him a shake. She's treating him now as if he were a careless construction worker. "Get in the truck, and we'll take you to the doctor."

"No," the boy wails finally. It's the doctor and his waiting room, the smell of pain, maybe, and the glint of needles that set him off. Thank God, thinks Barry, the kid's human. In a few moments they are off, with not a word to Barry. He thinks suddenly — it comes with the visual force of hallucination — that this town is someone's miniature, exposed from above. He looks into the sky and half expects to see an enormous moon-eyed face blotting out the sun.

He's weaving on the sidewalk when this vision passes, and he looks up in surprise to see the little girl standing in front of him, her overalls straps loose on her tiny arms. She's dirt-streaked and is holding a filthy pink blanket with tattered strings of satin binding, but her hair is perfect under two purple barrettes.

"The boy's going to be all right," Barry calls out. "Wendall is going to be fine." He doesn't know why he says this, except that whenever something frightening or bad happens around Gay and Pattie, he tells them it will be all right. He tells them this even as he sinks into despair. Four children killed by stray bullets in a single night, his girls hear on the radio, and Dad says, "It's all right. They're in Heaven."

The girl asks, "Are you in the army?"

"No," Barry says, not unfamiliar with the abruptness of a four-year-old's conversation.

"Will you play with me for these many minutes?" The girl holds up a sticky palm with all five digits spread.

"How many is that?" Barry asks encouragingly.

"Eight."

A voice comes from across the street just as Barry is ready to smile. "Winona! Don't talk to that man. Come here."

Barry figures the woman is just a little paranoid, and tries not to take it personally; he's a stranger, even if he did just save the life or eye or something of one of this town's sons. "That's right," he says to the girl. "Don't talk to strangers."

"Winona!"

The girl hesitates just long enough to exert a measure of independence. Barry gives a wave over toward the green ranch house: he thinks it's obvious that his wave means that he is a parent, too, that of course she shouldn't talk to him. But the mother takes his wave for a signal that she must act very quickly, and she runs over to swoop up the girl as if rescuing her from the path of a flood. It seems an overorchestrated gesture to Barry. The mother and girl reach the far side of the street, and the woman turns to defy him straight on, large breasts pushed out like musculature. When she's satisfied that Barry has been warned away sufficiently, she pulls the little girl back into the house. Barry sees then that what he took for flowers in her yard is actually litter: waxed cardboard from frozen vegetable packs, tufts of white tissue, the orange spiral from a box of Tide.

Barry stands there flushed with anger. He cannot imagine how he could be treated as dangerous to small children. Everyone says he's great with kids. He cannot deny that he's a little uninvolved with his own daughters' daily experiences — Polly is a superb mother, really quite remarkable — but he's always figured he'll weigh in strongly when they're teenagers or young adults. He's getting more and more indignant as he climbs back into his car: he's *from* this town, for God's sake. Sort of. He heads into the prairie. He thinks back to the directions the waitress gave him to his grandfather's spread — go west and go left. He likes the sound of it; he relaxes his anger and makes himself laugh heartily at the thought of these directions becoming some sort of credo for his grandfather, something for his family crest.

Barry's mother's campaign to eradicate her father's memory had been so meticulous and so persistent that there was virtually nothing about his flight that Barry did not know. It began in 1930 with an empty place at the head of the dinner table in Hartford, a setting of china and silver removed by the maid halfway through soup. Lobster bisque, if Barry recalled correctly. He had always been quite fond of his grandmother, a gutsy lady, and had suspected that she was happier to have her husband gone. But for years, dutifully, he had taken his mother's side in this matter, and even now, a pilgrim to the man's final place of rest, Barry can't imagine him being called affectionately "a funny old prairie dog."

He comes to a gravel road, about a mile beyond the point
where he had found the children, and takes a left. The wheel
tracks are deep as wagon trails, and the grass and brush bend
under the car. He drives slowly, up over one rise and down into
a deep basin. He seems not to be getting anywhere, for all this
motion; the land just keeps rising and falling endlessly.

He drives on, and is finally aware of a different quality in the
light behind the next rise, strands of luminescence. He reaches
the crest and is immediately dazzled by a thousand shards of sun.
Then, as his eyes adjust, he sees the source of all this confused
display. He understands what the waitress meant when she said
the old man collected cars. There are hundreds of them following the contours of this bowl, automobiles and vehicles of other
sorts, things on wheels of every possible type. The sun finds the
untarnished surfaces on all of them — chrome bumpers, head-
lamps and rearview mirrors, still lustrous hoods and metallic-
flaked fenders. The place is spotless and beautiful, as beautiful
as anything he has seen on his trip through unrelieved decay and
decline. Barry is stunned and uplifted by this dreadful vision. It
could be nothing but a junk yard, but the man was clearly up to
something, and whether or not he had thought of it this way, he
had left behind a monument.

Barry gets out of his car and sits, watching the sun mark an
hour or two on the face of this immense obsession. He tries hard,
with as much concentration as he has put into anything in the
past few months, to figure out what it means. He has not felt so
refreshed in many days, has not sensed so many options since he
was a teenager. There are invitations on the tip of each blade of
grass, enticements everywhere.

After a while the rush passes. If there was a sign for him in
this, he has not found it, or has not divined its meaning. He
hasn't exactly decided what to do next, so he thinks he will return
to the town. No doubt there will be someone who wants to thank
him for bringing in the child. Perhaps the waitress will be on
duty, and he can report back that he has visited Old Gordon's
place.

There is no one in the Virginian. Barry grabs a newspaper — it's
a few days old — and feels bold enough to go over to his table

against the back wall and crack open the storm shutter. A shaft of white light cuts out a wedge of the greasy surface. He unfolds his paper and reads about the high school sports, and then the social news. At one point a man comes in and walks straight to the bar to pour himself a draught beer with all the familiarity of someone getting water at his own kitchen sink; he stands for a moment, gives Barry a canine stare over the rim of his glass, finishes, and then slaps a handful of change on the bar before leaving. The bartender returns an hour or so later, sees the money, and drops it, coin by coin, into the separate bins of his cash register. It doesn't sound to Barry like much of a gross receipt for a long afternoon, and, in fact, the bartender glares at Barry, as if he damn well could have contributed something himself.

Barry goes back to his paper, and in a few more minutes the door opens and the waitress comes in. He is surprised by the strong nod of recognition he gets, and is flattered when she walks quickly to his table. She's wearing a name tag now, pinned to her gray sweatshirt — something more formal for supper, perhaps. Her name is May. "You brought Wendall Peters in. That was you."

Barry had forgotten, for these few moments, about the boy, and the modest surprise he shows is genuine. "Oh, that! Yes, I guess I did. Quite a thing."

"I can't believe it." She's very upset.

"How is he?" asks Barry.

"You don't know?"

"What?" he asks. How could he know anything? He could have been two hundred miles away by now.

"He's going to lose the eye. They're taking it out right now up to Good Shepherd." She turns to blow her nose.

Barry believes this; the boy was too still and didn't cry. Their pediatrician always made a joke about that: "The louder they cry . . ." He thinks of the boy's almost rancid odor. The feeling of the spiky hair against his arm comes back, and with it Barry's recognition that he had been *hoping* for something dramatic out of all this, something more than a few stitches in the boy's eyebrow. "It didn't seem that bad," Barry says, defending himself against his thoughts.

"I told them it was dangerous," says May.

Barry reflects that she had not sounded alarmed or nervous at lunch when she described to him what the children were doing. "Of course you did. One of my daughters is a hell-raiser," he adds, trying to remember whether he had told her before that he was a parent. He's been doing a good bit of lying out here — things like pretending he served in Vietnam, during Tet or in the Delta, or saying that he grew up in Arizona — harmless lies, just to ease his way among strangers.

May smiles, finally. "My boy, Everett, is so cautious he scares himself when he sneezes. He's six," she adds.

Wendall, Everett, Winona. What's with the names in this town? he wonders. "So he wasn't there?"

She seems slightly insulted by this deduction. "Well, sure he was there." She wrings a red dishtowel that she has been holding the whole time. "It gives me shivers." She produces a real shiver, a trembling in her shoulders, and when it is done she asks, "Do you want a beer, an Olympia?"

Barry nods, suddenly feeling utterly at home. He has never had a regular eating place, or a regular bar, and has never felt like a patron of any establishment, except perhaps for the paper stand at the mouth of his subway stop. But in this one day he has started to act as if he owned this table, and the people who have been drifting into the bar seem to expect to see him sitting there. He begins to feel a permanence, as if the accidents of the day could not have occurred to a mere passerby. He likes May. Besides, he has been watching her thin-hipped body and is very turned on by her. He has never been unfaithful to Polly, but this could be different — physical and free. His saliva becomes electric at the hard-core images in his mind.

May brings him a beer and then recommends he order the pork chops. "Sure," he says.

Suddenly, the door of the Virginian bursts open, and Barry recognizes the man who had served himself at the bar earlier. He wavers in the doorway and then appears to remind himself to shout out hysterically, "They saved it! They think they saved the eye!"

There is a moment of reduced conversational hum. The man is obviously Wendall's father, quite a bit older than the wife who had claimed the boy earlier and driven off with a younger man.

"That's good, Frank," says one male voice, but it is followed by a few snickers. It turns out that the medical report is the product of a drunk's extravagant, self-serving imagination. Frank weaves slightly but holds his place, as if he still expected to be mobbed at the door and carried aloft to the bar for a celebration. At last, May takes the man's hand and leads him over. The bartender shares a look with May, and then pours half a draught beer.

Barry himself is drinking more tonight than he has for weeks, months; he had lost the taste for it just about the time he hit the road. May brings his supper, and then checks back with him in the course of the evening, bringing him beers, giving him the quick line on the other customers, most of them men. There's not much else for her to do. One of the drunks yells at May to get her "skinny ass over here," and he makes a grab for her when she goes by. Barry knows he must accept the fact that she could not possibly have any interest in him. However this woman lives her life, it won't be him she's sleeping with tonight. He is beginning to crash, falling back on nothing but the foul breath of his night's drinking. He thinks about unrolling his sleeping bag and starts to look forward with dread to the morning's heavy dew.

"Where are you staying?" asks May. It's now just about closing time, and he's one of the last people left in the Virginian. The man who grabbed for her has gone. "Going to Rylla or something?"

Barry says, "Sure." Maybe that's it, a motel in Rylla.

"Well, you know," she says.

Barry reads May's hooded, apologetic eyes and slightly set lips, and is stunned to realize that all his unspoken prayers have been answered. She's going to ask him to stay — if not with her, then at least at her place. And she does.

"I've got a spare bedroom."

He accepts. She goes about her cleanup duties, and she makes no attempt at all to hide him; there is nothing furtive here, nothing to apologize for, as if everyone in the room would wish her well in finding a little unexpected companionship.

The air in May's house — one of two small bungalows behind the church — is stuffy with the chemical odors of carpeting. Most of the living room is taken up with a wooden-armed Colonial sofa, covered with a print of New England village scenes. The lamps and shades are part of the same set, and everything is very neat; the walls and ceiling are the same unfortunate light green. A man hasn't lived here in a long time — maybe never. There is a collection of china farm animals, and miniatures on a small hanging bookshelf. Barry pictures her adding to this collection, buying a new piece in Rylla and carrying it home in a box of cotton, taking it out and finding the best place for it on the shelf beside the other knickknacks, the woolly lamb, and the tea set for six. He sits on the sofa, following her with his ears as she wakes her boy, carries him to the toilet so he can pee, returns him to bed, and then begins to make coffee in the kitchen. There seems to have been no babysitter. Barry tries to figure out where the spare bedroom must be.

May talks to him from the kitchen — a confident intimacy, as if he had always been where she expects him to be and always would be. "You know, I'm still real skittish about that accident."

Barry yells back, "Yeah. There's something really frightening about an eye injury. Eyes seem so vulnerable, anyway."

She is obviously so struck by the aptness of this comment that she leans her head around the door to answer. "That's a real interesting point."

Barry is quite amazed that he is doing so well; it really has been some time since he's tried to converse. "Eyes are so important," he yells back, now that she has returned to the stove. There is a clinking of cups and the rattle of a burner grate on a cheap range.

Barry scouts around the room, looking at the tabletops and the shallow window wells; except for a telephone book, there isn't a single printed word in the house, as far as he can tell. He finds that comforting. "This is very kind of you." He yells again. "This is a very nice home." He's learned in his travels to use the word "home" and not "house," to say "sack" for "paper bag," and to pump his own gas without paying first.

She comes in with coffee, looks around the room, and it's clear that she, too, is comforted by what she sees. "I like things to be nice," she says. She's relaxed in her private space; he thinks of Polly. He is upset, but then relieved to find that he can't really recall her face.

May shakes him out of his thoughts; he must have been quiet for a beat too long.

"I guess at noontime when you drove in you never thought you'd get involved in something like this," she says.

He isn't sure what she means by "this": her or the town. "You never know."

"It's not always exciting around here." She begins this statement quite straight, but realizes halfway through that it's funny.

"How can you stand it?" says Barry, and they both laugh. He hasn't used irony in weeks; at home, everything that everyone — his friends, people at work, Polly — says is indirect. May eyes him as if she had just realized that he's been holding out on her, that he's been playing possum behind all his Eastern reserve. He can tell the idea of making love to him is in her mind.

"Have you ever thought of leaving here?" he asks.

She's already told him she grew up on the other side of the Commerce Building, in a house that burned down. She shakes her head and shrugs at the same time. "It ain't the bright lights," she says, suddenly undreamy and unchildlike and very defensive, "but it's home."

Barry is busy slamming on the brakes. "Sure. You don't understand. I love it here."

"Mom?" It's Everett. His voice is just as fearful and squeaky as May made him sound in the café.

"Sh-h-h," says May to Barry, and crouches as if she were ducking the snare in her son's call.

"Mom? Who's there?"

She gives up. "No one, honey. Go to sleep."

The boy starts to cry — not an entirely convincing cry, to Barry's trained ear. "I had a nightmare. I dreamed grachity was letting go and we all started to float."

May looks at Barry apologetically and leaves him. When she comes back, after a longer interval than Barry anticipated, she is holding clean, folded sheets, a pillow, and a towel — not a good sign. His heart sinks. But she sits down again beside him and puts her foot up on the sofa cushion between them, close enough to touch him, and after a few silent moments he drops his hand onto her calf. They talk, and then lean forward and kiss. Her saliva has a slightly odd taste and her mouth feels very different from Polly's; her back is hard and taut to his touch, but maybe

she's just tense. They move to her bedroom, which is arranged
just like a motel room, with a low dresser with a mirror above it
along the wall opposite the bed. They start to unbutton and un-
zip each other's clothes, with a few nervous laughs, and then she
pulls herself away to the bathroom in disarray. Barry catches
sight of his reflection for a moment and tells himself, in a disbelieving and wildly thrilled way, that in a very few minutes it will
be happening: he will plunge over one of the edges of his life
with Polly. He wonders what it would be like to think of it as his
"former" life. May comes back in a pink terry cloth bathrobe, and
it opens, at one point, right up to her waist. She turns out the
light and slows things down, making him hold her in his arms for
a few minutes in the darkness. Barry is startled by how good this
feels — the pressure and heated silk of another's flesh. He has
not had sex — or "made love" or whatever he should call this —
in some weeks, and his stomach churns with desire; his ears seem
to ring when, finally, her hand brushes him. She has almost no
buttocks, and her stomach is as flat as a teenager's. He finds softness here and there on her body. When he enters her she feels
athletic, wiry as a runner, and she moves in pleasure. It makes
him think of Polly's fuller, more cushioned body, inertly receiv-
ing, but it ends with a long, almost sweet, chirping from May,
and his own surprised thank-yous.

Barry wakes up in the spare bedroom and looks out the window
at the early morning. He's looking directly into a cemetery, close
enough to read the names on many of the stones, to see the
carved image of Calvary etched in the pink granite of the most
recent gravestone. Beyond the barbed boundaries of this slightly
green plot the yellow plains stretch out to a bare, purple rise.
The events of the preceding day run quickly past his eyes — the
first sight of town, meeting May, the boy's eye, his grandfather's
cars: as recent as they are, Barry has the sensation that these random events have been awaiting him for many years. He looks at
a life-size statue of Jesus in the center of the graveyard. It stands
on a pedestal of rust-colored concrete marked with the phrase
"I Am the Life" arranged in a triangle of letters, a word to a
line.
    He dresses with as little sound as possible, not because he

wants to slip out but because he hears the boy out there. Soon there is the bustle of a child's being sent to school, and a door closing — presumably the bus is working again. Barry comes out at last. May is still in her bathrobe, and any embarrassment in this meeting is dispelled in a second. The kitchen's aluminum-legged table is set with two chairs, May's and Everett's. On the cramped counter behind her is a large school picture of the boy — he's nice-looking, with a very slender face — and Barry is relieved at not recognizing him from the roadside.

"You seem real rested," May says. It's clear she thinks it's her — and it is, in some part.

"Best I've felt in weeks."

"I slept pretty well myself," she says. She reaches back to rub her neck languidly.

"I like it here a lot," he says. He's sitting in Everett's seat. "I mean the land around here."

"Not much like home," she offers, although Barry doesn't remember telling her where home is. She assumes a position in front of the stove, waiting for his breakfast request.

"I can't explain it, but I feel there are answers here, on your plains. Do you know what I mean?"

She doesn't, really. She has turned her back to the stove.

"It may be a kind of unique place," he says.

Her expression darkens slightly as he tells her that the statue in the cemetery reminded him that Christ went out into the wilderness. "Forty days and forty nights," he hums, trying to get the melody of an old hymn.

"I wouldn't know," she says. "I'm not up on my Bible."

"Neither am I," he admits.

May is a little unnerved by this conversation; Barry sees this. She says, "When you're back with your wife and working at your new job you'll think of us. And Old Gordon's cars."

"I guess," he says. "But I think I'm going to stick around a little longer." Maybe it's time for him to admit — to himself, anyway — that he has left Polly and the girls for good, that he is never going back.

May rewraps her terry cloth bathrobe tightly across her front and tightens the cord. "Here?"

"Well, I don't mean freeloading off you."

"Hey," she says, "I like it. You just make it sound a little permanent."

"I just mean I'd like to look around. Maybe see what's up in real estate."

"Here?" she asks again.

"Pretty crazy, isn't it?"

"I just don't understand. You mean *move* here? Why would anyone *do* that?"

Barry is losing clarity somewhat. "I'm married," he says. "I have children." He doesn't know why he is telling her this again, after the night before, but it *is* a reason. Isn't it? "Hell," says Barry. He means — and she clearly understands him to mean — that anything is possible in this world, that anything could make sense. "I'm looking for investment possibilities."

"Not here," May says. "Not in my town. I didn't invite you here because I'm looking for new neighbors."

"I can't ask you to understand."

"We had a nice time, a really nice time, but shouldn't you go home? There's nothing for you here."

"Maybe you have to come from the outside."

"Well," she says. She shrugs. "This whole damn county, this whole state, is going down the tubes. You'd have to be nuts . . ." Her thought trails off. Barry can't debate with her. In fact, he's starting to feel quite pushed and frustrated by what she is saying: his chest tightens, which is exactly what happens when he's on the phone with Polly. Being alone, after all, means you can think your own thoughts without interference.

She goes to the sink to do dishes; he never even got a cup of coffee. He thinks of her body inside the bathrobe and wishes they could make love again. It could still happen; if he shows up at her door at ten tonight, she may tell him she's so glad he hasn't left yet, that she hopes he'll stay awhile longer. Or maybe during the day she'll think vaguely that he'll come back, but she'll be here in the evening and he'll be hundreds of miles away.

This morning, the time for them is past, though, that's for sure. He's said or done something a little weird — not that he knows exactly what it is. Now that everything is settled, now that she believes she'll never see him again, she's cheerful. "You going to see your granddad's place again on your way out? You sure seemed impressed."

He remembers that he carried on a bit about it after they were done with lovemaking. He doesn't answer, wondering if he should be angry about any of this, about May's sleeping with him and then throwing him out, about his grandfather's having left no message or sign for him but a field of junked cars, about Polly, a thin reed at the end of a telephone line, charting his decline like a stockbroker hoping to find his fifty-two-week low.

"Quite a place," says May. She is referring to his grandfather's.

Still in her bathrobe, May sees him out the door. A reddish sun is rising over a very cold morning. Barry walks down the dusty path by the church and comes out facing the middle of the Commerce Building. He can see a sign, an incongruously cute rebus, in one of the empty storefronts, "Fred and Alice's Used 🐝-4 Store." Quite a place, he thinks as he throws his toilet kit into the trunk of his car. He fishes for a map, not one for a specific state but the one he rarely uses: the western half of the country, from the Mississippi to the Pacific. It spreads out across the dashboard and fills the entire windshield. Thousands of shattered, ruined towns — pulses of light in his own darkened sky.

He turns, finally, for Rylla. It's west, and the sun pushes down on him. Two or three miles out of town he makes out a large shape on the side of the road. It's the school bus, the town's bus, and he assumes it has broken down again: the front door, the emergency exit, and the hood are all open. But as he draws close he sees no sign of the children; it's a little spooky, as if the bus had been waylaid. He gets out of his car and calls, but there is no answer. He pokes his head in the doorway of the bus and calls again. The key is in the ignition, and on an impulse he tries it, but the engine doesn't catch. He knows perfectly well that none of this is his business, and he is about to turn his back when he notices an end of a pink blanket peeping out into the aisle of haze-gray seats. He walks back and picks it up, recognizing it as the beloved and trusted friend of that little girl, Winona. For a moment his mind floods with images: ankle socks, size-six T-shirts, dolls, and vinyl purses shiny with sequins. He quickly drops the blanket back on the seat, and backs out the door into the prairie, and stands there surveying the bounds of this vast, ownerless domain, wondering if this is really the way these things happen, the way people run.

DAVID FOSTER WALLACE

Forever Overhead

FROM FICTION INTERNATIONAL

HAPPY BIRTHDAY. Your thirteenth is important. Maybe your first really public day. Your thirteenth birthday is the chance for people to recognize that important things are happening to you.

And things have been happening to you for the past half year. You have seven hairs in your left armpit now. Twelve in your right. Hard dangerous spirals of brittle black hair. Crunchy, animal hair. There are now more of the hard curled hairs around your privates than you can count without losing track. Other things. Your voice is rich and scratchy and moves between octaves without warning or pattern. Your face has begun to get shiny when you don't wash it. And two weeks of a deep and frightening ache this past spring left you with something dropped down from inside: your sack is now full and vulnerable, a commodity to be protected. Hefted and strapped in tight supporters that stripe your buttocks red. You have grown into a new fragility.

And dreams. For months past, there have been dreams like nothing before: moist and busy and distant, full of yielding curves, frantic pistons, soft warmths and great fallings; and you have awakened through fluttering lids to a rush and a gush and a toe-curling scalp-snapping jolt of feeling from an inside deeper than you knew you had, spasms of a deep sweet hurt, the streetlights through your window blinds cracking into sharp stars against the black bedroom ceiling, and on you a dense white jam that lisps between trembling legs, trickles and sticks, cools on you, hardens and clears until there is nothing but gnarled knots of pale solid animal hair in the morning shower, and in the wet tangle a clean sweet smell you can't believe comes from anything you made inside you.

The smell is, more than anything, like this swimming pool: a bleached sweet salt detergent, a flower with chemical petals. The pool has a strong clear blue smell, though you know the smell is never as strong when you are actually in the blue water, as you are now, all swum out, resting back along the shallow end, the hip-high water lapping at your locus of change.

Around the deck of this old public pool on the western edge of Tucson is a cyclone fence, the color of pewter, decorated with a bright tangle of locked bicycles. Beyond this a hot black parking lot full of white lines and glittering cars. A dull field of dry grass and hard weeds, old dandelions' downy heads exploding and snowing up in a rising wind. And past all this, reddened by a round slow September sun, are mountains, jagged, their tops' sharp angles darkening into definition against a deep red tired light. Against the retreating red their sharp connected tops form a spiked line, a graph, an electrocardiagram of a dying day.

The clouds are taking on color by the rim of the sky. The water is bright spangles off soft blue, five-o'clock warm, and the pool's smell, like the other smell, connects with a chemical haze inside you, an interior dimness that bends light to its own ends, softens the difference between what leaves off and what begins.

Your party is tonight. This afternoon, on your birthday, you have asked to come to the pool. You wanted to come alone, but a birthday is a family day, your family wants to be with you. This is nice, and you can't talk about why you wanted to come alone, and really truly maybe you didn't want to come alone, so they are here. Sunning. Both your parents sun. Their deck chairs have been marking time all afternoon, rotating, tracking the sun's curve across a desert sky heated to an eggy film. Your sister plays Marco Polo near you in the shallows with a group of loud thin girls from her grade. She is being blind now, her Marco's being Polo-ed. She is shut-eyed, twirling to calls, spinning at the hub of a wheel of shrill girls in bathing caps. Her cap has raised rubber flowers. There are limp old pink petals that shake as she lunges at blind sound.

There at the other end of the pool is the diving tank and the high board's tower. Back on the deck behind is the SN CK BAR, and on either side, bolted above the cement entrances to dark wet showers and lockers, are gray metal bullhorn speakers that send out the pool's radio music, the jangle flat and tinny thin.

Your family likes you. You are bright and quiet, respectful to elders — though you are not without spine. You are largely good. You look out for your little sister. You are her ally. You were six when she was zero and you had the mumps when they brought her home in a soft yellow blanket; you kissed her hello on her feet out of concern that she not catch your mumps and your pain. Your parents say that this augured well. That it set the tone. They now feel they were right. In all things they are proud of you, satisfied, and they have retreated to the warm distance from which pride and satisfaction travel. You all get along well.

Happy Birthday. It is a big day, big as the roof of a whole Southwest sky. You have thought it over. There is the high board. They will want to leave soon. Climb out and do the thing.

Shake off blue clean. You're half-bleached, loose and soft, tender, pads of fingers gently wrinkled. The mist of the too-clean smell is in your eyes; it breaks light into gentle color. Knock your head with the heel of your hand. One side has a flabby echo. Cock your head to the side and hop: sudden heat in your ear, delicious, and brain-warmed water turns cold on the soft nautilus of your ear's outside. You can hear harder tinnier music, closer shouts, much movement in much water.

The pool is crowded late. Here are thin children. Hairy animal men. Disproportionate boys, all legs and necks and knobby joints, shallow-chested, vaguely birdlike. Like you. Here are old people moving tentatively through shallows on stick legs, feeling at the water with their hands, out of several elements at once.

And girl-women, women, evokers of wows, curved like fruit or instruments, skin burnished brown-bright as staircases of old wonder, suit tops held by delicate knots of fragile colored string against the pull of soft mysterious weights, suit bottoms riding low over the gentle juts of hips totally unlike your own, immoderate swells and swivels that melt in light into a surrounding space that cups and accommodates the soft curves as things precious. You almost understand.

The pool is a system of event. Here now there are: laps, splash fights, divings, corner tag, sharks and minnows, Marco Polo (your sister still the blind player, halfway to tears, the game teetering on the edge of cruelty, odd man out, not your business to save or embarrass). Two clean little bright-white boys, caped in cotton towels, run along the poolside with tiny steps until the guard stops them dead with a shout through his bullhorn. The guard is as brown as a tree, blond hair in a vertical line on his stomach, his head in a jungle explorer hat, his nose a white triangle of cream. A girl has an arm around a leg of his little tower. He's bored.

Get out now and go past your parents, who are sunning and reading, not looking. Forget your towel. Stopping for the towel means talking, and talking means thinking. You have decided that being scared is caused mostly by thinking. Go right by, toward the tank at the deep end. Over the tank is a great iron tower of dirty white. A board protrudes from the top of the tower like a tongue. The pool's concrete deck is rough and hot against your soft bleached feet. Each of your footprints is thinner and fainter. Each shrinks behind you on the hot stone and disappears.

Lines of plastic wieners bob around the tank, which is its own field, empty of the rest of the pool's convulsive ballet of heads and arms. The tank is as blue as energy, small and deep and perfectly square, flanked by lap lanes and SN CK BAR and rough hot deck and the bent late shadow of the tower and board. The tank is quiet and still and healed between fallings.

There is a rhythm to it. Like breathing. Like a machine. The line for the board curves back from the tower's ladder. The line moves in its curve, straightens as it nears the ladder. One by one, people reach the ladder and climb. One by one, spaced by the beats of hearts, they reach the tongue of the board at the top. And once on the board they pause, exactly the same tiny heartbeat pause. And their legs take them to the end, where they all give the same stomping hop, arms curving out as if to describe something circular, total; they come down heavy on the edge of the board and make it throw them up and off.

It's a swooping machine, lines of stuttered movement in a sweet late bleach mist. You can watch from the deck as they hit the cold blue sheet of the tank. Each falling makes a white that plumes and falls into itself and spreads and fizzes. Then blue clean comes up from the deep in the middle of the white and spreads like thick smooth pudding, making it all new. The tank heals itself. Three times as you go by.

You are in line. Look around. Look bored. Few talk in the line. Everyone seems by himself. Most look at the ladder, look bored. You almost all have crossed arms, chilled by a late dry rising wind on the constellations of blue-clean chlorine beads that cover your backs and shoulders. Beside you is the edge of the tower's shadow, the tilted black tongue of the board's image. The system of shadow is huge, long, off to the side, joined to the tower's base at a sharp late angle.

Almost everyone in line for the board watches the ladder. Older boys watch older girls' bottoms as they go up. The bottoms are in soft thin cloth, tight nylon plastic stretch. The good bottoms move up the ladder like pendulums in soft liquid, a gentle uncrackable geometric code. The girls' legs make you think of deer. Look bored.

Look past it. Look across. You can see so well. Your mother is in her deck chair, reading, squinting, her face tilted up to get light on her cheeks. She hasn't looked to see where you are. She sips something sweet out of a bright can. Your father is on his big stomach, back like the hint of a hump of a whale, shoulders curling with animal spirals, skin oiled and soaked red-brown with too much sun. Your towel is hanging off your chair and a corner of the cloth now moves — your mother hit it as she waved away a sweat bee that likes what she has in the can. The bee is back right away, seeming to hang motionless over the can in a blurred sweet air. Your towel is one big face of Yogi Bear.

At some point there got to be more line behind you than in front of you. Now no one in front except three on the slender ladder. The woman right before you is on the low rungs, looking up, wearing a tight black nylon suit that is all one piece. She climbs. From above there is a falling, then a plume and a healing. Now two on the ladder. The pool rules say one on the ladder at a time, but the guard never shouts about it. The guard makes the rules by shouting or not shouting.

This woman above you should not wear a suit as tight as the

suit she is wearing. She is as old as your mother, and as big. She is too big and too white. Her suit is full of her. The backs of her thighs are squeezed by the suit and look like cheese. Her legs have abrupt little squiggles of cold blue shattered vein under the white skin, as if something were broken, hurt, in her legs. Her legs look like they hurt to be squeezed, full of curled Arabic lines of cold broken blue. Her legs make you feel like your legs hurt.

The rungs are very thin. It's unexpected. Thin round iron rungs laced in slick wet Safe-T felt. You taste metal from the smell of wet iron in shadow. Each rung presses into the bottoms of your feet and dents them. The dents feel deep and they hurt. You feel heavy. How the big woman over you must feel. The hand bars along the ladder's sides are also so thin. It's like you might not hold on. You've got to hope the woman holds on, too. And of course it looked like fewer rungs from far away. You are not stupid.

Get halfway up, in the open, big woman placed above you, and a solid bald muscular man on the ladder underneath your feet. The board is still high overhead, invisible from here. But it rumbles, and flaps, and a boy you can see for a few contained feet through the thin rungs falls in a flash of a line, a knee held to his chest, doing a splasher. There is a huge exclamation point of foam into your field of sight, then scattered claps into a great fizzing. Then the silent sound of the tank healing to new blue.

More thin rungs. Hold on tight. The radio is loudest here, one speaker at ear level over a concrete locker room entrance. Grab the thin bars tight and twist and look down behind you and you can see people buying snacks below. You can see down into it: the clean white top of the vendor's billed cap, tubs of ice cream, steaming brass freezers, scuba tanks of soft drink syrup, snakes of soda hose, bulging boxes of salty popcorn kept hot in the sun. Now that you're overhead you can see the whole thing.

There's wind. It's windier the higher you get on the ladder. The wind is thin; through the shadow it's cold on your wet white skin. It makes a shivered whistle in your ears. Four more rungs to the top of the white tower. The rungs hurt your feet very much. They are thin and let you know just how much you weigh. You have real weight on the ladder. The ground wants you back.

Now you can see just over the top of the ladder. You can see the board. The woman is there. There are two ridges of red, hurt-looking callused skin on the backs of her ankles. She stands at the beginning of the board, your eyes on her ankles. The solid man under you is looking through the rungs into the contained space the woman's fall will pass through.

She pauses for just that beat of a pause. There's nothing slow about it at all. It makes you cold. In no time she's at the end of the board, up, down on it, it bends low like it doesn't want her. Then it flaps and throws her up and out, away, her arms opening out to inscribe that circle, and gone. She disappears in a dark blink. And there's time before you hear the hit below.

Listen. It does not seem good, the way she disappears into a time that passes before she sounds. Like a stone down a well. But you think she did not think so. She was part of a rhythm that excludes thinking. And you have made yourself part of it, too. The rhythm seems blind. Like ants. Like a machine.

You decide this needs to be thought about. It may, after all, be all right to do something scary without thinking, but not when the scariness is the not thinking itself. Not when not thinking turns out to be wrong. Here wrongnesses have piled up blind: affected boredom, weight, thin rungs, hurt feet, space cut into laddered parts that melt together only in a disappearance that takes time. The wind on the ladder not what anyone would expect. When it all turns out to be different you should get to think. It should be required.

The ladder is full behind you. It is fed by a solid line that stretches away and curves into the dark of the tower's skewed shadow. People's arms are crossed. It is a machine that moves only forward.

You climb up onto the thing's tongue. The board turns out to be long. As long as the time you stand. Time slows. It thickens around you as your heart gets more and more beats out of every second, every movement in the system below you.

The board is long. From where you stand it stretches into a nothing. It is a flatness covered with a rough white plastic stuff. The rough white surface is freckled and lined with pale watered red: drops of pool water that are catching low light over sharp

mountains. The rough white stuff of the board is wet. And cold.
Your feet are hurt from the thin rungs and have a great ability to
feel. They feel your weight. There are handrails running above
the beginning of the board. They are set low, and you almost
have to bend over to hold on to them. They are just for show, no
one holds them. Holding on shakes the rhythm of the machine.

It is a long cold rough white plastic fiberglass board, veined
with the sad pink color of old candy.

But at the end of the white board, the edge, where you go off,
there are two areas of darkness. Two flat shadows in the broad
light. Two vague black ovals. The end of the board has two dirty
spots.

They are from people before you. Your feet as you stand here
are tender and soft and dented, hurt by the rough wet surface,
and you see that the two dark spots are from people's skin. They
are skin, abraded from feet by the violence of the disappearance
of people with weight. More people than you could count without losing track. The suddenness of their disappearing leaves little bits of soft tender feet behind, bits and shards and curls of
skin that dirty and darken and tan as they lie tiny and smeared
in the sun at the end of the board. They pile up and get smeared
and mixed together. They get dark in circles.

No time is passing outside you at all. It is amazing. The late ballet
below is slow motion, the broad movements of mimes in blue
jelly. If you wanted you could really stay here forever, vibrating
so fast you float still and magic in time, like a bee over something
sweet.

But they should clean the board. Anybody who thought about
it for even a second would think that they should clean the board
of people's skin, of two black collections of what's left of before,
spots that look like eyes, like blind cross-eyed eyes.

Where you are now is still and quiet. Wind radio shouting
splashing not here. No time and no real sound but your blood
squeaking wild in your head.

Overhead here means sight and smell. The smells are intimate, newly clear. The smell of bleach's special flower, but out of
it other things rise to you like a weed's seeded snow. You smell

deep yellow popcorn. Sweet tan oil, hot coconut, a shiny sugared memory. Either hot dogs or corn dogs. A thin, cruel hint of dark Pepsi in paper cups. And the unique smell of tons of water off tons of heated skin, rising like steam off a new bath. Animal heat. From overhead it is more real than anything.

See it all. You can see the whole thing, blue and white and brown and white, soaked in a watery spangle of deepening red. Everyone. This is a view. And you knew that from below you wouldn't look nearly so high overhead. You know now how high you are. You knew from underneath no one could tell.

He says it behind you, his eyes around your ankles, the solid bald man, Hey kid. They want to know. Do your plans up here involve the whole day or what exactly is the story. Hey kid are you okay.

There's been time this whole time. You can't kill time with your heart. Everything takes time. Bees have to move to stay still.

Hey kid he says Hey kid are you okay.

Metal flowers bloom on your tongue. No more time for thinking. Now that there is time you don't have time.

Hey.

Slowly now, across everything, there's a watching that spreads like silent energy pudding. Watch it. Your sighted sister and her thin white pack, pointing. Your mother looks to the shallows where you used to be, then makes a visor of her hand. The whale stirs and jiggles. The guard looks up, the girl around his leg looks up, he reaches for his horn.

Forever below is rough deck, snacks, thin metal music, where you used to be; the line is solid and has no reverse gear; and the water, of course, is only soft when you're inside it. Look. Now it moves in sun, full of hard coins of light that shimmer red as they stretch away into a mist that is your own sweet salt. The coins crack into early moons, long pins of light from the hearts of sad stars. The square tank is a cold blue sheet. Cold is just a kind of hard. A kind of blind. You have been taken off guard. Happy Birthday. Did you think it over. Yes and no. Hey kid.

Two black spots, violence, and disappear into a well of time. Height is not the problem. It all changes when you get back down. With your weight.

But so which is the lie? Hard or soft? Silence or time?

The lie is that it's one or the other. A still, floating bee is moving faster than it can think. From overhead the sweet drives it crazy.

The board will nod and you will go, and black eyes of skin can cross blind into a cloud-blotched sky, punctured light emptying behind sharp stone that is forever. That is forever. Step into the skin and disappear.

Hello.

KATE WHEELER

Under the Roof

FROM BLACK WARRIOR REVIEW

MOIST, lead-lemon Bangkok dawn: Miss Bi Chin's Chinese alarm clock goes off, a harsh metallic sound, like tiny villagers beating pans to frighten the dragon of sleep. She opens her eyes and sees a big fire ant crawling up her yellow mosquito net; feels how the black earth's chill has penetrated her hipbones. At first she does not know where she is.

Tuk-tuks, taxis and motorbikes already roar behind the high garden wall; but the air is still sweet, yesterday's fumes brought down by the dew. She has slept outside, behind her house, under the sal tree. All around her lie pink, fleshy blossoms, fallen during the night.

She lies still on her side, allowing last night's trip to Dom Muang airport to bloom in her mind, seeing the American monk stalk from the barrier, his brown robe formally wrapped to form a collar and tight scroll down his right arm. Straight out of Burma. It delights her to remember his keen, uncertain look as he scanned the crowd for her unfamiliar face. Then she waved, and he smiled. On the way home, the taxi driver charged them only half price.

She heaves up to sitting; the monk, who is standing now at her screened upstairs window, sees her hips' awkward sideways roll, her hands pressing the small of her back. Both of them have the same thought: the body is a heap of suffering! The monk steps back quickly, lest Miss Bi Chin catch him gazing out the window — worrying about what will become of him out here in the world. As he moves into the shadow, he suddenly realizes that the worry itself is the world's first invasion, and again he is struck with gratitude for his robes. Having to be an example for others protects me, too, he thinks. It works from the outside in, the way forcing yourself to smile can make you feel happy.

Miss Bi Chin rolls up her straw sleeping mat and hurries into the house with it under her arm. Her bones ache, but she takes joy in that. Why should she rent a hotel room when she can sleep for free in her own back yard? It's not the rainy season. She will earn great merit for helping the monk to sleep as the rules require, under a roof where there is no woman. By now he must have completed his morning meditation.

In her mind she sees the Thai monks going for alms food right now all over the city: hundreds of them in bright orange robes, bare feet stepping over broken glass and black street garbage. They shave their heads only on full moon day, they have TVs and they seduce American tourists. They don't care if the tourists are women or men. Thai people crave too much for sense pleasures. Miss Bi Chin would not donate so much as an orange to Thai monks; she saves her generosity for the good, clean monks trained in Burma.

As she lights the gas under the huge aluminum teakettle, the old man comes shuffling into the dark kitchen. He pulls the light cord, searing the room with jerks of blue fluorescence. "Why do you cook in the dark, Chinese sow," he says in Malay. He is her mother's second husband's brother and lived off the family for years in Penang. Now he has come here to torture her and make her life miserable.

"Shh," she says, motioning with her head. The American monk sits cross-legged at a low table in the next room. His eyes are downcast and a small smile curves his lips. Beautifully white, he resembles the marble Buddhas they sell in Rangoon.

"So what? He doesn't understand me," the old man says. "Why don't you bring in a real man for a change? You'd be a lot less religious if you were satisfied." And I'd be happier living here, he thinks, if she were a normal woman, not lost in pious dreams.

His words roll off her mind like dew from the petals of a white lotus. "You will go to all the hells," she predicts. "First the hot and then the cold."

The old man laughs. "I am Muslim. Will I go to the same hell as you and your rag-wrapped *farang*? I am waiting for my breakfast." He walks in and shows all his teeth to the American monk. "Goo mornin sah!"

"Hey," the monk says. "Thanks for the bed. I slept great."

The old man can only nod. He doesn't understand English. Miss Bi Chin bites her tongue, deciding it is better for the monk's peace of mind not to know it was her bed that he slept in. Of course, she moved it into the sewing room.

This American monk is the favorite of the Rangoon abbot, Miss Bi Chin has heard. He's been in intensive meditation for three years, completing two levels of insight practice and the concentrations on the four heavenly abodes. But the monastery's friend in the Department of Religious Affairs lost his position in November, and the monk's last visa renewal application was rejected. He has come to Thailand to apply for re-entry into Burma; approval will take at least three months, if it comes at all. Conditions in Burma are unstable; the government has had to be very strict to maintain order, and it does not want too many foreign witnesses to its methods. Recently, they changed the country's name to Myanma, as if this would solve its problems.

If the monk cannot return, the abbot may send him back to America to found a monastery. The monk has not been told. The streams of defilements are strong in the West: all the American monks that the abbot has known disrobe soon after they go home, so they can enjoy sense pleasures. Ideally, the monk should stay in Burma a few more years; but the abbot hasn't worn robes all his life to forget that the world is not ideal. This monk is addicted to pondering, a common Western vice, but he has a devoted heart, and his practice has been good. Pork should fry in its own fat; the American devotees cry out for a monastery. This monk may be the perfect candidate.

The abbot sees no reason to make a decision yet. He's asked Miss Bi Chin, the monastery's great supporter, to report on the monk's behavior: whether living unsupervised in capitalist Bangkok becomes his downfall.

Seeing him wait for his food, so still, Miss Bi Chin has no worries. She's studied his face, too, according to Chinese physiognomy. A broad forehead means calm, the deep lines at each side of the mouth mean kindness.

"Breakfast for you." She kneels at the monk's side, offering the dishes from a cubit's distance, as the Buddha prescribed. The monk touches each plate and she sets it on the table. Wheaties, instant Nescafé with condensed milk, sliced mango, lemon cookies from England, and a bowl of instant ramen noodles.

He hasn't seen such food in three years. He smiles in gratitude at Miss Bi Chin and begins eating.

Miss Bi Chin sits on one side with her feet tucked behind her and her hands in the respectful position. Rapture arises in her mind. She has helped Western monks before, and she knows they do not do well on the diet in Rangoon — too much oil and hot pepper. This monk is bony, his skin rough. She will buy chicken extract, milk powder, and vitamins for him, she will take early lunch hours to come and cook his lunch: monks eat no solid food between noon and dawn.

She stops her ears against the sound of the old man, slurping in the kitchen like a hungry ghost.

The monk wipes his mouth. He has finished everything except the noodles, which remind him too much of Burmese food. Miss Bi Chin notices. She'll reheat them for herself with fish paste; the monk's future breakfasts will be entirely Western.

Because the monk is American, he sometimes feels unworthy of being bowed to and, living on donations, guilty about the extent to which he has learned to enjoy such treatment. Miss Bi Chin, for example, is not rich. She works as a secretary at American Express, and says she refused promotion twice so that she can feel free to neglect her job when monks need help. He'd like to thank her for the food, for everything she is going to do for him, but this is not allowed.

If he were still a carpenter, he'd build her a kitchen countertop; as a monk, example and guidance are the only returns he can offer — they're what she expects, he reminds himself, slipping again into the Asian part of his mind. Her donations bring her merit. She supports what I represent, the possibility of enlightenment: not me specifically.

He clears his throat. "Where did you learn such good English?"

"Oh! My mother sent me to a British school in Penang."

"And you speak Burmese, Thai, and what else?"

"Malay, Cantonese, a little Mandarin."

The monk shakes his head. "Amazing. You're one smart lady."
Miss Bi Chin laughs in embarrassment. "I am Chinese, but my
family moved to Malaysia, and we had to learn all the languages
on the way. If you had my same *kamma*, you would know them,
too."

"Listen." The monk laughs. "The abbot did his best to teach
me Burmese." It's hard for him to imagine that this woman is
also a foreigner here.

"Better for you," Miss Bi Chin says promptly. "For a monk it is
most important to maintain virtue and concentration. Learning
languages is only worldly knowledge. The Burmese won't let
you alone if they know you can speak. When I go to meditate at
Pingyan Monastery, I have to hide in my room." She laughs.

The monk smiles, charmed. Faith makes Miss Bi Chin glow
like a smooth golden cat; yet her black eyes sparkle wickedly. He
will have to be careful to see her as his older sister, or even as a
future corpse.

He'd be surprised to know that Miss Bi Chin thinks of herself
as ugly. As a child, her mother would tweak her arm hairs and
say, "No one will marry you, Black Dog. Better learn English so
you can feed yourself." True, no Asian men want Miss Bi Chin,
but the reason may not be her skin — there are plenty of married women as dark. No, she is too well educated, too sharp-
tongued, and most of all too religious. From her own side, the
only Asian men she is interested in are celibate, monks. She had
a long relationship with an American, Douglas, the heir to a toy
fortune who does business in Bangkok and Singapore. He
smokes Dunhills in a holder, and sponsors the publication of
Buddhist texts. Younger than she, he left her a year ago for a
glamorous twenty-year-old Thai. She still sees him sometimes at
Buddhist meetings, drawling his reactionary opinions. How she
ever was involved with him is a mystery to her.

Now she cries, "What is there in this world worth talking
about? Everything is only blah, blah, blah. I must go to work now
and type meaningless reports so that I can sustain my life and
yours. I will come back to cook your lunch. Please use my house
as you wish. I have many Buddhist books in English. The old
man will not bother you."

She shuffles toward the monk on her knees, to remove the

plates. Not to introduce the old man as her uncle is one of her secret acts of revenge.

How terrible my life would be without monks, she thinks.

The monk paces slowly up and down Miss Bi Chin's unfurnished living room. His body feels soft and chaotic among the sharp corners, the too shiny parquet, the plastic flowers under a tinted portrait of his abbot, the most famous teacher in Burma. This photograph shows the abbot's terrifying side, when his eyes, hard and sharp, pierce into each person's heart to lay bare its secret flaws. The monk prefers his tenderness, eyes that make you want to fall over sideways.

This is the first day in three years the monk has not been surrounded by other monks, living the life called "pure and clean as a polished shell": its ten precepts, 227 rules, daily alms round, chanting at dusk. The monastery wall was like a mirror facing inward; beyond it was another barrier, the national boundary of Burma. He often used to speculate on what disasters could be happening in the outside world without his knowing. Meanwhile, cocooned within the walls, the discipline of the robes, and the fierce certainties of his teacher, the monk's mind grew dextrous, plunged into nothingnesses too subtle to remember. He was merely left with a yearning to go back to them; now ordinary happiness feels harsh and coarse.

Outside, traffic roars like storm surf. What a city! He was a different man when he passed through on the way to Rangoon, drank a Singha beer at the airport bar, defiantly toasting his future as a renunciate. Even then he'd been shocked by Bangkok — everything for sale: plastic buckets, counterfeit Rolexes, bootleg software; and of course the women, dressed as primly as third-grade teachers, hoping a client will choose to marry them.

Burma may attack your health, he thinks, but Bangkok will suck you to your doom.

What if his visa is denied?

Will he disrobe? His civilian clothes are even now in a suitcase in the monastery's strong room: they must be eaten up by mildew. He's not ready to go back home as a shaven-headed, toga-wearing freak. No way would the abbot let him stay and practice under a Thai, not down here where they've got monks running around claiming to be reincarnations of Gotama the Buddha. There's a Burmese center in Penang, which Miss Bi Chin supported before she moved up to Bangkok; but she said last night it's near a huge highway and so is unsuitable for the absorption practices; plus, she added confidentially, the head monk in Penang hates Westerners. She ought to know: he's her cousin. If I get sent to Penang, the monk thinks, I'll be able to practice patience for about two weeks and then I'll be out of the robes. I was never a lifer, anyway. Or was I?

I know this is only a form.

For sure, he isn't ready just yet to lose the peace, the certainty of being a monk; nor to be separated from the abbot, his teacher: the only man on earth, he's often told himself, he truly, deeply respects. And loves.

He catches himself planning to sneak across the border at Chiang Rai and run up to Rangoon through the forest with help from Karen insurgents. Bowing three times at the abbot's feet. Here I am. In his mind the abbot laughs at him and says, Peace is not in Burma or in Bangkok. Peace comes from dropping one's preferences. That is why we beg for our food, we take what is given.

The monk stops in front of the abbot's portrait and makes the gesture of respect, palms together.

He feels the world stretching out around him. I'm here, he thinks; suddenly he's in his body again, feeling its heaviness and insubstantiality.

He can even feel the strengthening effect of the milk in the Wheaties he just ate. Conditions in Thailand are good for healing the old bod; he can make it a project. In the States he ran and did yoga fairly regularly; in Burma he never exercised. He was never alone, and people would gossip if they saw him in an undignified posture.

Carefully he spreads his sitting cloth, a maroon-and-orange patchwork square, on the straw mat where he ate breakfast; now he lies flat on it, easing the bunched muscles of his shoulders. Slowly he raises his legs to vertical, letting the small of his back flatten against the cool straw. His sacrum releases with a loud pop.

He tucks the skirt of his robe between his knees and raises his buttocks off the ground, until he is in full shoulder stand, the queen of poses, the great redistributor of psychic energy. His mind flies, faster than light, to Vermont.

He's lived as if he'll never go back to where people know him as Tom Perkins, a carpenter and the more or less unreliable lover of Mary Rose Cassidy, who still lives in Brattleboro, where she's a partner in a cooperative restaurant. She's known he would ordain ever since they came East together in seventy-three. They were both moved by the calm faces of monks they saw; but only he had that realization at the great dome of Borobudur in Java. Tapped it, and said, "Empty. That's it! There's nothing inside." Mary Rose saw in his face that it was a deep moment for him. After coming home, they learned to meditate together at a center in western Mass. She kept saying the tradition was sexist and stifled your *joie de vivre;* Tom wondered if she did it only to keep him from getting too far away.

And she didn't expect him to be gone this long. He's written her four letters saying: my practice is getting deep, it's fascinating, I want to renew my visa.

He should've broken up with her. A year ago he knew: but it seemed cruel to cut her off by mail, and more appropriate as a monk to be vaguely affectionate, vaguely disconnected, than to delve into his past and make a big mess. He halfway hoped she'd lose patience and break up with him herself; but she says she's had no other lover since he left, and she sends a hundred dollars every other month to the monastery treasurer for his support. It's more than enough.

She would have stopped sending money. He would've had to be supported entirely by the Burmese. God knows they have little enough to spare. Think what his plane ticket to Bangkok would have cost in kyat. Four months' salary for the average worker, even at the official rate; at the black market rate, the real value of Burmese money: three years' salary.

He lowers his legs as slowly as he can, feeling unfamiliar pulls in his belly and chest.

He turns to look out the large front window — the old man is staring in at him. He's been sweeping dead leaves off the cement courtyard. He wears ancient blue rubber thongs and a checked sarong; his fine-skinned purplish breasts sag over his ribs. His gaze is clouded and fierce, an old man's rage. The monk has assumed that he is some sort of servant, a trusted retainer of Miss Bi Chin's; he didn't quite take the old man into consideration. Now, this stare rips away all barriers between them.

Lying on the floor, his robes in disarray, he's Tom again, for the first time since he ordained.

With as much dignity as he can muster, he gets to his feet and goes out the back door, into the tiny walled garden where Miss Bi Chin slept. The old man has swept the pink sal flowers into a pile. The fresh ones look like parts of Mary Rose; the decaying ones, black and slimy, remind him of things the abbot says about sensuous desire. He watches one blossom fall, faster than he'd expect. It's heavy, the petals thick as blotting paper. He picks it up, rubs one petal into bruised transparency.

I should call Mary Rose while I've got the Thai phone system, he thinks. I need to tell the truth.

Now he wishes he'd studied the rules, for he doesn't know if using the phone would break the precept against taking what is not given. It's a subtle thing, but how impeccable does he have to be? Miss Bi Chin offered her house, but then steered him into her library. She surely expects to do all his telephoning. Surprising Mary Rose with an overseas collect charge isn't too monkly, except that she still considers him her lover. The irony of this is not lost on him.

Well, it's ten P.M. in Brattleboro. If he waits until Miss Bi Chin comes home it'll be too late, and what's more, she'll overhear everything: the phone is in the kitchen where she'll be cooking lunch. He walks around the corner of the house and asks the old man's permission to use the phone.

The old man waggles his head as if his neck had lost its bones. He says in Malay, "I don't understand you, and you don't understand me!"

The monk decides that this weird movement contains some element of affirmation. In any case, his mind is made up.

As he watches his hand travel toward the phone, he remembers the abbot talking about the gradations of defilement. Desire shakes the mind. The body moves, touches the object, touches it, causing the object to move. When he touches the receiver, he picks it up quickly and dials.

"Tom?" The satellite transmission is so clear, Mary Rose sounds like she's in the next room. "Oh, it's fantastic to hear your voice!"

When he hangs up, an hour later, he feels sick — he can't help imagining her expression when she gets the phone bill. Yet he has to admit, he's intensely alive, too, as if he'd stuck his fingers in a socket, as if someone had handed him a sword.

He thinks: Maybe this will create a vacuum that my visa will rush into.

He goes up to Miss Bi Chin's sewing room and closes the door. Cross-legged on his sitting cloth, he tries to cut off all thoughts of Mary Rose so he can send loving-kindness to the abbot, his benefactor. At first tears come, his body feels bludgeoned by emotion; but then his loving feeling strengthens, the abbot's presence hardens in his mind. Suddenly he and the abbot are welded together, a bond tighter than Krazy Glue. The monk's lips curve up: here there is no grief.

Miss Bi Chin and the old man are eating dinner, chicken and Chinese cabbage in ginger sauce; the monk is upstairs reading a list of the Twenty-Four Mental States Called Beautiful.

"Your monk talked on the phone for two hours," the old man says slyly. "He put his feet above his head and then pointed them at the portrait of Pingyan Sayadaw."

It is not true that the monk pointed his feet at the portrait, but as soon as the old man says so, he begins to believe himself. He's tired of having monks in the house, tired of the prissy, superior way his step-niece behaves when these eunuchs are about. What good do they do? They live off other people, beg for their food, they raise no children. The old man has no children either, but he can call himself a man. He was a policeman for six years in Malaysia, until a bullet lodged near his spine.

Miss Bi Chin pretends he does not exist, but he pinches her bicep, hard.

"Ow!" she cries, and jerks her arm away. "I *told* him he could use the house as he pleased." Too late, she realizes she shouldn't have descended to arguing: it causes the old man to continue.

"Well, he did that. He only waited for you to leave before changing his behavior. I think he's a very loose monk. He wandered up the stairs, down the stairs, examining this and that. Out

into the garden to stare at the sky and pick up flowers. Then he
got on the phone. He'll be poking in the refrigerator tomorrow,
getting his own food."

"You just hate monks."

"Wait and see," the old man says lightly. "Have you noticed his
lower lip? Full of lust and weakness."

Miss Bi Chin lowers her face until all she can see is her bowl of
soupy cabbage. The old man is her curse for some evil deed in
the past. How he abuses her, how he tries to poison her mind!
She tells herself that the old man's evil speech is a sign of his own
suffering, yet he seems to cause her more pain than he feels himself. Sometimes she enjoys doing battle with him — and she has
developed great strength by learning to seal off her mental state
so that he cannot infiltrate. This strength she uses on different
occasions: on a crowded bus when an open sore is thrust beneath
her nose, or when her boss at American Express overloads her
with work. At other times the old man defeats her, causes her
defilements to arise. Hatred. Fear. A strange sadness, like home-
sickness, when she thinks of him helpless in the grip of his obses-
sions.

She could never kick him out. Crippled, too old to learn Thai
or get a job, how would he survive in Bangkok? And he does
make himself useful, he tends the garden and cleans the floors
and bathrooms. Even more important, without him as witness,
she and her monks would not be allowed to be in the same house
together. The Buddha knew human nature very well when he
made those rules, she thinks.

Washing up, she hears that the old man has turned on his TV
and is watching his favorite talk show, whose host gained fame
after a jealous wife cut off his penis, and he had it sewn on again.

"Why do you have to watch that!" she scolds at his fat, unre-
sponsive back.

She goes up to the sewing room in a fury, which dissipates into
shame as soon as she sees the monk reading. The light from the
window lies flat and weak on the side of his shaven head. His
pallor makes him look as if he has just been peeled; her ex-lover
Douglas had a similar look, and it gives her a shiver. She turns
on the yellow electric lamp so he will not ruin his eyes and leaves
the door wide open, as is necessary when a monk and a woman
are together in a room.

"Hello, sister," he says. The edges of his eyelids feel burnt by tears; Miss Bi Chin notices redness, but thinks it is from ill health.

She begins to speak even before she has finished her three bows. "Please instruct me, sir, I am so hateful. I should practice meditation for many years, like you, so I can attain the *anagami* stage where anger is uprooted forever. But I am tied to my six sense doors, I cannot become a nun, I must live in this world full of low people. I think also, if I quit my job, who will support you monks when you come to Bangkok?"

As she speaks he takes the formal posture, and unconsciously sets his mouth in the same line as the abbot's in the portrait downstairs. Usually when someone bows to him, the beauty of the ancient hierarchy springs up like cool water inside him. Today he'd like to run from this woman, bunched up on the floor, getting ready to spill out her hot, messy life.

But he has to serve her, or else why give up Mary Rose?

"I'm not *anagami*. I'm just an American monk." He waggles his head from side to side, trying to look cheerful, maybe even throw her off track.

"You are so humble!" she says, looking up at him with eyes tormented and devoted as a dog's.

Oh my God, he thinks. Mary Rose. He forces himself to go on. "I understand your wish to renounce the world. Look at me, I left behind a very good woman to do this. I don't regret it," he adds quickly.

She thinks, he should not be talking about his woman; and then: who was she? He must have loved her, to look so regretful even after three years.

"Of course not. Monks enjoy a higher happiness," she says.

"But you don't need to be a nun to purify your mind. Greed, hatred, and delusion are the same whether you are in robes or not. Don't be hard on yourself. We all get angry."

"I am hard because hatred is hard." She says something in Pali, the scriptural language. But he can tell she's relieved, she's heard something that has helped her. She goes on more softly, "Sometimes I want to strike out against one person."

Miss Bi Chin feels a great relief as she confesses this, as if a rusty pin had been removed from her flesh.

"You'll also hurt yourself." The monk regrets his occasional cruelties to Mary Rose. Once, feeling perverse, he called her a cow, only because he knew she was sensitive about her big breasts. The word, the moment, the look on her face, have come back to his mind hundreds of times. And today she said that he wasted three years of her life, that he is a coward, that he insulted her by not speaking sooner.

"I know! I know!" Miss Bi Chin falls silent.

The monk tries for a better topic. "Who's the old man you have living with you? He gave me quite a look through the window."

He has the psychic powers, Miss Bi Chin thinks. "You've guessed my enemy. My step-uncle. My mother sent him to me. I cannot get rid of him." She picks like a schoolgirl at the hem of her dress, hearing the old man's mocking voice: "If you don't have the guts to throw me out, you deserve whatever you get."

The monk sees her face go deep red. That horrible old man! He sees him staring in the window again, his rheumy, cruel eyes. I'd better be careful though. Maybe they've slept together. You never know, when two people live in the same house.

"Every personal relationship brings suffering," he says cautiously.

"Better to live alone if one wants to free the mind," Miss Bi Chin quotes from the admonitions of the abbot. "Should I ask Uncle to leave?"

"Um, any reason why you can't?"

"Why not!" She giggles. She is not so much planning to kick out the old man as letting herself fall just a little in love with this monk. He is so breezy and American, like a hero in the movies; yet he has much wisdom. "Well, he has to stay here until you get your visa, because you and I would not be able to be in the house alone."

The monk smiles uncertainly. "I may not get a visa."

"Of course you will. You have good *kamma* from practice."

"Yet we never know when our *kamma* will ripen, do we. Good or bad."

They both nod slowly, looking into each other's eyes.

"What will you do if you can't go back?" She really wants to know; and it gives her a thrill to talk about this, knowing that the monk is ignorant of the abbot's intentions. Perhaps she'll report the answer to Rangoon.

"I'll try to remain in equanimity."

That's a good answer for the abbot, she thinks, but it's not enough for me. She extends herself: "Would you like to go back to your country and begin a monastery?"

"Oh, no," he says lightly.

"Why?"

"I have no interest in making others follow rules. I'm not a cop, basically."

"Don't you miss your home?"

"Yes, but . . ."

"I should have offered you to use the phone. Maybe you want to call your parents."

"I've already used it. I hope that's all right."

A shock runs down Miss Bi Chin's back. So it's true what the old man says. "You used the phone?"

"It was sort of urgent. I had to make a call. I did it collect, there'll be no charge to you. Maybe I should call Penang and confess?"

"Oh, no, no, no," she says. "I offered you to use my house as you wished. Who did you talk to?"

"Well, my old girlfriend from the States," and he finds himself describing the whole situation to Miss Bi Chin, confessing. Recklessly, he even says he might have postponed breaking up because he was afraid to lose a supporter. Because Miss Bi Chin is a stranger — and because she knows so much more about being a monk than he does — he feels compelled to expose his worst motivations. If forgiving words come out of these quietly smiling lips, he'll be exonerated. If her face turns from gold to brass and she casts him out, that will be right also.

As he speaks, Miss Bi Chin feels she is walking through a huge house, where rooms open up unexpectedly one after another. When she was in the British school, she had to read a poem about the East being East and the West being West, and never the twain shall meet. This is not true: she knows she can follow this monk far into his labyrinth, and maybe get lost. For him it is the simplest thing to say: the old man is bad, ask him to leave. But for himself, it is so complicated. In one room of his mind he is a monk, and using the phone was an error; in another room calling was the right thing to do. First he is too strict with himself, then he lets go of the rules altogether.

Should she tell the abbot? What would there be to tell? That the monk used the telephone after she had already given permission? That he was impatient to perform a wholesome act?

Miss Bi Chin has a water heart: it flows in uncontrollable sympathy toward the monk. She knows he was afraid to be forgotten when he went so far from home. That is the true reason he did not cut off this girlfriend, but he is a man and cannot admit such kind of fears.

She interrupts. "If I were Mary Rose," she tells him, "if Mary Rose were Burmese, or even Thai, as soon as you ordained, her reason for sending money would change. She would donate to earn merit for herself. You would then feel grateful but not indebted. You would feel to strive hard in meditation, to make her sacrifice worthwhile. And I think that your mind is very pure and you are trying to perform your discipline perfectly, but because you were in intensive practice you do not know in precise way what monks should do and not do when they are in ordinary life. Therefore I think you should spend your time here studying the texts in my library and learning what you did not learn."

At the end of this speech she is breathless, shocked to hear herself admonishing a monk.

"Thank you," he says. "That's great." His face is broken up by emotion; he looks as if he might weep.

Now, she thinks, should I tell the abbot that his monk is falling apart?

Not yet. It's only his first day.

Within a week it is obvious to the old man that Miss Bi Chin and the monk are in love.

"I should call Rangoon," he teases Miss Bi Chin. They both know he will never do so, if only because he will not know how to introduce the topic to a person he has never met. But the threat gives him power over her. Miss Bi Chin now ignores it when he fails to sweep or clean the bathrooms. The monk sometimes sweeps away the blossoms under the sal tree; the old man stands at the window of the sewing room, enjoying this spectacle. Miss Bi Chin made loud remarks about the toilet but ended up cleaning it herself. She also serves the old man his meals before going in and prattling with the monk. The old man has never felt so satisfied since he moved in here two years ago.

Miss Bi Chin, too, is happy. These days she feels a strange new kind of freedom. She and the monk are so often in the same room — he sits in the kitchen while she cooks, and otherwise they go to the sewing room and study or meditate — that the old man has fewer opportunities to pinch or slap. In the past she even feared that the old man might kill her, but he seems calmed by the monk's purity of mind.

The monk actually wants to know what she thinks about this and that. When she comes home from work, he asks respectfully how her day was, and they discuss her problems. He sees so clearly people's motivation! Then they go to the texts and try to look behind the surface to see what is the effect on the mind of each instruction, always asking, what did the Buddha intend? When they disagree with each other, they don't let each other off the hook: sometimes their arguments are fierce, exciting.

"Why do Burmese and Thais call each other lax?" he asks one night. "The Thais accuse the Burmese because Burmese monks will take stuff straight out of a woman's hand. Then the Burmese turn around and say Thais drink milk after noon. Can't they see it's all relative?"

"You don't know Thai monks," she replies hotly. "Won't take a pencil from a woman's hand but you don't know what they take from her other parts."

"Yeah, but not all Thai monks are bad. What about those old Ajahns up north? They live under trees."

"Insects also live under trees! Burmese get good results in their meditation, in the city or in the forest. You better listen to your own teacher to know what is right. No one reaches enlightenment by saying 'it is all relative.' "

His lips go tight, but then he nods. "You're right. Pingyan Sayadaw says Western skepticism makes people sour inside. You stay at the crossroads and never go anywhere. 'I don't believe this path, I don't believe that path.' Look at the power of mind he has."

"Such a strong monk," she says joyously.

No man has ever yielded to her thinking; it fills her heart with cold, delicious fire.

"Incredible," the monk replies, his pale eyes shining.

Then they meditate together, and her mind becomes so fresh.

She feels she is living in the time of the Buddha with this monk. When the old man accuses her of being in love, she retorts that she's always been in love with the truth.

The monk is getting healthy, eating Wheaties and doing yoga every day. Miss Bi Chin often asks if there's anything he needs, so he can say "A bottle of vitamin C" or "A new pair of rubber thongs" without feeling strange. He feels pleasantly glutted with conversation. In Burma, he never sifted through his thoughts, the idea was simply to take in as much as he could. At Miss Bi Chin's, he can sort, digest, refine. She helps direct his studies, she's almost as good as a monk; and in turn he's helping her figure out how to deal with daily life.

A perfect marriage would be like this, he thinks, except sex would screw it up with expectations. At times his feelings for Miss Bi Chin do grow warm, and he tosses on her bed at night; but there's no question in his mind about these feelings. They'll go away at the third stage of enlightenment. Having left Mary Rose, he feels more like a monk than ever. It's good exercise for him to see Miss Bi Chin's loveliness with detachment, as if she were a flower or a painting in a museum. When she exclaims that she's ugly and dark, he corrects her, saying, "All self-judgment reinforces the ego."

He writes the abbot every week. "Living in the world is not as difficult as I feared, but maybe this is because Miss Bi Chin's house is like a monastery. I am studying in her library. Her support is generous and her behavior is impeccable. She sleeps outside, under a tree. One night it rained and she went straight out to a hotel."

The monk has only two fears during this period. One is that the embassy of Myanma will not approve his visa. The other is that it will. When he thinks of Pingyan Monastery, he remembers its discomforts: diarrhea in the Rains, in April prickly heat.

I have my head in the sand, he thinks; or, I am asleep between my mother's breasts.

Miss Bi Chin is showing the monk a large bruise on her upper arm. It is the blue-black of an eggplant and has ugly spider's legs spreading in all directions around it. If he were not a monk, he'd touch it gently with his finger.

"I can't believe he does this to you," he says. "Don't you want him to leave? I'll be there when you say it. I'll stand over him while he packs."

"If he left, you'd have to go also. Where? He'd come back the next day. He was in the narcotics squad in Malaysia. I don't know what he would do. I think something. He has his old gun in a sack. It is broken but he could fix it."

Hearing about the gun makes the monk's stomach light with horror. Human beings, what they'll do to each other. Imagine a rapist's mind, a murderer's. Delusion, darkness, separation. How has Miss Bi Chin let this evil being stay in the house? How has she been able to live under the roof with such fear?

"He's got to go. If I'm still here he'd be less likely to bother you," the monk says. "I'm an American, after all. He'd get into big trouble if he pulled anything. Now that I can use the phone" — he laughs a little — "I can get on the horn to the embassy."

"But he is my step-uncle," Miss Bi Chin says weakly. She doesn't really want the monk to be proposing this. He sounds not like a monk, but like any other American boasting about his country's power.

"Look," the monk says. "I'll sleep outside. I'll eat outside. I'll stay outside all day. We can leave the gate open so people in the street can see us. I think this thing with the old man is more serious than you think. We can work out the monk part. The Patimokkha only talks about sleeping under the same roof and sharing a secluded seat, and in the second case a woman follower has to accuse me of seducing you."

"Okay. I'll get you a tent," Miss Bi Chin says.

"No way. You didn't have one," the monk retorts. "Why don't you find him a job instead?"

The old man knows something is wrong: when he comes back from the soda shop at six, the two of them are sitting in the patio chairs side by side, facing the gate, like judges.

"You must leave this house tomorrow," Miss Bi Chin says. The monk's face bears a look the old man knows is dangerous: determination mixed with terror, the look of a young boy about to pull a trigger. In a flash he calculates his chances. The monk is not healthy and probably knows no dirty fighting tricks, but is thirty years younger and much larger. He must have been a laborer

once, his arms and chest show signs of former strength; and he's
been exercising every day.

The old man makes his hands into claws. "Heugh!" he cries,
and fakes a pounce: only six inches forward. Of course, the
monk leaps to his feet. The old man laughs. This kind of thing
brings vigor in old age.

"So you lovebirds want privacy?" he says. "Watch out I don't
take the kitchen knife to you tonight. I'm old but I'm still a
man."

"I got you a job guarding the Chinese market," Miss Bi Chin
says. "They'll give you a room in back." She was surprised how
easy this solution was, once the monk opened her mind to it.
Now she owes the monk her happiness. Her house suddenly
seems vast; her nostrils fill with the sweet scent of sal flowers, as
if the old man were a fire emitting sharp smoke which had been
put out.

The next morning she calls a taxi. All of the old man's clothes
fit into a vinyl sports bag, but his TV is too big to carry on the
bus.

Watching him go, old and crooked, out the gate, Miss Bi Chin
feels bad. Her mother will not understand. Loyalty is important
in a family. She's been living in this house with the American
monk, who tells her about the youth revolution when everyone
decided their parents were wrong. This was the beginning of
meditation in America; even the monk got interested in spiritual
things at first because of drugs.

Now the monk meets her in the garden. He's smiling softly.
"Remember the test of loving-kindness?" he asks her. "You're sitting under a tree with a neutral person, a friend, and an enemy,
and a robber comes and says you have to choose who he'll kill?"

"I remember," she says dully. "I refuse the decision."

The abbot's letter has taken a month to arrive. He writes through
an interpreter: "My son in robes: I hope you get a visa soon. I am
glad you keep good morality. Miss Bi Chin says you are suitable
to be a teacher and your speeches are refined. I praise her for
sleeping outside, but maybe it is your turn. Be careful of desire
and pride, and do not think too much."

Miss Bi Chin has sent several glowing reports by aerogram.

Now she is not so sure. She hates sleeping in the bed, she feels she has lost her power in some obscure way. She and the monk are trying hard to keep the rules. They avoid being in the house together, but there are too many robbers in Bangkok to leave the street gate open, so they rely on the fact that they're always visible from the second floor of the elementary school across the street. They joke about their debt to one small, distracted boy who's always staring out the window; but this is almost like a lovers' joke. Miss Bi Chin feels disturbed by the monk's presence now. When he looks at her with soft eyes she feels nothing but fear. Perhaps he is in love with her. Perhaps he thinks of her at night. She dreads his quick buzz of the doorbell, announcing he's coming in to use the bathroom.

One morning at work she types an aerogram to the abbot. It makes her happy to see the clarity of the Selectric type on the thin, blue paper. "I worry about the American monk. We're alone together in my compound ever since he asked my uncle to leave my house. We try to keep his precepts, but I want your opinion. He spoke about his personal life. There was a woman in love with him at home. He said the precepts are relative, what is most important is the effect on the mind."

She tosses this in her Out box and watches the office boy take it away with her boss's letters to America. For some reason, she thinks of the gun lying in the bottom of the old man's sports bag as he walked off down the street.

"Don't you want to go home and teach your own people?" Miss Bi Chin asks again.

She's brought up this subject many times, and the monk always says no. But today his answer surprises both of them. With the old man gone, things have fallen into place. He likes sleeping under the sal tree, the same kind of tree under which the Buddha was born and died. Monks did this in ancient times, dwelt at the roots of trees. He loves its glossy green leaves and pink flowers; he imagines it is the tradition, and at night his roots go down with its roots, deep into the black soil. "Maybe I'm in a special position," he says. "Americans are hungry for truth. Our society is so materialistic."

"You don't want to be an abbot though," Miss Bi Chin says. "It is too tiring."

"I don't know," he says. "If my teacher asked me to I guess I'd have to go."

"Well, an abbot wouldn't be staying here alone with me, I can tell you that much," Miss Bi Chin bursts out.

That night he lies awake under the sal tree. Why didn't she tell him sooner, if it wasn't proper for him to stay? Is she in love with him? Or is she teaching him step by step?

He remembers the rules he's studied. Miss Bi Chin herself could be the woman follower who accuses him of seduction. Even though they haven't shared a seat, it's possible that if she brings a charge against him, there'd be no power in his denial, since they've been rather secluded together in her compound.

He understands something new: a monk's life has to be absolutely clear-cut. These rules were made for a reason. Ambiguous situations mean murky feelings, subterranean defilements. Again he can thank Miss Bi Chin for showing him how to go.

Whether he gets his visa or not is unimportant. He must go to Penang and live with other monks and prepare for the responsibilities of the future. If the Penang abbot hates Westerners, it's probably because he's never met one who appreciates the robes. If it's difficult to be there, it will develop his mental strength.

He imagines himself a monk in old age. The stubble on his head will grow out white, he'll laugh at the world like his teacher. Old Burmese monks are so very much alive, he thinks. Their bodies are light, their skin emits a glow. If you can feel free amid restrictions you truly are free.

In the morning he is quiet as Miss Bi Chin serves his breakfast on the front patio.

He is red now, not white: his blood is healthy. He keeps his eyes down as she hands him the plates. Wheaties, mango, cookies, Nescafé. Talk to me, she cries inside herself. She stares at his mouth, seeing its weakness and lust. It shows the part of him she loves, the human part.

She hasn't slept all night, and her mind is wild as an untamed elephant. Maybe the abbot will get her aerogram and make the monk disrobe. He'll stay in her house and live a lay life; they can make love after having their conversations. I could call the embassy and withdraw his visa application, she thinks. What is the worst that could happen? That I am reborn as a nun who'll be seduced by a foreigner?

At last she understands the old man, who said once he didn't care if *kamma* punished him in a future life, as long as he got to do what he wanted to in this life. How can we know who we'll be, or who we were? We can only try to be happy.

Frightened by her thoughts, she watches the monk bite a U shape out of this toast. He's being careful, moving stiffly as a wooden puppet; and he must have shaved his head this morning, it is shiny, hairless, there is a small bloody nick over his ear.

She knows she won't be able to cancel his visa application; and that her aerogram will result, not in the monk's disrobing, but in his being sent to Penang and forbidden to stay with her again. She hasn't accused him of downfall offenses, or disgusting offenses. So he'll go on with his practice and maybe become an abbot, or a fully liberated arhat. At least I was full of wholesome moral dread when I wrote that aerogram, she thinks. When the benefits come, I can enjoy them without guilt. Such as they'll be. Someone will give me a new Buddha image, I'll be offered another promotion and refuse it. She laughs under her breath. Is this what I was looking for when, as a young girl, I began running from temple to temple and lost all my friends?

"What are you laughing about," the monk says.

"I was thinking of something."

"I have to go to Penang," he says. His voice is low and hollow, so neither of them is sure he's actually spoken.

"I am sorry my house is unsuitable for you to stay."

"No, it's been wonderful to be here. But I need to be around other monks. I feel like we've been playing with the rules a little bit. We're in a gray area."

He smiles at her coaxingly, but she refuses the bait. "I'll buy you a ticket to Penang this afternoon."

How can she be so cold suddenly? She's pulling him out, compelling him to make the contact. "I'll miss you. Don't tell the abbot, okay?"

"If there is no lust, a monk may say he will miss."

"I want this to stay between us," he says. "You've been like my sister. And teacher. I'm sorry I have to go."

"Every personal relationship brings suffering," she says, but she's smiling at him, finally, a tiny complicated smile he'd never believe could appear on her golden face. Suddenly he sees her eyes are full of tears, and he knows he'll be lonely in Penang, not only for Miss Bi Chin but for Mary Rose, who also fixed things so he could ask for whatever he wanted.

Nothing changes, the old man thinks. There they are, sitting in the front courtyard, talking about nothing. He's standing at the jalousied window of the third-grade classroom, during the children's first morning recess. He knew this was the time. Bi Chin doesn't go to work until nine-thirty.

He woke up in a rage that drove him to the bus stop, still not knowing what he would do — something: he has his pistol in the sports bag. He had it fixed, and late at night he practices shooting at bottles floating in the *khlong* past the Chinese market. His aim isn't what it was. The pistol is heavier than he remembered, his eyes are bad, his arm shakes.

He knew an idea would come when he was actually standing at the window, and it has. He sees one thing he can succeed at. He can at least hit that plate glass window, shatter it behind their heads. He sees it clearly, bursting, shower of light. They run inside and slam the door. Miss Bi Chin in her terror grabs the monk. Ha! They find themselves embracing. That'll be a good one, if he doesn't miss and blow one of their heads off.

Happy with this solution, the old man begins to hum as he unzips the sports bag. The gun's cold oil smell reaches his nostrils, making him sharp and powerful. He's always wanted to break that window, he doesn't know why. Just to see it smash. I'm an evil old man, he thinks. Good thing I became a cop.

ELIZABETH WINTHROP

The Golden Darters

FROM AMERICAN SHORT FICTION

I WAS TWELVE YEARS OLD when my father started tying flies. It was an odd habit for a man who had just undergone a serious operation on his upper back, but, as he remarked to my mother one night, at least it gave him a world over which he had some control.

The family grew used to seeing him hunched down close to his tying vise, hackle pliers in one hand, thread bobbin in the other. We began to bandy about strange phrases — foxy quills, bodkins, peacock hurl. Father's corner of the living room was off limits to the maid with the voracious and destructive vacuum cleaner. Who knew what precious bit of calf's tail or rabbit fur would be sucked away never to be seen again.

Because of my father's illness, we had gone up to our summer cottage on the lake in New Hampshire a month early. None of my gang of friends ever came till the end of July, so in the beginning of that summer I hung around home watching my father as he fussed with the flies. I was the only child he allowed to stand near him while he worked. "Your brothers bounce," he muttered one day as he clamped the vise onto the curve of a model-perfect hook. "You can stay and watch if you don't bounce."

So I took great care not to bounce or lean or even breathe too noisily on him while he performed his delicate maneuvers, holding back hackle with one hand as he pulled off the final flourish of a whip finish with the other. I had never been so close to my father for so long before, and while he studied his tiny creations,

I studied him. I stared at the large pores of his skin, the sleek black hair brushed straight back from the soft dip of his temples, the jaw muscles tightening and slackening. Something in my father seemed always to be ticking. He did not take well to sickness and enforced confinement.

When he leaned over his work, his shirt collar slipped down to reveal the recent scar, a jagged trail of disrupted tissue. The tender pink skin gradually paled and then toughened during those weeks when he took his prescribed afternoon nap, lying on his stomach on our little patch of front lawn. Our house was one of the closest to the lake and it seemed to embarrass my mother to have him stretch himself out on the grass for all the swimmers and boaters to see.

"At least sleep on the porch," she would say. "That's why we set the hammock up there."

"Why shouldn't a man sleep on his own front lawn if he so chooses?" he would reply. "I have to mow the bloody thing. I might as well put it to some use."

And my mother would shrug and give up.

At the table when he was absorbed, he lost all sense of anything but the magnified insect under the light. Often when he pushed his chair back and announced the completion of his latest project to the family, there would be a bit of down or a tuft of dubbing stuck to the edge of his lip. I did not tell him about it but stared, fascinated, wondering how long it would take to blow away. Sometimes it never did and I imagine he discovered the fluff in the bathroom mirror when he went upstairs to bed. Or maybe my mother plucked it off with one of those proprietary gestures of hers that irritated my brothers so much.

In the beginning, Father wasn't very good at the fly-tying. He was a large, thick-boned man with sweeping gestures, a robust laugh, and a sudden terrifying temper. If he had not loved fishing so much, I doubt he would have persevered with the fussy business of the flies. After all, the job required tools normally associated with woman's work. Thread and bobbins, soft slippery feathers, a magnifying glass, and an instruction manual that read like a cookbook. It said things like, "Cut off a bunch of yellowtail.

Hold the tip end with the left hand and stroke out the short hairs."

But Father must have had a goal in mind. You tie flies because one day, in the not-too-distant future, you will attach them to a tippet, wade into a stream, and lure a rainbow trout out of his quiet pool.

There was something endearing, almost childish, about his stubborn nightly ritual at the corner table. His head bent under the standing lamp, his fingers trembling slightly, he would whisper encouragement to himself, talk his way through some particularly delicate operation. Once or twice I caught my mother gazing silently across my brothers' heads at him. When our eyes met, she would turn away and busy herself in the kitchen.

Finally, one night, after weeks of allowing me to watch, he told me to take his seat. "Why, Father?"

"Because it's time for you to try one."

"That's all right. I like to watch."

"Nonsense, Emily. You'll do just fine."

He had stood up. The chair was waiting. Across the room, my mother put down her knitting. Even the boys, embroiled in a noisy game of double solitaire, stopped their wrangling for a moment. They were all waiting to see what I would do. It was my fear of failing him that made me hesitate. I knew that my father put his trust in results, not in the learning process.

"Sit down, Emily."

I obeyed, my heart pounding. I was a cautious, secretive child, and I could not bear to have people watch me doing things. My piano lesson was the hardest hour in the week. The teacher would sit with a resigned look on her face while my fingers groped across the keys, muddling through a sonata that I had played perfectly just an hour before. The difference was that then nobody had been watching.

"— so we'll start you off with a big hook." He had been talking for some time. How much had I missed already?

"Ready?" he asked.

I nodded.

"All right then, clamp this hook into the vise. You'll be making the golden darter, a streamer. A big flashy fly, the kind that imitates a small fish as it moves underwater."

Across the room, my brothers had returned to their game, but their voices were subdued. I imagined they wanted to hear what was happening to me. My mother had left the room.

"Tilt the magnifying glass so you have a good view of the hook. Right. Now tie on with the bobbin thread."

It took me three tries to line the thread up properly on the hook, each silken line nesting next to its neighbor. "We're going to do it right, Emily, no matter how long it takes."

"It's hard," I said quietly.

Slowly I grew used to the tiny tools, to the oddly enlarged view of my fingers through the magnifying glass. They looked as if they didn't belong to me anymore. The feeling in their tips was too small for their large, clumsy movements. Despite my father's repeated warnings, I nicked the floss once against the barbed hook. Luckily it did not give way.

"It's Emily's bedtime," my mother called from the kitchen.

"Hush, she's tying in the throat. Don't bother us now."

I could feel his breath on my neck. The mallard barbules were stubborn, curling into the hook in the wrong direction. Behind me, I sensed my father's fingers twisting in imitation of my own.

"You've almost got it," he whispered, his lips barely moving. "That's right. Keep the thread slack until you're all the way around."

I must have tightened it too quickly. I lost control of the feathers in my left hand, the clumsier one. First the gold mylar came unwound and then the yellow floss.

"Damn it all, now look what you've done," he roared, and for a second I wondered whether he was talking to me. He sounded as if he were talking to a grown-up. He sounded the way he had just the night before when an antique teacup had slipped through my mother's soapy fingers and shattered against the hard surface of the sink. I sat back slowly, resting my aching spine against the chair for the first time since we'd begun.

"Leave it for now, Gerald," my mother said tentatively from the kitchen. Out of the corner of my eye, I could see her sponging the kitchen counter with small, defiant sweeps of her hand. "She can try again tomorrow."

"What happened?" called a brother. They both started across the room toward us but stopped at a look from my father.

"We'll start again," he said, his voice once more under control. "Best way to learn. Get back on the horse."

With a flick of his hand, he loosened the vise, removed my hook, and threw it into the wastepaper basket.

"From the beginning?" I whispered.

"Of course," he replied. "There's no way to rescue a mess like that."

My mess had taken almost an hour to create.

"Gerald," my mother said again. "Don't you think —"

"How can we possibly work with all these interruptions?" he thundered. I flinched as if he had hit me. "Go on upstairs, all of you. Emily and I will be up when we're done. Go on, for God's sake. Stop staring at us."

At a signal from my mother, the boys backed slowly away and crept up to their room. She followed them. I felt all alone, as trapped under my father's piercing gaze as the hook in the grip of its vise.

We started again. This time my fingers were trembling so much that I ruined three badger hackle feathers, stripping off the useless webbing at the tip. My father did not lose his temper again. His voice dropped to an even, controlled monotone that scared me more than his shouting. After an hour of painstaking labor, we reached the same point with the stubborn mallard feathers curling into the hook. Once, twice, I repinched them under the throat, but each time they slipped away from me. Without a word, my father stood up and leaned over me. With his cheek pressed against my hair, he reached both hands around and took my fingers in his. I longed to surrender the tools to him and slide away off the chair, but we were so close to the end. He captured the curling stem with the thread and trapped it in place with three quick wraps.

"Take your hands away carefully," he said. "I'll do the whip finish. We don't want to risk losing it now."

I did as I was told, sat motionless with his arms around me, my head tilted slightly to the side so he could have the clear view through the magnifying glass. He cemented the head, wiped the excess glue from the eye with a waste feather, and hung my golden darter on the tackle box handle to dry. When at last he pulled away, I breathlessly slid my body back against the chair. I was still conscious of the havoc my clumsy hands or an unexpected sneeze could wreak on the table, which was cluttered with feathers and bits of fur.

"Now, that's the fly you tied, Emily. Isn't it beautiful?"

I nodded. "Yes, Father."

"Tomorrow, we'll do another one. An olive grouse. Smaller hook but much less complicated body. Look. I'll show you in the book."

As I waited to be released from the chair, I didn't think he meant it. He was just trying to apologize for having lost his temper, I told myself, just trying to pretend that our time together had been wonderful. But the next morning when I came down, late for breakfast, he was waiting for me with the materials for the olive grouse already assembled. He was ready to start in again, to take charge of my clumsy fingers with his voice and talk them through the steps.

That first time was the worst, but I never felt comfortable at the fly-tying table with Father's breath tickling the hair on my neck. I completed the olive grouse, another golden darter to match the first, two muddler minnows, and some others. I don't remember all the names anymore.

Once I hid upstairs, pretending to be immersed in my summer reading books, but he came looking for me.

"Emily," he called. "Come on down. Today we'll start the lead-winged coachman. I've got everything set up for you."

I lay very still and did not answer.

"Gerald," I heard my mother say. "Leave the child alone. You're driving her crazy with those flies."

"Nonsense," he said, and started up the dark, wooden stairs, one heavy step at a time.

I put my book down and rolled slowly off the bed so that by the time he reached the door of my room, I was on my feet, ready to be led back downstairs to the table.

Although we never spoke about it, my mother became oddly insistent that I join her on trips to the library or the general store.

"Are you going out again, Emily?" my father would call after me. "I was hoping we'd get some work done on this minnow."

"I'll be back soon, Father," I'd say. "I promise."

"Be sure you do," he said.
And for a while I did.

Then at the end of July, my old crowd of friends from across the lake began to gather and I slipped away to join them early in the morning before my father got up.

The girls were a gang. When we were all younger, we'd held bicycle relay races on the ring road and played down at the lakeside together under the watchful eyes of our mothers. Every July, we threw ourselves joyfully back into each other's lives. That summer we talked about boys and smoked illicit cigarettes in Randy Kidd's basement and held leg-shaving parties in her bedroom behind a safely locked door. Randy was the ringleader. She was the one who suggested we pierce our ears.

"My parents would die," I said. "They told me I'm not allowed to pierce my ears until I'm seventeen."

"Your hair's so long, they won't even notice," Randy said. "My sister will do it for us. She pierces all her friends' ears at college."

In the end, only one girl pulled out. The rest of us sat in a row with the obligatory ice cubes held to our ears, waiting for the painful stab of the sterilized needle.

Randy was right. At first my parents didn't notice. Even when my ears became infected, I didn't tell them. All alone in my room, I went through the painful procedure of twisting the gold studs and swabbing the recent wounds with alcohol. Then on the night of the club dance, when I had changed my clothes three times and played with my hair in front of the mirror for hours, I came across the small plastic box with dividers in my top bureau drawer. My father had given it to me so that I could keep my flies in separate compartments, untangled from one another. I poked my finger in and slid one of the golden darters up along its plastic wall. When I held it up, the mylar thread sparkled in the light like a jewel. I took out the other darter, hammered down the barbs of the two hooks, and slipped them into the raw holes in my earlobes.

Someone's mother drove us all to the dance, and Randy and I pushed through the side door into the ladies' room. I put my hair up in a ponytail so the feathered flies could twist and dangle above my shoulders. I liked the way they made me look — free and different and dangerous, even. And they made Randy notice.

"I've never seen earrings like that," Randy said. "Where did you get them?"

"I made them with my father. They're flies. You know, for fishing."

"They're great. Can you make me some?"

I hesitated. "I have some others at home I can give you," I said at last. "They're in a box in my bureau."

"Can you give them to me tomorrow?" she asked.

"Sure," I said with a smile. Randy had never noticed anything I'd worn before. I went out to the dance floor, swinging my ponytail in time to the music.

My mother noticed the earrings as soon as I got home.

"What has gotten into you, Emily? You know you were forbidden to pierce your ears until you were in college. This is appalling."

I didn't answer. My father was sitting in his chair behind the fly-tying table. His back was better by that time, but he still spent most of his waking hours in that chair. It was as if he didn't like to be too far away from his flies, as if something might blow away if he weren't keeping watch.

I saw him look up when my mother started in with me. His hands drifted ever so slowly down to the surface of the table as I came across the room toward him. I leaned over so that he could see my earrings better in the light.

"Everybody loved them, Father. Randy says she wants a pair, too. I'm going to give her the muddler minnows."

"I can't believe you did this, Emily," my mother said in a loud, nervous voice. "It makes you look so cheap."

"They don't make me look cheap, do they, Father?" I swung my head so he could see how they bounced, and my hip accidentally brushed the table. A bit of rabbit fur floated up from its pile and hung in the air for a moment before it settled down on top of the foxy quills.

"For God's sake, Gerald, speak to her," my mother said from her corner.

He stared at me for a long moment as if he didn't know who I was anymore, as if I were a trusted associate who had committed some treacherous and unspeakable act. "That is not the purpose for which the flies were intended," he said.

"Oh, I know that," I said quickly. "But they look good this way, don't they?"

He stood up and considered me in silence for a long time across the top of the table lamp.

"No, they don't," he finally said. "They're hanging upside down."

Then he turned off the light and I couldn't see his face anymore.

TOBIAS WOLFF

Firelight

FROM STORY

MY MOTHER SWORE we'd never live in a boardinghouse again, but circumstances did not allow her to keep this promise. She decided to change cities; we had to sleep somewhere. This boardinghouse was worse than the last one, unfriendly, funereal, heavy with the smells that disheartened people allow themselves to cultivate. On the floor below ours a retired merchant seaman was coughing his lungs out. He was a friendly old guy, always ready with a compliment for my mother as we climbed past the dim room where he sat smoking on the edge of his bed. During the day we felt sorry for him, but at night, as we lay in wait for the next racking seizure, feeling the silence swell with it, we hated him. I did, anyway.

My mother said this was just temporary. We were definitely getting out of there. To show me and maybe herself that she meant business, she went through the paper during breakfast every Saturday morning and circled the advertisements for furnished apartments that sounded, as she put it, "right for our needs." I liked that expression. It made me feel as if our needs had some weight in the world, and would have to be reckoned with. Then, putting on her shrewd face, my mother compared the apartments for price and culled out the most expensive and also the very cheap ones. We knew the story on those, the dinky fridge and weeping walls, the tub sinking through the bathroom floor, the wife beater upstairs. We'd been that route. When my

mother had five or six interesting places, she called to make sure
they were still open and we spent the day going from one to another.

We couldn't actually take anything. The landlords wanted first
and last month's rent, plus cleaning deposit, and it was going to
be a while before my mother could put all that together. I understood this, but every Saturday my mother repeated it again so I
wouldn't get carried away. We were just looking. Getting a feel
for the market.

There is pleasure to be found in the purchase of goods and
services. I enjoy it myself now, playing the part of a man who
knows what he wants and can take it home with him. But in
those days I was mostly happy just to look at things. And that
was lucky for me, because we did a power of looking, and no
buying.

My mother wasn't one of those comparison shoppers who
head straight for the price tag, shaking their faces and beefing
about the markup to everyone in sight. She had no great interest
in price. She had no money, either, but it went deeper than that.
She liked to shop because she felt at home in stores and was interested in the merchandise. Sales clerks waited on her without
impatience, seeing there was nothing mean or trivial in her curiosity, this curiosity that kept her so young and drove her so hard.
She just had to see what was out there.

We'd always shopped, but that first fall in Seattle, when we
were more broke than we'd ever been, we really hit our stride.
We looked at leather luggage. We looked at televisions in large
Mediterranean consoles. We looked at antiques and Oriental
rugs. Looking at Oriental rugs isn't something you do lightly, because the men who sell them have to work like dogs, dragging
them down from these tall teetering piles and then humping
them over to you, sweating and gasping, staggering under the
weight, their faces woolly with lint. They tend to be small men.
You can't be squeamish. You have to be free of shame, absolutely
sure of your right to look at what you cannot buy. And so we
were.

When the new fashions came in my mother tried them on
while I watched. She had once been a model and knew how to

strike attitudes before the mirror, how to walk casually away and
then stop, canting one hip and glancing over her shoulder as if
someone had just called her name. When she turned to me I ex-
pressed my judgments with a smile, a shrug, a sour little shake of
the head. I thought she was beautiful in everything but I felt
obliged to discriminate. She didn't like too much admiration. It
suffocated her.

We looked at copper cookware. We looked at lawn furniture
and pecan dining room sets. We spent one whole day at a marina,
studying the inventory of a bankrupt Chris-Craft dealership.
"The Big Giveaway," they called it. It was the only sale we ever
made a point of going to.

My mother wore a smart gray suit when we went house hunting.
I wore my little gentleman outfit, a V-neck sweater with a bow
tie. The sweater had the words "Fraternity Row" woven across
the front. We looked respectable, as, on the whole, we were. We
also looked solvent.

On this particular day we were touring apartments in the university district. The first three we looked at were decent enough,
but the fourth was a wreck — the last tenant, a woman, had lived
here like an animal in a cave. Someone had tried to clean it up,
but the job was hopeless. The place smelled like rotten meat,
even with the windows open and the cool air blowing through.
Everything felt sticky. The landlord said that the woman was depressed over the breakup of her marriage. He talked about a
paint job, new carpets, but he seemed discouraged and soon fell
silent. The three of us walked through the rooms, then back outside. The landlord could tell we weren't biting. He didn't even
offer us a card.

We had one more apartment to look at, but my mother said
she'd seen enough. She asked me if I wanted to go down to the
wharf, or home, or what. Her mouth was set, her face drawn.
She tried to sound agreeable, but she was in a black mood. I
didn't like the idea of going back to the house, back to the room,
so I said why didn't we walk up to the university and take a look
around.

She squinted up the street. I thought she was going to say no,
but she said, "Sure. Why not? As long as we're here."

We started walking. There were big maples along the sidewalk. Fallen leaves scraped and eddied around our legs as the breeze gusted.

"You don't *ever* let yourself go like that," my mother said, hugging herself and looking down. "There's no excuse for it."

She sounded mortally offended. I knew I hadn't done anything, so I kept quiet. She said, "I don't care what happens, there is no excuse to give up like that. Do you hear what I'm saying?"

"Yes, ma'am."

A group of Chinese came up behind us, ten or twelve of them, all young men, talking excitedly. They parted around us, still talking, and rejoined like water flowing around a stone. We followed them up the street and across the road to the university, where we wandered among the buildings as the light began to fail and the wind turned raw. This was the first really cold day since we'd moved here, and I wasn't dressed for it. But I said nothing because I still didn't want to go home. I had never set foot on a campus before and I was greedily measuring it against my idea of what it should look like. It had everything. Old-looking buildings with stone archways and high, arched windows. Rich greenswards. Ivy. The leaves of the ivy had turned red. High on the west-facing walls, in what was left of the sunshine, the red leaves glittered as the wind stirred them. Every so often a great roar went up from Husky Stadium, where a game was in progress. Each time I heard it I felt a thrill of complicity and belonging. I believed that I was in place here, and that the students we passed on the brick walkways would look at me and see one of themselves — "Fraternity Row" — if it weren't for the woman beside me, her hand on my shoulder. I began to feel the weight of that hand.

My mother didn't notice. She was in good spirits again, flushed with the cold and with memories of days like this at Yale and Trinity, when she used to get free tickets to football games from a girlfriend who dated the players. She had dated one of the players herself, an all-American quarterback from Yale named Dutch Diefenbacker. He'd wanted to marry her, she added carelessly.

"You mean he actually asked you?"

"He gave me a ring. My father sold it to him. He'd bought it for this woman he had a crush on, but she wouldn't accept it. What she actually said was, 'Why, I wouldn't marry an old man like you.' " My mother laughed.

"Wait a minute," I said. "You had a chance to marry an all-American from Yale?"

"Sure."

"Well, why didn't you?"

We stopped beside a fountain clotted with leaves. My mother stared into the water. "I don't know. I was pretty young then, and Dutch wasn't what you'd call a scintillating guy. He was nice . . . just dull. Very dull." She drew a deep breath and said, with some violence, "God, he was boring!"

"I would have married him," I said. I had never known this before. It was outrageous that my mother, out of schoolgirl snobbery, had deprived me of an all-American father from Yale. I would be rich now, and have a collie. Everything would be different.

We circled the fountain and headed back the way we'd come. When we reached the road, my mother asked me if I wanted to look at the apartment we'd skipped. "Oh, what the heck," she said, seeing me hesitate. "As long as we're here we might as well make a clean sweep."

I was cold, but because I hadn't said anything so far I thought it would sound phony if I complained now, phony and babyish. She stopped two girls wearing letter sweaters — *coeds*, I thought, finding excitement in the word — and while they gave her directions I studied a display of books in a shop window, as if I just happened to be standing beside this person who didn't know her way around.

The evening was clear and brief. At a certain moment the light flared weakly, and then it was gone. We walked several blocks, to a neighborhood of Victorian houses whose windows, seen from the empty street, glowed with rich, exclusive light. The wind blew at our backs. I was starting to shake. I still didn't tell my mother. I knew I should have said something earlier, that I'd been stupid not to, and now I fastened all my will on the effort to conceal this stupidity by maintaining it.

We stopped in front of a house with a turret. The upper story was dark. "We're late," I said bitterly.

"Not that late," my mother said. "Besides, the apartment's on the ground floor."

She walked up to the porch while I waited on the sidewalk. I heard the muted chime of bells and watched the windows for movement.

"Nuts . . . I should have called," my mother said. She'd just turned away when one of the two doors swung open and a man leaned out, a big man silhouetted in the bright doorway.

"Yes?" he said. He sounded impatient, but when my mother turned to face him he added, more gently, "What can I do for you?" His voice was so deep I could almost feel it, like coal rumbling down a chute.

She told him we were here about the apartment. "I guess we're a little late," she said.

"An hour late," he said.

My mother exclaimed surprise, said we'd been walking around the university and completely lost track of time. She was very apologetic but made no move to go, and it must have been clear to him that she had no intention of going until she'd seen the apartment. It was clear enough to me. I came down the walkway and up the porch steps.

He was big in every direction, tall, wide, rotund, with a massive head, a trophy head. He had the kind of size that provokes, almost inevitably, the nickname "Tiny," but I'm sure nobody called him that. He was too solemn, preoccupied, like a buffalo in the broadness and gravity of his face. He looked down at us through black-framed glasses. "Well, you're here," he said, not unkindly, and we followed him inside.

The first thing I saw was the fire. I was aware of other things, furniture, the churchlike expanse of the room, but my eyes went straight to the flames. They burned with a hissing sound in a fireplace I could have walked into without stooping, or just about. The logs were snapping like grease. A girl lay on her stomach in front of the fire, one bare foot raised and slowly twisting, her chin propped in her hand. She was reading a book. She went on reading it for a few moments after we came in, then sat up and said, very precisely, "Good evening." She had boobs. I could see them pushing at the front of her blouse. But she wasn't pretty. She was owlish and large and wore the same kind of glasses as the man, whom she closely and unfortunately resembled. She blinked constantly. I felt immediately at ease with her.

I smiled and said "Hi" instead of assuming the indifference, even hostility, with which I treated pretty girls.

Something was in the oven. Something chocolate. I went over to the fire and stood with my back to it, flexing my hands behind me.

"Oh yes, it's quite comfortable, very comfortable," the man said in answer to a comment of my mother's. He peered around curiously as if surprised to find himself here. The room was big, the biggest I'd ever seen in an apartment. We could never afford to live here, but I was already losing my grip on that fact.

"I'll go get my wife," the man said, but he stayed where he was, watching my mother. She was turning slowly, nodding to herself in a pensive way as if making calculations in her head.

"All this room," she said. "It makes you feel so free. How can you bear to give it up?"

At first he didn't answer. The girl started picking at something on the rug. Then he said, "We're ready for a bit of a change. Aren't we, Sister?"

She nodded without looking up.

A woman came in from the next room, carrying a plate of brownies. She was tall and thin. Deep furrows ran down her cheeks, framing her mouth like parentheses. Her gray hair was pulled into a ponytail. She moved toward us with slow, measured steps, as if carrying gifts to the altar, and set the plate on the coffee table. "You're just in time to have some of Dr. Avery's brownies," she said.

I thought she was referring to a recipe. Then the man hurried over and scooped up a handful, and I understood. I understood not only that he was Dr. Avery, but that the brownies belonged to him; his descent on the plate bore all the signs of jealous ownership. I was nervous about taking one, but Sister did it and survived, and even went back for another. I had a couple myself. As we ate, the woman slipped her arm behind Dr. Avery's back and leaned against him. The little I'd seen of marriage had disposed me to view public affection between husbands and wives as pure stagecraft — *Look, this is a home where people hug each other* — but she was so plainly happy to be where she was that I couldn't help feeling happy with her.

My mother prowled the room restlessly. "Do you mind if I look around?" she said.

Mrs. Avery asked Sister to show us the rest of the apartment.

More big rooms. Two of them had fireplaces. Above the mantel in the master bedroom hung a large photograph of a man with dark, thoughtful eyes. When I asked Sister who it was, she said, a shade importantly, "Gurdjieff."

I didn't mind her condescension. She was older, and bigger, and I suspected smarter than me. Condescension seemed perfectly in order.

"Gurdjieff," my mother said. "I've heard of him."

"*Gurdjieff*," Sister repeated, as though she'd said it wrong.

We went back to the living room and sat around the fire, Dr. and Mrs. Avery on the couch, my mother in a rocking chair across from them. Sister and I stretched out on the floor. She opened her book, and a moment later her foot rose into the air again and began its slow twisting motion. My mother and Mrs. Avery were talking about the apartment. I stared into the flames, the voices above me pleasant and meaningless until I heard my name mentioned. My mother was telling Mrs. Avery about our walk around the university. She said that it was a beautiful campus.

"Beautiful!" Dr. Avery said. "What do you mean by beautiful?"

My mother looked at him. She didn't answer.

"I assume you're referring to the buildings."

"Sure. The buildings, the grounds. The general layout."

"Pseudo-Gothic humbug," Dr. Avery said. "A movie set."

"Dr. Avery believes that the university pays too much attention to appearances," Mrs. Avery said.

"That's all they pay attention to," Dr. Avery said.

"I wouldn't know about that," my mother said. "I'm not an expert on architecture. It looked nice enough to me."

"Yes, well that's the whole point, isn't it?" Dr. Avery said. "It *looks* like a university. The same with the so-called education they're selling. It's a counterfeit experience from top to bottom. Utterly hollow. All *materia*, no *anima*."

He lost me there, and I went back to looking at the flames. Dr. Avery rumbled on. He had been quiet before, but once he got started he didn't stop, and I wouldn't have wanted him to. The sound of his voice made me drowsy with assurance. It was like

the drone of a car engine when you're lying on the backseat,
going home from a long trip. Now and then Mrs. Avery spoke
up, expressing concord with something the doctor had said,
making her complete agreement known; then he resumed. Sister
shifted beside me. She yawned, turned a page. The logs settled
in the fireplace, very softly, like some old sleeping dog adjusting
his bones.

Dr. Avery talked for quite a while. Then my mother said my
name. Nothing more, only my name. Dr. Avery went on as if he
hadn't heard. He was leaning forward, one finger wagging to the
cadence of his words, glasses glinting as his great head shook. I
looked at my mother. She sat stiffly in the rocker, her hands
kneading the purse in her lap. Her face was bleak, frozen. It was
the expression she wore when she got trapped by some diehard
salesman or a pair of Mormons who wouldn't go away. She
wanted to leave.

I did not want to leave. Nodding by the fire, torpid and content, I had forgotten that this was not my home. The heat and
the firelight worked on me like Dr. Avery's voice, lulling me into
a state of familial serenity such as these people seemed to enjoy.
I even managed to forget that they were not my family, and that
they too would soon be moving on. I made them part of my story
without any sense that they had their own to live out.

What that was, I don't know. We never saw them again. But
now, so many years later, I can venture a guess. My guess is that
Dr. Avery had been denied tenure by the university, and that this
wasn't the first university to prove itself unequal to him, nor the
last. I see him carrying his fight against mere appearances from
one unworthy institution to the next, each of them refusing, with
increasing vehemence, his call to spiritual greatness. Dr. Avery's
colleagues, small minds joined to small hearts, ridicule him as
a nuisance and a bore. They imply that his high-mindedness
is a cover for lack of distinction in his field, whatever that is.
Again and again they send him packing. Mrs. Avery consoles his
wounded *anima* with unfailing loyalty, and ministers to his swell-
ing *materia* with larger and larger batches of brownies. She believes in him. Her faith, whatever its foundation, is heroic. Not
once does she imagine, as a lesser woman might, that her chances
for common happiness — old friends, a place of her own, a life

rooted in community — have been sacrificed not to some higher truth but to vanity and arrogance.

No, that part belongs to Sister. Sister will be the heretic. She has no choice, being their child. In time, not many years after this night, she will decide that the disappointments of her life can be traced to their failings. Who knows those failings better than Sister? There are scenes. Dr. Avery is accused of being himself, Mrs. Avery of being herself. The visits home from Barnard or Reed or wherever Sister's scholarship takes her, and then from the distant city where she works, become theatrical productions. Angry whispers in the kitchen, shouts at the dinner table, early departure. This goes on for years, but not forever. Sister makes peace with her parents. She even comes to cherish what she has resented, their refusal to talk and act as others do, their endless moving on, the bright splash of their oddity in the muddy flow. She finds she has no choice but to love them, and who can love them better than Sister?

It might have gone this way, or another way. I have made these people part of my story without knowing anything of theirs, just as I did that night, dreaming myself one of them. We were strangers. I'd spent maybe forty-five minutes in their apartment, just long enough to get warm and lose sight of the facts.

My mother spoke my name again. I stayed where I was. Usually I would have gotten to my feet without her saying anything else, not out of obedience but because it pleased me to anticipate her, to show off our teamwork. But this time I just stared at her sullenly. She looked wrong in the rocking chair. She was too glamorous for it. I could see her glamor almost as a thing apart, another presence, a brassy impatient friend just dying to get her out of here, away from all this domesticity.

She said we ought to think about getting home. Sister raised her head and looked at me. I still didn't move. I could see my mother's surprise. She waited for me to do something, and when I didn't she rocked forward slowly and stood up. Everyone stood with her except me. I felt foolish and bratty sitting on the floor all by myself, but I stayed there anyway while she made the final pleasantries. When she was about to leave I got up, mumbled my good-byes, and followed her back outside.

Dr. Avery held the door for us.

"I still think it's a pretty campus," my mother said.

He laughed — Ho ho ho. "Well, so be it," he said. "To each his own." He waited until we reached the sidewalk, then turned the light off and closed the door. It made a solid bang behind us.

"What was that all about?" my mother said.

I didn't answer.

"Are you feeling okay?"

"Yes." Then I said, "I'm a little cold."

"Cold? Why didn't you say something?" She tried to look concerned but I could see that she was glad to have a simple answer for what had happened back in the house.

She took off her suit jacket. "Here."

"That's okay."

"Put it on."

"Really, Mom. I'll be okay."

"Put it on, dimwit!"

I put the coat on. We walked for a while. "I look ridiculous," I said.

"So . . . who cares?"

"I do."

"Okay, you do. *Sorry.* Boy, you're a regular barrel of laughs tonight."

"I'm not wearing this thing on the bus."

"Nobody said you had to wear it on the bus. You want to grab something to eat before we head back?"

I told her sure, fine, whatever she wanted.

"Maybe we can find a pizza place. Think you could eat some pizza?"

I said I thought I could.

A black dog with gleaming eyes crossed the street in our direction.

"Hello, sport," my mother said.

The dog trotted along beside us for a while, then took off.

I turned up the jacket collar and hunched my shoulders.

"Are you still cold?"

"A little." I was shivering like crazy. It seemed to me I'd never been so cold, and I blamed my mother for it, for taking me outside again, away from the fire. I knew it wasn't her fault but I blamed her anyway. I blamed her for this and the wind in my face and for every nameless thing that was not as it should be.

"Come here." When I kept my distance she pulled me over and began to rub her hand up and down my arm. I leaned away but she held onto me and kept rubbing. It felt good. I wasn't really warm, but I was as warm as I was going to get.

"Just out of curiosity," my mother said, "what did you think of the campus? Honestly."

"I liked it."

"I thought it was great," she said.

"So did I."

"That big blowhard," she said. "Where does he get off?"

I have a fireplace myself now. Where we live, the winters are long and cold. The wind blows the snow sideways, the house creaks, the windows glaze over with ferns of ice. After dinner I lay the fire, building four walls of logs like a roofless cabin. That's the best way. Only greenhorns use the tepee method. My children wait behind me, jockeying for position, furiously arguing their right to apply the match. I tell them to do it together. Their hands shake with eagerness as they strike the matches and hold them to the crumpled paper, torching as many spots as they can before the kindling starts to crackle. Then they sit back on their heels and watch the flame engulf the cabin walls. Their faces are reverent.

My wife comes in and praises the fire, knowing the pride it gives me. She lies on the couch with her book but doesn't read it. I don't read mine, either. I watch the fire, watch the changing light on the faces of my family. I try to feel at home. And I do, mostly. It is a sweet time. But in the very heart of it I catch myself bracing a little, as if in fear of being tricked. As if to really believe in it will somehow make it vanish, like a voice waking me from sleep.

Contributors' Notes

*100 Other Distinguished
Stories of 1991*

Editorial Addresses

Contributors' Notes

ALICE ADAMS is the author of five collections of short stories and seven novels, most recently *Caroline's Daughters*. She lives in San Francisco.
• I wrote this story after going to a lunch in Stinson Beach, where I did indeed meet a series of people whom I had known before, in one way or another — some of them not exactly welcome apparitions. But I do not know how I came up with the Mexican doctor, except that at the time I was writing a book about Mexico. I liked the idea of the city itself, San Francisco, being a more or less offstage character in the story.

RICK BASS is most recently the author of *The Ninemile Wolves*, as well as four other books of natural history and a story collection, *The Watch*. He lives in Montana and is working on a novel.
• I am a sloth. I am a pig, a cretin, a laze-about, an editor's wastrel. A thug. As my friend Bonky, age six, says: "A bad, bad, very bad, not good" editor. How much easier it is to turn in a raw chunk of story and let the various editors labor over it, kneading and pummeling the writer's dull and torpid psyche, like a masseuse wrenching all the limbs back into their proper and useful alignments: leaning over the writer's ear, perhaps, and whispering (with an editor's — or masseuse's — perverse mix of tenderness and ferocity), *But what about this? Why does Mack love Laura? And, Do you really think Jean is frightened, or just lonely? And, What if? And, This logic needs reversing.* And (wrenching the shoulder nearly all the way out), *Cut, cut, cut — the story doesn't begin until page ten.*
All of my short stories, I feel, have in their basement of sin a huge and embarrassing cloacal growth of clumsiness and goofiness and just plain wrongheadedness. And so around and around we go, the editors and I, and usually it takes between ten and fifteen drafts to get on track. It's not that I can't *learn* to edit and think like an editor: I'm just lazy. Why

bother doing it when the magazine or quarterly editor (in this case, Don Lee) or my agent or my wife or a friend or even a stranger on the street — there's always someone to sponge off of — can do all that hard fine-tuning stuff for me?

It makes me sick to my stomach to realize what a pig I am. It's a sickness that I can't help. Or, maybe I enjoy it. Maybe I secretly despise editors and like to see them scramble and work until beads of blood pop from their brows. Left to my own devices, I am too "relaxed" (lazy) and do not bear down hard enough. Especially in the rewrites. ("Fatigue makes cowards of us all," said the late Vince Lombardi, coach of the Green Bay Packers.)

"Days of Heaven" began with the notion of helplessness, of dependency: of how the narrator needed dark woods in which to hide and calm his sometimes angry but other times frightened soul. So in the beginning it was an easy story. The textbooks say to set into action forces which will try to take away that solace, that refuge. And then the books say to have the narrator struggle to retain that peace, those days of heaven. I thought it was an okay story, and Don Lee at *Ploughshares* was generous to take it. At that point it hadn't occurred to me to look for unexpected seams and brushier trails in the story. The easy thing to do was to have the narrator fight the proposed development actively, textbookedly, rather than hiding and watching and learning.

In my usual fashion, I hadn't yet shown the story to Carol Smith, my fiction editor at Norton. Too often I send off a story while tanked up on the lovely intoxicating juices of having just completed it, when all the characters are heroes for having made it through to the end — and the writer's head is full of what Barry Hannah calls "that exquisite, silvery gas." I'd done it again here. As an afterthought I sent a copy of the story to Carol, mentioning that it was about to be published and that maybe she'd be able to pick up a few comma cuts, that kind of thing.

Rather than patting me on the back, Carol ripped the stuffing out of the story, sent it back via Federal Express, and made clear her disgust that the story was going to see print in its draft form. As usual in an early draft, my characters were one-dimensional, and the narrator was too dreamy-moony, too detached.

Let's say it: too lazy.

In the meantime, while the story was going to galleys, Don Lee was looking at it again and composing his own editorial letter. Carol had had to rush to fix the story as best she could. While Don Lee's kind and cruel revision was tumbling toward me, I used Carol's notes to patch the biggest leaks and sent a revision off to Don Lee. Most of Carol's outrage had to do with what came in the first half of the story.

In the meantime, of course, Mr. Lee had come to his senses. His severely marked copy arrived the day after I sent out the patched version. Most of Lee's fury was directed at the second half of the story.

Around and around we went, Fed-Exing and UPS-Second-Daying like crazy, doing two and three drafts a day — I'd do one in the morning, run up and make a phone call, come back and do another at lunch, drive up to the phone and call again, and then come back home and do the third draft after supper. One of my perversities is that when I get something "right" in a revision, it usually unravels and makes "wrong" two things that earlier in the text had been "right," so then the editors have to go back in and put out *those* brush fires . . .

Faxes began to get involved (a ninety-five-mile round trip, for me), and then, *raw* telephone calls. Calls to Don's house made, again, from that lonely pay phone in Yaak. ("Oh, is it two A.M. in Massachusetts? I'm sorry, it's only midnight here.")

Don was fatigued, if not cross, having been through all this with me a couple of years earlier with my story "The History of Rodney," the last page of which we'd ended up resetting at the last second (in a different typeface! My fault!). For some reason, the *true* ending of "The History of Rodney" was not revealed to me until the last possible second — making it necessary for me to call Don at his home at three A.M.

We did the same thing with "Days of Heaven." Again, I got lucky with my thirteenth and final draft. The story was slotted to be last in the issue, which meant that this time we could still call the typesetter after it had already gone to press (at my considerable expense; the burden of being a pig) and tell him to hold off setting the last page (this after he'd *already* reset the story). We finally got it right, all three of us, and why I can't just take my time and get it right without pressure and panic swirling all around, I don't know. Carol says tactfully that it is because I get in a hurry and get confused, and Don says, also tactfully, that it is because it takes me a while to see what the story is, but I say it is because I am a pig and that I like to use editors like a crutch or an illegal drug, and I owe them a thank-you for this story, as for too many others. The more supportive they are, the sloppier I get. But it is fun, too. Actually it is great fun, watching them race around all crazy and upset, all *concerned,* doing back flips to help your story — all for your story's well-being, all for art. It's fun. It's messy. Another thank-you. And another.

T H O M A S B E L L E R coedits the magazine *Open City* and plays drums and writes lyrics for the band *Honus Wagner.* His stories have appeared in *The New Yorker, Mademoiselle,* and *Epoch.* A graduate of Vassar College, he has an M.F.A. in creative writing from Columbia University. He was born and raised in New York City, where he currently lives.

▪ I have no idea how this story came to be written; the genesis of the story and the ideas in it are a mystery to me, which is probably just as well. What I do remember quite vividly, however, was how much I disliked it for most of its early stages. I kept putting it away and revisiting it and putting it away. This went on for a long period of time. I'm not sure at what stage it started to come together, but I remember one particularly long and miserable night during which a number of things in the story started to come into focus, and during that night I recall getting up repeatedly to pace around the room and mutter, and for some reason I kept reading and rereading this poem, "The Lace Makers," which is in a collection titled *The Intelligence of Clouds*, by Stanley Moss. I just went and looked at that poem for the first time in quite a while and was reminded of how obsessed I had been with this one phrase: "Things obsolete, improper."

AMY BLOOM's short stories have been published in *Room of One's Own*, *Story*, and *River City* and reprinted in various places, including last year's *Best American Short Stories*. Her collection of short stories will be brought out by Edward Burlingame Books/Harper Collins in 1993.

▪ The grief, love, and exhaustion of life with schizophrenics is so close to unbearable that I can only admire, and want to sing for, the afflicted and their families.

ROBERT OLEN BUTLER is the author of the novels *The Alleys of Eden*, *Sun Dogs*, *Countrymen of Bones*, *On Distant Ground*, *Wabash*, and *The Deuce*. "A Good Scent from a Strange Mountain" is the title story from his recent collection of short fiction (Henry Holt, 1992). His stories have appeared in many literary magazines, including *The Sewanee Review*, *The Hudson Review*, *The Southern Review*, *New England Review*, and *The Virginia Quarterly Review*, where he won the Emily Clark Balch Award, and have been anthologized in *The Best American Short Stories 1991* and *New Stories from the South* in both 1991 and 1992. He served with the U.S. Army in Vietnam as a Vietnamese linguist and is a charter recipient of the Tu Do Chinh Kien Award for outstanding contributions to American culture by a Vietnam veteran. He teaches creative writing at McNeese State University in Lake Charles, Louisiana.

▪ These things are true: Ho Chi Minh was once a pastry chef under the great Escoffier at the Carlton Hotel in London; he once worked retouching photographs in Paris; he showed up at the Hall of Mirrors during the signing of the Treaty of Versailles to enlist Woodrow Wilson's support in winning certain modest rights for the Vietnamese in French Indochina; after the Second World War he once again hoped that America would be an ally in his cause. From all of this I could see these concrete images for the man who was actively vilified in America for more than a decade, and I carried them in my head for a long time: Ho painting the blush into the cheeks of a Frenchman; Ho chafing in a suit of rented clothes and a bowler hat; Ho lifting his hands, powdered from his pastry work, in the bustle of a hotel kitchen.

These images then awaited the aesthetic dialectic that eventually came from an old man in a back alley in Saigon who translated for me the four Chinese characters on the Buddhist shrine in his tiny sleeping room. This, he said, is the mystery of life, all that we need ever to consider: "A good scent from a strange mountain." It took nearly twenty years for me to put all of this together, to understand the vision of a peace that struggled to harmonize these two men, and, happily, that articulated the overarching vision of the book of short fiction that this eponymous story completed.

I finally began to hear the voice of this tale when I found an occasion — the traditional formal leave-taking with their friends and family that Vietnamese often make at the end of their lives — and when I found a first sentence, spoken in the voice of a man nearly one hundred years old, "Ho Chi Minh came to me again last night, his hands covered with confectioners' sugar." After that, it was simply a matter of letting the old man speak.

MAVIS GALLANT was born in Montreal and worked as a feature writer there before giving up newspaper work to devote herself to fiction. She left Canada in 1950 and after extensive travel settled in Paris. She is a regular contributor to *The New Yorker* and currently is working on a major account of the Dreyfus case and on a novel.

TIM GAUTREAUX is a native of southern Louisiana. He has a Ph.D. in English from the University of South Carolina and has studied under James Dickey, George Garrett, and Walker Percy. His fiction has appeared in *Massachusetts Review, Kansas Quarterly, Crescent Review, Louisiana Life, Stories,* and *The Atlantic Monthly.* A novel, *A Life of Hard Work,* won the Deep South Writers' Conference Novel Competition. Recently he received a Louisiana Division of the Arts fellowship for his fiction. For twenty years he has taught creative writing at Southeastern Louisiana University, where he edits *Louisiana Literature.*

• I'm big on telling students to incorporate their own fascinations into the fabric of their writing, whether it's mounting butterflies or collecting toilet bowls. I've also taught them that they should write about what goes on in their own back yards. On the first count, I've always been fascinated by obsolete machinery, so I decided to write a story set in the Depression about a man who repaired the gas engines that powered well pumps. On the second count, I decided to set the story in the community I've lived in for twenty years, a sandy pine barren of gravel pits, strawberry patches, and pulpwood yards which never before seemed worthy of turning into fiction.

I talked to old people about the engines on their farms, what things sounded like at night sixty years ago, the geography of their crops and of their lives. I consulted old railroad schedules and tales of venerable Italian strawberry farmers. With just a little research I had the parts of a kit, which, when assembled, would be the mechanism of my story. I put Harry Lintel, a traveling repairman who followed droughts, and Ada, a murderously bored farmer's wife, together early in the story and let things happen. The setting, the time, the details, informed by my research, shaped the action; facts taken from old farmers seemed to make the movement of the story inevitable. Early in the first draft, Ada's husband's death was an accident. As I wrote the end, the repairman and I realized, "Hell, she killed him." This murder was what everything, including her hard life, and her desires, pointed to. I was astounded by what was happening while I was writing it. After finishing the tale, I realized that some of the best stories come from attention to culture and history, and that no person and no place, even the dull backwoods or the bland suburb, is devoid of those aspects.

The first ending was a passive literary-magazine nonending. Thanks to the fine sensibility of C. Michael Curtis at *The Atlantic*, who told me the ending "turned talky and petered out," I was able to write an action ending that continued Ada's killer tradition, a logical continuation of what the story was about, a hard heart pushed by a hard life toward malignant action.

DENIS JOHNSON, born in Munich, Germany, in 1949, was raised in Tokyo, Manila, and the suburbs of Washington, D.C. He received his B.A. and M.F.A. from the University of Iowa. His four books of poetry include *The Man Among the Seals, Inner Weather, The Incognito Lounge,* and *The Veil.* He has also published four novels: *Angels,* which won the Sue Kaufman Prize for First Fiction of the American Academy and Institute of Arts and Letters; *Fiskadoro; The Stars at Noon;* and *Resuscitation of a Hanged Man.* Among his other awards are fellowships from the National Endowment for the Arts, the Guggenheim Foundation, and the Robert

Frost Award. The story "Emergency" is included in a collection called *Jesus' Son,* to be published this year by Farrar, Straus & Giroux.

• I have several stories now about this young man, who doesn't seem to go by any name except the insulting one of "Fuckhead." Like the others, this one is a series of improvisations set down on paper at different times (in this case, over a period of about two years) with very little revision. In the early seventies I did in fact work as a clerk in a hospital emergency room in Iowa City. This story strings together a lot of anecdotes I heard or things I experienced there — a good deal of it actually happened. In October 1991 I read the story in front of an audience in Iowa City, and afterward a physician introduced himself to me and told me that only a few days before he'd been to a slide lecture at that same hospital. He said they'd shown a picture of the man with the knife sticking out of his head.

THOM JONES is a graduate of the Iowa Writer's Workshop. A collection of his stories will be published by Little, Brown in the fall of 1993. Mr. Jones lives in Olympia, Washington, with his wife and daughter.

• There has been such superlative work written about Vietnam that I never considered writing about that war until the Persian Gulf War of recent times coincided with the birthday of a Marine buddy who died in Vietnam. At that point I sat down and wrote "The Pugilist at Rest," essentially in a single sitting.

Michael Herr, Tim O'Brien, Robert Stone, and Wallace Terry, to name a few, wrote definitive books on the Vietnam War. Before these fine writers, James Jones, William Manchester, and Norman Mailer wrote powerful and compelling books about World War II. There were military novels and stories by William Goldman, William Styron, and Richard Yates that affected me deeply, and most of all there was Erich Maria Remarque. I do not pretend to belong in this hallowed company, but I would like to acknowledge these writers since my story came only after having read them and having for years carried the memories of the wonderful people I knew who died in Vietnam.

MARSHALL N. KLIMASEWISKI was born and raised in rural western Connecticut. He received his B.A. from Carnegie Mellon University in Pittsburgh and his M.F.A. from Bowling Green University in Ohio. His stories have appeared in *The New Yorker, Ploughshares* (1988 "Fiction Discovery" issue), *Quarterly West,* and elsewhere. In 1991 he was the Fletcher Pratt Scholar in Fiction at the Bread Loaf Writers' Conference in Vermont. He is completing a collection of stories to be titled *Astonishment.*

▪ Trying to trace the origins of this story proved more difficult than I expected. It reminded me of interpreting a strange dream — while I was able to link some elements directly to my waking life, most seemed to have come from nothing I know. I have done a lot of hiking in the White Mountains of New Hampshire, I have experienced the disorientation and peculiar mental fatigue that Tanner experiences in the last scene, and I've worked summers in the same machine shop that I picture Tanner in. Those are the easy ones — but they are all surface details, well removed from either JunHee or her child.

Because this is the third story I wrote about Tanner and JunHee, most of its origins were in the realm of fiction. Because I have never written a successful first draft that I was in control of, both of the characters had already startled me on several occasions. They had taken on their own identities and distanced themselves from me. And though the revision process generally requires that I take back a good deal of that control, I suppose I return to the more romantic, removed perspective once the story is finished. This is all pretend, I know, but I don't want to try to figure out where JunHee or her child came from. I want to say, here are this story's origins: There is a Korean woman who is married to a man from Vermont. They live together here in Connecticut. When they had been married for six years, she became unexpectedly pregnant and had a miscarriage. She will tell you the rest.

LORRIE MOORE is the author of a novel, a children's book, and two collections of stories. She is also editor of the recent anthology *I Know Some Things: Stories About Childhood by Contemporary Writers.*

▪ This is a story about the various ingredients in one woman's life, particularly those involving her sense of foreignness, un-at-homeness, and as a result her disablingly intermittent lunges at love, inclusion, helpfulness. I thought of this as a kind of figure and ground problem, like a painting. How did I come to write it? I discovered certain things to be on my mind (uprootedness, assorted municipal expressions of dislocation and anachronism, bats). Which is, of course, how anyone comes to write anything.

ALICE MUNRO's most recent collection of stories is *Friend of My Youth* (Knopf, 1990). Born in Wingham, Ontario, Ms. Munro now lives in Clinton, Ontario. She has received Canada's Governor General's Award for two of her books.

▪ I heard a story about a librarian from the town where I live who had supposedly been kidnapped by bandits in Albania during a trip to Europe in the early years of this century. I could never find out if this story was true, but it got me interested in librarians and Albania. So eventually I wrote another story about Albania because my librarian got involved in her own affairs. I had a pretty realistic story going about World War I, small-town industry, the kind of accidents they had, the boss, the workers. But all the time I felt a parallel story going, in which the accident never happened and another reality developed with the same kind of detail, mundane detail, and the librarian getting access to this 'other' in an accidental, rather ordinary way. It gave me a lot of trouble because I didn't want the point to be the "ghost" (I hate even calling him that) but something interchangeable, some way in which events, even drastic ones, do, and don't, matter. That's all I can say about it.

JOYCE CAROL OATES is the author of a number of novels, short story collections, and volumes of criticism, poetry, and plays. She is a recipient of the National Book Award for her novel *them* and is a member of the American Academy and Institute of Arts and Letters. Other awards include the 1990 Heideman Award for One-Act Plays (cowinner), the 1990 Rea Award for the Short Story, and the 1990 Bobst Lifetime Award from New York University. Her novel *Because It Is Bitter, and Because It Is My Heart* was nominated for the 1990 National Book Award. Joyce Carol Oates is the Roger S. Berlind Distinguished Professor in the Humanities at Princeton University and is a coeditor of *The Ontario Review*. Her most recent novels are *Snake Eyes* (under the pseudonym "Rosamond Smith") and *Black Water* (1992).

▪ "Is Laughter Contagious?" was a painful story to compose because it seemed to me to somehow be about madness. The dissolution of the ego. The threat of the dissolution of civilization. *What if we all just suddenly started laughing, not* with, *but* at, *one another?* I envisioned a nightmare world in which the social fabric of tact, courtesy, kindness, and human sympathy was rent by the sudden force of derision. Who could bear to live in such a world?

Though it is a concept story (by "concept story" I mean a fiction whose genesis is in an idea, not images or people), it is as realistic a story as I could make it, set in an upscale-Caucasian-suburban community like Princeton, New Jersey, in which I've lived since 1978. Not all of it *is* fiction, but, when certain of these events occurred, we didn't laugh. At least, I didn't hear anyone laugh. Nor did I laugh myself. I think.

Obviously the story has its visionary, or at least its allegorical, aspirations. There are some fictions that so typify Idea, they can be most effectively rendered in generic, symbolic, allegorical terms — which doesn't make them less "real."

I wrote the story in a concentrated burst, or outburst, of feeling. I doubt that I smiled once. I can hardly bring myself to read the story again, unless I tell myself I'm checking out sentence structure, typos. It's just too painful. I hope it isn't "prophetic." I don't want to be here, if ever, in Princeton or elsewhere, it is.

REYNOLDS PRICE was born in Macon, North Carolina, in 1933. Reared and educated in the public schools of his native state, he earned a A.B. from Duke University. In 1955 he traveled as a Rhodes Scholar to Merton College, Oxford University, to study English literature. After three years, and the B.Litt. degree, he returned to Duke, where he continues to teach as James B. Duke Professor of English.

In 1962 his novel *A Long and Happy Life* received the William Faulkner Award for a notable first novel. He has published other novels — *Blue Calhoun* (May 1992) is the ninth — and in 1986 his *Kate Vaiden* received the National Book Critics Circle Award. He has also published volumes of short stories; plays; essays; translations from the Bible; a memoir, *Clear Pictures* (a finalist for the Pulitzer Prize), and he has written for the screen and for television. He is a member of the American Academy and Institute of Arts and Letters, and his books have appeared in sixteen languages.

▪ Like many children of my time and place — the upper South in the thirties and forties — I only learned the plight of the races in slow, untutored silence. None of my white kin sat me down and drew the lines of demarcation for me — us here, blacks there. No one said we were better or even luckier than they, though with a child's fear of deprivation and a keen appraising eye, I quickly gathered we were in a run of luck compared to the black men and women we knew. Every time I rode with my father at night as he took the cook home, I silently compared her unplumbed shack with our own quarters, hardly deluxe but warm and dry. Once when I was five and saw a black woman in a funny hat, I said, "Look at that lady's hat," and an older cousin said, "That's a woman, not a lady." Again with my father, when he visited the home of an ancient black woman who'd nursed him in childhood (a woman part-Indian and almost surely born a slave), I recorded the utterly foreign state of her hot rooms — walled with newspaper, floorboards scrubbed bone-white with lye, and the wild scent of fig preserves from the small iron stove.

I was well on the way to adolescence, though, before I glimpsed the mystery that started my story "The Fare to the Moon." I was with my mother in a grocery store. She'd finished her shopping and we were waiting at the one cash register. A man and a woman walked into the store from the cold, grim day and went straight over to the produce counter to pick their way through rutabagas and sweet potatoes. In some strong sense, they were clearly a pair. Their contingency burned a hot light around them. He was white and handsome; she was colored a high live shade of copper, officially black. No one but me seemed to note them at all, though such a publicly flaunted bond was so nearly non-existent in our tame world as to be a crucial discovery for me — one or more lives could be freely led in the teeth of whatever, and the world well lost.

That night at supper my mother told my father briefly that Mr. X and his "common-law wife" were in the store this afternoon. Father nodded and said he'd heard they'd lived together for more than a year, far out in the country. The man was younger than my father, but they knew each other. No further discussion, no apparent judgment on a choice at absolute odds with our world, and no further effort by me (who couldn't drive on explorations) to learn more facts about the bond. Forty-odd years on in my life though, their image — upright, there in the produce — burned back up in my mind so clearly that I had little choice but to set their reckless mystery down, inventing all the absent facts (which were 99 percent) in the hope of finding some clue to the beauty they constituted for a lonely, puzzled boy like me, who'd secretly wished them well that day when a whole white town merely blinded itself to the adamant fact they lodged among us.

ANNICK SMITH is a writer and filmmaker who lives in western Montana. She was the executive producer of *Heartland,* a feature film about a woman homesteader's life on the Great Plains, and helped to develop Robert Redford's forthcoming film, *A River Runs Through It,* based on the novella by Norman Maclean. Smith was coeditor with William Kittredge of *The Last Best Place,* an anthology of Montana writing. She has published personal essays in magazines and anthologies. "It's Come to This" is her first published short story.

▪ The heart of "It's Come to This" is true to my life; the rest is fiction. I am a widow, born in Paris of Hungarian parents, and I have raised four boys on a quarter-section homestead near Potomac, Montana, in the valley of the Big Blackfoot River. My husband, David Smith, died of a heart attack in the kitchen of our log house in May 1974. I'd tried to write about this life-changing trauma in poems, in essays, in my mind, but never could get it right.

Years later, in a Missoula bar called The Top Hat, a drunk old cowboy tapped me on the shoulder. His right hand was shrunken and deformed, but we danced until we were out of breath and sweating. When

I joined my friends at the bar I nearly burst into tears. "It's come to this," I said.

Another year my longtime companion Bill Kittredge and I danced at the Turah Pines bar in what would be one of Ernest Tubb's last concerts. Still later we saw a rainbow at midnight over the Clark's Fork River near its juncture with Rock Creek, where my young family once lived in a bungalow owned by a woman named Mary-Dell, who was in love with horses. When I started to write a story about Mary-Dell and the old drunken cowboy, all these elements came together, along with a great imaginary logger-lover named Frank.

CHRISTOPHER TILGHMAN's first collection of stories, *In a Father's Place*, appeared in 1990. He is at work on a novella and a new story collection.

▪ I composed "The Way People Run" as a collage of visual images I had collected on the northern Plains. It was satisfying to write, but when I finished I had no idea what it meant. I started adding characters and scenes, hoping that I'd get some direction, some meaning. When I succeeded in destroying everything that I liked, I put the whole mess in the filing cabinet. About a year later I was driving through the boarded-up towns of rural Virginia (it could have been anywhere in the U.S.A., of course), and my character Barry came back to me as a simple image of economic decline and moral exhaustion. I realized my story was not about the West, where it is set, but about the coasts, from which Barry has run. The fact of decay seemed to offer its own sufficient reason, so I polished up the first draft and sent it off. I don't like describing things that are falling apart — it's the shape of the story that bothers me more than the pessimism — but I'm afraid we'd all better get used to it.

DAVID FOSTER WALLACE is the author of a novel, *The Broom of the System;* a story collection, *Girl with Curious Hair;* and, with Mark Costello, a book-length essay on race and music called *Signifying Rappers.* He lives in Boston and is at this very moment restructuring his whole c.v. around inclusion in this anthology.

▪ This is a bit embarrassing, and I'd rather not discuss it, but will, since certain authorities have been polite but firm about these little post-story discussions being strongly encouraged, and I'd probably submit with cheer to way more embarrassing requirements if it meant getting the old snout into the *B.A.S.S.* trough.

The embarrassing issue here is I'm not all that crazy about this story. It's one of very few autobiographically implicated things I've ever tried. I did, like probably lots of kids, have a high-dive trauma. My real trauma was much more plain-old-sphincter-loosening-fear-based than the existential conundra this story's kid encounters. I basically got to the top, with a long line of jaded souls behind me, and changed my mind about going off. It was excruciatingly shaming, but in no way deeply or exceptionally shaming. I think it wasn't the memory of the shame so much as current shame that allowed so pedestrian a shame still to haunt my esteem-centers, prompting me to make the story so heavy, meditative, image-laden, swinging for the fence on just about every pitch. The thing seems to me a performative index of every weakness I have as a writer and as a person. And God knows why I let my desire for an Alienated Narrative Persona lead me to use the second-person point of view; now I'm scared people will read this and think I'm just a McInerney imitator in a black turtleneck, a copy of Kierkegaard under my arm.

The thing went through dozens of drafts, the first of which still sits in the pages of my undergraduate "Stories That'll Prove I'm a Genius" notebook. I went to grad school in Tucson, which is where I guess the thing picked up its setting: you can't spit in Tucson without hitting a pool, though darn few are public like this one is public.

I completely deny ever once kissing any part of my sister's feet at any time whatsoever.

I'm noticing that, with respect to any piece of fiction, my dissatisfaction with the final draft is directly proportional to the excitement that precedes the first draft. I remember doing the tortured artist thing back in school, all ego and caffeine, and thinking I had a genuine Big Idea for this story here, and seeing it finished, Big, published, lauded as Important by bearded titans. This was before I even bothered to start to try writing the thing. I preconceived it as deeply moving and imposingly cerebral at the same time, at once tender-psyche'd and tough-minded, just the sort of thing Eminences would pluck out of the glabrous herd by choosing for a prestigious anthology. By the second draft, my head was more or less permanently attached to the wall I'd been pounding it on. In black-lit contrast to the timelessly Big thing I'd preconceived, the actual ink-on-paper story seemed pretentious and trendy and jejune and any number of bad things: it seemed like the product of a young writer who was ashamed of a personal trauma and who was straining with every fast-twitch fiber to make that trauma sound way deeper and prettier and Big than anything true could ever really be. And here I mean "true" both artistically and historically.

I don't know why I kept putting the thing through drafts. I kept getting late-night twinges of that original preconceptual excitement. I kept seeing the thing as maybe just one image or two epiphanies away from blossoming, from honoring its entelechy of Bigness. Six years and many other completed projects later, I sent this story out in the old brown envelope. I sent it out for the same reason most young writers I know send stuff out: to have an excuse to quit thinking about it. My surprise when *Fiction International* took the thing was nothing compared to my feelings about the august endorsement that occasions this wordy little confession. Do not get me wrong: qualms about the story's failure to be anything more than a lumpy ghost of what I remain convinced was its initial promise of Bigness have not inhibited me from calling pretty much everybody I know and casually working in the *B.A.S.S.*-selection news. I'm extremely and yet of course also humbly grateful and moved and etc. I'm just coming to realize that I have very little personal clue about whether the stuff I do is good or bad or successful or not successful* which like most bits of self-knowledge is both mortifying and kind of a relief. It makes me glad I have opinionated critical friends and politely firm editors, not necessarily in that order.

*Is "successful" the same as "good," here? Does inclusion in *B.A.S.S.* render a story de facto "good" the way a human reverend's pronouncement effects a legally binding union?

KATE WHEELER has won the O. Henry and Pushcart prizes and has published half a dozen short stories and essays in literary journals. She grew up in South America and has traveled widely.

▪ I might still be a nun in Rangoon had there not, in August 1988, been riots attempting to overthrow the military government. I wrote "Under the Roof" after disrobing and returning to the West, during a gloomy winter in Boston. Having surrendered as entirely as possible to Burmese Theravadin Buddhism, and, even more narrowly, to my monastery's meditation style, which was highly precise and technical, based on a fifth-century Sri Lankan text, I found I had my being in several different, internally consistent, mutually contradictory modes. This is surely true for anyone, but since I grew up "overseas" — "overseas" from the U.S., which is "overseas" from "overseas" — my personal history emphasizes this point: I live simultaneously; and must, at times, try to discover what is universal.

I'd like to say "I met those people," but I'd have to add that I started meeting them as a child, and will continue to meet them until I die. Traveling in Buddhist Asia, I did come to know women of superhuman energy, generosity, and devotion. Monasteries could not exist without them. Some of my friends and I might not have survived Rangoon without their shipments of powdered milk, Nescafé, and antibiotics. The American monk, of course, represents me and all my Western comrades, in particular a couple of male friends who tried to negotiate the demands of a monk's life (nuns are not taken as seriously, so we had more freedom). Imagining my way through a Western man's relation to Theravadin robes helped me to comprehend why I did not remain as a nun, come to the U.S. and found a monastery, as my preceptor hoped I might.

I submitted this story to twenty-three journals before J. R. Jones took it for *Black Warrior*. My gratitude to him, to Robert Stone, and to everyone who enjoys it. I'd come to believe it was too slow, too long and serious. Its microscopic complexity certainly reflects the meditation I was practicing, which involves slowing down one's physical movements to maintain a precise, moment-to-moment awareness of the mind and body. It touches my heart whenever I see that care is valued in a world where things often seem so quick, so overwhelming.

Sometimes my stories become prophetic: events I imagine actually come to pass in my life, years later. That has been the case with "Under the Roof."

ELIZABETH WINTHROP is the author of *In My Mother's House* and of more than thirty books for children of all ages. Her latest children's novel, *The Castle in the Attic*, has been nominated for nineteen state book awards and recently won the Dorothy Canfield Fisher Award in Vermont and the Young Reader's Award in California. Ms. Winthrop has twice won the PEN Syndicated Fiction Contest, once in 1985 with her story "Bad News" and again in 1990 with "The Golden Darters." She lives in New York City.

▪ One summer four years ago, I was between two projects and determined to take a rest from writing and from thinking about writing. So, for the first time in years, I did not bring my computer with me when I went up to spend August on a small island off the coast of Connecticut. But stories seem to happen to writers when we least expect them, even when we try to shut the door on them.

I dropped by to have dinner with some old friends and after we ate, the husband gave me a tour of his fly-tying corner. Joe is my idea of a Renaissance man. He paints and takes martial arts and Italian lessons and plays the piano. He is also a hunter and an avid fly fisherman. So on one hand it was not surprising that he had chosen fly-tying as a way of passing the hours of his convalescence from a disk operation. But tying flies seemed to be such a fussy womanish business for a man as normally robust and active as Joe. I was impressed with his patience, his perseverance, and his small motor control. When he saw that my interest seemed to go beyond the usual polite responses of dinner guests, he invited me to sit down and tie a streamer with him.

It was a grown woman who accepted the invitation but a twelve-year-old girl who lowered herself into that chair. A girl who used to hate to perform in front of any kind of audience, no matter how small or how encouraging, unless she was assured of success. A girl who forced herself to listen to a grown man's quietly delivered, yet imperative, instructions because she was so frightened of failing him and yet so angry at being put in that position. And at the end of the evening, it was a grown woman with an aching back and a story starting in her head who stood up from the chair, whispered her good-byes, and with her golden darter tucked safely in a pocket, crawled home to bed.

In the days that followed, the story made its slow way on to paper. With no computer, I wrote it in longhand on a yellow legal pad. My friend Joe has seen it in its various drafts and we have cheerfully argued back and forth about the direction it took. I think he wanted a story that dealt with trout season and hatching mayflies and a man's love of the river. But as I pointed out to him, I couldn't write that story because it was not mine. Mine was about a girl's coming of age and her rebellion against control. Perhaps for Joe, my story "hung upside down," but it was the only one I knew how to tell, a point which he finally and just as cheerfully conceded.

TOBIAS WOLFF's most recent book is *This Boy's Life*. Winner of the 1985 PEN/Faulkner Award, he is also the author of a novel, *The Barracks Thief*, and two collections of short stories, *In the Garden of the North American Martyrs* and *Back in the World*. "Firelight" is from a collection in progress. He lives in Syracuse, New York.

▪ The origins of my stories are always hard for me to pin down because the act of writing them inevitably tangles history and imagination in a way impossible for me to untangle later on. All I have left is the story. This one has a few autobiographical elements but is mostly imagined. What is not imagined, and what impelled me to write it in the first place, is its emotional core — that sense, hardly unique to me, of being somehow outside the circle of light, a feeling so pernicious that even when you are where you want to be you shy away from the joy of it and begin to fear banishment and loss.

100 Other Distinguished Stories of 1991

SELECTED BY KATRINA KENISON

SETTLE, MARY LEE
Dogs. *Virginia Quarterly Review,*
Winter.
SILBER, JOAN
Lake Natasink. *The New Yorker,*
July 8.
SMILEY, JANE
Fahrvergnügen. *Playboy,* December.
SMITH, CURTIS
What About Meg? *Antietam Review,*
Spring.
SMITH, LEE
The Bubba Stories. *The Southern
Review,* Winter.
SPARK, DEBRA
The Year of Our Father. *Prairie
Schooner,* Fall.
SPENCER, DARRELL
Union Business. *Prairie Schooner,*
Spring.
STARK, SHARON SHEEHE
Kerflooey. *The Antioch Review,*
Spring.

TALLENT, ELIZABETH
Black Dress. *ZYZZYVA,* Spring.
THOMAS, ABIGAIL
A Tooth for Every Child. *The
Missouri Review,* Vol. 13, No. 3.

THOMAS, MARIA
Back Bay to the Bundu. *The New
Yorker,* April 22.

UPDIKE, JOHN
The Other Side of the Street. *The
New Yorker,* October 28.
Ferrell's Caddie. *The New Yorker,*
February 25.

VERGHESE, ABRAHAM
Lilacs. *The New Yorker,* October 14.
The Agent of His Death Is a White
Woman. *Black Warrior Review,*
Spring/Summer.

WETHERELL, W. D.
Wherever That Great Heart May
Be. *American Short Fiction,* Vol. 1,
No. 2.
WHEELER, KATE
Improving My Average. *The
Missouri Review,* Vol. 14, No. 2.
WICKERSHAM, JOAN
Lena. *Story,* Summer.
WILLIAMS, LYNNA
Sole Custody. *The Atlantic Monthly,*
September.

Editorial Addresses of American and Canadian Magazines Publishing Short Stories

When available, the annual subscription rate, the average number of stories published per year, and the name of the editor follow the address.

Agni Review
Creative Writing Department
Boston University
236 Bay State Road
Boston, MA 02115
$12, 10, Askold Melnyczuk

Alabama Literary Review
Smith 253
Troy State University
Troy, AL 36082
$9, Theron E. Montgomery

Alaska Quarterly Review
Department of English
University of Alaska
3221 Providence Drive
Anchorage, AK 99508
$8, 28, Ronald Spatz

Alfred Hitchcock's Mystery Magazine
Davis Publications, Inc.
380 Lexington Avenue

New York, NY 10017
$25.97, 130, Cathleen Jordan

Ambergris
P.O. Box 29919
Cincinnati, OH 45229
$6, 8, Mark Kissling

Amelia
329 East Street
Bakersfield, CA 93304
$27, 9, Frederick A. Raborg, Jr.

American Literary Review
University of North Texas
P. O. Box 13615
Denton, TX 76203
$10, 7, James Ward Lee

American Short Fiction
Parlin 108
Department of English
University of Texas at Austin

Austin, TX 78712-1164
$24, 32, Laura Furman

American Voice
332 West Broadway
Louisville, KY 40202
$12, 20, Sallie Bingham, Frederick Smock

Analog Science Fiction/Science Fact
380 Lexington Avenue
New York, NY 10017
$34.95, 70, Stanley Schmidt

Antaeus
26 West 17th Street
New York, NY 10011
$30, 6, Daniel Halpern

Antietam Review
82 West Washington Street
Hagerstown, MD 21740
$5, 8, Suzanne Kass

Antioch Review
P.O. Box 148
Yellow Springs, OH 45387
$20, 11, Robert S. Fogarty

Apalachee Quarterly
P.O. Box 20106
Tallahassee, FL 32316
$12, 10, Barbara Hardy et al.

Ascent
English Department
University of Illinois
608 South Wright Street
Urbana, IL 61801
$3, 8, group editorship

Atlantic Monthly
745 Boylston Street
Boston, MA 02116
$15.94, 13, C. Michael Curtis

Aura Literary/Arts Review
P.O. Box University Center
University of Alabama
Birmingham, AL 35294
$6, 10, rotating editorship

Belles Lettres
11151 Captain's Walk Court
North Potomac, MD 20878
$20, 2, Janet Mullaney

Bellowing Ark
P.O. Box 45637
Seattle, WA 98145
$15, 7, Robert R. Ward

Beloit Fiction Journal
P.O. Box 11, Beloit College
Beloit, WI 53511
$9, 14, Clint McCown

Black Warrior Review
P.O. Box 2936
Tuscaloosa, AL 35487-2936
$7.50, 13, Alicia Griswold

BOMB
New Art Publications
594 Broadway, 10th floor
New York, NY 10012
$16, 4, Betsy Sussler

Border Crossings
Y300-393 Portage Avenue
Winnipeg, Manitoba
R3B 3H6 Canada
$18, 12, Robert Enright

Boston Review
33 Harrison Avenue
Boston, MA 02111
$15, 6, editorial board

Boulevard
2400 Chestnut Road, Apt. 2208
Philadelphia, PA 19103
$12, 17, Richard Burgin

Bridge
14050 Vernon Street
Oak Park, MI 48237
$8, 10, Helen Zucker

Brooklyn Free Press
268 14th Street
Brooklyn, NY 11215
$1, 10, Raphael Martinez Alequin

Buffalo Spree
4511 Harlem Road, P.O. Box 38
Buffalo, NY 14226
$8, 16, Johanna Shotell

BUZZ
11835 West Olympic Blvd.
Suite 450
Los Angeles, CA 90064
$12, 5, Renee Vogel

California Quarterly
100 Sproul Hall
University of California
Davis, CA 95616
$14, 4, Elliott L. Gilbert

Callaloo
Johns Hopkins University Press
701 West 40th Street, Suite 275
Baltimore, MD 21211
$20.50, 6, Charles H. Rowell

Calyx
P.O. Box B
Corvallis, OR 97339
$18, 11, Margarita Donnelly

Canadian Fiction
Box 946, Station F
Toronto, Ontario
M4Y 2N9 Canada
$36, 23, Geoffrey Hancock

Capilano Review
Capilano College
2055 Purcell Way
North Vancouver,
British Columbia
V7J 3H5 Canada
$12, 5, Pierre Coupey

Carolina Quarterly
Greenlaw Hall 066A
University of North Carolina
Chapel Hill, NC 27514
$10, 13, Lisa Carl

Changing Men
306 North Brooks Street
Madison, WI 53715
$24, 2, Jeff Kirsch

Chariton Review
Division of Language & Literature
Northeast Missouri State University
Kirksville, MO 63501
$9, 6, Jim Barnes

Chattahoochee Review
DeKalb Community College
2101 Womack Road
Dunwoody, GA 30338-4497
$15, 21, Lamar York

Chelsea
P.O. Box 5880
Grand Central Station
New York, NY 10163
$11, 6, Sonia Raiziss

Chicago Review
5801 South Kenwood
University of Chicago
Chicago, IL 60637
$20, 20, Elizabeth Arnold

Christopher Street
P.O. Box 1475
Church Street Station
New York, NY 10008
$27, 50, Tom Steele

Cimarron Review
205 Morrill Hall
Oklahoma State University
Stillwater, OK 74078-0135
$12, 15, Gordon Weaver

Clockwatch Review
Department of English
Illinois Wesleyan University
Bloomington, IL 61702
$8, 6, James Plath

Columbia
404 Dodge
Columbia University
New York, NY 10027
$11, 14, rotating editorship

Commentary
165 East 56th Street
New York, NY 10022
$39, 5, Norman Podhoretz

Concho River Review
English Department
Angelo State University
San Angelo, TX 76909
$12, 7, Terence A. Dalrymple

Confrontation
English Department
C. W. Post College of Long Island
  University
Greenvale, NY 11548
$8, 25, Martin Tucker

Conjunctions
New Writing Foundation
866 Third Avenue
New York, NY 10022
$16, 12, Bradford Morrow

Crab Creek Review
4462 Whitman Avenue North
Seattle, WA 98103
$8, 3, Linda Clifton

Crazyhorse
Department of English
University of Arkansas
Little Rock, AR 72204
$8, 13, David Jauss

Cream City Review
University of Wisconsin, Milwaukee
P.O. Box 413
Milwaukee, WI 53201
$10, 30, Ellen Barclay, Sanford Tweedy

Crescent Review
P.O. Box 15065
Winston-Salem, NC 27113
$10, 23, Guy Nancekeville

Critic
205 West Monroe Street, 6th floor
Chicago, IL 60606-5097
$17, 4, John Sprague

Crosscurrents
2200 Glastonbury Road
Westlake Village, CA 91361
$18, 38, Linda Brown Michelson

Crucible
Barton College
College Station
Wilson, NC 27893
Terence L. Grimes

Cut Bank
Department of English
University of Montana
Missoula, MT 59812
$9, 20, rotating editorship

Delos
P.O. Box 2800
College Park, MD 20741
$20, Reed Whittemore

Denver Quarterly
University of Denver
Denver, CO 80208
$15, 5, Donald Revell

Descant
P.O. Box 314, Station P
Toronto, Ontario
M5S 2S8 Canada
$26, 20, Karen Mulhallen

Dialogue
University Station
UMC - 7805
Logan, UT 84332
*$25, F. Ross Peterson,
Mary Kay Peterson*

Elle
1633 Broadway
New York, NY 10019
$24, 2

Epoch
251 Goldwin Smith Hall
Cornell University
Ithaca, NY 14853-3201
$11, 23, Michael Koch

Esquire
1790 Broadway
New York, NY 10019
$17.94, 6, Rust Hills

Essence
1500 Broadway
New York, NY 10036
$12.96, 6, Stephanie Stokes Oliver

event
c/o Douglas College
P.O. Box 2503
New Westminster, British Columbia
V3L 5B2 Canada
$13, 18, Maurice Hodgson

Fantasy & Science Fiction
P.O. Box 56
Cornwall, CT 06753
$21, 75, Edward L. Ferman

Farmer's Market
P.O. Box 1272
Galesburg, IL 61402
$8, 10, Jean C. Lee

Fiction
Fiction, Inc.
Department of English
The City College of New York
New York, NY 10031
$7, 15, Mark Mirsky

Fiction International
Department of English and
Comparative Literature
San Diego State University
San Diego, CA 92182
$14, Roger Cunniff and Edwin Gordon

Fiction Network
P.O. Box 5651
San Francisco, CA 94101
$8, 25, Jay Schaefer

Fiddlehead
Room 317, Old Arts Building
University of New Brunswick
Fredericton, New Brunswick
E3B 5A3 Canada
$16, 20, Don McKay

Florida Review
Department of English
University of Central Florida
P.O. Box 25000
Orlando, FL 32816
$7, 14, Pat Rushin

Folio
Department of Literature
The American University
Washington, D.C. 20016
$10, 12, Lisa Norris

Four Quarters
LaSalle University
20th and Olney Avenues
Philadelphia, PA 19141
$8, 10, John J. Keenan

Free Press
268 14th St.
Brooklyn, NY 11215
$25, 10, Raphael Martinez Alequin

Gamut
1218 Fen Tower
Cleveland State University
Cleveland, OH 44115
$15, 4, Louis T. Milic

Georgia Review
University of Georgia
Athens, GA 30602
$12, 10, Stanley W. Lindberg

Gettysburg Review
Gettysburg College
Gettysburg, PA 17325
$15, 10, Peter Stitt

Glamour
350 Madison Avenue
New York, NY 10017
$20.50, 3, Laura Mathews

Glimmer Train Stories
812 SW Washington Street
Suite 1205
Portland, OR 97205
$36, 40, Joyce Thompson

Good Housekeeping
959 Eighth Avenue
New York, NY 10019
$17.97, 7, Arleen L. Quarfoot

GQ
350 Madison Avenue
New York, NY 10017
$19.97, 12, Thomas Mallon

Grain
Box 1154
Regina, Saskatchewan
S4P 3B4 Canada
$15, 21, Geoffrey Ursell

Grand Street
135 Central Park West
New York, NY 10023
$24, 20, Jean Stein

Granta
250 West 57th Street, Suite 1316
New York, NY 10107
$28, Anne Kinard

Gray's Sporting Journal
20 Oak Street
Beverly Farms, MA 01915
$34.95, 4, Edward E. Gray

Great River Review
211 West 7th
Winona, MN 55987
$9, 6, Ruth Forsythe et al.

Green Mountain Review
Box A 58
Johnson State College
Johnson, VT 05656
$4, 8, Tony Whedon

Greensboro Review
Department of English
University of North Carolina
Greensboro, NC 27412
$5, 16, Jim Clark

Habersham Review
Piedmont College
Demorest, GA 30535-0010

*$8, David L. Greene, Lisa Hodgens
Lumkin*

Hadassah
50 West 58th Street
New York, NY 10019

Harper's Magazine
666 Broadway
New York, NY 10012
$18, 9, Lewis H. Lapham

Hawaii Review
University of Hawaii
Department of English
1733 Donaghho Road
Honolulu, HI 96822
*$15, 18, Susan Ginoza and Tamara
Moan*

Hayden's Ferry Review
Matthews Center
Arizona State University
Tempe, AZ 85287-1502
$10, 8, Barbara Nelson, Dianne Nelson

High Plains Literary Review
180 Adams Street, Suite 250
Denver, CO 80206
$20, 7, Robert O. Greer, Jr.

Holdout
P.O. Box 963, Back Bay Station
Boston, MA 02117
$8, 6, Glenn Stout

Hudson Review
684 Park Avenue
New York, NY 10021
$20, 8, Paula Deitz, Frederick Morgan

Idler
255 Davenport Road
Toronto, Ontario
M5R 1J9 Canada
$24, 3, Paul Wilson

Indiana Review
316 North Jordan Avenue
Bloomington, IN 47405
$12, 13, Jon Tribble

Addresses of American and Canadian Magazines

Innisfree
P.O. Box 277
Manhattan Beach, CA 90266
$22, 100, Rex Winn

Interim
Department of English
University of Nevada
4505 Maryland Parkway
Las Vegas, NV 89154
$8, A. Wilber Stevens

Iowa Review
Department of English
University of Iowa
308 EPB
Iowa City, IA 52242
$15, 10, David Hamilton

Iowa Woman
P.O. Box 680
Iowa City, IA 52244
$15, 15, Marianne Abel

Isaac Asimov's Science Fiction
Davis Publications, Inc.
380 Lexington Avenue
New York, NY 10017
$25.97, 27, Gardner Dozois

Italian Americana
University of Rhode Island
College of Continuing Education
199 Promenade Street
Providence, RI 02908
$25, 6, Carol BonoMo Ahearn

Jewish Currents
22 East 17th Street, Suite 601
New York, NY 10003-3272
$15, 8, editorial board

Journal
Department of English
Ohio State University
164 West 17th Avenue
Columbus, OH 43210
$8, 5, Michelle Herman

Kalliope
Florida Community College

3939 Roosevelt Blvd.
Jacksonville, FL 32205
$10.50, 12, Mary Sue Koeppel

Kansas Quarterly
Department of English
Denison Hall
Kansas State University
Manhattan, KS 66506
$20, 18, Harold Schneider

Karamu
English Department
Eastern Illinois University
Charleston, IL 61920
Peggy L. Brayfield

Kenyon Review
Kenyon College
Gambier, OH 43022
$20, 15, David H. Lynn

Kinesis
P.O. Box 4007
Whitefish, MT 59937-4007
$10, 6, Austin B. Byrd

Konch
Ishmael Reed Publishing Co.
P.O. Box 3288
Berkeley, CA 94703
$14.95, 6, Ishmael Reed

Laurel Review
Department of English
Northwest Missouri State University
Maryville, MO 64468
$8, 20, Craig Goad and David Slater

Lilith
The Jewish Women's Magazine
250 West 57th Street
New York, NY 10107
$14, 5, Julia Wolf Mazow

Literary Review
Fairleigh Dickinson University
285 Madison Avenue
Madison, NJ 07940
$18, 10, Walter Cummins

Lost Creek Letters
Box 373A
Rushville, MO 64484
$15, 10, Pamela Montgomery

McCall's
230 Park Avenue
New York, NY 10169
$13.95, 6, Kathy Sagan

Mademoiselle
350 Madison Avenue
New York, NY 10017
$28, 10, Eileen Schnurr

Madison Review
University of Wisconsin
Department of English
H. C. White Hall
600 North Park Street
Madison, WI 53706
$7, 8, Sara Goldberg

Malahat Review
University of Victoria
P.O. Box 1700
Victoria, British Columbia
V8W 2Y2 Canada
$15, 20, Constance Rooke

Manoa
English Department
University of Hawaii
Honolulu, HI 96822
$12, 12, Robert Shapard

Maryland Review
Department of English and
  Languages
University of Maryland, Eastern
  Shore
Princess Anne, MD 21853
*$6, 7, Chester M. Hedgepeth, Jr.,
Cary C. Holladay*

Massachusetts Review
Memorial Hall
University of Massachusetts
Amherst, MA 01003
$14, 3, Mary Heath

Matrix
c.p. 100 Ste.-Anne-de-Bellevue
Quebec
H9X 3L4 Canada
$15, 8, Linda Leith

Metropolitan
6307 North 31st Street
Arlington, VA 22207
$7, 13, Jacqueline Bergsohn

Michigan Quarterly Review
3032 Rackham Building
University of Michigan
Ann Arbor, MI 48109
$18, 10, Laurence Goldstein

Mid-American Review
106 Hanna Hall
Department of English
Bowling Green State University
Bowling Green, OH 43403
$8, 11, Ken Letko

Minnesota Review
Department of English
State University of New York
Stony Brook, NY 11794-5350
$8, 10, Fred Pfeil and Tony Vaver

Mirabella
200 Madison Avenue
New York NY 10016
$17.98, 6, Pat Towers

Mississippi Review
University of Southern Mississippi
Southern Station, P.O. Box 5144
Hattiesburg, MS 39406-5144
$10, 25, Frederick Barthelme

Missouri Review
Department of English
231 Arts and Sciences
University of Missouri
Columbia, MO 65211
$12, 23, Speer Morgan

Mother Jones
1663 Mission Street
2nd floor

San Francisco, CA 94103
$24, 3, Douglas Foster

Ms.
230 Park Avenue
New York, NY 10169
$45, 7, Robin Morgan

Nebraska Review
Writers' Workshop
ASH 212
University of Nebraska
Omaha, NE 68182-0324
$6, 10, Art Homer, Richard Duggin

Negative Capability
62 Ridgelawn Drive East
Mobile, AL 36605
$12, 15, Sue Walker

New Delta Review
Creative Writing Program
English Department
Louisiana State University
Baton Rouge, LA 70803
$7, 9, David Tilley

New Directions
New Directions Publishing
80 Eighth Avenue
New York, NY 10011
$11.95, 4, James Laughlin

New England Review
Middlebury College
Middlebury, VT 05753
$18, 9, T. R. Hummer

New Letters
University of Missouri
4216 Rockhill Road
Kansas City, MO 64110
$17, 10, James McKinley

New Mexico Humanities Review
P.O. Box A
New Mexico Tech
Socorro, NM 87801
$8, 15, John Rothfork

New Orleans Review
P.O. Box 195
Loyola University
New Orleans, LA 70118
$25, 4, John Biguenet, John Mosier

New Quarterly
English Language Proficiency
  Programme
University of Waterloo
Waterloo, Ontario
N2L 3G1 Canada
$14, 15, Peter Hinchcliffe

New Renaissance
9 Heath Road
Arlington, MA 02174
$11.50, 10, Louise T. Reynolds

New Yorker
25 West 43rd Street
New York, NY 10036
$32, 50, Robert Gottlieb

Nimrod
Arts and Humanities Council of
  Tulsa
2210 South Main Street
Tulsa, OK 74114
$10, 10, Francine Ringold

North American Review
University of Northern Iowa
Cedar Falls, IA 50614
$11, 13, Robley Wilson, Jr.

North Atlantic Review
15 Arbutus Lane
Stony Brook, NY 11790-1408
$13, 9, editorial board

North Dakota Quarterly
University of North Dakota
P.O. Box 8237
Grand Forks, ND 58202
$10, 13, Robert W. Lewis

North Stone Review
Box 14098, D Station

Minneapolis, MN 55414
$15, 4, James Naiden

Northwest Review
369 PLC
University of Oregon
Eugene, OR 97403
$11, 10, Cecelia Hagen

Ohio Review
Ellis Hall
Ohio University
Athens, OH 45701-2979
$12, 10, Wayne Dodd

Old Hickory Review
P.O. Box 1178
Jackson, TN 38301
$4, 6, Dorothy Starfill

Omni
1965 Broadway
New York, NY 10023-5965
$24, 20, Patrice Adcroft

Ontario Review
9 Honey Brook Drive
Princeton, NJ 08540
$10, 8, Raymond J. Smith

Open City
118 Riverside Drive, Suite 14A
New York, NY 10024
$20, 12, Thomas Beller

Other Voices
University of Illinois at Chicago
Department of English
(M/C 162) Box 4348
Chicago, IL 60680
$16, 30, Sharon Fiffer, Lois Hauselman

Oxalis
Stone Ridge Poetry Society
P.O. Box 3993
Kingston, NY 12401
$14, 12, Shirley Powell

Paris Review
541 East 72nd Street
New York, NY 10021
$20, 10, George Plimpton

Parting Gifts
3006 Stonecutter Terrace
Greensboro, NC 27405
Robert Bixby

Partisan Review
236 Bay State Road
Boston, MA 02215
$4, 4, William Phillips

Passages North
Kalamazoo College
1200 Academy Street
Kalamazoo, MI 49007
$5, 8, Mary LaChapelle

Playboy
Playboy Building
919 North Michigan Avenue
Chicago, IL 60611
$24, 10, Alice K. Turner

Ploughshares
Emerson College
100 Beacon Street
Boston, MA 02116
$15, 15, DeWitt Henry

Potpourri
P.O. Box 8278
Prairie Village, KS 66208
48, Polly W. Swafford

Prairie Schooner
201 Andrews Hall
University of Nebraska
Lincoln, NE 68588-0334
$17, 20, Hilda Raz

Prism International
Department of Creative Writing
University of British Columbia
Vancouver, British Columbia
V6T 1W5 Canada
$16, 20, Francie Greenslade

Product
Center for Writers
University of Southern Mississippi
Hattiesburg, MS 39401
$8, 9, Paul Karon

Puerto del Sol
P.O. Box 3E
Department of English
New Mexico State University
Las Cruces, NM 88003
*$7.75, 12, Kevin McIlvoy, Antonya
   Nelson*

Quarry Magazine
P.O. Box 1061
Kingston, Ontario
K7L 4Y5 Canada
$18, 20, Steven Heighton

Quarterly
Vintage Books
201 East 50th Street
New York, NY 10022
$36, 81, Gordon Lish

Quarterly West
317 Olpin Union
University of Utah
Salt Lake City, UT 84112
$8.50, 10, David Stevenson

Raritan
Rutgers University
31 Mine Street
New Brunswick, NJ 08903
$16, 5, Richard Poirier

RE:AL
School of Liberal Arts
Stephen F. Austin State University
P.O. Box 13007, SFA Station
Nacogdoches, TX 75962
$6, 5, Lee Schultz

Redbook
959 Eighth Avenue
New York, NY 10017
$11.97, 10, Dawn Raffel

River Styx
Big River Association
14 South Euclid
St. Louis, MO 63108
$20, 30, Lee Schreiner

Room of One's Own
P.O. Box 46160, Station G
Vancouver, British Columbia
V6R 4G5 Canada
$20, 12, rotating editorship

Salmagundi
Skidmore College
Saratoga Springs, NY 12866
$15, 4, Robert Boyers

San Jose Studies
c/o English Department
San Jose State University
One Washington Square
San Jose, CA 95192
$12, 5, Fauneil J. Rinn

Santa Clara Review
Santa Clara University
500 El Camino Real 3212
Santa Clara, CA 95053

Santa Monica Review
Center for the Humanities
Santa Monica College
1900 Pico Boulevard
Santa Monica, CA 90405
$10, 16, Jim Krusoe

Saturday Night
511 King Street West, Suite 100
Toronto, Ontario
M5V 2Z4 Canada
$26.45, 7, Robert Weaver

Seattle Review
Padelford Hall, GN-30
University of Washington
Seattle, WA 98195
$8, 12, Charles Johnson

Seventeen
850 Third Avenue
New York, NY 10022
$13.95, 8, Bonni Price

Sewanee Review
University of the South
Sewanee, TN 37375-4009
$15, 10, George Core

Shenandoah
Washington and Lee University
P.O. Box 722
Lexington, VA 24450
$11, 17, Dabney Stuart

Sinister Wisdom
P.O. Box 3252
Berkeley, CA 94703
$17, 25, Elana Dykewoman

Snake Nation Review
2920 North Oak
Valdosta, GA 31602
$12, 16, Roberta George

Sonora Review
Department of English
University of Arizona
Tucson, AZ 85721
$8, 12, Martha Ostheimer, Laurie Schorr

South Dakota Review
University of South Dakota
P.O. Box 111 University Exchange
Vermillion, SD 57069
$15, 15, John R. Milton

Southern California Anthology
ᶜ/o Master of Professional Writing
   Program
WPH 404
University of Southern California
Los Angeles, CA 90089
$7.95, 18, Richard P. Aloia, Jr.

Southern Exposure
P.O. Box 531
Durham, NC 27702
$24, 12, Susan Ketchin

Southern Humanities Review
9088 Haley Center
Auburn University
Auburn, AL 36849
$12, 5, Dan R. Latimer, Thomas L.
   Wright

Southern Review
43 Allen Hall
Louisiana State University

Baton Rouge, LA 70803
$15, 17, James Olney, Dave Smith

Southwest Review
Southern Methodist University
P.O. Box 4374
Dallas, TX 75275
$16, 15, Willard Spiegelman

Sou'wester
School of Humanities
Department of English
Southern Illinois University
Edwardsville, IL 62026-1438
$10, 10, Fred Robbins

Spirit That Moves Us
P.O. Box 820
Jackson Heights, NY 11372-0820
$7, 11, Morty Sklar

Stories
14 Beacon Street
Boston, MA 02108
$18, 12, Amy R. Kaufman

Story
1507 Dana Avenue
Cincinnati, OH 45207
$17, 52, Lois Rosenthal

Story Quarterly
P.O. Box 1416
Northbrook, IL 60065
$12, 20, Anne Brashler, Diane Williams

Sun
107 North Roberson Street
Chapel Hill, NC 27516
$28, 30, Sy Safransky

Tampa Review
P.O. Box 19F
University of Tampa
401 West Kennedy Boulevard
Tampa, FL 33606-1490
$7.50, 2, Andy Solomon

Thema
Box 74109

Metairie, LA 70053-4109
$16, Virginia Howard

Threepenny Review
P.O. Box 9131
Berkeley, CA 94709
$12, 10, Wendy Lesser

Tikkun
5100 Leona Street
Oakland, CA 94619
$30, 10, Michael Lerner

Touchstone
Tennessee Humanities Council
P.O. Box 24767
Nashville, TN 37202
Robert Cheatham

TriQuarterly
2020 Ridge Avenue
Northwestern University
Evanston, IL 60208
$18, 15, Reginald Gibbons

Turnstile
175 Fifth Avenue, Suite 2348
New York, NY 10010
$24, 12, group editorship

University of Windsor Review
Department of English
University of Windsor
Windsor, Ontario
N9B 3P4 Canada
$10, 6, Joseph A. Quinn

Vincent Brothers Review
4566 Northern Circle
Mad River Township
Dayton, OH 45424
$4.50, 12, Kimberly A. Willardson

Virginia Quarterly Review
One West Range
Charlottesville, VA 22903
$15, 14, Staige D. Blackford

Vogue
Condé Nast Building
350 Madison Avenue

New York, NY 10017
$24, 4, Nancy Nicholas

Voice Literary Supplement
842 Broadway
New York, NY 10003
$17, 8, M. Mark

Wascana Review
English Department
University of Regina
Regina, Saskatchewan
S4S 0A2 Canada
$7, 8, J. Shami

Weber Studies
Weber State College
Ogden, UT 84408
$5, 2, Neila Seshachari

Webster Review
Webster University
470 East Lockwood
Webster Groves, MO 63119
$5, 2, Nancy Schapiro

Wellspring
770 Tonkawa Road
Long Lake, MN 55356
$8, 10, Maureen LaJoy

West Branch
Department of English
Bucknell University
Lewisburg, PA 17837
$5, 10, Robert Love Taylor

West Wind Review
Stevenson Union, Room 321
Southern Oregon State College
1250 Siskiyou Boulevard
Ashland, OR 97520
$6, 11, Dale Vidmar, Catherine Ordal

Western Humanities Review
University of Utah
Salt Lake City, UT 84112
$18, 10, Barry Weller

Whetstone
Barrington Area Arts Council
P.O. Box 1266

Barrington, IL 60011
Marsha Portnoy

William and Mary Review
College of William and Mary
Williamsburg, VA 23185
$4.50, 4, William Clark

Willow Springs
MS-1
Eastern Washington University
Cheney, WA 99004
$7, 8, Kristen Birchett

Wind
RFD Route 1
P.O. Box 809K
Pikeville, KY 41501
$7, 20, Quentin R. Howard

Witness
31000 Northwestern Highway,
  Suite 200
Farmington Hills, MI 48018
$16, 15, Peter Stine

Worcester Review
6 Chatham Street
Worcester, MA 01690
$10, 8, Rodger Martin

Writ
Innis College
University of Toronto
2 Sussex Avenue
Toronto, Ontario
M5S 1J5 Canada
$12, 7, Roger Greenwald

Writers Forum
University of Colorado
P.O. Box 7150
Colorado Springs, CO 80933-7150
$8.95, 15, Alexander Blackburn

Xavier Review
Xavier University
Box 110C
New Orleans, LA 70125
6, Thomas Bonner, Jr.

Yale Review
1902A Yale Station
New Haven, CT 06520
$20, 12, J. D. McClatchy

Yankee
Yankee Publishing, Inc.
Dublin, NH 03444
$22, 4, Judson D. Hale, Sr.

Yellow Silk
P.O. Box 6374
Albany, CA 94706
$30, 10, Lily Pond

Yokoi
415 E. Olive
Bozeman, MT 59715
$16, 5, Marjorie Smith

ZYZZYVA
41 Sutter Street, Suite 1400
San Francisco, CA 94104
$20, 12, Howard Junker